The Abbess of Vlaye

Stanley John Weyman

"HE HAD DISMOUNTED, AND HAD HIS HAT IN HIS HAND"

[*Page 113*]

THE ABBESS
OF VLAYE

BY

STANLEY J. WEYMAN

*Author of " Under the Red Robe," "A Gentleman of France,"
" My Lady Rotha," " The Red Cockade," " Count
Hannibal," " The Castle Inn," etc.*

LONGMANS, GREEN, AND CO.

91 AND 93 FIFTH AVENUE, NEW YORK

LONDON AND BOMBAY

1904

ROBERT DRUMMOND, PRINTER, NEW YORK.

TO

HUGH STOWELL SCOTT,

IN REMEMBRANCE OF LONG SUMMER DAYS SPENT WITH HIM

AMID THE SCENES WHICH SUGGESTED IT,

THIS STORY IS

AFFECTIONATELY DEDICATED BY HIS FRIEND.

CONTENTS.

THE ABBESS OF VLAYE.

INTRODUCTION.

A KING IN COUNCIL.

MONSIEUR DES AGEAUX was a man of whom his best friends could not say that he shone, or tried to shine, in the pursuit of the fair sex. He was of an age, something over thirty, when experience renders more formidable the remaining charms of youth; and former conquests whet the sword for new emprises. And the time in which he lived and governed the province of Périgord for the King was a time in which the favour of ladies, and the good things to be gained thereby, stood for much, and morality for little. So that for the ambitious the path of dalliance presented almost as many chances of advancement as the more strenuous road of war.

Yet des Ageaux, though he was an ambitious man and one whose appetite success—and in his degree he had been very successful—had but sharpened, showed no inclination to take that path, or to rise by trifling. Nay, he turned from it; he shunned if he did not dislike the other sex. Whether he doubted his powers—he was a taciturn, grave man—or he had energy only for the one pursuit he loved, the government of men, the thing was certain. Yet he was not unpopular even at Court, the lax Court of Henry the Fourth. But he was known for a thoughtful, dry man, older than his years and no favourite with great ladies; of whom some dubbed him shy, and some a clown, and all—a piece of furniture.

None the less, where men were concerned, he passed for a man more useful than most; or, for certain, seeing that he boasted no great claims, and belonged to no great family, he had not been Governor of a province. Governors of provinces in those days were of the highest; cousins of the King, when these could be trusted, which was rare; peers and Marshals of France, great Dukes with vast hereditary possessions, old landed Vicomtes, and the like. Only at the tail of the list came some half-dozen men whom discretion and service, or the playfulness of fortune had—*mirabile dictu*—raised to office. And at the tail of all came des Ageaux; for Périgord, his province, land of the pie and the goose liver, was part of the King's demesne, the King was his own Governor in it, and des Ageaux bore only the title of "Lieutenant for the King in the country of Périgord."

Yet was it a wonderful post for such a man, and many a personage, many a lord well seen at Court, coveted it. All the same the burden was heavy; a thing not to be dismissed in a moment. The King found him no money, or little; no men, or few. Where greater Governors used their own resources he had to use—economy. And to make matters worse the man was just; it was part of his nature, it was part of his passion, to be just. So where they taxed not legally only, but illegally, he scrupled, he held his hand. And, therefore, though his dignity was almost as high as office could

make it, and his power in his own country not small, no
man who ever came to Court went with less splendour
in the streets of Paris, or with a smaller following.
Doubtless, as a result of this, a few despised him; a few
even, making common cause with the Court ladies, and
being themselves semi-royal, and above retort, flouted
him as a thing negligible.

But, on the whole, he passed, though dry and grave,
for a man to be envied, the ladies notwithstanding.
And he held his own tolerably, and his post handsomely
until a certain day in the summer of 1595, when word
came to the young Governor to cross half France to meet
the King at Lyons; where, in the early part of that year,
Henry the Fourth lay, and was ill-content with a world
which, on the surface, seemed to be treating him well.

But on the surface only. The long wars of religion,
midway in which the Massacre of Bartholomew stands
up, like some drear gibbet landmark in a waste, were,
indeed, virtually over. Not only had Henry come to
the throne, but Paris, his capital, was his at last; had
he not bought it eighteen months before by that mass,
that abjuration of Protestant errors, of which the world
has heard so much? And not Paris only. Orleans
and Bourges, and this good city of Lyons, and Rouen, all
were his now, and in their Notre-Dames or St.-Etiennes
had sung their *Te Deums*, and more or less heartily
cried "God save the King!" At last, after six years
of fighting, of wild horse forays, that flamed across the
Northern corn-lands, after a thousand sleepless nights
and as many days of buying and bartering—at last the
lover of Gabrielle, who was also the most patient and
astute of men, was King of France and of Navarre, lord
of all this pleasant realm.

Or, not lord; only over-lord, as six times a day they made him know. Nor even that, of all. For in Brittany a great noble still went his own way. And in Provence a great city refused to surrender. And north-eastwards Spain still clung to his border. Nevertheless it was none of these things filled Henry, the King, with discontent. It was at none of these things that he swore in his beard as he sulked at the end of the long Council Table this June morning; while des Ageaux, from his seat near the bottom of the board, watched his face.

In truth Henry was discovering, that, having bought, he must pay; that so great was the mortgage he had put on his kingdom, the profits belonged to others. Overlord he was—lord, no; except perhaps in Lyons where he lay, and where for that reason the Governor had to mind his manners. But in smiling Provence to south of him? Not a whit. The Duke of Epernon ruled the land of Roses, and would rule until the young Duke of Guise, to whom His Majesty had given commission, put him out; and then Guise would rule. In Dauphiny the same. In Languedoc, the great middle province of the south, Montmorency, son to the old Constable, was King in fact; in Guienne old Marshal Matignon. In Angoumois —here Epernon again; so firmly fixed that he deigned only to rule by quarterly letters from his distant home. True in Poitou was an obedient Governor, but the house of Trémouille from their red castle of Thouars outweighed his governorship. And in rocky Limousin the Governor could keep neither the King's peace nor his own.

So it was everywhere through the wide provinces of France; and Henry, who loved his people, knew it, and sulkily fingered the papers that told of it. Not that he had need of the papers. He knew before he cast eye on them in what a welter of lawlessness and disorder, of private feud and public poverty, thirty years of civil war had left his kingdom. One province was in arms, torn asunder by a feud between two great houses. Another laboured in the throes of a peasant rising, its hills alight night after night with the flames of burning farmsteads. A third was helpless in the grip of a gang of brigands, who held the roads. A fourth was beset by disbanded soldiers. The long wars of religion had dissolved all ties. Everywhere monks who had left their abbeys and nuns who had left their convents swarmed on the roads, with sturdy beggars, homeless peasants, broken gentry. Everywhere, beyond the walls of the great cities, the law was paralysed, the great committed outrage, the poor suffered wrong, the excesses of war enured, and, in this time of fancied peace, took grimmer shape.

He whom God had set over France, to rule it, knew these things and sat hopeless, brooding over the papers; hampered on the one side by lack of money, on the other by the grants of power that in evil days had bought a nominal allegiance. He began to see that he had won only the first bout of a match which must last him his life. Nor would it have consoled him much to know that in the college of Navarre that day played a little lad, just ten years old, whose frail white hand would one day right these things with a vengeance.

His people cried to him, and he longed to help them and could not. From a thousand market-places, splayed wooden shelters, covering each its quarter-acre of ground, their cry came up to him: "Give us peace, give us law!" and he could not. No wonder that he brooded over the papers, while the clerks looked askance at him, and the

great lords who had won what he had lost whispered or
played tric-trac at the board. Those who sat lower, and
among these M. des Ageaux, were less at their ease.
They wondered where the storm would break, and feared
each for his own head.

Presently M. de Joyeuse, one of the great nobles,
precipitated the outburst. "You have heard," said he,
twiddling a pen between his delicate fingers, "what
they call these peasants who are ravaging Poitou, sire?"

Before the King could answer the Governor of Poitou
protested from his place lower down the table. "They
are none of mine," he said. "It is in the Limousin next
door to me that they are at work. I wash my hands of
them!"

"They are as bad on your side as on mine!" he of
the barren Limousin retorted.

"They started with you!" Poitou rejoined. "Who
kindles a fire should put it out."

The King raised his hand for silence. "No matter
who is responsible, the fact remains!" he said.

"But you have not heard the jest, sire," Joyeuse struck
in. His thin handsome face, pale with excess, belied
eyes thoughtful and dreamy, eyes that saw visions.
He had been a King's favourite, he had spent years in
a convent, he had come forth again, now he was head
of the great Joyeuse house, lord of a third of Languedoc.
By turns "Father Angel"—for he had been a noted
preacher—and Monseigneur, there were those who pre-
dicted that he would some day return to the cloister
and die in his hood. "They call them the Tards-
Avisés," he continued, "because they were foolish
enough to rise when the war was over."

"God pity them!" the King said.

"*Morbleu!* Your Majesty is pitiful of a sudden!" The speaker was the Constable de Montmorency. He was a stout, gruff, choleric man, born, as the Montmorencys were, a generation too late.

"I pity them!" the King answered a trifle sharply. "But you"—he spoke to the table—"neither pity them nor put them down."

"You are speaking, sire," one asked, "of the Crocans?" It was so; from the name of a village in their midst, they called these revolted peasants of the Limousin of whom more will be said.

"Yes."

"They are not in my government," the speaker replied.

"Nor in mine!"

"Nor mine!" And so all, except the Governor of the Limousin and the Governor of Poitou, who sat sulkily silent.

Another of the great ones, Marshal Matignon, nodded approval. "Let every man shoe his own ass," he said, pursing up his lips. He was a white-haired, red-faced, apoplectic man of sixty, who thought that in persuading the Estates of Bordeaux to acknowledge Henry he had earned the right to go his own way. "Otherwise we shall jostle one another," he continued, "and be at blows before we know it, sire! They are in the Limousin; let the Governor put them down. It is his business and no other's."

"Except mine," the King replied, with a frown of displeasure. "And if he cannot, what then?"

"Let him make way, sire, for one who can," the Constable answered readily. "Your Majesty will not have far to look for him," he continued in a playful tone. "My nephew, for instance, would like a government."

"A truce to jesting," Henry said. "The trouble began, it is true, in the Limousin, but it has spread into Poitou and into the Angoumois"—he looked at Epernon's
agent, for the Duke of Epernon was so great a man he had
not come himself. "Gentlemen," the King continued,
sitting back in his great chair, "can you not come to
some agreement? Can you not mass what force you
have, and deal with them shortly but mercifully? The
longer the fire burns, the more trouble will it be to extinguish it, and the greater the suffering."

"Why not let it burn out, sire?" Epernon's agent
muttered with thinly veiled impudence. "It will then
burn the more rubbish, with your Majesty's leave!"

But, the words said, he quailed. For, under his
aquiline nose, the King's mustaches curled with rage.
There were some with whom he must bear, lords who
had brought him rich cities, wide provinces; and others
whose deeds won them licence. But this man? "There
spoke the hireling!" he cried. And the stroke went
home, for the man was the only one at the table who had
no government of his own. "I will spare your attendance, sir," the King continued, with a scornful gesture.
"M. de Guise will answer such questions as arise on your
master's late government—of Provence. And for his
other government——"

"I represent him there also," the man muttered
sulkily.

"Then you can represent his absence," Henry retorted
with quick wit, "since he is never there! I need you
not. Go, sir, and see that within three hours you are
without the walls of Lyons!"

The man rose, divided between fear of the King and
fear of the master to whom he must return. He paused

an instant, then went down the room slowly, and went out.

"Now, gentlemen," Henry continued, with hard looks, "understand. You may shoe each his own ass, but you must shoe mine also. There must be an end put to this peasant rising. Who will undertake it?"

"The man who should undertake it," Matignon answered, "for the ass is of his providing, is the gentleman who has gone out."

"He is naught!"

"He is for much in this."

"How? Sometimes," the King continued irritably, "I think the men are shod, and the asses come to my Council Table!"

This was a stroke of wit on a level with the Constable's discernment; he laughed loudly. "Nevertheless," he said, "Matignon's right, sire. That man's master is for a good deal in this. If he had kept order his neighbour's house would not be on fire."

For the first time M. des Ageaux ventured a word from the lower end of the table. "Vlaye!" he muttered.

The Constable leaned forward to see who spoke. "Ay, you've hit on it, my lad, whoever you are. Vlaye it is!" And he looked at Matignon, who nodded his adhesion.

Henry frowned. "I am coming to the matter of Vlaye," he said.

"It is all one, sire," Matignon replied, his eyes half shut. He wheezed a little in his speech.

"How?"

The Constable explained. He leant forward and prodded the table with a short, stout finger—not over-clean according to the ideas of a later time. "Angoumois is there," he said. "See, your Majesty. And Poitou is here"—with a second prod an inch from the first. "And the Limousin is here! And Périgord is there! And see, your Majesty, where their skirts all meet in this corner—or as good as meet—is Vlaye! Name of God, a strong place, that!" He turned for assent to old Matignon, who nodded silently.

"And you mean to say that Vlaye——"

"Has been over heavy handed, your Majesty. And the clowns, beginning to find the thing beyond a joke, began by hanging three poor devils of toll gatherers, and the thing started. And what is on everybody's frontier is nobody's business."

"Except mine," the King muttered drily. "And Vlaye is Epernon's man?"

"That is it, sire," the Constable answered. "Epernon put him in the castle six years back for standing by him when the Angoulême people rose on him. But the man is no Vlaye, you understand. M. de Vlaye was in that business and died of his wounds. He had no near heirs, and the man whom Epernon put in took the lordship as well as the castle, the name and all belonging to it. They call him the Captain of Vlaye in those parts."

The King looked his astonishment.

"Oh, I could give you twenty cases!" the Constable continued, shrugging his shoulders. "What do you expect, sire, in such times as these?"

"Ventre St. Gris!" Henry swore. "And not content with what he has got, he robs the poor?"

"And the rich, too," Joyeuse murmured with a grin, "when he gets them into his net!"

Henry looked sternly from one to another. "But what do you while this goes on?" he said. "For shame!

You, Constable? You, Matignon?" He turned from one to the other.

Matignon laughed wheezily. "Make me Governor in Epernon's place, sire," he said, "and I will account for him. But double work and single pay? No, no!"

The Constable laughed as at a great joke. "I say the same, sire," he said. "While Epernon has the Angoumois it is his affair."

The King looked stormily at the Governor of Poitou. But Poitou shook his head. "It is not in my government," he said moodily. "I cannot afford, sire, to get a hornets' nest about my ears for nothing."

He of the Limousin fidgeted. "I say the same, sire," he muttered. "Vlaye has three hundred spears. It would need an army to reduce him. And I have neither men nor money for the task."

"There you have, sire," the delicate-faced Joyeuse cried gaily, "three hundred and one good reasons why the Limousin leaves the man alone. For the matter of that"—he tried to spin his pen like a top—"there is a government as deeply concerned in this as any that has been named."

"Which?" Henry asked. He was losing patience. That which was so much to him was nothing to these.

"Périgord," Joyeuse answered with a bow. And at that several laughed softly—but not the King. He was himself, as has been said, Governor of Périgord.

Here at last, however, was one on whom he could vent his displeasure; and he would vent it! "Stand up, des Ageaux!" he cried harshly. And he scowled as des Ageaux, who was somewhat like him in feature, rose from his seat. "What have you to say, man?" Henry cried. "For yourself and for me! Speak, sir!"

But before des Ageaux could answer, the King broke
out anew—with abuse, with reproaches, giving his passion rein; while the great Governors listened and licked
their lips, or winked at one another, when the King hit
them a side blow. Presently, when des Ageaux would
have defended himself, alleging that he was no deeper
in fault than others,

"Ventre St. Gris! No words, sir!" Henry retorted.
"I find kings enough here, I want not you in the number!
I made not you that I might have your nobility cast
in my teeth! You are not of the blood royal, nor
even," leaning a little on the word, "Joyeuse or Epernon!
Man, I made you! And not for show, I have enough
of that—but to be of use and service, for common needs
and not for parade—like the gentleman," bitterly, "who
deigns to represent me in the Limousin, or he who is
so good as to sign papers for me in Poitou! Man alive, it
might be thought you were peer and marshal, from
your way of idling here, while robbers ride your marches,
and my peasants are driven to revolt. Go to, do you
think you are one of these?" He indicated by a gesture
the great lords who sat nearest him. "Do you think that
because I made you, I cannot unmake you?"

The man on whom the storm had fallen bore it not
ignobly. It has been said that he featured Henry himself, being prominent of nose, with a grave face, a brown
beard, close-cropped, and a forehead high and severe.
Only in his eyes shone, and that rarely, a gleam of
humour. Now the sweat stood on his brow as he
listened—they were cruel blows, the position a cruel one.
Nevertheless, when the King paused, and he had room
to answer, his voice was steady.

"I claim, sire," he said, "no immunity. Neither that,

nor aught but the right of a soldier, who has fought for France——"

"And gallantly!" struck in one, who had not yet spoken—Lesdiguières, the Huguenot, the famous Governor of Dauphiny. He turned to the King. "I vouch for it, sire," he continued. "And M. de Joyeuse, who has the better right, will vouch for it, too."

But Joyeuse, who was sulkily prodding the table with his spoiled pen, neither lifted his eyes nor gave heed. He was bitterly offended by the junction of his name with that of Epernon, who, great and powerful as he was, had had a notary for his father. He was silent.

Des Ageaux, who had looked at him as hoping something, lifted his eyes. "Your Majesty will do me the justice to remember," he said, "that I had your order to have a special care of my province; and to mass what force I could in Périgueux. Few men as I have——"

"You build them up within walls!" Henry retorted.

"But if I lost Périgueux——"

The King snarled.

"Or aught happened there?"

"You would lose your head!" Henry returned. He was thoroughly out of temper. "By the Lord," he continued, "have I no man in my service? Must I take this fellow of Vlaye into hire because I have no honest man with the courage of a mouse! You call yourself Lieutenant of Périgord, and this happens on your border. I have a mind to break you, sir!"

Henry seldom let his anger have vent; and the man who stood before him knew his danger. From a poor gentleman of Brittany with something of pedigree but little of estate, he had risen to this post which eight out of ten at that table grudged him. He saw it slipping away; nay, falling from him—falling! A moment might decide his fate.

In the pinch his eyes sought Joyeuse, and the appeal in them was not to be mistaken. But the elegant sulked, and would not see. It was clear that, for him, des Ageaux might sink. For himself, the Lieutenant doubted if words would help him, and they might aggravate the King's temper. He was bravely silent.

It was Lesdiguières, the Huguenot, who came to the rescue. "Your Majesty is a little hard on M. des Ageaux," he said. And the King's lieutenant in Périgord knew why men loved the King's Governor in Dauphiny.

"In his place," Henry answered wrathfully, "I would pull down Vlaye if I did it with my teeth. It is easy for you, my friend, to talk," he continued, addressing the Huguenot leader. "They are not your peasants whom this rogue of a Vlaye presses, nor your hamlets he burns. I have it all here—here!" he repeated, his eyes kindling as he slapped with his open hand one of the papers before him, "and the things he has done make my blood boil! I swear if I were not King I would turn Crocan myself! But these things are little thought of by others. M. d'Epernon supports this man, and"—with a sudden glance at Matignon—"the Governor of Guienne makes use of his horses when he travels to see the King."

Matignon laughed something shamefacedly. "Well, sire, the horses have done no harm," he said. "Nor he in my government. He knows better. And things are upside down thereabouts."

"It is for us to right them!" Henry retorted. And then to des Ageaux, but with less temper. "Now, sir,

I lay my order on you! I give you six weeks to rid
me of this man, Vlaye. Fail, and I put in your place
a man who will do it. You understand, Lieutenant?
Then do not fail. By the Lord, I know not where I
shall be bearded next!"

He turned then, but still muttering angrily, to other
business. Matignon and the Constable were not concerned in this; and as soon as the King's shoulder was
towards them they winked at one another. "Your
nephew will not have long to wait," Matignon whispered,
"if a lieutenancy will suit him."

"'Twould be a fair start," the Constable answered.
"But a watched pot—you know the saying."

"This pot will boil at the end of six weeks," Matignon
rejoined with a fat chuckle. "Chut, man, with his wage
a year in arrear, and naught behind his wage, where is
he to find another fifty men, let alone three or four
hundred? He will need five and twenty score for this,
and he dare not move a man!"

"He might squeeze his country?" the Constable objected.

"Pooh! He is a fool of the new school! He will go
back to his cabbages before he will do that! I tell you,"
he continued, laying his hand on the other's knee, "he
has got Périgord, the main part of it, into order! Ay,
into order! And if he don't go, we shall have to mend
our manners," with a grin, "and get our governments
into order, too!"

"By the Lord, there is no finger wags in my country
unless I will it!" the Constable rejoined with some
tartness. "Since he"—he indicated Joyeuse—"came
over to us, at any rate! Don't think it! But there it is.
If there were no whifflesnaffles here and there, and no

blood-letting, it would not suit us very well, would it?
You don't want to go to cabbage planting, Marshal, more
than I do?"

The Marshal smiled.

.   .   .   .

Late that night the young Duke of Joyeuse, leaving
his people at the end of the street, went by himself to
the house in which des Ageaux lodged in Lyons. A
woman answered his summons, and not knowing the
young grandee—for he was cloaked to the nose—fetched
the Bat, an old, lean, lank-visaged captain who played
squire of the body to des Ageaux. The Bat knew the
Duke in spite of his cloak; perhaps he had him for a
certain reason in his mind. And he bowed his long, stiff
back before him, and would have fetched lights; yet with
a glum face. But the Duke answered him shortly that
he wanted no more than a word with his master, and
would say it there.

On which, "You are too late, my lord," the Bat rejoined; and Joyeuse saw that with all his politeness he
was as gloomy as his name. "He left Lyons this afternoon."

"With what attendance?" the Duke asked in great
surprise. For he had not heard of it.

"Alone, my lord Duke."

"Does he return to-morrow?"

"I know not."

"But you know something!" the young noble retorted
with more of vexation than the circumstances seemed to
justify.

"My lord, nothing," the Bat answered, "save that
we are ordered to follow him to-morrow by way of Cler-
mont."

"To his province?"

"Even so, my lord."

Joyeuse struck his booted foot against the pavement, and the sombre Bat, whose ears—some said he got his name from them—were almost as long as his legs, caught the genial chink of gold crowns. It was such music as he seldom heard, for he had a vision of a heavy bag of them; and his eyes glistened.

But the chink was all he had of them. Joyeuse turned away, and with a stifled sigh and a shrug went back to the play-table at the Archbishop's palace. Sinning and repenting were the two occupations in which he had spent one half of his short life; and if there was a thing which he did with greater ardour than the first—it was the second.

CHAPTER I.

VILLENEUVE-L'ABBESSE.

THE horse looked piteously at the man. Blood oozed from its broken knees and its legs quivered under it. The man holding his scratched and abraded hand to his mouth returned the beast's look, at first with promise of punishment, but by and by less unkindly. He was a just man, and he saw that the fault was his; since it was he who, after crossing the ridge, had urged the horse out of the path that he might be spared some part of the weary descent. Out of the path, and cunningly hidden by a tuft of rough grass, a rabbit-hole had lain in wait.

He contented himself with a word of disgust, therefore, chucked the rein impatiently—since justice has its limits —and began to lead the horse down the descent, which a short sward rendered slippery. But he had not gone many paces before he halted. The horse's painful limp and the sweat that broke out on its shoulders indicated that two broken knees were not the worst of the damage. The man let the rein go, resigned himself to the position, and, shrugging his shoulders, scanned the scene before him.

The accident had happened on the south side of the long swell of chalk hills which the traveller had been mounting for an hour past; and scarcely a stone's-throw

18

below the ruined wind-mill that had been his landmark
for leagues. To right and left of him, under a pale-blue
sky, the breezy, open down, carpeted with wild thyme
and vetches, and alive with the hum of bees, stretched in
long soft undulations, marred by no sign of man save a
second and a third wind-mill ranged in line on the
highest breasts. Below him the slope of sward and fern,
broken here by a solitary blackthorn, there by a clump
of whin and briars, swept gently down to a shallow wide
valley—almost a plain—green and thickly wooded,
beyond which the landscape rose again slowly and
imperceptibly into uplands. Through this wide valley
flowed from left to right a silvery river, its meandering
course marked by the lighter foliage of willows and
poplars; and immediately below the traveller a cluster
of roofless hovels on the bank seemed to mark a ford.

On all the hill about him, on the slopes of thyme, and
heather, and yellow gorse, the low sun was shining—
from his right, and from a little behind him, so that his
shadow stretched far across the sward. But in the valley
about the river and the ford evening was beginning to
fall, grey, peaceful, silent. For a time his eyes roved
hither and thither, seeking a halting-place of more
promise than the ruined cots; and at length they
found what they sought. He marked, rising from a
mass of trees a little beyond the ford, a thin curl of
smoke, so light, so grey, as to be undiscoverable by
any but the sharpest eyes—but his were of the sharpest. The outline of the woods at the same point indicated a clearing within a wide loop of the river; and
putting the one with the other, des Ageaux—for it was
he—came to a fair certainty that a house of some mag-
nitude lay hidden there.

At any rate he saw no better chance of shelter. It was that of the ruined hovels and the roadside, and taking the rein once more, he led the horse down the hill, and in the first dusk of the evening crossed the pale clear water on stepping-stones. He suffered the horse to stand awhile in the stream and drink and cool its legs amid the dark, waving masses of weed. Then he urged it up the bank, and led it along the track, that was fast growing dim, and grey, and lonesome.

The horse moved painfully, knuckling over at every step. Yet night had not quite fallen when the traveller, plodding along beside it, saw two stone pillars standing gaunt and phantom-like on the left of the path. Each bore aloft a carved escutcheon, and in that weird half-light and with a backing of dark forest trees the two might have been taken for ghosts. Their purpose, however, was plain, for they flanked the opening, at right angles to his path, of a rough road, at the end of which, at a distance of some ten score paces from the pillars, appeared an open gateway framed in a dim wall. No more than that, for above was the pale sky, and on either hand the black line of trees hedged the narrow picture.

The traveller peered awhile at the escutcheons. But gathering darkness and the lichens which covered the stone foiled him, and he was little the wiser when he turned down the avenue. When he had traversed a half of its length the trees fell back on either hand, and revealed the sullen length of a courtyard wall, and rising within it, a little on his right, a dark mass of building, compact in the main of two round towers, of the date of Philip Augustus, with some additions of more modern times. The effect of the pile, viewed in that half-light, was gloomy if not forbidding; but the open gateway, the sled-marks that led to it, and the wisps of hay which strewed the road, no less than the broken yoke that hung in the old elm beside the entrance—all these, which the Lieutenant's eyes were quick to discern, seemed to offer a more homely and more simple welcome.

A silent welcome, nevertheless, borne on the scent of new-mown, half-gathered hay; a scent which des Ageaux was destined to associate ever after with this beginning of an episode, and with his entrance in the gloaming, amid quiet things. Slowly he passed under the gateway, leading the halting horse. Fallen hay, swept from the cart by the brow of the arch, deadened his footfalls, and before he was discovered he was able to appreciate the enclosure, half courtyard, half fold-yard, sloping downward from the house and shut in on the other sides by a tile-roofed wall. At the lower end on his left were stalls, and sheds, and stables, and a vague, mysterious huddle of ploughs and gear, and feeding beasts, and farm refuse. Between this mass—to which the night began to lend strange forms—and the great, towered house which loomed black against the sky, lay the slope of the court, broken midway by the walled marge of a swell something Italian in fashion, and speaking of more prosperous days. On this there sat, as the traveller saw, two figures.

And then one only. For as he looked, uncertain whether to betake himself first to the stables of the house, one of the two figures sprang from the wall-edge, and came bounding to him with hands upraised, flying skirts, a sharp cry of warning.

"Oh, take care, Charles!" it cried. "Go back before M. le Vicomte comes!"

Then, at six paces from him, she knew him for a stranger, and the last word fell scarcely breathed from her lips; while he, knowing her for a girl, and young by her voice, uncovered. "I seek only a night's shelter," he said stiffly. "Pardon me, mademoiselle, the alarm I fear I have caused you. My horse slipped on the hill, and is unable to travel farther."

She stood staring at him in astonishment, and until her companion at the well came forward made no reply. Something in the movements of this second figure as it crossed the court struck the eye as abnormal, but it was only when it came quite close that the stranger discovered that the lad before him was slightly hump-backed.

"You have met with a mischance," the youth said with awkward diffidence.

"Yes."

"Whatever the cause, you are welcome. Go, Bonne," the young man continued, addressing the girl, "it is better you went—and tell my father that a gentleman is here craving shelter. When I have stabled his horse I will bring him in. This way, if you please!" the lad continued, turning to lead the way to the stables, but casting from moment to moment timid looks at his guest. "The place is rough, but such as it is, it is at your service. Have you ridden far to-day, if it please you?"

"From Rochechouart."

"It is well we had not closed the gates," the youth answered shyly; "we close them an hour after sunset by rule. But to-day the men have been making hay, and we sup late."

The stranger expressed his obligation, and, following his guide, led his horse through one of the doors of a long range of stabling built against the western wall of the courtyard. Within all was dark, and he waited while his companion fetched a lanthorn. The light, when it came, disclosed a sad show of empty mangers, broken racks, and roof beams hung with cobwebs. Rain and sunshine, it was evident, entered through more holes than one, and round the men's heads a couple of bats, startled by the lanthorn-light, flitted noiselessly to and fro.

At the farther end of the place, the roof above three or four stalls showed signs of recent repair; and here the young man invited his guest to place his beast.

"But I shall be turning out your horses," the stranger objected.

The youth laughed a little awry. "There's but my father's gelding," he said, "and old Panza the pony. And they are in the ox-stable where they have company. This," he added, pointing to the roof, "was made good for my sister the Abbess's horses."

The guest nodded, and, after examining his beast's injuries, bathed its knees with fresh water; then producing a bandage from his saddle-bag he soaked it in the water and skilfully wound it round the strained fetlock. The lad held the lanthorn, envy, mingled with admiration, growing in his eyes as he watched the other's skilled hands and method.

"You are well used to horses?" he said.

"Tolerably," des Ageaux answered, looking up. "Are not you?" For in those days it was an essential part of a gentleman's education.

The lad sighed. "Not to horses of this sort," he said, shrugging his shoulders. And des Ageaux took note of the sigh and the words, but said nothing. Instead he removed his sword and pistols from his saddle, and would have taken up his bags also, but the young man interposed and took possession of them. A moment and the two were crossing the darkened courtyard. The light of the lanthorn made it difficult to see aught beyond the circle of its rays, but the stranger noticed that the château consisted half of a steep-roofed house, and half of the two round towers he had seen; house and towers standing in one long line. Two rickety wooden bridges led across a moat to two doors, the one set in the inner of the two towers—probably this was the ancient entrance—the other in the more modern part.

On the bridge leading to the latter two serving-men with lights were awaiting them. The nearer domestic advanced, bowing. "M. le Vicomte will descend if"— and then, after a pause, speaking more stiffly, "M. le Vicomte has not yet heard whom he has the honour of entertaining."

"I have no pretensions to put him to the trouble of descending," the traveller answered politely. "Say if you please that a gentleman of Brittany seeks shelter for the night, and would fain pay his respects to M. le Vicomte at his convenience."

The servant bowed, and turning with ceremony, led the way into a bare, dimly-lit hall open to its steep oaken roof, and not measurably more comfortable or less draughty than the stable. Here and there dusty blazonings looked down out of the darkness, or rusty weapons left solitary in racks too large for them gave back gleams of light. In the middle of the stone floor a trestle table such as might have borne the weight of huge sirloins and great bustards, and feasted two score men-at-arms in the days of the great Francis, supported a litter of shabby odds and ends; old black-jacks jostling riding-spurs, and a leaping-pole lying hard by a drenching-horn.

An open door on the tower side of the hall presented the one point of warmth in the apartment, for through it entered a stream of ruddy light and an odour that announced where the kitchen lay.

But if this were the dining-hall? If the guest felt alarm on this point he was soon reassured. The servant conducted him up a short flight of six steps which rose in one corner. The hall, in truth, huge as it seemed in its dreary emptiness, was but one half of the original hall. The leftward half had been partitioned off and converted into two storeys—the lower story raised a little from the ground for the sake of dryness—of more modern chambers. More modern; but if that into which the guest was ushered, a square room not unhandsome in its proportions, stood for sample, scarcely more cheerful. The hangings on the walls were of old Sarazinois, but worn and faded to the colour of dust. Carpets of leather covered the floor, but they were in holes and of a like hue; while the square stools clad in velvet and gilt-nailed, which stood against the walls, were threadbare of stuff and tarnished of nails. In winter, warmed by the ruddy blaze of a generous fire, and well sconced, and filled with pleasant company seated about a well-spread board, the room might have passed muster and even conduced to ease. But as the dusky frame of a table, lighted by four poor candles—that strove in vain with the vast obscurity—and set with no great store of provision, it wore an air of meagreness not a whit removed from poverty.

The man who stood beside the table in the light of the candles, and formed the life of the picture, blended well with the furnishings. He was tall and thin, with stooping shoulders and a high-nosed face, that in youth

had been masterful and now was peevish and weary.
He wore a sword and much faded lace, and on the appearance of his guest moved forward a pace and halted,
with the precision and stiffness of clockwork. "I have
the honour," he began, "to welcome, I believe——"

"A gentleman of Brittany," des Ageaux answered,
bowing low. It by no means suited his plans to be
recognised. "And one, M. le Vicomte, who respectfully craves a night's hospitality."

"Which the château of Villeneuve-l'Abbesse," the
Vicomte replied with grandeur, "has often granted to
the greatest, nor"—he waved his hand with formal grace
—"ever refused to the meanest. They have attended, I
trust," he continued with the air of one who, at the
head of a great household, knows, none the less, how to
think for his guests, "to your people, sir?"

"Alas, M. le Vicomte," des Ageaux answered, a faint
twinkle in his eyes belying the humility of his tone, "I
have none; I am travelling alone."

"Alone?" The Vicomte repeated the word in a tone
of wonder. "You have no servants with you—at all?"

"Alas—no."

"Is it possible?"

Des Ageaux shrugged his shoulders, and spread out
his hands. "In these days, M. le Vicomte, yes."

The Vicomte seemed by the droop of his shoulders to
admit the plea; perhaps because the other's eyes strayed
involuntarily to the shabby furniture. He shook his
head gloomily. "Since Coutras——" he began, and
then, considering that he was unbending too soon, he
broke off. "You met with some accident, I believe,
sir?" he said. "But first, I did not catch your name?"

"Des Voeux," the Lieutenant answered, adopting on

the spur of the moment one somewhat like his own. "My horse fell and cut its knees on the hill about a mile beyond the ford. I much fear it has also strained a fetlock."

"It will not be fit to travel to-morrow, I doubt?"

The guest spread out his hands, intimating that time and the morrow must take care of themselves; or that it was no use to fight against fate.

"I must lend you something from the stables, then," the Vicomte answered; as if at least a score of horses stood at rack and manger in his stalls. "But I am forgetting your own needs, sir. Circumstances have thrown my household out of gear, and we sup late to-night. But we shall not need to wait long."

He had barely spoken when the two serving-men who had met the Lieutenant on the bridge entered, one behind the other, bearing with some pomp of circumstance a couple of dishes. They set these on the board, and withdrawing—not without leaving behind them a pleasant scent of new-mown hay—returned quickly bearing two more. Then falling back they announced by the mouth of the least meagre that my lord was served.

The meal which they announced, though home-grown and of the plainest, was sufficient, and des Ageaux, on the Vicomte's invitation, took his seat upon a stool at a nicely regulated distance below his host. As he did so the girl he had seen in the courtyard glided in by a side door and silently took her seat on the farther side of the table. Apparently the Vicomte thought his guest below the honour of an introduction, for he said nothing. And the girl only acknowledged the Lieutenant's respectful salutation by a bow.

The four candles shed a feeble light on the table, and left the greater part of the room in darkness. Des Ageaux could not see the girl well, and he got little more than an impression of a figure moderately tall and somewhat plump, and of a gentle, downcast face. Form and face owned, certainly, the charm of youth and freshness. But to eyes versed in the brilliance of a Court and the magnificence of *grandes dames* they lacked the more striking characteristics of beauty.

He gave her a thought, however, pondering while he gave ear to the Vicomte's querulous condescensions how so gentle a creature—for her gentleness and placidity struck him—came of so stiff and peevish a father. But that was all. Or it might have been all if as the thought passed through his mind his host had not abruptly changed the conversation and disclosed another side of his character.

"Where is Roger?" he asked, addressing the girl with sharpness.

"I do not know, sir," she murmured.

A retort seemed hovering on the Vicomte's lips, when the youth who had taken the guest to the stable, and had stayed without, perhaps to make some change in his rustic clothes, entered and slid timidly into his place beside his sister. He hoped, probably, to pass unseen, but the Vicomte, his great high nose twitching, fixed him with his eyes and pointed inexorably at him, with a spoon held delicately between thumb and finger. "You would not think," he said with grim abruptness, "that that—that, M. des Voeux, was son of mine?"

Des Ageaux started. "I fear," he said hastily, "that it was I, sir, who made him late. He was good enough to receive me."

"I can only assure you," the Vicomte replied with cruel wit, "that whoever made him late, it was not I who made him—as he is! The Villeneuves, till his day, I'd have you know, sir, have been straight and tall, and men of their hands, as ready with a blow as a word! Men to make their way in the world. But you see him! You see him! Can you," he continued, his eyes half-closed, dwelling on the lad, whose suffering was evident, "at Court? Or courting? Or stepping a *pavanne?* Or——"

"Father!"

The word burst from the girl's lips, drawn from her by sheer pain. The Vicomte turned to her with icy courtesy. "You spoke, I think?" he said in a tone which rebuked her for the freedom on which she had ventured. "Just so. I was forgetting. We live so quietly here, we use so little ceremony with one another, that even I forget at times that family matters are not interesting to a stranger. Were my elder daughter here, M. des—ah, des Voeux, yes—my daughter the Abbess, who knows the world, and has some tincture of manners, and is not taken commonly for a waiting-woman, she would be able to entertain you better. But you see what we are. For," with a smirk, "it were rude not to include myself with my family."

No wonder, the guest thought, as he listened, full of pity—no wonder the lad had spoken timidly and shyly, if this were the daily treatment he received! If poverty, working on pride, had brought the last of a great family to this—to repaying on the innocents who shared his decay the slings and arrows of unkind fortune! The girl's exclamation, wrung from her by her brother's suffering, had gone to the Lieutenant's heart, though that heart was not of the softest. He would have given something to silence the bitter old tyrant. But experience told him that he might make matters worse. He was no knight-errant, no rescuer of dames; and, after all, the Vicomte was their father. So while he hesitated, seeking in vain a safe subject, the sharp tongue was at work again.

"I would like you to see my elder daughter," the Vicomte resumed with treacherous blandness. "She has neither a ploughboy's figure, nor," slowly, "a dairymaid's speech. Her manners are quite like those of the world. She might go anywhere, even to Court, where she has been, without rendering herself the subject of ridicule and contempt. It is truly unfortunate for us"—with a bow—"that you cannot see her."

"She is not at home?" the Lieutenant said for the sake of saying something. He was full of pity for the girl whose face, now red, now pale, betrayed how she suffered under the discipline.

"She does not live at home," the Vicomte answered. And then—with curious inconsistency he now hid and now declared his poverty—"We have not much left of which we can be proud," he continued, "since the battle of Coutras seven years back took from the late King's friends all they had. But the Abbey of Vlaye is still our appanage. My elder daughter is the Abbess."

"It lies, I think, near Vlaye?"

"Yes, some half-league from Vlaye and three leagues from here. You have heard of Vlaye, then, Monsieur—Monsieur des Voeux?"

"Without doubt, M. le Vicomte."

"Indeed! In what way, may I ask?" There was a faint tinge of suspicion in his tone,

"At Rochechouart I was told that the roads in that direction were not over safe."

The Vicomte laughed in his sardonic fashion. "They begin to cry out, do they?" he said. "The fat burgesses who fleece us? Not very safe, ha, ha! The roads! Not so safe as their back-shops where they lend to us at cent per cent!"—with bitterness. "It is well that there is some one to fleece them in their turn!"

"They told me as much as that," des Ageaux replied with gravity. "So much, indeed, that I was surprised to find your gates still open! They gave me to understand that no man slept without a guard within four leagues of Vlaye."

"They told you that, did they?" the Vicomte answered. And he chuckled, well satisfied. It pleased him to think that if he and his could no longer keep Jacques Bonhomme in order, there were others who could. "They told you not far from the truth. A little later, and you had been barred out even here. Not that I fear the Captain of Vlaye. Hawks pike not out hawks' eyes," with a lifting of the head, and an odd show of arrogance. "We are good friends, M. de Vlaye and I."

"Still you bar your gates, soon or late?" the Lieutenant replied with a smile.

A shadow fell across the Vicomte's face. "Not against him," he said shortly.

"No, of course not," des Voeux replied. "I had forgotten. You have the Crocans also at no great distance. I was forgetting them."

The sudden rigidity of his younger listeners, and the silence which fell on all, warned him, as soon as he had spoken, that he had said something amiss. Nor was the silence all. When his host next spoke—after an interval

—it was with a passion as far removed from the cynical rudeness to which he had treated his children as are the poles apart. "That name is not named in this house!" he cried, his voice thin and tremulous. "By no one!" he struck the table with a shaking hand. "Understand me, sir, by no one! God's curse on them! Ay, and on all who——"

"No, sir, no!" The cry came from the girl. "Do not curse him!"

She was on her feet. For an instant the Lieutenant, seeing her father's distorted face, feared that he would strike her. But the result was different. The opposition that might have maddened the angry man, had the effect of sobering him. "Sit down!" he muttered, passing his napkin over his face. "Sit down, fool! Sit down! And you"—he paused a moment, striving to regain the gibing tone that was habitual to him—"you, sir, may now see how it is. I told you we had no manners. You have now the proof of it. I doubt I must keep you, until the Abbess, my daughter, pays her next visit, that you may see at least one Villeneuve who is neither clown nor dotard!"

Man of the world as he was, the King's Lieutenant knew not what to say to this outburst. He murmured a vague apology, and thought how different all was from the anticipations which the scent of hay and the farm-yard peace had raised in him on his arrival. This old man, rotting in the husk of his former greatness, girding at his helpless children, gnawing, in the decay of his family's grandeur, on his heart and theirs, returning scorn for scorn, and spite for spite, but on those who were innocent of either, ignorant of either—this was a picture to the painting of which the most fanciful must have brought some imagination.   Under the surface lay something more; something that had to do with the Crocans. He fancied that he could make a guess at the secret; and that it had to do with the girl's lover.   But the meal was closing, the Vicomte's rising interrupted his thoughts, and whatever interest the question had for him, he was forced to put it away for the time.

The Vicomte bowed a stiff good-night.   "Boor as he is, I fear that you must now put up with my son," he said, smiling awry.   "He has the Tower Room, where, in my time, I have known the best company in the province lie, when good company was; it has been scarce," he continued bitterly, "since Coutras.   He will find you a lodging there, and if the accommodation be rough, and your room-fellow what you see him," shrugging his shoulders, "at least you will have space enough and follow good gentry.   I have known the Governor of Poitou and the Lieutenant of Périgord, with two of the Vicomtes of the Limousin, lie there—and fourteen truckle-beds about them.   In those days was little need to bar our gates at night.   Solomon! The lanthorn, fool!   I bid you good-night, sir!"

Des Ageaux bowed his acknowledgements, and following in the train of an older serving-man than he had yet seen; who, bearing a lanthorn, led him up a small staircase.   Roger the hapless followed.   On the first floor the guest noted the doors of four rooms, two on either side of a middle passage, that got its light from a window at the end of the house.   Such rooms—or rooms opening one through the other—were at that date reserved for the master and mistress of the château, and their daughters, maiden or married.   For something of the old system which secluded women, and a century before had forbidden their appearance at Court, still prevailed; nor was the Lieutenant at all surprised when his guide, turning from these privileged apartments, led him up a flight of four or five steps at the hither end of the passage. And so through a low doorway.

He passed the door, and was surprised to find himself in the open air on the roof of the hall, the stars above him, and the night breeze cooling his brow. The steeply-pitched lead ended in a broad, flat gutter, fenced by a rail fixed in the parapet. The servant led him along the path which this gutter provided to a door in the wall of the great round tower that rose twenty feet above the house. This gave entrance to a small chamber—one of those commonly found between the two skins of such old buildings—which served both for landing and ante-room. From it the dark opening of a winding staircase led upwards on one hand; on the other a low-browed door masked the course of the downward flight.

Across this closet—bare as bare walls could make it— the grey-bearded servant led him in two strides, and opening a farther door introduced him into the chamber which had seen so much good company. It was a gloomy, octagonal room of great size, lighted in the day-time by four deep-sunk windows, and occupying—save for such narrow closets as that through which they entered—a whole storey of the tower. The lanthorn did but make darkness visible, but Solomon proceeded to light two rushlights that stood in iron sconces on the wall, and by their light the Lieutenant discerned three truckle-beds laid between two of the windows. He could well believe, so vast was the apartment, that fourteen had not cumbered its bareness. At this date a couple of chests, as many stools, a bundle of old spears and a heavy three-legged table made up, with some dingy, tattered hangings, the whole furniture of the chamber.

The old serving-man set down the lanthorn and looked about him sorrowfully.

"Thirty-four I've seen sleep here," he said. "The Governor of Poitou, and the Governor of Périgord, and the four Vicomtes of the Limousin, and twenty-eight gentles in truckles."

"Twenty-eight?" the Lieutenant questioned, measuring in some astonishment the space with his eye. "But your master said——"

"Twenty-eight, by your leave," the man answered obstinately. "And every man his dog! A gentleman was a gentleman then, and a Vicomte a Vicomte. But since that cursed battle at Coutras set us down and put these Huguenots up, there is an end of gentry almost. Ay, thirty—was it thirty, I said?"

"Four, you said. Thirty-four," des Ageaux answered, smiling. "Good-night."

The man shook his head sombrely, bade them good-night, and closed the door on them.

An instant later he could be heard groping his way back through the closet and over the roof. The Lieutenant, as soon as the sound ceased, looked round and thought that he had seldom lain in a gloomier place. The windows were but wooden lattices innocent of glass, and through the slats of the nearest a strong shoot of ivy grew into the room. The night air entered with it and stirred the ragged hangings that covered a part of the walls; hangings that to add to the general melancholy had once been black, a remnant, it is possible, of the funeral trappings of some dead Vicomte. Frogs croaked in a puddle without; one of the lattices creaked open at intervals, only to close again with a hollow report; the rushlights flared sideways in the draught. Des Ageaux had read of such a room in the old romances, in *Bevis of Hampton*, or the *History of Armida;* a room of shadows and gloom, owl-flittings and dead furnishings. But he smiled at the thoughts it called up. He had often lain in his cloak under the sky amid dead men. Nevertheless, "Do you sleep here alone?" he asked, turning to his companion, who had seated himself despondently on one of the beds.

The lad, oppressed by what had gone forward downstairs, barely looked up. "Yes," he began, "since"— and then, breaking off, he added sullenly, "Yes, I do."

"Then you don't lack courage!" des Ageaux replied.

"People sleep well when they are tired," the youth returned, "as I am to-night." .

The Lieutenant accepted the hint, and postponed until the morrow the questions he had it in his mind to ask. Nodding a good-humoured assent he proceeded to his simple arrangements for the night, placed his sword and pistols beside the truckle-bed, and in a few minutes was sleeping as soundly on his thin palliasse as if he had been in truth the poverty-stricken gentleman of Brittany he once had been and still might be again.

CHAPTER II.

THE TOWER CHAMBER.

An hour or two later the Lieutenant awoke suddenly. He rose on his elbow, and listened. Inured to a life of change which had cast him many times into strange beds and the company of stranger bed-fellows, he had not to ask himself where he was, or how he came to be there. He knew these things with a soldier's instinct, before his eyes were open. That which he did ask himself was, what had roused him.

For it was still the dead of night, and all in the château, and all without, save the hoarse voices of the frogs, seemed quiet. Through the lattice that faced him the moonbeams fell on the floor in white, criss-cross patterns; which the pointed shape of the windows made to resemble chequered shields—the black and white escutcheons of his native province. These patches of light diffused about them a faint radiance, sufficient, but no more than sufficient, to reveal the outlines of the furniture, the darker masses of the beds, and even the vague limits of the chamber. He marked nothing amiss, however, except that which had probably roused him. The nearest lattice, that one through which he had noted the ivy growing, stood wide open. Doubtless the breeze, light as it was, had swung the casement inwards, and the creak of the hinge, or the coolness of the un-broken stream of air which blew across his bed, had disturbéd him.

Satisfied with the explanation, he lay down with a sigh of content, and was about to sink into sleep when a low, sibilant sound caught his ear, fretted him awhile, finally dragged him up, broadly awake. What was it? What caused it? The gentle motion of the loosened ivy on the sill? Or the wind toying with the leaves outside? Or the stir of the ragged hangings that moved weirdly on the wall? Or was some one whispering?

The last was the fact, and, assured of it, des Ageaux peered through the gloom at the nearer pallet, and discovered that it was empty. Then he reflected. The ivy, which grew through the window, must have held the lattice firm against a much stronger breeze than was blowing. It followed that the casement had been opened by some one; probably by some one who had entered the room that way.

It might be no affair of his, but on the other hand it might be very much his affair. He looked about the room, making no sound, but keeping a hand raised to seize his weapons on the least alarm.

He could discover neither figure nor any sign of movement in the room. Yet the whispering persisted. More puzzled, he raised himself higher, and then a streak of light which the low, lumpy mass of one of the truckle-beds had hidden, broke on him. It shone under the door by which he had entered, and proceeded, beyond doubt, from a lanthorn or rushlight in the ante-chamber.

What was afoot? It is not as a rule for good that men whisper at dead of night, nor to say their prayers that they steal from their beds in the small hours. Des Ageaux was far from a timid man—or he had not been Lieutenant-Governor of Périgord—but he knew himself alone in a strange house, and a remote corner of that house; and though he believed that he held the map of the country he might be deceiving himself. Possibly, though he had seen no sign of it, he was known. His host styled himself the Captain of Vlaye's friend; he might think to do Vlaye a kindness at his guest's expense. Nor was that all. Lonely travellers ran risks in those days; it was not only from inns that they vanished and left no sign. He bore, it was true, not much of price about him, and riding without attendance might be thought to have less. But, all said and done, the house was remote, the Vicomte poor and a stranger. It might be as well to see what was passing.

He rose noiselessly to his feet, and, taking his sword, crept across the floor. He had lain down in the greater part of his clothes, and whatever awaited him, he was ready. As he drew near the door, the whispering on the farther side persisted. But it was low, the sound lacked menace, and before he laid his ear to the oak some shame of the proceeding seized him.

His scruples were wasted. He could not, even when close, distinguish a word; so wary were the speakers, so low their voices. Then the absurdity of his position, if he were detected and the matter had naught to do with him, took him by the throat. The chamber, with its patches of moonlight and its dim spaces, was all quiet about him, and either he must rest content with that, or he must open and satisfy himself. He took his resolution, found the latch, and opened the door.

He was more or less prepared for what he saw. Not

so the three whom he surprised in their midnight conference. The girl whom he had seen at supper sprang with a cry of alarm from the step on which she had her seat, and retreating upwards as quickly as the cloak in which she was muffled would let her, made as if she would escape by the tower stairs. The two men—Roger, the son of the house, and another, a taller youth, who leant against the wall beside him—straightened themselves with a jerk; while the stranger, who had the air of being two or three years older than Roger, laid his hand on his weapon. A lanthorn which stood on the stone floor between the three, and was the only other object in the closet, cast its light upwards; which had the effect of distorting the men's features, and exaggerating looks already disordered.

The Lieutenant, we have said, was not wholly surprised. None the less the elder of the two young men was the first to find his tongue. "What do you here?" he cried, his eyes gleaming with resentment. "We came to be private here. What do you wish, sir?"

Des Ageaux took one step over the threshold and bowed low. "To offer my apologies," he replied, with a tinge of humour in his tone, "and then to withdraw. To be plain, sir, I heard whispering, and, half-roused, I fancied that it might concern me. Forgive me, mademoiselle," he continued, directing an easy and not ungraceful gesture to the shrinking girl, who cowered on the dark stairs as if she wished they might swallow her. "Your pardon also, Monsieur Charles."

"You know my name?" the stranger exclaimed, with a swift, perturbed glance at the others.

"Your name and no more," des Ageaux answered, smiling and not a whit disturbed. His manner was perfectly easy. "I heard it as I opened. But be at rest, that which is not meant for me I do not keep. You will understand that the hour was late, I found the window open, I heard voices—some suspicion was not unnatural. Have no fear, however. To-morrow I shall only have had one dream the more."

"But dream or no dream," the person he had addressed as Charles blurted out, "if you mention it——"

"I shall not mention it."

"To the Vicomte even?"

"Not even to him! The presence of mademoiselle's brother," des Ageaux continued, with a keen glance at Roger, "were warrant for silence, had I the right to speak."

The girl started and the hood of her cloak fell back. With loosened hair and parted lips she looked so pretty that he was sorry he had struck at her ever so slightly. "You think, sir," she exclaimed in a tone half-indignant, half-awestruck, "that this is my lover?"

His eyes passed from her to the taller young man. He bowed low. "I did," he said, the courtesy of his manner redoubled. "Now I see that he is your brother. Forgive me, mademoiselle, I am unlucky this evening. Lest I offend again—and my presence alone must be an offence—I take my leave."

Charles stepped forward. "Not," he said somewhat peremptorily, "before you have assured us again of your silence! Understand me, sir, this is no child's play! Were my father to hear of my presence, he would make my sister suffer for it. Were he to discover me here—you do not know him yet—it might cost a life!"

"What can I say more," des Ageaux replied with a

little stiffness, "than I have said? Why should I betray you?"

"Enough, sir, if you understand."

"I understand enough!" And then, "If I can do no more than be silent——"

"You can do no more."

"I take my leave." And, bowing, with an air of aloofness he stepped back and closed the door on them.

When he had done so the three looked eagerly at one another. But they did not speak until his footsteps on the chamber floor had ceased to sound. Then, "What is this?" the elder brother muttered, frowning slightly at the younger. "There is something here I do not understand. Who is he? What is he? You told me that he was some poor gentleman adventuring alone, and without servants, and staying here for the night with a lame horse and an empty purse. But——"

"He was not like this at supper," Roger replied, excusing himself.

"But he has nothing of the tone of the man you described."

"Not now," Bonne said. "But at supper he was different in some way." And recalling how he had looked at her when he thought that Charles was her lover, she blushed.

"He is no poor man," Charles muttered. "Did you mark his ring?"

"No."

"May-be at supper it was turned inward, but as he stood there with his hand on the door post, the light fell on it. *Three leopards passant or on a field vert!* I have seen that coat, and more than once!"

"But why should not the poor gentleman wear his

coat?" Bonne urged. "Perhaps it is all that is left of his grandeur."

"In gold on green enamel?" Charles asked, raising his eyebrows. "Certainly his sword was of the plainest. But I don't like it! Why is he here? What is he doing? Can he be friend to Vlaye, and on his way to help him?"

Abruptly the girl stepped forward, and flinging an arm round her brother's neck, pressed herself against him. "Give it up! Give it up!" she murmured. "Charles! Dear brother, listen to me. Give it up!"

"It were better you gave me up," he replied in a tone between humour and pathos, as he stroked her hair. "But you are Villeneuve at heart, Bonne——"

"Bonne by nature, Bonne by name!" Roger muttered, caressing her with his eyes.

"And stand by those you love, whatever come of it!" Charles continued. "Would you then have me leave those"—with a grimace which she, having her face on his shoulder, could not see—"whom, if I do not love, I have chosen! Leave them because danger threatens? Because Vlaye gives the word?"

"But what can you do against him?" she answered in a tearful tone. "You say yourself that they are but a rabble, your Crocans! Broken men, beggars and what not, peasants and ploughboys, ill-armed and ill-fed! What can they do against men-at-arms? Against Vlaye? I thought when I got word to you to come, in order that I might tell you what he was planning—I thought that you would listen to me!"

"And am I not listening, little one?" he replied, fondling her hair.

"But you will not be guided?"

"That is another thing," he replied more soberly.
"Had I known, it is true, what I know now, had I known
of what sort they were to whom I was joining myself,
I might not have done it. I might have borne a little
longer"—his tone grew bitter—"the life we lead here!
I might have borne a little longer to rust and grow
boorish, and to stand for clown and rustic in M. de
Vlaye's eyes when he deigns to visit us! I might have
put up a little longer with the answer I got when I
craved leave to see the wars and the world—that as my
fathers had made my bed I must lie on it. Ay, and
more! If he—I will not call him father—had spared me
his sneers only a little, if he had let a day go by without
casting in my face the lack that was no fault of mine,
I would have still tried to bear it. But not a day did
he spare me! Not one day, as God is my witness!"

Her sorrowful silence acknowledged the truth of his
words. At length, "But if these folk," she said timidly,
"are of so wretched a sort, Charles?"

"Wretched they are," he answered, "but their cause
is good. Better fall with them than rise by such deeds
as have driven them to arms. I tell you that the things
I have heard, as I sat over their fires by night in the
caves about Bourdeilles where they lie, would arm not
men's hands only, but women's! Would spoil your
sleep of nights, and strong men's sleep! Poor cottars
killed and hamlets burned, in pure sport! Children flung
out and women torn from homes, and through a whole
country-side corn trampled wantonly, and oxen killed to
make a meal for four! But I cannot tell you what they
have suffered, for you are a woman and you could not
bear it!"

Bonne forgot her fears for him. She leant forward—

she had gone back to her seat on the stairs—and clenched her small hands. "And M. de Vlaye it is," she cried, "he who has done more than any other to madden them, who now proposes to rise upon their fall? Monsieur de Vlaye it is who, having driven them to this, will now crush them and say he does the King service, and so win pardon for a thousand crimes?"

But the light had gone out in Charles's eyes. "Ay, and win it he will. So it will go," he said moodily. "So it will happen! He has seen afar the chance of securing himself, and he will seize it, by doing what, for the time, no other has means to do."

"He who kindled the fire will be rewarded for putting it out?"

"Just so!"

"But can you do nothing against him?" Roger muttered.

"We may hold our own for a time, in the caves and hills about Brantôme perhaps," the elder brother answered. "But after a while he will starve us out. And in the open such folks as we have, ill-armed, ill-found, with scarce a leader older than myself, will melt before his pikes like smoke before the wind!"

Roger's eyes glistened. "Not if I were with you," he muttered. "There should be one blow struck before he rode over us! But"—he let his chin sink on his breast —"what am I?"

"Brave enough, I know," Charles answered, putting his hand affectionately on the lad's shoulder. "Braver than I am, perhaps. But it is not the end, be the end what it may, good lad, that weighs me down and makes me coward. It is the misery of seeing all go wrong hour by hour and day by day! Of seeing the cause

with which I must now sink or swim mishandled! Of
striving to put sense and discipline into the folk who are
either clowns, unteachable by aught but force, or a rabble
of worthless vagrants drawn to us as to any other cause
that promises safety from the gallows. And yet, if I
were older and had seen war and handled men, I feel
that even of this stuff I could make a thing should
frighten Vlaye. Ay, and for a time I thought I could,"
he continued gloomily. "But they would not be driven,
and short of hanging half a dozen, which I dare not
attempt, I must be naught!"

"Do you think," Roger muttered, "that if you had me
beside you—I have strong arms——"

"God forbid!" Charles answered, looking sadly at
him. "Dear lad, one is enough! What would Bonne
do without you? It is not your place to go forth."

"If I were straight!"

The girl leaned forward and took his hand. "You
are straight for me," she said softly. "Straight for me!
More precious than the straightest thing in the world!"

He sighed and Bonne echoed the sigh. It was the
first time the three had met since Charles's flight; since,
fretted by inaction and stung beyond patience by the
gibes of the father—who, while he withheld the means
of making a figure in the world, did not cease to sneer
at supineness—he had taken a step which had seemed
desperate, and now semed fatal. For if this Crocan
rising were not a Jacquerie in name, if it were not
stained as yet by the excesses which made that word
a terror, it was still a peasant-rising. It was still a
revolt of the canaille, of the mob; and more indulgent
fathers than the Vicomte would have disowned the son
who, by joining it, ranged himself against his caste.

The younger man had known that when he took the step; yet he had been content to take it. The farther it set him from the Vicomte the better! But he had not known nor had Bonne guessed how hopeless was the cause he was embracing, how blind its leaders, how shiftless its followers, how certain and disastrous its end! But he knew now. He knew that, to the attack which M. de Vlaye meditated, the mob of clods and vagrants must fall an easy prey.

Young and high-spirited, moved a little by the peasants' wrongs, and more by his own, he had done this thing. He had rushed on ruin, made good his father's gibes, played into M. de Vlaye's hands—the hands of the man who had patronised him a hundred times, and with a sneer made sport of his rusticity. The contempt of the man of the world for the raw boy had sunk into the lad's soul, and he hated Vlaye. To drag Vlaye down had been one of Charles's day-dreams. He had pined for the hour when, at the head of the peasants who were to hail him as their leader, he should tread the hated scutcheon under foot.

Now he saw that all the triumph would be M. de Vlaye's, and that by his bold venture he had but added a feather to the hated plume. And Bonne and Roger, mute because their love taught them when to speak and when to refrain, gazed sadly at the lanthorn. The silence lasted a long minute, and was broken in the end, not by their voices, but by the distant creak of a door.

Bonne sprang to her feet, the colour gone from her face. "Hush!" she cried. "What was that? Listen."

They listened, their hearts beating. Presently Roger, his face almost as bloodless as Bonne's, snatched up the lanthorn. "It is the Vicomte!" he gasped. "He is coming! Quick, Charles! You must go the way you came!"

"But Bonne?" his brother muttered, hanging back. "What is she to do?"

Roger, his hand on the door of the Tower Chamber, stood aghast. Charles might escape unseen, there was still time. But Bonne? If her father found the girl there? And the stranger was in the Tower Room, she could not retreat thither. What was she to do?

The girl's wits found the answer. She pointed to the stairs. "I will hide above," she whispered. "Do you go!" It was still of Charles she thought. "Do you go!" But the terror in her eyes—she feared her father as she feared no one else in the world—wrung the brothers' hearts.

Charles hesitated. "The door at the top?" he babbled. It is locked, I fear!"

"He will not go up!" she whispered. "And while he is in the Tower Room I can escape."

She vanished as she spoke, in the darkness of the narrow winding shaft—and it was time she did. The Vicomte was scarce three paces from the outer door when the two who were left sprang into the Tower Chamber.

The Lieutenant was on his feet by the side of his bed. He had not gone to sleep, and he caught their alarm, he had heard the last hurried whispers, he had guessed their danger. He was not surprised when Charles, without a word, crossed the floor in a couple of bounds, flung himself recklessly over the sill of the window, clung an instant by one hand, then disappeared. A moment the shoot of ivy that grew into the chamber jerked violently, the next the door was flung wide open, and the

Vicomte, a gaunt figure bearing a sword in one hand, a lanthorn in the other, stood on the threshold. The light of the lanthorn which he held above his head that he might detect what was before him, obscured his face. But the weapon and the tone of his voice proclaimed the fury of his suspicions. "Who is here?" he cried. "Who is here?" And again, as if in his rage he could frame no other words, "Who is here, I say? Speak!"

Roger, on his feet, the tell-tale lanthorn in his hand, could not force a word. He stood speechless, motionless, self-convicted; and had all lain with him, all had been known. Fortunately des Ageaux took on himself to answer.

"Who is here, sir?" he said in a voice a tone louder and a shade easier than was natural. "The devil, I think! For I swear no one else could climb this wall!"

"What do you mean?"

"And climb it," des Ageaux persisted, disregarding the question, "very nearly to this sill! I heard him below five minutes ago. And if I had not been fool enough to rouse your son and bid him light we had had him safe by now on this floor!"

The Vicomte glared. The story was glib, well told, animated; but he doubted it. He knew what he had expected to find. "You lit the lanthorn?" he snarled. "When?"

"Two minutes back—it might be more," des Ageaux replied. "Now he is clean gone. Clean gone, I fear," he added as he stepped into the embrasure of the window and leant forward cautiously, is if he thought a shot from below a thing not impossible. "I hear nothing, at any rate."

The Vicomte, struggling with senile rage, stared about

him. "But I saw a light!" he cried. "In the outer room!"

"The outer room!"

"Under the door."

"Shone under both doors, I suppose," des Ageaux replied, still intent to all appearance on the dark void outside. "I'll answer for it," he added carelessly as he turned, "that he did not go out by the door."

"He will not go out now," the Vicomte retorted with grim suspicion, "for I have locked the outer door." He showed the key hung on a finger of the hand which held the lanthorn.

The sight was too much for Roger; he understood at once that it cut off his sister's retreat. A sound between a groan and an exclamation broke from him.

The Vicomte lifted the lanthorn to his face. "What now, booby?" he said. "Who has hurt you?" And, seeing what he saw, he cursed the lad for a coward.

"I did not feel over brave myself five minutes ago," the Lieutenant remarked.

The Vicomte turned on him as if he would curse him also. But, meeting his eyes, he thought better of it, and swallowed the rage he longed to vent. He stared about him a minute or more, stalking here and there offensively, and trying to detect something on which to fasten. But he found nothing, and, having flung the light of his lanthorn once more around the room, he stood an instant, then, turning, went sharply—as if his suspicions had now a new direction—towards the door.

"Good-night!" he muttered churlishly.

"Good-night!" the Lieutenant answered, but in the act of speaking he met the look of horror in Roger's eyes, remembered and understood. "She is still there," the lad's white lips spelled out, as they listened to the grating noise of the key in the lock. "She could not escape. And he suspects. He is going to her room."

Des Ageaux stared a moment nonplussed. The matter was nothing to him, nothing, yet his face faintly mirrored the youth's consternation. Then, in a stride, he was at his bedside. He seized one of the horse-pistols which lay beside his pillow, and, before the lad understood his purpose, he levelled it at the open window and fired into the night.

The echoes of the report had not ceased to roll hollowly through the Tower before the door flew wide again, and the Vicomte reappeared, his eyes glittering, his weapon shaking in his excitement. "What is it?" he cried, for at first he could not see, the smoke obscured the room. "What is it? What is it?"

"A miss, I fear," des Ageaux answered coolly. He stood with his eyes fixed on the window, the smoking weapon in his hand. "I fear, a miss—I had a notion all the time that he was in the ivy outside, and when he poked up his head——"

"His head?" the Vicomte exclaimed. He was shaking from head to foot.

"Well, it looked like his head," des Ageaux replied more doubtfully. He moved a step nearer to the window. "But I could not swear to it. It might have been an owl!"

"An owl?" the Vicomte answered in an unsteady tone. "You fired at an owl?"

"Whatever it was I missed it," des Ageaux answered with decision, and in a somewhat louder tone. "If you will step up here—but I fear you are not well, M. le Vicomte?"

He spoke truly, the Vicomte was not well. He had
had a shock. Cast off his son as he might, hate him as
he might—and hate him he did, as one who had turned
against him and brought dishonour on his house—that
shot in the night had shaken him. He leant against the
wall, his lips white, his breath coming quickly. And a
minute or more elapsed before he recovered himself and
stood upright.

He kept his eyes averted from des Ageaux. He
turned instead to Roger. Whether he feared for himself
and would not be alone, or he suspected some complicity
between the two, he signed to the lad to take up the
lanthorn and go before him. And, moving stiffly and
unsteadily across the floor, he got himself in silence to
the door. With something between a bow and a glance
—it was clear that he could not trust his tongue—he was
out of the room.

The Lieutenant sat on his bed for some time, expecting
Roger to return. But the lad did not appear, and after
an interval des Ageaux took on himself to search the
staircase. It was untenanted. The girl, using the
chance he had afforded her, had escaped.

CHAPTER III.

STILL WATERS TROUBLED.

HAD Bonne de Villeneuve, a day earlier, paid a visit much in fashion at that time, and consulted the "dark man" who, in an upper room on the wall of Angoulême, followed the stars and cast horoscopes, and was reputed to have foretold the death of the first Duke of Joyeuse as that nobleman passed southwards to the field of Coutras, she might have put faith in such of the events of the night as the magic crystal showed her; until it came to mirror, faint as an evening mist beside the river, her thoughts after the event. Then, had it foretold that, as she lay quaking in her bed, she would be thinking neither of the brother, whose desperate venture wrung her heart, nor of Roger, her dearer self, but of a stranger—a stranger, whose name she had not known six hours, and of whose past she knew nothing, she would have paused, refusing credence. She would have smiled at the phantasm of the impossible.

Yet so it was. Into the quiet pool of her maiden heart had fallen in an hour the stone that sooner or later troubles the sweet waters. As she lay thinking with wide-open eyes, her mind, which should have been employed with her brother's peril, or her own escape, or her father's rage, was busy with the stranger who had dropped so suddenly into her life, and had begun on the instant to play a sovereign part. She recalled his aspect as he looked in on them, cool and confident, at their midnight conference. She heard his tone as he baffled her father's questions with cunning answers. She marvelled at the wit that in the last pinch had saved her from discovery. He seemed to her a man of the world such as had not hitherto come within the range of her experience. Was he also the perfect knight of whom she had not been woman if she had not dreamed?

What, she wondered, must his life have been, who, cast among strange surroundings, bore himself so masterfully, and so shrewdly took his part! What chances he must have seen, what dangers run, how many men, how many cities visited! He might have known the Court, that strange *mélange* of splendour and wickedness, and mystery and valour. He might have seen the King, shrewdest of captains, bravest of princes; he might have encountered eye to eye men whose names were history. He came out of the great outer world of which she had visions, and already she was prepared to invest him with wonderful qualities. Her curiosity once engaged, she constructed for him first one life and then another, and then yet another—all on the same foundation, the one fact which he had told them, that he was a poor gentleman of Brittany. She considered his ring, and the shape of his clothes, and his manner of eating, which she found more delicate than her brothers'; and she fancied, but she told herself that she was foolish to think it, that she detected under his frigid bearing a habit of command that duller eyes failed to discern.

She was ashamed at last of the persistence with which her thoughts ran on him, and she tried to think of other things, and so thought of him again, and, awaking to the fact, smiled. But without blushing; partly because, whatever he was, he stood a great way from her, and partly because it was only her fancy that was touched, and not her heart; and partly again because she knew that he would be gone by mid-day, and could by no possibility form part of her life. Nevertheless, it was not until her time for rising came that anxiety as to her brother's safety and her father's anger eclipsed him. Then, uncertain how much the Vicomte knew, how near the truth he guessed, she forgot her hero, and thought exclusively of her father's resentment.

She might have spared her fears. The Vicomte was a sour and embittered man, but neither by nature nor habit a violent one. Rage had for an hour rendered him capable of the worst, capable of the murder of his son if, having an arm in his hand, he had met him, capable of the expulsion of his daughter from his house. But the fit was not natural to him; it was not so that he avenged the wrongs which the world had heaped upon him—since Coutras. He fell back easily and at once into the black cynical mood that was his own. He was too old and weak, he had too long brooded in inaction, he had too long wreaked his vengeance on the feeble to take strong measures now, whatever happened to him.

But some hours elapsed before Bonne knew this, or how things would be. It was not her father's custom to descend before noon, for with his straitened means and shrunken establishment he went little abroad; and he would have died rather than stoop to the rustic tasks which Roger pursued, and of which Bonne's small brown hands were not ignorant. She had not seen him when, an hour before noon, she repaired to a seat in the most remote corner of the garden, taking with her some household work on which she was engaged.

The garden of the château of Villeneuve—the garden proper that is, for the dry moat which divided the house from the courtyard was planted with pot-herbs and cabbages—formed a square, having for its one side the length of the house. It lay along the face of the building remote from the courtyard, and was only accessible through it. Its level, raised by art or nature, stood more than a man's height above the surrounding country; of which, for this reason, it afforded a pleasant and airy prospect. The wall which surrounded and buttressed it stood on the inner side no more than three feet high, but rose on the outer from a moat, the continuation of that which has just been mentioned.

The pleasaunce thus secured on all sides from intrusion consisted first of a paved walk which ran under the windows of the château, and was boarded by a row of ancient mulberry-trees; secondly, beyond this, of a strip of garden ground planted with gooseberry-bushes and fruit-trees, and bisected by a narrow walk which led from the house to a second terrace formed on the outer wall. This latter terrace lay open towards the country and at either end, but was hidden from the prying eyes of the house by a line of elms, poled and cut espalier fashion. It offered at either extremity the accommodation of a lichen-covered stone bench which tempted the old to repose and the young to reverie. The east bench enabled a person seated sideways on it—and so many had thus sat that the wall was hollowed by their elbows—to look over the willow-edged river and the tract of lush meadows which its loop enclosed. The western seat had not this poetic advantage, but by way of compensation afforded to sharp eyes a glimpse of the track—road it could not be called—which after passing the château wound through the forest on its course to Vlaye and the south.

From childhood the seat facing the river had been Bonne's favourite refuge. Before she could walk she had played games in the dust beneath it. She had carried to it her small sorrows and her small joys, her fits of nursery passion, her moods as she grew older. She had nursed dolls on it, and fancies, dreamed dreams and built castles; and in a not unhappy, thought neglected girlhood, it had stood for that sweet and secret retreat, the bower of the budding life, which remains holy in the memory of worn men and women. The other bench, which commanded a peep of the road, had been more to her elder sister's taste; nor was the choice without a certain bearing on the character of each.

This morning, she had not been five minutes at work before she heard footsteps on the garden path. The sun, near its highest, had driven her to the inner end of the seat, where the elm in summer leaf straggled widely over it, growing low, as elms will. She knew that whoever came she would see before she was seen.

It turned out as she expected. M. des Ageaux lounged onto the terrace, and shading his eyes from the sun's rays, gazed on the prospect. She judged that he thought himself alone, for he took a short turn this way and that. Then, after a casual glance at the empty seats—empty as he doubtless judged, though she from her arbour of leaves could watch his every movement— he wheeled about, and, facing the château, seemed to satisfy himself that the wall of pollard elms sheltered him from sight.

His next proceeding was mysterious. He drew from his breast a packet, of parchment or paper, unfolded it, and laid it flat on the wall before him. Then he stooped and after poring over it, glanced at the view, referred again to the paper, then again to the lie of the country, and the course of the river which flowed on his left. Finally he measured off a distance on the map. For a map it was, beyond doubt.

A shadow fell on her as she watched him. Nor did his next movement dispel the feeling. Folding up the map he replaced it in his breast, and leaning over the wall he scrutinised the outer surface of the brickwork. Apparently he did not discover what he sought, for he raised himself again, and with eyes bent on the tangle of nettles and rough herbage that clothed the bottom of the moat, he moved slowly along the terrace towards her. He reached, without seeing her, the seat on which she sat, knelt on it with one knee, and leaning far over the moat, allowed a low laugh to escape him.

She fought the faint suspicion that, unwelcome, asserted itself. He had behaved so honourably, so reticently, in all that had happened that she was determined not to believe aught to his discredit. But her folly, if foolish she was, must not imperil another. She made a mental note that there was one thing she must not tell him. Very quickly that reflection passed through her brain. And then—

"Why do you laugh?" she said.

He wheeled about so sharply that in another mood she must have laughed, so much she had the advantage of him. For an instant he was so taken aback that he did not speak. Then, "Why did you startle me?" he asked, his eyes smiling.

"Because—yes, my brother came in that way."

"I know it," he answered; "but not why you startled me, mademoiselle, a minute ago."

"Nor I," she retorted, smiling faintly, "why you were so inquisitive, M. des Voeux?"

"I am going to tell you that," he said. He seated himself on the bench so as to face her, and doffing his hat, held it between his face and the sun. He was not, we know, very amenable to the charms of women, and he saw in her no more than a girl of rustic breeding, comely and gentle, and something commonplace, but a good sister whose aid with her brother he needed. "I am going to tell you," he said; "because I am anxious to meet your brother again and to talk with him."

She continued to meet his eyes, but her own were clouded. "On what subject," she asked, "if I am not too curious?"

"The Crocans."

On her guard as she was, the word put her out of countenance. She could not hide, and after one half-hearted attempt did not try to hide, her dismay. "The Crocans?" she said. "But why do you come to me?" her colour coming and going. "What have we to do with them, if you please? Or my brother?"

"He has been banished from his home for some offence," the Lieutenant answered quietly. "Your father forbids the mention of the name Crocans. It is reasonable to infer that the offence is connected with them, and, in a word, that your brother has done what any young man with generous instincts and a love of adventure might do. He has joined them. I do not blame him."

"You do not blame him?" she murmured. Never

had she heard such words of the Crocans—except from her brother. "You mean that?"

"I say it and mean it," the Lieutenant replied. But he spoke without emotion, emotion was not his forte. "Nor am I alone," he went on, "in holding such opinions. But the point, mademoiselle, is this. I wish to find a means of communicating with them, and he can and probably will be willing to aid me. For certain, if the worst comes to the worst, I can aid him."

Bonne's heart beat rapidly. She did not—she told herself that she did not distrust him. Had it been her own secret he was seeking she would have delivered it to him freely. But the manner in which he had borne himself while he thought himself alone, the possession of the map, and the shrewdness with which he had traced her brother's movement and surprised a secret that was still a secret from the household, frightened her. And her very inexperience made her pause.

"But first, I take it, you need his aid?" she murmured.

"I wish to speak with him."

"Have you seen my father?"

He opened his eyes and bent a little nearer. "Do you mean, mademoiselle——"

"I mean only," she said gently, "that if you express to him the views on the Crocans which you have just expressed to me, your opportunities of seeing my brother will be scant."

He laughed. "I have not opened them to him," he said. "I have seen him, and whether he thinks that he was a little more exigent last night than the danger required, or he desires to prove to me that midnight alarms are not the rule at Villeneuve, he has not given me notice to go. His invitation to remain is not, perhaps," he smiled slightly, "of the warmest. But if you, mademoiselle, will second it——"

She muttered—not without a blush—that it would give her pleasure. And he proceeded, "Then no difficulty on that point will arise."

She stooped lower over her work. What was she to do? He wanted that which she had decided she must not give him. Just that! What was she to do?

She was so long in answering, that he dubbed her awkward and mannerless. And thought it a pity, too; for she was a staunch sister, and had shown herself resourceful; and in repose her face, though brown and sunburnt, was not without grace. He came to the point. "May I count on you for this?" he asked bluntly.

"For—what?"

"That as soon as you can you will bring me face to face with your brother?"

She looked up and met his gaze. "As soon as I think it safe to do so," she said, "I will. You may depend on me."

He had not divined her doubt, nor did he discern her quibble. Still, "Could I not go to him to-day?" he said. "If he is still in the neighbourhood?"

She shook her head. "I do not know where he is," she answered, glad that she could say so much with truth. "But if he show himself, and it be safe, I will let you know. Roger——"

"Ha! To be sure, Roger may know?"

She smiled. "Roger and I are one," she said. "You must not expect to get from him what I do not give." She said it naïvely, with just so much of a smile as showed her at her best, and he hastened to say that he left him-

self in her hands. She blushed through her sunburn at
that, but clung to her quibble, telling herself that this
was a stranger, the other a brother, and that if she
destroyed Charles she could never forgive herself.

He saw that she was disturbed, and he changed
the subject. "You have always lived here?" he
asked.

"Yes," she answered, "but I can remember when
things were different with us. We were not always so
broken. Before Coutras—but," with a faint smile, "you
have heard my father on that, and will not wish to hear
me."

"The Vicomte was present at the battle?"

"Yes, he was in the centre of the Catholic army with
the Duke of Joyeuse. He escaped with his life. But
we lay in the path of the pursuit after the flight, and
they sacked the house, and burned the hamlet by the
ford—the one you passed—and the two farms in the
bend of the river—the two behind you. They swept off
every four-legged thing, every horse, and cow, and sheep,
and left us bare. One of the servants who resisted was
killed, and—and my mother died of the shock."

She broke off with an uncontrollable shiver. She was
silent. After a pause, "Perhaps you were at Coutras,
M. des Voeux?" she said, looking up.

"I was not of the party who sacked your house," he
answered gravely.

She knew then that he had fought on the other side;
and she admired him for the tact with which he made it
known to her. He was a soldier then. She wondered,
as she bent over her work, if he had fought elsewhere,
and under whom, and with what success. Had he
prospered or sunk? He called himself a poor gentleman

of Brittany, but that might have been his origin only, he might be something more now.

In the earnestness of her thoughts she turned her eyes on his ring, and she blushed brightly when with a quick, almost rude movement he hid his hand. "I beg your pardon!" she murmured. "I was not thinking."

"It is I should beg yours," he said quietly. "It is only that I do not want you to come to a false conclusion. This ring—in a word I wear it, but the arms are not mine. That is all."

"Does that apply also," she asked, looking at him ingenuously, "to the pistols you carry, M. des Voeux? Or should I address you—for I saw last evening that they bore a duke's coronet—as your Grace?"

He laughed gaily. "They are mine, but I am not a duke," he said.

"Nor are you M. des Voeux?"

Her acuteness surprised him. "I am afraid, mademoiselle," he said, "that you have a mind to exalt me into a hero of romance—whether I will or no."

She bent over her work to hide her face. "A duke gave them to you, I suppose?" she said.

"That is so," he replied sedately.

"Did you save his life?"

"I did not."

"I have heard," she returned, looking up thoughtfully, "that at Coutras a gentleman on the other side strove hard to save the Duke of Joyeuse's life, and did not desist until he was struck down by his own men."

"He looked to make his account by him, no doubt," the Lieutenant answered coldly. "Perhaps," with a scarcely perceptible bitterness, "the Duke, had he lived, would have given him—a pair of pistols!"

"That were a small return," she said indignantly, "for such a service!"

He shrugged his shoulders. And to change the subject—

"What are the grey ruins," he asked, "on the edge of the wood?"

"They are part of the old Abbey," she answered without looking up, "afterwards removed to Vlaye, of which my sister is Abbess. There was a time, I believe, when the convent stood so close to the house that it was well-nigh one with it. There was some disorder, I believe, and the Diocesan obtained leave to have it moved, and it was planted on lands that belonged to us at that time."

"Near Vlaye?"

"Within half a league of it."

"Your sister, then, is acquainted with the Captain of Vlaye?"

She did not look up. "Yes," she said.

"But you and your brothers?"

"We know him and hate him—only less than we fear him!" She regretted her vehemence the moment she had spoken.

But he merely nodded. "So do the Crocans, I fancy," he said. "It is rumoured that he is preparing something against them."

"You know that?" she exclaimed in surprise.

"Without being omniscient," he answered smiling. "I heard it in Barbesieux. It was that, perhaps," he continued shrewdly, "which you wished to tell your brother yesterday."

On that she was near confessing all to him and telling him, in spite of her resolutions, where on the next day he could find her brother. But she clung to her decision, and a minute later he rose and moved away in the direction of the house.

When they met at table the mystery of the Vicomte's sudden impulse to hospitality, which was something of a puzzle to her, began to clear.

It had its origin in nothing more substantial than his vanity; which was tickled by the opportunity of talking to a man who, with some pretensions to gentility, could be patronised. A little, too, he thought of the figure he had made the night before. It was possible that the stranger had been unfavourably impressed. That impression the Vicomte thought he must remove, and to that end he laboured, after his manner, to be courteous to his guest. But as his talk consisted, and had long consisted, of little but sneers and gibes at the companions of his fallen fortunes, his civility found its only vent in this direction.

Des Ageaux indeed would gladly have had less of his civility. More than once—though he was not fastidious—his cheek coloured with shame, and willingly would he, had that been all, have told the Vicomte what he thought of his witticisms. But he had his cards sorted, his course arranged. Circumstances had played for him in the dangerous game on which he was embarked, and he would have been unworldly indeed had he been willing to cast away, for a point of feeling—he who was no knight-errant—the advantages he had gained.

Not that he did not feel strongly for the two whose affection for one another touched him. Roger's deformity appealed to him, for he fancied that he detected in the lad a spirit which those who knew him better, but knew only his gentler side, did not suspect.

And the girl who had grown from child to woman in
the rustic stillness of this moated house—that once had
rung with the tread of armed heels and been gay with
festive robes and tourneys, but now was sinking fast
into a lonely farmstead—she too awakened some interest in the man of the world, who smiled to find himself embedded for the time in a life so alien from his
every-day experiences. Concern he felt for the one and
the other; but such concern as weighed light in the
balance against the interests he held in his hands, or
even against his own selfish interest.

It soon appeared that the Vicomte had another motive
for hospitality, in the desire to dazzle the stranger by
the splendours of his eldest daughter, on whom he continued to harp. "There is still one of us," he said with
senile vanity—"I doubt if, from the specimens you have
seen, you will believe it—who is not entirely as God made
her! Thank the Lord for that! Who is neither clod
nor clout, sir, but has as much fashion as goes to the
making of a modest gentlewoman."

His guest looked gravely at him. "I look forward
much to seeing her, M. le Vicomte!" he said for the
tenth time.

"Ay, you may say so!" the Vicomte answered. "For
in her you will see a Villeneuve, and the last of the line!"
with a scowl at Roger. "Neither a lout with his boots
full of hay-seeds—pah! nor a sulky girl with as much
manner as God gave her, and not a jot to it! Nice
company I have, M. des Voeux," he continued
bitterly. "Did you say des Voeux—I never heard the
name?"

"Yes, M. le Vicomte."

"Nice company, I say, for a Villeneuve in his old age!

What think you of it? Before Coutras, where was an end of the good old days, and the good old gentrice——"

"You were at Coutras?"

"Ay, to my cost, a curse on it! But before Coutras, I say, I had at least their mother, who was a Monclar from Rouergue. She had at any rate a tongue and could speak. And my daughter the Abbess takes after her, though may-be more after me, as you will think when you see her. She will be here, she says, to-morrow, for a night or two." This he told for the fifth time that evening.

"I am looking forward to seeing her!" the guest repeated gravely—also for the fifth time.

But the Vicomte could not have enough of boasting, which was doubly sweet to him; first because it exalted the absent, and secondly because it humiliated those who were present. "Thank God, she at least is not as God made her!" he said again, pleased with the phrase. "At Court last year the King noticed her, and swore she was a true Villeneuve, and a most perfect lady without fault or blemish!"

"His Majesty is certainly a judge," the listener responded, the twinkle in his eye more apparent than usual.

"To be sure!" the old man returned. "Who better? But, for the matter of that, I am a judge myself. My daughter—for there is only one worthy of the name"—with a withering glance at poor Bonne—"is not hand in glove with every base-born wench about the place, trapesing to a christening in a stable as readily as if the child were a king's son! Ay, and as I am a Catholic, praying beside old hags' beds till the lazy priest at the chapel has nought left to do for his month's meal! Pah!"

"Ranks are no doubt of God's invention," des Voeux said with his eyes on the table.

The Vicomte struck the board angrily. "Who doubts it?" he exclaimed. "Of God's invention, sir? Of course they are!"

"But I take it that they exist, in part at least," des Ageaux answered, "as a provision for the exercise of charity; and of——" he hesitated, unwilling—he read the gathering storm on the Vicomte's brow—to give offence; and, by a coincidence, he was saved from the necessity. As he paused the door flew open, and a serving-man, not one of the two who had waited on the table, but an uncouth creature, shaggy and field-stained, appeared gesticulating on the threshold. He was out of breath, apparently he could not speak; while the gust of wind which entered with him, by blowing sideways the long, straggling flames of the candles, and deepening the gloom of the ill-lit room, made it impossible to discern his face.

The Vicomte rose. They all rose. "What does this mean?" he cried in a rage. "What is it?"

"There's a party ringing at the gate, my lord, and—and won't take no!" the man gasped. "A half-dozen of spears, and others on foot and horse. A body of them. Solomon sent me to ask what's to do, and if he shall open."

"There's a petticoat with them," a second voice answered. The speaker showed his face over the other's shoulder.

"Imbeciles!" the Vicomte retorted, fired with rage. "It is your lady the Abbess come a day before her time! It is my daughter and you stay her at the door!"

"It is not my lady," the second man answered timidly.

"It might be some of her company, my lord, but 'tis not her. And Solomon——"

"Well? Well?"

"Says that they are not her people, my lord."

The Vicomte groaned. "If I had a son worthy the name!" he said, and then he broke off, looking foolish. For Roger had left the room and des Ageaux also. They had slipped by the men while the Vicomte questioned them, and run out through the hall and to the gate—not unarmed. The Vicomte, seeing this, bade the men follow them; and when these too had vanished, and only four or five frightened women who had crowded into the room at the first alarm remained, he began to fumble with his sword, and to add to the confusion by calling fussily for this and that, and to bring him his arquebus, and not to open—not to open till he came! In truth years had worked imperceptibly on him. His nerves, like many things about him, were not what they had been—before Coutras. And he was still giving contrary directions, and scolding the women, and bidding them make way for him—since it seemed there was not a man to go to the gate but himself—when approaching voices broke on his ear and silenced him. An instant later one or two men appeared among the women in the doorway, and the little crowd fell back in wonder, to make room for a low dark man, bareheaded and breathing hard, with disordered hair and glittering eyes, who, thrusting the women to either side, cried—not once, but again, and yet again:—

"Room! Room for the Countess of Rochechouart! Way for the Countess!"

At the third repetition of this—which he seemed to say mechanically—his eyes took in the scene, the table,

the room, and the waiting figure of the scandalized
Vicomte, and his voice broke. "Saved!" he cried,
flinging up his arms, and reeling slightly as if he would
fall. "My lady is saved! Saved!"

And then, behind the low, dark man, who, it was plain,
was almost beside himself, the Vicomte saw the white
face and shrinking form of a small, slight girl little
more than a child, whose eyes were like no eyes but a
haunted hare's, so large and bright and affrighted were
they.

CHAPTER IV.

THE DILEMMA.

SHEER amazement held the Vicomte silent. The Countess of Rochechouart, of the proud house of Longueville, that in those days yielded place to scarce a house in France—the Countess of Rochechouart to be seeking admittance at his door! And at this hour of the night! She, who was of the greatest heiresses of France, whose hand was weighted with a hundred manors, and of whose acquaintance the Abbess had lately boasted as a thing of which even a Villeneuve might be proud, she to be knocking at his gate in the dark hours! And seeking help! The Countess—his head went round. He was still gazing speechless with surprise when the short dark man who had entered with her fell on his knees before the girl, and seizing her hand mumbled upon it, wept on it, babbled over it, heedless alike of the crowd of gazers who pressed upon him, and of the master of the house, who stared aghast.

The Vicomte's amazement began at that to give place to perplexity. The Abbess, had she been here, would have known how to entertain such a guest. But Bonne and Roger—they were naught. Yet he must do something. He found his voice. "If I have, indeed," he said, for he was still suspicious of a trick, so forlorn and

childish seemed the figure before him—"if I have indeed
the honour," he repeated stiffly, "to address the Countess
of Rochechouart, I—I bid her welcome to my poor
house."

"I am Mademoiselle de Rochechouart," the girl murmured, speaking faintly. "I thank you."

It was apparent that she could say no more. Her
face was scratched and bleeding, her hair was loose, her
riding-dress, stained to the throat with dirt, was torn
in more places than one. There were other signs that,
frail as she was, she had ridden hard and desperately;
ridden to the end of her strength.

But the Vicomte thought, not of her, but of himself, as was his custom; not of her plight, but of the
figure he was making before his people, who stared
open-mouthed at the unwonted scene. "Time was,
mademoiselle," he replied, drawing himself up, "before
Coutras, when I could have offered you"—with a bow—
"a more fitting hospitality. Time was when the house
of Villeneuve, which has entertained four kings, could
have afforded a more fitting reception to—hem—to
beauty in distress. But that was before Coutras. Since
Coutras, destined to be the grave of the nobility of
France—I—— What is it?"

"I think she is faint, sir," Bonne murmured timidly.
She, with a woman's eye, saw that the Countess was
swaying, and she sprang forward to support her. "She
is ill, sir," she continued hurriedly and with greater
boldness. "Permit me, I beg you, sir, to take her to
my room. She will be better there—until we can ar-
range a chamber." Already the child, half-fainting,
was clinging to her, and but for her must have fallen.

The Vicomte, taken aback by his daughter's presumption, could only stare. "If this be so," he said grudgingly, "certainly! But I don't understand. How comes all this about? Eh? How——" But he found that the girl did not heed him, and he turned and addressed the attendant. "How, you, sir, comes your mistress here? And in this plight?"

But the dark man, as deaf as his mistress to the question, had turned to follow her. He seemed indeed to have no more notion of being parted from her than a dog which finds itself alone with its master among strangers. Bonne at the door discovered his presence at her elbow, and paused in some embarrassment. The Vicomte saw the pause, and glad to do something— he had just ordered off the women with fleas in their ears—he called loudly to the man to stand back. "Stand back, fellow," he repeated. "The Countess will be well tended. Let two of the women be sent to her to do what is needful—as is becoming."

But the Countess, faint as she was, heard and spoke. "He is my foster-father," she murmured without turning her head. "If he may lie at my door he will heed no one."

Bonne, whose arm was round her, nodded a cheerful assent, and, followed by two of the women, the three disappeared in the direction of the girl's chamber. The Vicomte, left to digest the matter, sniffed once or twice with a face of amazement, and then awoke to the fact that Roger and his guest were still absent. Fortunately, before he had done more than give vent to peevish complaints, they entered.

He waited, with his eyes on the door. To his surprise no one followed them—no steward, no attendant. "Well?" he cried, withering them with his glance.

"What does this mean? Where are the others? Is there no one in the Countess's train of a condition to be presented to me? Or how comes it that you have not brought him, booby,"—this to Roger—"to give me some account of these strange proceedings? Am I the last to be told who come into my house? But God knows, since Coutras——"

"There is no one, M. le Vicomte," the Lieutenant answered.

The Vicomte glared at him. "How? No one?" he retorted pompously. "Impossible! Do you suppose that the Countess of Rochechouart travels with no larger attendance than a poor gentleman of Brittany? You mean, sir, I take it, that there is no one of condition, though that is so contrary to rule that I can hardly believe it. A countess of Rochechouart and no gentlemen in her train! She should travel with four at the least!"

"I only know that there is no one, sir."

"I do not understand!"

"Neither do we," the Lieutenant of Périgord returned, somewhat out of patience. "The matter is as dark to us as it is to you, sir. It is plain that the Countess has experienced a serious adventure, but beyond that we know nothing, since neither she nor her attendant has spoken. He seems beside himself with joy and she with fatigue."

"But the spears?" his host retorted sharply. "The men on horse and foot who alarmed the porter?"

"They vanished as soon as we opened. One I did delay a moment, and learned—though he was in haste to be gone—that they fell in with the lady a half mile from here. She was then in the plight in which you have seen her, and it was at her attendant's prayer, who informed them of her quality, that they escorted her to this house. They learned no more from him than that the lady's train had been attacked in the woods between this and Vlaye, and that the man got his mistress away and hid with her, and was making for this house when the horsemen met them."

"Incredible!" the Vicomte exclaimed, stalking across the hearth and returning in excitement. "Since Coutras I have heard no such thing! A Countess of Roche-chouart attacked on the road and put to it like a common herdgirl. It must be the work of those cursed—peasants! It must be so! But, then, the men who brought her to the door and vanished again, who are they? Travellers are not so common in these parts. You might journey three days before you fell in with a body of men-at-arms to protect you on your way."

"True," des Ageaux answered. "But I learned no more from them."

"And you, Master Booby?" the Vicomte said, addressing Roger with his usual sarcasm. "You asked nothing, I suppose?"

"I was busied about the Countess," the lad muttered. "It was dark, and I heard no more than their voices."

"Then it was only you who saw them?" the Vicomte exclaimed, turning again to des Ageaux. "Did you not notice what manner of men they were, sir, how many, and of what class? Strange that they should leave a warm house-door at this hour! Did you form no opinion of them? Were they"—he brought out the word with an effort—"Crocans, think you?"

The Lieutenant replied that he took them for the armed attendants of a gentleman passing that way, and the Vicomte, though ill-content with the answer, was obliged to put up with it. "Yet it seems passing strange to me," he retorted, "that you did not think their drawing off a little beside the ordinary. And who travels at this hour of the night, I would like to know?"

The Lieutenant made no answer, and the Vicomte too fell silent. From time to time serving-women had passed through the room—for, after the awkward fashion of those days, the passage to the inner apartments was through the dining-hall—some with lights, and some with fire in pans. The draught from the closing doors had more than once threatened to extinguish the flickering candles. Such flittings produced an air of bustle and a hum of preparation long unknown in that house; but they were certainly more to the taste of the menials than the master. At each interruption the Vicomte pished and pshawed, glaring as if he would slay the offender. But the women, emboldened by the event and the presence of strangers, did not heed him, and after some minutes of silent sufferance his patience came to an end.

"Go you," he cried to Roger, "and bid the girl come to me."

"The Countess, sir?" the lad exclaimed in astonishment.

The Vicomte swore. "No, fool!" he replied. "Your sister! Is she master of the house, or am I? Bid her descend this instant and tell me what is forward and what she has learned."

Roger, with secret reluctance, obeyed, and his father, sorely fretting, awaited his return. Two minutes elapsed, and three. Seldom stirring abroad, the Vicomte had, in spite of all his talk about Coutras, an overweening sense of his own importance, and he was about to break out in fury when Bonne at length entered. She was followed by Roger.

It was clear at a glance that the girl was frightened; less clear that mixed with her fear was another emotion. "Well," the Vicomte cried, throwing himself back in his great chair and fixing her with his angry eyes. "What is it? Am I to know nothing—in my own house?"

Bonne controlled herself by an effort. "On the contrary, sir, there is that which I think you should know," she murmured. "The Countess has told me the story. She was attacked on the road, some of her people she fears were killed, and all were scattered. She herself escaped barely with her life."

The Vicomte stared. "Where?" he said. "Where was it?"

"An hour from here, sir."

"Towards Vlaye?"

"Yes, sir."

"And she barely escaped?"

"You saw her, sir."

"And who—who does she say dared to commit this outrage?"

Bonne did not answer. Her eyes sought her brother's and sank again. She trembled.

The Vicomte, though not the keenest of observers, detected her embarrassment. He fancied that he knew its origin, and the cause of her hesitation. In a voice of triumph, "Ay, who?" he replied. "You don't wish to say. But I can tell you. I read it in your face. I can tell you, disobedient wench, who alone would be guilty of such an outrage. Those gutter-sweepings"—

his face swelled with rage—"made up of broken lacqueys and ploughboys, whom they call Crocans! Eh, girl, is it not so?" he continued savagely. "Am I not right?"

"No, sir," she murmured without daring to look up.

His face fell. "No?" he repeated. "No? But I don't believe you! Who then? Don't lie to me! Who then?" He rapped the table before him.

"The Captain of Vlaye," she whispered.

The Vicomte sank back in his chair. "Impossible!" he cried. Then in a much lower tone: "Impossible!" he repeated. "You dream, girl. M. de Vlaye has done some things not quite—not regular. But—but in cases perfectly different. To people of—of no consequence! This cannot be!"

"I fear it is so, sir," she whispered, without raising her eyes. "Nor is that—the worst."

The Vicomte clenched his fingers about the arms of his chair and nodded the question he could not frame.

"It was with the Abbess, sir—with my sister," Bonne continued in a low tone, "that the Countess was to stay the night. I fear that it was from her that he learned where and how to beset her."

The Vicomte looked as if he was about to have a fit.

"What?" he cried. "Do you dare, unnatural girl, to assert that your sister was privy to this outrage?"

"Heaven forbid, sir!" Bonne answered fervently. "She knew naught of it. But——"

"Then why——"

"But it was from her, I fear, that he learned where the child—she is little more—could be surprised."

The Vicomte glared at her without speaking. The Lieutenant, who had listened, not without admiration of the girl's sense and firmness, seized the opening to intervene. "Were it not well, sir," he said, his matter-of-fact tone calming the Vicomte's temper, "if mademoiselle told us as nearly as possible what she has heard? And, as she has been somewhat shaken, perhaps you will permit her to sit down! She will then, I think, be able to tell us more quickly what we want." .

The Vicomte gave a surly assent, and the Lieutenant himself placed a stool for the girl where she could lean upon the table. Her father opened his eyes at the attention, but something in des Ageaux's face silenced the sneer on his lips, and he waited untl Bonne began.

"The Countess lay at Pons last night, sir," she said in a low tone. "There the lady who was formerly her *gouvernante*, and still rules her household, fell ill. The plague is in Western Poitou, and though the Countess would have stayed, her physician insisted that she should proceed. Accordingly she left the invalid in his charge and that of some of her people, while she herself pursued her way through Jonsac and Barbesieux with a train reduced to fourteen persons, of whom eight were well armed."

"This is what comes of travelling in such a fashion," the Vicomte said contemptuously. "I remember when I never passed the gates without—but go on!"

"She now thinks that the *gouvernante's* food was tampered with. Be that as it may, her company passed our ford in the afternoon, and an hour later reached the ascent a league this side of Vlaye. They were midway on the ascent, when half a dozen shots were fired. Several of their horses were struck, and the rest seized by a number of men who sprang from the undergrowth. In the panic those who were at the rear attempted to turn, but found their retreat cut off. The Countess alone, who rode in the middle with her steward, escaped through the devotion of a servant, who thrust his horse before the leader of the bandits and brought him down. Fulbert, her steward, saw the opportunity, seized her rein, and, plunging into the undergrowth, reached by good luck the bottom of the hill, and, hidden by the wood, gained a start. He knew, however, that her strength would not hold out, and at the first sound of pursuit he alighted in a coppice, drove on the horses, and crept away with her through the underwood. He hoped to take shelter here, but passed the entrance in the darkness and walked into the midst of a party of men encamped at the ford. Then he thought all lost, deeming them the band that had waylaid the Countess——"

"And who were they, if they were not?" the Vicomte asked, unable to restrain his curiosity. "Eh? They were camping at the ford?"

"Some riders belonging to the household of the Lieutenant of Périgord, sir, on their way to join him in his government. They were so honest as to guard the Countess hither——"

"And go again? The good Lord!" the Vicomte cried irritably. "Why?"

"I do not know, sir."

"Go on, then. Why do you break off? But—enough!" The Vicomte looked at the other listeners with an air of triumph. "Where is Vlaye in this? Because it was within a league of his castle, you put it on him, you baggage?"

"No, sir, indeed!" Bonne cried anxiously. "But Fulbert the steward knows M. de Vlaye well, and recognised him. He wore a mask, it seems, but when his horse fell, the mask slipped, and Fulbert saw his face and knew him. Moreover——"

"Well?"

"One of the band rode a bald-faced black horse, which the steward saw in M. de Vlaye's troop at Angoulême two months back, and to which he says he could swear among ten thousand."

The Vicomte swore as one among a large number. But at length, "And what is this to do with me?" he fumed. "What is this to me? Time was, before Coutras, when I might have been expected to—to keep the roads, and stay such things! But now—body of Satan, what is it to me?"

No one spoke, and he looked about him angrily, resenting their silence. "What is it?" he snarled. "What are you keeping back?"

"Nothing, sir," Bonne answered.

"Then what would you?"

"If," Bonne ventured desperately, "M. de Vlaye come to-morrow with my sister—with the Abbess, sir, as is not unlikely—and find the Countess here, will she be safe?"

The Vicomte's mouth opened, and slowly consternation settled upon his features. "*Mon Dieu!*" he muttered. "I had not thought of that. But here—no, no, he would not dare! He would not dare!"

"He went very far to-day, sir," Bonne objected, gaining courage from his face. "So far that he must go farther to ensure himself from the consequences."

The Vicomte was silent.

The Lieutenant coughed. "If his object," he said, "be to force a marriage with the Countess——"

The Vicomte, with an oath, cut him short. "A

marriage?" he said. "A marriage? When he and my daughter the Abbess are—but who said aught of the kind? Who said aught of a marriage?"

The Lieutenant did not answer, and the Vicomte, after growling in his beard, turned to him. "Why," he demanded in a tone that, though ungracious, was no longer violent, "why do you say that that was his object?"

"Because," the Lieutenant answered, "I happen to know that M. de Longueville, who is her guardian, has his hands full. His wife and children are prisoners with the Spaniards, and he is moving heaven and earth and the court to procure their release. He has no thought to spare for the Countess, his cousin; and were she once married, however violently, I doubt if he or any would venture to dispute her possessions with a Vlaye, whose resources her wealth would treble. Such knights-errant," he continued drily, "are not very common, M. le Vicomte. Set M. de Vlaye's strength at three hundred men-at-arms——"

"Four!" the Vicomte muttered, despite himself. .

"Then double the four—as such a marriage, however effected, would double them—and I doubt," with a courteous bow, "if even a Villeneuve would find it easy to avenge a wrong!"

The Vicomte fidgeted in his seat. "You seem to know a vast deal about it, sir," he said, with ill-feigned contempt.

"I should feel it an honour," the Lieutenant answered politely, "to be permitted to join in the defence."

"Defence!" the Vicomte exclaimed, staring at him in astonishment. "You go fast, sir! Defence? What do you mean?"

"If M. de Vlaye learn that the Countess has taken refuge here—I fear it will come to that."

"Pooh! Impossible! Defence, indeed! What are you dreaming of?"

But the guest continued to look grave, and the Vicomte, after muttering incoherently, and drumming on the table with his fingers, condescended to ask with a sneer what *he* would do—in the circumstances.

"I should keep her presence from him," des Ageaux answered. "I have no right, I know," he continued, in a more conciliatory tone, "to give counsel to one of your experience, M. le Vicomte. But I see no choice save to do what I suggest, or to pull up the drawbridge."

The Vicomte sat up straight. Pull up the drawbridge? Was he dreaming—he who had sat down to sup without a thought of misfortune? He with four hundred yards of wall to guard, and some seven pikes to hold it—to defy Vlaye and his four hundred ruffians? Body of Satan, he was not mad! Defy Vlaye, whom he feared even while he sneered at him as an adventurer? Vlaye, in whose star he believed even while he sneered. Or would he have dreamed of giving him his daughter? Pull up the drawbridge? Never!

"I am not mad," he said coldly. But his hands trembled.

"Then, M. le Vicomte, it remains to keep it from him."

"How? You talk at random," the exasperated man answered. "Can I close the mouth of every gossip in the house? Can I cut out every woman's tongue, beginning with that girl's? How can I keep out his men, or stop their ears over the wine-pot?"

"Could you not admit him only?"

"And proclaim from the housetop," the Vicomte retorted with contempt, "that I have something to hide?"

The Lieutenant did not reply at once, and it was plain that he was puzzled by this view of the position. "Certainly that has to be borne in mind," he said. "You are quite right."

"To be sure it has!" the Vicomte answered brusquely, glad to have the opportunity of putting this over-zealous adviser in his right place. But the satisfaction of triumph faded quickly, and left him face to face with the situation. He cursed Vlaye for placing him in the dilemma. He cursed the Countess—why could she not have taken refuge elsewhere? Last of all, he cursed his guest, who, after showing himself offensively able to teach him his duty, failed the moment it came to finding an expedient.

The solution of the riddle came from a quarter whence —at any rate by the Vicomte—it was least expected. "May I say something?" Roger ventured timidly.

His father glared at him. "You?" he exclaimed. And then ungraciously, "Say on!" he growled.

"We have cut half the grass in the long meadow," the lad answered. "And to-morrow we ought to be both cutting and making, while it is fine. Last year, as we were short-handed, the women helped. If you were to order all but Solomon to the hay-field to-morrow—it is the farthest from here, beside the river—there would be no one to talk or tell, sir."

Des Ageaux struck his leg in approbation. "The lad has it!" he said. "With your permission, M. le Vicomte, what could be better?"

"Better?" the Vicomte retorted, throwing himself

back in his chair. "What? I am to open my gate with my own hands?"

"Solomon would open. And he can be trusted."

"Receive my daughter without man or maid?" the Vicomte cried. "Show myself to strangers without my people? Appear like one of the base-born beggarly ploughmen with mud in their veins, with whom you love to mix? What mean you, sirrah, by such a suggestion? Shame on you, unnatural fool!"

"But, M. le Vicomte," the Lieutenant remonstrated, "if you will not do that——"

"Never! Never!"

"Then," des Ageaux answered, more stiffly, "it remains only to pull up the drawbridge. Since, I presume," he continued, his tone taking insensibly a note of disdain, "you do not propose to give up the young lady, or to turn her from your door."

"Turn her from my door?"

"That being at once to help M. de Vlaye to this marriage, and to drag the name of Villeneuve in the mud! But"—breaking off with a bow—"I am sure that the honour of the family is safe in your hands, M. le Vicomte."

"It is well you said that!" the Vicomte cried, his face purple, his hands palsied with rage. "It is well you broke off, sir, or I would have proved to you that my honour is safe with me. Body of Satan, am I to be preached to by everybody—every brainless lad," he continued, prudently diverting his tirade to the head of the unlucky Roger, "who chooses to prate before his elders! *Mon Dieu!* There was a time when children sat mute instead of preaching. But that was before Coutras!"—bitterly—"when most things came to an end."

This time des Ageaux had the shrewdness to be silent, and he garnered the reward of his reticence. The Vicomte, rant as wildly as he might, was no fool, though vanity was hourly putting foolish things into his mouth. He was not blind—had he not "since Coutras" always on his lips?—to the changes which time had wrought in the world, and he knew that face to face with his formidable neighbour he was helpless. Nor was he in the dark on Vlaye's character. So far the adventurer had respected him, and in presence, and at a distance, had maintained an observance and a regard that was flattering to the decayed gentleman. But the Vicomte had seen the fate of others who crossed the Captain of Vlaye. He knew how impotent the law had proved to save them, how slack their friends—in a word, how quickly the waters had rolled over them. And he was astute enough to see, with all his conceit, that as it had been with them, it might be with him, if he stood in M. de Vlaye's way.

On the other hand, had he been mean enough to deliver up the Countess, he dared not. In the first place, to do so would, at the best, be hazardous; she had powerful friends, and whether she escaped or married her captor she might not forgive him. In the second place, he did not lightly resign the plan, which he had conceived, of uniting his favourite daughter to the rising adventurer. True, M. de Vlaye's position was anomalous, was precarious. But a day, a bribe, a turn of the cards might legalise it and place him high in Court favour. And then——

The Vicomte's train of thought ran no farther in silence. With an oath and an ill grace he bade them do as they would. "Things," he cried, "are come to a pass indeed when guests——"

"A thousand pardons, M. le Vicomte!"

"And children dictate what is to be done and what to be left undone!" He looked older as he spoke; more broken and more peevish. "But since Coutras the devil has all, I think."

CHAPTER V.

THE CAPTAIN OF VLAYE.

DANGER, that by night sends forth a vanguard of fears, and quells the spirits before it delivers the attack, pursues a different course by day, seeking to surprise rather than to intimidate. Seldom had June sun shone on a fairer scene than that which the lifting of the river mists delivered to the eyes of the dwellers in the château on the following morning, or on one more fit to raise the despondent courage. The tract of meadow land that, enfolded by the river, formed the only clear ground about the house lay in breezy sunshine, which patches of shadow, flung on the sward by such of the surrounding trees as rose a little higher than the ordinary, did but heighten. The woods which enclosed this meadow land, here with a long straight wall of oaks, there with broken clumps of trees that left to view distant glades and alleys, sparkled, where the sun lighted their recesses, with unnumbered dew-drops, or with floating gossamers, harbingers of a fair day. The occasional caw of a rook flying fieldward over the open, or the low, steady coo of the pigeons in the great stone cote beside the gate, added the last touch of peace to the scene; a scene so innocent that it forbade the notion of danger and rendered it hard to believe that

88

amid surroundings like these, and under the same sky of blue, man's passions were, in parts not distant, turning an earthly heaven to a hell.

Access to these meadows was by a sled-road, which, starting from the great gate, wound round the wall of the courtyard, and then, turning its back on the house, passed by a small stone bridge over the brook which had once supplied the moat. From the bridge the track ran across the meadows to the abandoned farms which stood on the river bank half a mile from the château. The only building among these which retained a roof was a long wooden barn, still used to contain waste fodder and the like.

It was from this bridge, a narrow span of stone, that Bonne, the following morning, gazed on the scene, her hand raised to shade her eyes from the sun. The whole of the Vicomte's household, with the exception of a deaf cook and of Solomon, who could be trusted, were gone to the hay-field; some with delight, as welcoming any change, and some with whispers and surmises. Thence their shrill voices and laughter were borne by the light breeze to the girl's ears.

Nothing had been heard of the Countess's train, and her concealment during the hours of danger had perplexed both the Vicomte and his advisers. His pride would not permit him to make her privy to the coming visit, or the precautions which it rendered needful. Yet without acknowledging his inability to protect her, it was not easy to confine her to one room. For, with the elasticity of youth, she had risen little the worse for her adventures.

The council sat long, and in the end the better course seemed to be to invite her to the hay-field. As it fell out, a small matter gave a natural turn to the proposal. Her riding-dress—and more of her dress than that—was so stained and torn as to be unwearable. And Bonne could not help her, for the child, though perfectly formed, and of a soft prettiness, was cast in a smaller mould. Here, then, was a Countess without so much as a stocking, had not Bonne thought of a little waiting-girl of about the same shape and size. This girl's holiday attire was borrowed, and found to be a charming fit— at least in the eyes of Roger. For the lad, because the Countess was shy, had become, after a sort, her protector.

The child's timidity was at standing odds with her rank, and on first descending in this dress she had been on the point of tears, as infants cry when they think themselves the objects of ridicule. A very little and she had fled. But a moment later, whether she read something that was not ridicule in the lad's eyes, as she walked up and down the terrace, or youth stirred in her and raised a childish pleasure in the masquerade, she preened herself, blushing, and presently she was showing herself off. So that at the first word she fell in with the notion of completing her make-believe by spending the day in the hay.

Fortunately, Fulbert, the steward, who attended her like a dog, and like a dog glared suspicion on all who approached her, raised no objection. And about three hours before noon the move was made. Bonne had gone with Mademoiselle as far as this bridge, where she now stood, and thence had sent her forward with Roger and Fulbert on the plea that she must herself attend to household cares. Nevertheless, as the three receded in the sun's eye, she lingered awhile looking thoughtfully after them.

The dainty creature, tripping in her queer travesty between her foster-father and Roger's misshapen form, showed like a fairy between two gnomes. Bonne watched and smiled, and presently the smile became a tear, for Roger's sake. She had other and more pressing cares, other and heavier burdens this morning; but her heart was warm for him. She had been mother as well as sister to him, and the reflection that his deformity—once she had heard a peasant call him goblin—would probably for ever set him apart and deprive him of the joys of manhood touched her with grief as she stood.

The tear was still on her lid when she heard a step behind her, turned and saw des Ageaux—to her des Voeux. He read trouble in her clear, youthful face, fancied she was in fear, and paused to reassure her. "Why so sad, mademoiselle," he asked, "when she"—with a good-humoured nod in the direction of the Countess—"who has so much more to fear, trips along gaily? She is another being to-day."

"I have others to fear for," she replied.

"Your brother?"

She fancied that he was about to press her to bring him to Charles, and to change the subject she avowed her trouble. Why, heaven knows; for though her presence of mind the previous evening had won a meed of admiration from him, he had made no sign.

"I was not thinking of him," she confessed. "I was thinking of Roger. I was thinking how sad it is—for him."

He understood her. "You make too much of it," he said lightly. "He has health and strength, and a good spirit when your father is not present. His arm is long, and will always keep his head. Have you never heard what M. de Gourdon, Governor of the March, who is—who is like your brother, you know—once said of himself? 'My back?' quoth he to one who mentioned it. 'My friends mind it not, and my enemies have never seen it!'"

She flushed and a light came into her eyes. "Oh, brave!" she cried. "Brave! And you think that Roger——"

"I think that Roger may some day make himself feared. And he who is feared," the Lieutenant continued, with a half cynical, half whimsical smile, "has ever love on his other hand—as surely as dog follows the hand that feeds it."

The words had barely left his lips when a wolf-hound, whose approach they had not noticed, darted upon them, and, leaping up at the Lieutenant's face, nearly overthrew him. Bonne recoiled, and with a cry looked round for help. Then she perceived that it was with joy, not with rage, that the dog was beside himself; for again and again, with sharp shrill cries of pleasure, it leapt on the Lieutenant, striving to lick his hands, his face, his hair. In vain he bade it "Down! Down, dog!" In vain he struck at it. It set its paws against his breast, and though often repulsed, as often with slobbering mouth and hanging tongue sought his face.

When he had a little calmed its transports and got it to heel, he turned to her, and for once showed an embarrassed countenance. "It is a dog," he said, "a dog of mine that has followed me."

"I see that," she replied, smiling with something of mischief in her looks.

"It must have followed me——"

"A full mile this morning," she said, stooping and patting the hound, which, with a dubious condescension, permitted the greeting. "It is both fed and dry. And its name is——"

He looked at her, but did not answer.

"Does this often happen to you?" she continued, feeling on a sudden a strange freedom with him. "To talk of dogs and they appear? Have you the habit when your horse falls lame of tying your dog to a tree, and placing a sufficiency of food and water by it to last it two days?" And then, when he did not answer her, "Who are you, M. des Voeux?" she said in a different tone. "Whence do you come, and what is your business?"

"Have I not told you," he answered, "that I wish to communicate through your brother with the Crocans? That is my business."

"But you did not know when you came to us that I had a brother," she replied, "or that he had joined the Crocans, or that we were like to be in these straits. So that you did not come for that. Why did you come?" confronting him with clear eyes. "Are we to count you friend or enemy? Be frank with me and I will be frank with you."

He looked at her with the first gleam of admiration in his eyes. But he hesitated. In the candour of a young girl who, laying aside coquetry and advantage, speaks to a man as to a comrade there lies a charm new to him who has not known a sister; more new to him, more surprising to him whose wont has lain among the women of a court—women whose light lives and fickle ambitions mark them of those who are but just freed from the seraglio. He smiled at her, openly acknowledging by his silence and his air that he had a secret; acknowledging also, and in the same way, that he held her equal. But he shook his head. "In a little time I will be frank with you, mademoiselle," he said. "It is true I have a secret, and at this moment I cannot tell it safely."

"You do not trust me?"

"I trust no one at this moment," he answered steadily.

It was not the answer she expected. She had thought he would quibble. She was impressed by his firmness, but she did not betray the feeling. "Good!" she said, with the least possible lifting of her head. "Then you must not expect to be trusted, or that I shall bring you to my brother."

"But you promised, mademoiselle."

"That I would do so when I could do so—safely," she retorted with mischievous emphasis. "It is your own word, sir, and I shall not feel that I can do so—safely—until I learn who you are. I suppose if my brother were here you would tell him?"

"Possibly."

Her colour rose. "You would tell him, and you will not tell me!" she cried indignantly.

"Now you are angry," he replied smiling. "How can I appease you?"

She was not really angry. But she turned on her heel, willing to let him think it. "By hiding yourself until this is over," she answered. And leaving him standing on the bridge, where he had found her, she made her way back to the house, where the only man left was Solomon in his hutch beside the gate. He was an old servant, a garrulous veteran of high renown for the enormous fables he had ever on his lips—particularly when the

Vicomte reverted to the greatness of the house before Coutras. Mademoiselle as she entered paused to speak to him. "Have you seen a strange dog, Solomon?" she asked.

"This morning, my lady?" he exclaimed in his shrill voice. "Strange dog? No, not I! Has one frightened you? Dog? Few dogs I see these sad days," he continued, with a gesture scornful of the present. "Dogs, indeed? Times were when we had packs for everything, for boars, and wolves, and deer, and hares, and vermin, and"—pausing in sheer inability to think of any other possible pack—"ay, each a pack, and more to them than I could ever count, or the huntsman either!"

"Yes, I know, Solomon. I have heard you say so at least. But you have not seen a strange dog this morning?"

"The morn! No, no, my lady! But last night I mind one—was't a deer-hound?"

"Yes, a deer-hound."

"Well, then, I can tell you," with a mysterious nod, "and no one else. It was with the riders who brought the young lady. But I'm mum," winking. "Not a word will they get out of me. Secrets? Ay, I'm the man can keep a secret. Why, I remember, talking of secrets and lives—and often they are all one——"

"But what became of the deer-hound?" she asked, ruthlessly cutting him short.

"Became of the dog?"—more shrilly than usual—he was a little hurt. "Is that all you want? It went with them as brought it, I do suppose. It didn't stop, anywise. But as I was saying about secrets—the secrets I have kept in old days—when there was no family had so many as ours——"

But she was gone. She had discovered what she wanted. And she was midway across the courtyard when the shrill sound of a hawk-whistle caught her ear. Turning she went through the gate again, and listened —not without a nervous feeling. Presently she could distinguish the dull tramp of a number of horses moving on the sward, the gay jingle of bit and spur, and mingled with these sounds the voices of a number of persons talking at their ease.

Warmly as the sun shone, she was aware of a shiver; of a presentiment that gripped and chilled her. Whatever it portended, however, whatever misfortune was in the air, the risk could not now be evaded. Already bright patches of moving colour glanced among the trees at the end of the approach, and steel points glittered amid the foliage, and feathers waved gaily above the undergrowth. She had barely time to tell Solomon to run and apprise her father of the arrival, when the head of the cavalcade wheeled, talking and laughing, into the avenue, and her sister, who rode in the van by the side of M. de Vlaye, espied her standing before the gate and waved a greeting.

Behind the Abbess rode a couple of women, one in the lay costume, liberally interpreted, of her order, the other of the world confessed; following close on their heels half a dozen horsemen completed the first party. The young Abbess bore a hooded hawk on her wrist, and the tinkle of its light silver bells mingled with the ripple of her voice as she approached, while two or three pairs of coupled hounds ran at her horse's heels. A little behind, separated from this select company by an interval of two score yards, followed the main body, a troop of some forty horse, in steel caps and corslets, with long swords swinging, and pistols in their holsters.

A more picturesque or more gallant company, as they swept by threes and fours into sight between the two grey pillars and rode towards the house under sun and shade, or a band that moved with a lordlier air, it had been hard to find, even in those days of show and pageantry, when men wore their fortunes on their backs. The Captain of Vlaye, stooping his sinewy figure to his companion, well became a horse that moved as he moved, and caracoled because he allowed it. His dark, keen face would have been as handsome as his form but for a blemish. In some skirmish of his youth he had lost the sight of an eye, and the blind orb gave his face a hard look which, so his enemies said, brought it into consonance with his character. He wore upturned moustaches without a beard, therein departing from the mode of the day. But his hunting-dress of white doeskin, with a fawn hat and belt, was in the fashion, and his horse's trappings shone almost as fine as the riding-dress of green and silver which set off his companion's tall figure and haughty face. In first youth a nose, too like her father's, and something over large in Odette de Villeneuve's frame, had foreshadowed charms not of the most feminine or the first order. But three years had supplied the carriage and the ripened and fuller contours that made her what she now was. To-day, if it pleased her to have at her beck one whose will was law, and whose stern manners invited few to intimacy— and in truth her infatuation for the successful adventurer knew no limits—he on his side found his account in parading, where he went, a woman whose beauty exceeded even her birth, and fell little short of her pride.

And she was content; she at least aimed at no more than setting on a safer basis the power she looked to share. It was she who, ignorant that her brother had joined them, had mentioned to her sister Vlaye's plan of suppressing the Crocans. That he had any other plan, that his views rose higher than a union with herself, that he hoped by a bold and secret stroke not only to secure what he had gained but to treble his resources—that his ambition, passing by a Villeneuve, dared to dream of an alliance with the ducal house of Longueville—of these things she had, as yet, no inkling. Not a jot, not a tittle. Nor was she likely to believe in their existence, save on evidence the clearest and most overwhelming.

Bonne knew more. She knew these things; and, as she went forward to meet the party, and after greeting her sister turned to her cavalier, the word "Welcome" stuck in her throat. She was conscious that her cheek grew a shade paler as she forced the word, that her knees shook. Her fear was that he would read the signs.

Ordinarily he would not have remarked them; partly because he was inured to meeting cowed looks, and partly because a careless scorn—masked where the Vicomte was concerned by a veneer of respect—was all to which he ever treated the Abbess's impoverished family. Crook-backed brother, tongue-tied sister, and the other fool, whose restive dislike had sometimes amused him—he held them all in equal and supreme contempt. But to-day he had his reasons for noting the girl more particularly; and the shadow of ill-temper that darkened his face lifted as her timid eye and fluttering colour confirmed his surmises.

"I thank you, I will not alight," he replied. "Your father is coming to the gate? M. le Vicomte is too kind, mademoiselle. But that being so, I will await him here."

The Abbess, with an air of patronage, touched Bonne's hair with the tip of her riding-switch. "Child, did you sleep in your clothes last night?" she said. "Or are you making hay with the kitchen-maids? See her blush, M. de Vlaye! What would you give me if I could blush as naïvely?" And her eyes rallied him, seeking a compliment in his. "But Abbesses who have been to Court——"

"Carry a court wherever they go," he replied. But his look did not leave Bonne's face. The Abbess's women and the rest of the company had drawn rein out of earshot, their horses making long necks that they might reach the grass, or poking their heads to crop a tender shoot. "I cannot alight," he continued, "for we are on an adventure, mademoiselle. I might almost say a pursuit."

"Do you know, child," her sister chimed in, "that Mademoiselle de Rochechouart never came to me last night? But you know nothing here—even, I daresay, that I expected her. How should you? You might as well live in a hole in the ground."

"She never came?" Bonne faltered, for the sake of saying something. The blush had subsided, leaving her paler than before.

"No, did I not say so? And she has not arrived to-day," the Abbess continued, flicking her horse's mane with her jewelled switch. "But some of her people were in by daylight this morning—from Heaven knows where—some hiding-place in the woods, I believe—·

making such a to-do as you would not credit. If they are to be believed, they were attacked near nightfall by the Crocans——"

"By the Crocans," M. de Vlaye repeated, nodding darkly at Bonne. He knew more than the Abbess knew of Charles's desperate venture.

"And M. de Vlaye," the Abbess continued, speaking in the negligent fashion, a trifle distant, in which she always addressed her family in his presence, "has most kindly sent out parties in search of her. Moreover, as I came this way on the same errand, he fell in with me, and came on—more, I believe, for her sake than mine"— with a look that called for contradiction—"to make inquiries in this direction. But on the way—but here is my father. Good morning, sir. M. de Vlaye——"

"Has been waiting some time, I fear," the Vicomte said hurriedly. He, too, was not free from embarrassment, but he hid it with fair success. "Why do you not alight and enter, my dear?"

"Because we have business, by your leave, sir," Vlaye answered, his politeness scarcely covering an undertone of meaning. And he told in a few words—while Bonne stood listening in an agony of suspense—what the Abbess had told her. "Fortunately, after I fell in with your daughter this morning," he proceeded, "I had news of the Countess. And where do you think, M. le Vicomte, we are told that she is?" he continued.

Fortunately the Vicomte, whose hands were beginning to tremble, and whose colour was mounting to his wrinkled cheek, could not immediately find his voice. It was his elder daughter who took on herself to answer. "Where do you think, sir?" she cried gaily. "In your hay-meadows—so M. de Vlaye says."

"Mademoiselle de Rochechouart?   In my hay-meadows?" the Vicomte faltered.

"Yes."

"In my hay-meadows?   It cannot be."

"It is so—or so we are told."

CHAPTER VI.

IN THE HAY-FIELD.

The Vicomte gasped; it was evident, it was certain, that M. de Vlaye knew all. What was he to say, what to do? While Bonne, though her ear hung upon his reply, was conscious only of a desperate search, a wild groping, after some method of giving the alarm to those whom it concerned—to Charles lurking in the barn beside the water, to the Countess making hay for sport and thinking no evil. She had heard of a woman who in such a strait sent a feather which put quick wits on the alert. But she had no feather, she had nothing, and if she had, at her first word of withdrawing M. de Vlaye, she knew, would interpose. At last—

"It must be!" the Vicomte exclaimed, taking a new line with some presence of mind. "But I would not believe it!"

"It must be? what must be, sir?" his daughter Odette rejoined.

"It must be the Countess!" the Vicomte repeated in a tone of surprise and conviction, not ill feigned. He saw that to persist in denying the truth—with the hayfield in sight—would not serve, and in the end must cover him with confusion. "Dressed in that fashion," he continued, "and with no attendant save one rough

102

clown, I—I could not credit her story. The Countess of Rochechouart! It seems incredible even now!"

"Yes, the Countess of Rochechouart," M. de Vlaye replied in a tone which proved that the Vicomte's sudden frankness did not deceive him. "With your permission we will wait on her, M. le Vicomte," he continued in the same tone, "and as soon as horses can be provided, I will escort her to a place of safety."

The Vicomte's face was a study of perplexity. "If you will alight," he said, slowly, "I will send and announce to the Countess—if Countess she really be—that you are here."

For an instant Bonne's heart stood still. If M. de Vlaye dismounted and entered, all things were possible. But the hope was dashed to the ground forthwith. "I thank you," Vlaye answered somewhat grimly, "but with your permission, M. le Vicomte, to business first. We will go to the meadows at once. It is not fitting that the Countess should be left for a minute longer than is necessary in a place so ill guarded. And, for the matter of that, things lost once are sometimes lost twice."

The Vicomte's nose twitched with rage; he was not a meek man. He understood M. de Vlaye's insinuation, he knew that M. de Vlaye knew; but he was helpless. On the threshold of his own house, on the spot where his ancestors' word had been law for generations—or a blow had followed the word—he stood impotent before this clever, upstart soldier who held him at mercy. And this the Abbess, had her affection for him been warm or her nature delicate, must have felt. Without a word spoken or a syllable of explanation, she must have perceived that she was witnessing her family's shame, and that her part in the scene was not with them.

But she, of them all, was the most in the dark, and her thoughts were otherwise bent. "You are very fearful for the young lady, M. de Vlaye," she said, turning to him, and speaking in a tone of mock offence. "I do not remember that you have ever been so over careful for me."

He bent his head and muttered something of which her sister caught not a word. Then, "But we must not waste time," he continued briskly. "Let us—with the Vicomte's permission—to the field! To the field!" And he turned his horse as he spoke into the sled-road that led around the courtyard wall; and by a gesture he bade his men follow. It was evident to Bonne, evident to her father, that he had had a spy on the house, and knew where his quarry harboured.

The girl wondered whether by flying through the house and dropping from the corner of the garden wall she could even now give the alarm. Then M. le Vicomte spoke. "I will come with you," he said in a surly tone that betrayed his sense of his position. "The times are indeed out of joint, and persons out of their places, but—Solomon, my staff! Daughter," to the Abbess, "a hold of your stirrup-leather! It is but a step, and I can still walk so far. If the field be unsafe for the guest,"—he added grimly—"it is fit the host should share the danger."

Bonne could have blessed him for the thought, for his offer bound the party to a walking pace, and something might happen. Vlaye, beyond doubt, had the same thought. But without breaking openly with the Vicomte —which for various reasons he was loth to do—he could not reject his company nor outpace him.

He raised no objection, therefore, and in displeased

silence the Vicomte walked beside his daughter's horse, Bonne accompanying him on the other hand. She knew more than he, and had reason to fear more; she was almost sick with anxiety. But he, perhaps, suffered more. Forced on his own ground to do that which he did not wish to do, forced to play a sorry farce, he felt, as he trudged in the van of the party, that he walked the captive in a Roman triumph. And he could have smitten the Captain of Vlaye across the face.

They passed only too quickly from the shelter of the house to the open meadows and the hot sunshine, and so over the stone bridge. Bonne knew that at this point they must become visible to the workers in the hay-field, and she counted on an interval of a few minutes during which the fugitives might take steps to hide themselves, or even to get over the river and bury themselves in the woods. She could have cried, therefore, when, without apparent order, a party from the rear cantered past the leaders and, putting their horses into a sharp hand-gallop, preceded them in their advance upon the panic-stricken haymakers, in the midst of whom they drew rein in something less than a minute.

The Vicomte halted as the meaning of the manœuvre broke upon him, and, striking his staff into the ground, he followed them with his eyes. "You seem fearful indeed," he growled, his high nose wrinkled with anger.

"Things happen very quickly at times," Vlaye answered, ignoring the tone.

"Take care, sir, take care!" the Abbess of Vlaye cried, addressing her lover. She little thought in her easy insouciance how near the truth she was treading. "If you show yourself so very anxious for the Countess's safety, I warn you I shall grow jealous."

"You have seen her," M. de Vlaye answered in a low tone, meant only for her ear; and he hung slightly towards her. "You know how little cause you have to fear."

"Fear?" the Abbess retorted rather sharply. "Know, sir," with a quick defiant glance, "that I fear no one!"

Apparently the handful of riders who had preceded the main body had no order but to stand guard over the workers. For having halted in the midst of the startled servants, who gazed on them in stupefaction, they remained motionless in their saddles. Meanwhile the Vicomte, with a surly face, was drawing slowly up to them. When no more than thirty or forty paces divided the two parties, the leader of the van wheeled about, and trotting to M. de Vlaye's side, saluted him.

"I do not see them, my lord," he muttered in a low tone.

The captain of Vlaye reined in his horse, and sitting at ease, cast an eagle glance over the terrified haymakers, who had instinctively fallen into three or four groups. In one part of the field the hay had been got into heaps, but these were of small size, and barely adequate to the hiding of a child. Nevertheless, look where he would—and his lowering brow bespoke his disappointment—he could detect no one at all resembling a Countess. A moment, and his glance passed from the open meadow to the ruined buildings, which stood on the brink of the stream. It remained fixed on them.

"Search that!" he said in a low tone. And raising his hand he pointed to the old barn. "They must be there! Go about it carefully, Ampoule."

The man he addressed turned, and summoning his party, cantered across the sward—never so green as

after mowing—towards the building. As the riders
drew near the river, Bonne could command herself no
longer. She uttered a low groan. Her face bespoke
her anguish.

M. de Vlaye did not see her face—it was turned from
him—but he caught the sound and understood it. "The
sun is hot," he said in a tone of polite irony. "You find
it so, mademoiselle? Doubtless the Countess has sought
protection from it—in the barn. She will be there, take
my word for it!"

Bonne made no reply. She could not have spoken for
her life; and he and they watched, shading their eyes
from the sun, she, poor girl, with a hand which shook.
The horsemen were by this time near the end of the
building, and all but one proceeded to alight. The rest
were in the act of delivering up their reins, and one had
already vanished within the building, when in full view
of the company, who were watching from the middle
of the field, a man sprang from an opening at the other
end of the barn, reached in three bounds the brink of
the stream, and even as Vlaye's shout of warning startled
the field, plunged from the bank, and was lost to sight.

"Holà! Holà!" M. de Vlaye cried in stentorian tones,
and, with his rowels in his horse's flanks, he was away
racing to the spot before his followers had taken the
alarm. The next moment they were thundering emu-
lously at his heels, their charge shaking the earth.
Even the men who had alighted beside the barn, and as
yet knew nothing of the evasion, saw that something
was wrong, took the alarm, and hurried round the
building to the river.

"He is there!" cried one, as they pulled up along the
bank of the stream. And the speaker, in his desire to

show his zeal, wheeled his horse about so suddenly that he well-nigh knocked down his neighbour.

"No, there! There!" cried another. And "There!" cried a third, as the fugitive dived, otter fashion, the willows of the stream affording him some protection.

Suddenly M. de Vlaye's voice rang above all. "After him!" he cried. "After him, fools, and seize him on the other side!"

In a twinkling three or four of the more courageous forced their horses into the stream, and began to swim across. Sixty yards below the spot where he had entered the water, the swimmer's head could be seen. He was being borne on a current towards a willow-bed which projected from the opposite bank, and offered a hiding-place. With wild cries those who had not entered the stream followed him along the bank, jostling and crossing one another, and marked him here and marked him there, while the baying of the excited hounds, restrained by their couples, filled the woods beyond the river with the fierce music of the chase.

Meantime the Vicomte and his younger daughter remained alone in the middle of the meadow; for the Abbess's horse had carried her after the others, whether she would or no, with her hawk clinging and screaming on her sleeve. Of the two who remained, the Vicomte was in a high rage. To be used after this fashion by his guests! To see strangers taking the law into their own hands on his land! To be afoot while hireling troopers spurned his own clods in his face, and all without leave or license, all where he and his forebears had exercised the low justice and the high for centuries! It was too much!

"What is it? Who is it?" he cried, adding in his

passion oaths and execrations then too common. "That is not the Countess! Are they mad?"

"It is Charles," she answered, weeping bitterly. "He was hiding there. And he thought that they were in search of him. Oh, they will kill him! They will kill him!"

"Charles?" the Vicomte exclaimed, and stood turned to stone. "Charles?"

"Yes!" she panted. "And, oh, sir, a word! He is your son, and a word may save him! He has done nothing—nothing that they should hunt him like a rat!"

But the Vicomte was another man now, moved, wrought on by Heaven knows what devils of pride and shame. "My son!" he cried, his rage diverted. "That my son? You lie, girl!" coarsely. "He is no son of mine. You wander. It is some skulking Crocan they have unharboured. Son of mine? Hiding on my land? No! You rave, girl!"

"Oh, sir!" she panted.

"Not a word!" He gripped her wrist fiercely and forced her to silence. "Do you hear me? Not a word. He is no son of mine!"

She clung to him, still imploring him, still trying to soften him. But he shook her off, roughly, brutally, raising his stick to her; and, blinded by her tears, unable to do more, she sank to the ground and buried her face, that she might not see, in a mass of hay. He, without a word, turned his back on her, on the crowd beside the river, on the groups of frightened haymakers—turned his back on all and strode away in the direction of the château, with those devils of shame and pride, which he had pampered so long, riding him hard. He had drained at last the cup of humiliation to the dregs.

He had seen his son hunted like a beast of vermin on his own land in his presence. And his one desire was to be gone. Rage with the cause of this last and worst disgrace dried up all natural feeling, all thought for his flesh and blood, all pity. He cared not whether his son lived or died. His only longing was to escape in his own person; to be gone from the place and scene of degradation, to set himself once more in a position, to —to be himself!

There are tones of the voice that in the lowest depth inspire something of confidence. Bonne, as she lay crushed under the weight of her misery, with the merciless sun beating down upon her neck, heard such a tone whispering low in her ear.

"Lie still, mademoiselle," it murmured. "Lie still! Where you are, you are unseen, and I must speak to you. The man, whoever he is, is taken. They have seized him."

She tried to rise. He laid his hand on her shoulder and held her down.

"I must go!" she gasped, still struggling to rise. "I must go! It is my brother!"

The Lieutenant—for he it was—muttered, it is to be feared, an oath. "Your brother!" he said. "It is your brother, is it? Ah, if you had trusted me! But all is not lost! Listen!" he continued urgently. "M. de Vlaye has bidden the men who have taken him— on the farther side of the river—to convey him along that bank to the ford, and so by the road to Vlaye. And —will you trust me now, mademoiselle?"

"I will, I will!" she sobbed. She showed him for one moment her tear-stained, impassioned face. "If you will help me! If you will help my brother!"

"I will!" he said, and then, and abruptly, he laid his hand on her and violently pressed her down. "Be still!" he muttered in a tone of sharp warning. "I have no more wish to be seen by Vlaye than your brother had!" Lying beside her, he peeped warily over the hay by which he was partly hidden; a slight hollow in which that particular cock rested served to shelter them somewhat, but the screen was slight. "I fear they are coming this way," he continued, his voice not quite steady. "I would I had my horse here, and sound, and I would trouble them little. But all is not lost, all is not lost," he repeated slowly, "till their hands are on us! Nor, may-be, even then!"

She understood, and lay trembling and hiding her face, unable to face this new terror. The thunder of hoofs, coming nearer and nearer, once more shook the earth. The horsemen were returning from the river.

"Lie low!" he repeated, more coolly. "They have spied the Countess. I feared they would. And they are hot foot after her—so ho! And we are saved! Yes," he continued, peeping again and more boldly, "we are saved, I think. They have stopped her, just as Roger and her man—clever Roger, he will make a general yet—were about to pass her over the bridge. Another minute and they had got her to cover in the house, and it had been my fate to be taken." -

She did not answer, her agitation was too great. And after a brief silence during which the Lieutenant watched what went forward at the end of the meadow: "Now, mademoiselle," he said in a more gentle tone, "it is for the Countess I want your help. I will answer for your brother. If no accident befall him he shall be free before many hours are over his head. Remember that!

But with Mademoiselle de Rochechouart—if she be once removed to Vlaye, and cast into this man's power, it will go hard. She is a child, little able to resist. Do you go to her, support her, speak for her, fight for her even—only gain time. Gain time! He will not resort to violence at once, or I am mistaken. He will not drag her away by force until he has exhausted all other means. He will suffer her to stay awhile if you play your part well. And you must play it well!"

"I will!" Bonne cried, all her forces rallied by hope. "I do not know who you are, but save my brother——"

"I will save him!"

"And I will bless you!"

"Do you save the Countess, and she will bless you!" he answered cheerfully. "Now to her, mademoiselle, and do not leave her. Go! Show yourself as brave there as here, and——"

He did not finish the sentence, but as she rose his hand, through some accident, or some impulse that surprised him—for such weaknesses were not in his nature —met hers through the hay and clasped it. The girl reddened to the brow, sprang up, and in a trice was hastening across the field towards the crowd that in a confused medley of horse and foot, peasants and troopers, was gathered about the stone bridge which spanned the brook. The sun beat hotly down on the little mob, but in the interest of the scene which was passing in their midst no one thought twice of the heat.

Bonne's spirits were in a tumult. She hardly knew what she thought or how she felt, or what she was going to do.

But one thing she knew. On one thing she set her foot with every step, and that was fear. A new courage, and a new feeling, filled the girl with an excitement half-painful, half-delightful. Whence this was she did not ask herself, nor why she rested so confidently on the guarantee of her brother's safety, which an untried stranger had given her. It was enough that he had given it. She did not go beyond that.

When she came, hot and panting, to the skirts of the crowd, she found that she must push her way between the horses of the troopers if she would see anything of what was passing. In the act she noticed that half the men were grinning, the others exchanging sly looks and winks. But she was through at last. Now she could see what was afoot.

On the bridge, three paces before her, stood M. de Vlaye with his back to her. He had dismounted, and had his hat in his hand. Beyond him, standing at bay, as it seemed, against the low side wall of the bridge, was the Countess, her small face white, and puckered, and sullen, and behind her again stood Roger, and Fulbert, the steward, with a wild-beast glare in his eyes.

"Surely, mademoiselle," Bonne heard M. de Vlaye say in honeyed accents, as she emerged from the crowd, "surely it were better you mounted here——"

"No!"

"And rode to the château. And then at your leisure——"

"No, I thank you. I will walk."

"But, Countess, you are not safe," he persisted, "on foot and in the open, after what has passed."

"Then I will go to the château," she replied, "but I can walk, I thank you." It was strange to see the firmness, ay, and dignity, that awoke in her in this extremity.

"That, of course," M. de Vlaye replied lightly. "Of

course. But seeing the Abbess on horseback, I thought that you might prefer to ride with her——"

"It is but a step."

"And I am walking," Bonne struck in, pushing to the front. "I will go with the Countess to the house." She spoke with a firmness which surprised herself, and certainly surprised M. de Vlaye, who had not seen her at his elbow. He hesitated, and partly in view of the Countess's attitude, partly of the fact that he had not precisely defined his next step if he got her mounted—he gave way.

"By all means," he said. "And we will form your guard."

Bonne passed her arm round the young Countess. "Come," she said. "I see my sister has preceded us to the house. The sun is hot, and the sooner we are under cover the better."

It was not the heat of the sun, however, that had driven the Abbess from the scene, but a spirit of temper. She had no suspicion of the truth—as yet. But the fuss which M. de Vlaye seemed bent on making about the little countess piqued her, and after looking on a minute or two, and finding herself still left in the background, she had let her jealousy have vent, had struck spur to her horse and ridden back to the house in a rage. This was the last thing she would have done had her eyes been open. Had she guessed how welcome to her admirer her retreat at that moment was, she would have risked a hundred sunstrokes before she went!

She had no notion of the real situation, however, and Bonne, who had, and with a woman's wit saw in her a potent ally, was too late to call her back, though she longed to do it. Between the bridge and the house-gate lay three hundred yards, every yard, it seemed to Bonne, a yard of peril to her charge; and the girl nerved herself accordingly. For Vlaye's darkening face sufficiently declared his perplexity. At any instant, at any point, he might throw off the mask of courtesy, use force, and ride off with his prey. And what could she do?

Only with a brave face walk slowly, slowly, talking as she went! Talking and making believe to be at ease; repressing both the treacherous flutter of her own heart and the little Countess's tendency to start at every movement M. de Vlaye made—as the lamb starts when the wolf bares its teeth! Bonne felt that to let him see that they expected violence was to invite it; and though, if he made a movement to seize her companion, she was prepared to cling and scream and fight with her very nails—she knew that such methods were the last desperate resource, to resort to which portended defeat.

He walked abreast of them, his rein on his arm, his haughty head bent. A little behind them on the left side walked Roger and the Countess's steward. Behind these again, at a short distance, followed the mob of troopers, grinning and nudging one another, and scarce deigning to hide their amusement.

Bonne guessed all, yet she talked bravely. "It is quite an adventure!" she said brightly. "We did but half believe it, M. de Vlaye! Until you told us, we thought mademoiselle must be romancing. That she could not be—oh, no, it seemed impossible that she could be the real Countess!"

"Indeed?" M. de Vlaye answered, measuring with his keen eye the distance to the corner of the court-yard. The girl's chatter embarrassed him. He could not weigh quite coolly the chances and the risks.

"It was after nine o'clock—yes, it must have been nearer midnight!" Bonne continued, with that woman's power of dissembling which puts men's acting to shame. "It was quite an alarm when she came! We thought we were to be robbed."

"It is for that reason," Vlaye said smoothly, "I wish the Countess to be placed in safety."

"Or that it was the Crocans——"

"Precisely—it might have been. And therefore I wish her to place herself without delay——"

"In proper clothes!" Bonne exclaimed cheerfully. "Of course! So she must, M. de Vlaye, and this minute! To think of the Countess of Rochechouart"—she laughed, and affectionately drew the girl nearer to her—"making hay in a waiting-woman's clothes! No wonder that she did not wish to be seen!"

M. de Vlaye looked at the chatterer askance, and mechanically gnawed his moustache. He believed, nay, he was almost sure that she knew all and was playing with him. If so she was playing so successfully that here they were at the corner of the courtyard and he no nearer a decision. They had but to pass along one wall, turn, and in forty paces they would be at the gate. He must make up his mind promptly, then! And, curse her! she talked so fast that he could not bring his mind to it, or weigh the emergencies. If he seized the girl here——

"Roger should not have let her try to cross the brook, M. de Vlaye, should he?" Bonne babbled. "He should have known better. Now she has wet her feet and must change her shoes! Yes," playfully, "you must, mademoiselle."

"I will," the Countess muttered with shaking lips.

One of the troopers who had been of the expedition the day before, and whom the situation tickled, laughed on a sudden outright. M. de Vlaye half halted, turned and looked back in wrath. Was he going to give the signal? Bonne's arm shook. But no, he turned again. And they were almost at the second corner; now they turned it, and her eyes sought the gate greedily, to learn who awaited them there. If the Vicomte was there, and her sister, it was so much in her favour. He would hardly dare to carry the girl off by force under their eyes.

But they were not there. Even Solomon was invisible; probably he had taken the Abbess's horse to the stable. Bonne was left to her own resources, therefore, to her own wits; and at the gate, at the moment of interest, at the last moment, the pinch would come.

And still, but with a dry throat, she talked. "To leave the sun for the shade!" she cried with a prodigious sigh as the western wall of the courtyard intervened and protected them from the sun's heat. "Is it not delightful! It was almost worth while to be so hot, to feel so cool! Are you cool, M. de Vlaye?"

"Yes," he replied grimly, "but——"

"Sommes-nous au milieu du bois?"

she sang, cutting him short—they were within seven or eight paces of the gateway, and she fancied that his face was growing hard, that she detected the movements of a man preparing to make his leap—

" Sommes-nous à la rive?
Sommes-nous au milieu du bois?
Sommes-nous à la rive?

A la rive! A la rive!" she chanted, her arm closing more tightly about the Countess. "*A la rive!*"

With the last word—*Pouf!*—she thrust the child towards the open gateway, and by the same movement dropped on her knees in front of M. de Vlaye, completely thwarting his first instinctive impulse, which was to snatch at the Countess. "It is my pin!" she cried, rising as quickly as she had knelt—the whole seemed but one movement. "Pardon, M. de Vlaye," she continued, but by that time the Countess was twenty paces away, and half-way across the court. "Did I interrupt you? How lucky to find it! I must have lost it yesterday!"

He did not speak, but his eyes betrayed his rage—rage not the less that his men had witnessed and understood the manœuvre; nay, dared by a titter to betray their amusement. For an instant he was tempted to seize her and crush the cursed pride out of her—he to be outwitted before his people by a woman! Or why should he not take her a hostage in the other's room?

Then he remembered that he needed no hostage; he had one already. In a voice that drove the blood from her cheeks, "Take care! Take care, mademoiselle!" he muttered. "Sometimes one pays too much for such a trifle as a pin. You might have hurt yourself, stooping so suddenly! Or hurt—your brother!"

Roger could no longer keep silence. "I can take care of myself, M. de Vlaye," he said, "and of my sister also, I would have you know."

But M. de Vlaye had himself in hand again. "It was not to you I referred," he said coldly and contemptuously. "Take me to your father."

They found the Vicomte awaiting them on the drawbridge at the farther side of the court. But the Countess had vanished; she had not lost a moment in hiding herself in the recesses of her room. For the first time in their intercourse M. de Vlaye approached his host without ceremony or greeting.

"The Countess must come with me," he said roughly and roundly. "She cannot stay here. This place," with a look of naked scorn, "is no place for her. Give orders, if you please, that she prepare to accompany me."

The Vicomte, shaken by the events of the morning, stood thunderstruck. His hand trembled on his staff, and for a moment he could not speak. At last—

"The Countess is in my care, and under my protection," he said, in a voice shrill with emotion.

"Neither of which would avail her in the least," M. de Vlaye answered brutally, "in the event of danger! But it is not to enter into an argument that I am here. I care nothing for the number of your household, or the strength of your house, M. le Vicomte, or," with a sneer, "what was the condition of either—before Coutras. The point is, this is no place for one in the Countess of Rochechouart's position. It is my duty to see her placed in a position of greater safety, and I intend to perform that duty!"

The Vicomte, powerless as he was, shook with passion. "Since when," he exclaimed, "has that duty been laid upon you?"

"It is laid on me," the Captain of Vlaye answered contemptuously, "by the fact that there is no one else in the district who can perform it."

"You will perform it at your peril," the Vicomte said.

"I shall perform it."

"But if the Countess prefers to stay here?" Roger cried, interfering hotly.

"It is a question of her safety, and not of her preference," Vlaye retorted, standing grim and cold before them. "She must come."

A dozen of his troopers had ridden into the courtyard, and from their saddles were watching the group on the drawbridge. The group consisted, besides the Vicomte, of Roger and his sister, old Solomon the porter, and the wild-looking steward. Roger, his heart bursting with indignation, measured with his eye the distance across the courtyard, and had thoughts of flinging himself upon Vlaye, bearing him to the ground, and making his life the price of his men's withdrawal. But he had no weapon, Solomon and Fulbert were in the like case, and the Captain of Vlaye, a man in the prime of life, and armed, was likely to prove a match for all three.

If the Vicomte's ancestors in the pride of their day and power had been deaf to the poor man's cry, if the justice-elm without the castle gates had received in the centuries past the last sighs of 'the innocent, if the towers of the old house had been built in groaning and cemented with blood, some part of the debt was paid this day on the drawbridge. To see the sacred rights of hospitality deforced, to stand by while the guest whom he could not protect—and that guest a woman of his rank and kind—was torn from his hearth, to be set for a laughing-stock to this canaille of troopers— such a humiliation should have slain the last of the Villeneuves where he stood.

Yet the Vicomte lived—lived, it is true, with twitching lips and shaking hands—but lived, and, after a few seconds of moody silence, stooped to parry the blow which he could not return.

"To-morrow—if you will wait until to-morrow," he

muttered, "she may be better prepared to—take the journey."

"To-morrow?"

"Yes, if you will give us till to-morrow"—reluctantly —"we may persuade her."

M. de Vlaye's answer was as unexpected as it was decisive. "Be it so!" he said. "She shall have till to-morrow." He spoke more graciously, more courteously, than he had yet spoken. "I have been—it is possible that in my anxiety for her safety, M. le Vicomte, I have been hasty. Once a soldier, always a soldier! Forgive me, and you, mademoiselle, the same; and I, on my side, will say to-morrow. There, I am not unreasonable," with a poor attempt at joviality. "Only I must leave with you ten or a dozen troopers for her safe keeping. And beyond to-morrow, in the present state of the country, I cannot spare them."

At the mention of the troopers the Vicomte's jaw fell. He stared.

"Will not that suit you?" M. de Vlaye said gaily. He had recovered his usual spirits. He spoke in his old tone.

"It must," the Vicomte answered sullenly. "But I could answer for her without your troopers."

M. de Vlaye shook his head. "Ah, no," he said. "I can say no better than that. With the Crocans so near, and growing in boldness every day, I am bound to be careful. I am told," with a peculiar smile, "that some ne'er-do-wells of birth have joined them in these parts. The worse for them!"

"Well, be it so," the Vicomte said with a ghastly smile. "Be it so! Be it so!"

"Good," Vlaye answered cheerfully—he grew more at his ease with every word. Some might have thought that he had gained all he wanted or saw a new and easy way to it. "Good, and as I must be returning, I will give the necessary orders at once."

He turned as he spoke, and crossing the courtyard, conferred awhile with Ampoule, his second in command. Hurriedly men were told off to this hand and that, some trotting briskly under the archway—where the hay of more peaceful days deadened the sound of hoofs, and the cobwebs almost swept their heads—and others entering by the same road. Presently M. de Vlaye, whose horse had been brought to him, got to his saddle, rode a few paces nearer the draw-bridge, and raised his hat.

"I have done as you wish," he said. "Until to-morrow, M. le Vicomte! Mademoise'le, I kiss your hands!" And wilfully blind to the coldness of the salutation made in return, he wheeled his horse grace-fully, called a man to his side, and rode out of the court.

The Vicomte let his chin fall upon his breast, and beyond a doubt his reflections were of the bitterest. But soon he remembered that there were strange eyes upon him, and he turned and went heavily into his house, the house that others now had in keeping. Old Solomon followed him with an anxious face, and Fulbert, ever desirous to be with his mistress, van-ished in their train. The troopers, after one or two glances at the two who remained on the drawbridge, and a jest at which some laughed outright and some made covert gestures of derision, began to lead their horses into the long stable.

Roger's eye met Bonne's in a glance of flame. "Do you see?" he said. "He was to leave twelve—at the most. He has left eighteen. Do you understand?"

She shook her head.

"I do!" he said. "I do! We may go to our prayers!"

CHAPTER VII.

A SOLDIERS' FROLIC.

A FEW hours later the château of Villeneuve, buried in the lonely woods, wore a strange and unusual aspect.

To all things there comes an end, even to long silences and the march of uneventful years. Summer evening after summer evening had looked its last through darkening tree-tops on the house of Villeneuve, and marked but a spare taper burning here and there in its recesses. Winter evening after winter evening had fallen on the dripping woods and listened in vain for the sounds of revelry that had once beaconed the lost wayfarer, and held wolves doubting on the extremest edge of pasture. Night after night for well-nigh a generation—with the one exception of the historic night of Coutras, when the pursuers feasted in its hall— the house had stood shadowy and silent in the dim spaces of its clearing, and prowling beasts had haunted without fear its threshold. A rotten branch, falling in the depth of the forest, now scared more than its loudest orgy; nay, the dead lords, at rest in the decaying graveyard where the Abbey had stood, made as much impression on the night—for often the will o' the wisp burned there—as their fallen descendants in his darkling house.

Until this night, when the wild things of the wood saw with wonder the glow in the tree-tops and cowered in their lairs, and the owl mousing in the uplands beyond the river shrank from the light in the meadows, and flew to shelter. Beside the well in the courtyard blazed such a bonfire as frightened the sparrows from the ivy; and the wolf had been brave indeed that ventured within half a mile of the singers, whose voices woke the echoes of the ancient towers.

> " Les femmes ne portent pas moustache,
>   Mordieu, Marion!
> Les femmes ne portent pas moustache!
>
> C'était des mûres qu'ell' mangeait
>   Mon dieu, mon ami!
> C'était des mûres qu'ell' mangeait!"

As the troopers, seated, some on the well-curb, and some on logs and buckets, beat out the chorus, or broke off to quarrel across the flames, a chance passer might have thought the night of the great battle come again. Old Solomon, listening to the roar of the wood, and watching the train of sparks fly upwards, trembled for his haystacks; nor would the man of peace have been a coward who, looking in at the open gate, preferred a bed in the greenwood to the peril of entrance. The more timid of the serving-men had hidden themselves with sunset; the dogs had fled to kennel with drooping tails. The noise was such that but for one thing a stranger must have supposed that a mutiny was on the point of breaking out. This was the cool demeanour of Ampoule, M. de Vlaye's lieutenant; who with a couple of confidants sat drinking in the outer hall, where the flames of an unwonted fire shone on torn pennons and dusty head-pieces. When asked by Roger to reduce the men to order, as the women could not sleep, he had shown himself offhand to the point of insolence, curt to the point of brutality. "Have a care of yourselves, and I'll have a care of my men!" he said. "You go to your own!" And he would hear no more.

The Vicomte for a while noticed none of these things. The events of the morning had aged and shaken him, and for hours he sat speechless, with dull eyes, thinking of God knows what—perhaps of the son he had cast off, or of his own fallen estate, or of the peril of his guest. In vain did Roger and his younger daughter try to rouse him from his reverie—try to gain some counsel, some comfort from him. They could not. But that which their timid efforts failed to effect, the rising tempest of joviality at last and suddenly wrought.

"Where is Solomon?" he cried, lifting his head as one awakened from sleep. And he looked about him in great wrath. "Where is Solomon? Why does he not put a stop to this babel? 'Sdeath, man, am I to put up with this? Do you hear me?" looking round. "Do you want them to bring the Abbess downstairs?"

Bonne and Roger, who were crouching with the little Countess in one of the two window-recesses that overlooked the courtyard, rose to go to him. But Solomon, who had been hiding in the shadows about the door, was before them. "To be sure, my lord, to be sure!" the old servant said gallantly, though his troubled face and twitching beard bespoke his knowledge of the real position. "To be sure, my lord, it is not the first time by a many hundred the knaves have forgot themselves, and I've had to go with a stirrup-leather and bring them to their senses! The liquor that has run in this house"—he lifted his hands in admiration—"'tis no wonder, my lord, it goes sometimes to the head!"

"Go out, man! Go out and put a stop to it!" the Vicomte retorted passionately. "Your chattering does but add to it!"

"To be sure, my lord, I am going," Solomon answered bravely. But his eyes asked Roger a question. "To be sure it is like old days, my lord, and I thought that may-be you would like them to have their way a while."

"I should like it, fool?"

"You might think it better——"

"Begone!"

"Nay," Roger said, approaching the Vicomte. "Nay, if any one goes, sir, I must. Solomon is old, and they may mishandle him."

"Mishandle him?" the Vicomte said, opening his eyes in astonishment. "Mishandle my steward? My——" He broke off, his hands feeling tremulously for the arms of his chair; he found them and sank back in it. "I—I had forgotten!" he muttered, his head sinking on his breast. "I had forgotten. I dreamt, and now I am awake. I dreamt," he continued, speaking with increasing bitterness, "that I was Seigneur and Vicomte of Villeneuve, and Baron of Vlaye! With swords at my will, and steeds in stall, and a lusty son to take him by the beard who crossed me! And I am a beggar! A beggar, with no son to call a son, with no sword but that old fool's blade! Mishandle him?" gloomily. "Ay, they may mishandle him!" he continued feebly, his head sinking yet lower on his breast. "But there. It is over. Let them do what they will!"

He continued to mutter, but incoherently, and

Roger, signing to Solomon to go to his place again, slunk back to the window recess. The lad had no hope of effecting more with Ampoule, a brutal man where rein was given him; and he crouched once more where he could see the dark figures carousing in the glare that reached to the range of stables. In order that those in the room might see without being seen, Solomon had lighted no more than two candles, and these were not behind the window, where Roger and the two girls sat in the shadow. They could therefore look out unchecked.

The day had been—and not many hours past—when the lad's cheek would have burned under the sneer just flung at him. Now, though a stranger and a girl had heard it, he was unmoved. For petty feelings of that kind his mind had no longer space. The conduct of the man whom Vlaye had left on guard, the increasing disorder and babel of the half-drunken troopers, awoke in him neither indignation nor anger, nor astonishment, but only fear. Not a fear that unmanned him, though he faced his first real peril, nor a fear that disarmed him, but one that braced him to do his best, that enabled him to think, and plan, and determine—crook-shouldered as he was—with a coolness which some day, as des Ageaux had said, might make of him a commander of men.

He was convinced that the men's unruliness was a thing planned and arranged. The Captain of Vlaye had conceived the wickedness of doing by others what he dared not do himself. The men, unless Roger was mistaken, would pass still more out of hand; the officer would profess himself impotent. Then, it might not be this evening, but to-morrow, or to-morrow evening at latest, the men would burst all bounds, cast aside respect, seize the young Countess, and bear her off. At the ford, or where you will, Vlaye would encounter them, rescue her, and while he gained a hold on her gratitude, would effect that which he had shrunk from doing openly.

It was a wicked, nay, a devilish plan, because in the course of its execution there must come a moment when all in the house—and not the young girl only at whom the plan was aimed—would lie at the men's mercy. For a time the men, half-drunk, must be masters. A moment there must be of extreme danger, threatening all, embracing all; and he, a lad, stood alone to meet it. Alone, save for one old man; for the Vicomte was past such work, and the servants had fled. And though Bonne, to whom as well as to the young Countess he had disclosed his fears, persisted in the hope of rescue, and based that hope on their strange guest's promise, he had little or no hope.

As he crouched with the two girls in the dark window recess, he faced the danger coolly, though the scene was one to depress an older heart. The scanty rays of the two candles which lighted a small part of the chamber fell full on the Vicomte, where he sat sunk low in his chair, a shiver passing now and again over his inert and feeble limbs. The only figure visible against the gloomy, dust-coloured hangings, he seemed the type of a race fallen hopelessly; his features, once imperious, hung flaccid, his hands clung weakly to the arms of his chair. He was capable still of one brief, foolish outburst, one passionate stroke; but no help or wise counsel could be expected from him. He was astonishingly aged in one day; even his power to wound the mind seemed near its end.

In contrast with that drooping figure, seated amid the shadows of the room in which generations of Ville-neuves had lorded it royally, the scene without struck with an appalling sense of virility. The lusty troopers lolling in the hot blaze of the bonfire, on which one or another constantly flung fresh wood, and now roaring out some gutter-stave, now flinging coarse badinage hither and thither, were such as years of license and cruel campaigning had made them; men such as it took a Vlaye or a Montluc to curb. And had the lad who watched them with burning eyes and a beating heart lacked one jot of the perfect courage, he had as soon thought of pitting himself against them as of raising dead bones to life.

But he had that thought, and even planned and plotted as he watched them. "Where is Odette?" he asked in a whisper. He had Bonne's hand in his, her other arm held the Countess to her. "They may be afraid of her. If she spoke to the officer, he might listen to her."

"She will not believe there is danger," Bonne answered with something like a sob. "She will not hear a word. I began to explain about the Countess and she flew into a passion. She has shut herself up and says that we are all mad, stark mad from living alone, and afraid of our shadows. And she and her women have shut themselves up in her chamber. I have been to the door twice, but she will hear nothing."

"She will hear too much by and by!" Roger muttered.

Then a thing happened. The light cast by the bon-fire embraced, it has been said, the whole of the courtyard. The men, confident in their strength, had left the gate open. As Roger ceased to speak, a single horseman emerged, silent as a spectre, from the low gateway, and advancing at a foot-pace three or four steps, drew rein, and gazed in astonishment at the scene of hilarity presented to him.

The three at the window were the first to see him. Roger's hand closed on his sister's; hers, so cold a moment before, grew on a sudden hot. "Who is it?" Roger muttered. "Who is it?" The court, which sloped a little from the house, was wide, but it might have been narrow and still he had asked, for the stranger wore—it was no uncommon fashion in those days—a mask. It was a slender thing, hiding only the upper part of the face, but it sufficed. "Who is it?" Roger repeated.

"M. des Voeux!" Bonne answered involuntarily. In their excitement the three rose to their feet.

Whether it were M. des Voeux or not, the masked man seemed in two minds about advancing. He had even turned his horse as if he would go out again, when some of the revellers espied him, and on the instant a silence, broken only by the crackling of the logs, and as striking as the previous din, proclaimed the fact.

The change seemed to encourage the stranger to advance. As he wheeled again and paced nearer, the men who sat on the farther side of the fire from him, and for that reason could not see him, rose and stood gaping at him through the smoke. He moved nearer to the outer ring.

"Who lives here, my good people?" he asked in a voice peculiarly sweet and clear; his tone smacked even a little womanish.

One of the men stifled a drunken laugh. Another turned, and after winking at his neighbours—who passed the joke round—advanced a pace or two, uncovered elaborately and bowed with ceremony to match. "M. le Vicomte de Villeneuve, if it please you, my lord—I should say your excellency!" with another low bow.

"Curse on it!" the stranger exclaimed.

The men's spokesman stared an instant, taken aback by the unexpected rejoinder. Then, aware that his reputation among his fellows was at stake, he recovered himself. "Did your excellency, my lord duke"— another delighted chuckle among the men—"please to speak?"

"Go and tell him I am here," the masked man answered, disregarding their horse-play; and he released his feet from the stirrups. The window of the dining-hall was open, and the three at it could mark him well, and hear every word of the dialogue.

"If your excellency—would enter?" the man rejoined with the same travesty of politeness. "The Vicomte would not wish you, I am sure, to await his coming."

"Very good. And do you, fellow, tell him that I crave the favour of a night's lodging. That I am alone, and my—but the rest I will tell him myself!"

The troopers nudged one another. "Go, Jasper," said the spokesman aloud, "and carry his excellency's commands to M. le Vicomte. Your horse, my lord duke, shall be taken care of! This way, if it please you my lord duke! And do some of you," turning, and making, unseen by the stranger, the motion of turning a key—"bring lights! Lights to the west tower, do you hear?"

The faces of the three within the window were pressed against the panes. "Who can he be?" Bonne muttered. "They call him——"

"They are fooling him!" Roger replied in wrath. "They know no more who he is than we do! He is not des Voeux. He has not his height, and not half his width. But what," angrily, "are they doing now? Where are they taking the man? Why are they taking him to the old tower?"

Why indeed?

Instead of conducting the guest over the bridge which led to the inhabited part of the house, the trooper, attended by four or five of his half-drunken comrades, was ushering him with ceremony to the lesser bridge which led to the western tower; the ground floor of which, a cold damp dungeon-like place, was used as a wood store. It had been opened a few hours before, that fagots might be taken from it, and this circumstance had perhaps suggested the joke to the prime conspirator.

"Lights are coming, my lord duke!" he said, taking a flaring brand from one of his comrades and holding it aloft. He was chuckling inwardly at the folly of the stranger in swallowing his egregious titles without demur. "The Vicomte shall be told. Beware of the step, my lord!" lowering his light that the other might see it. They were on the threshold now, and he pushed open the door that already stood ajar. "The step is somewhat awkward, your excellency! We have to go through the—it is somewhat old-fashioned, but craving your excellency's pardon for bringing you this way —Yah!"

With the word a sudden push thrust the unsuspecting

stranger forward. Involuntarily he stumbled, tripped and with a cry of rage found himself on his hands and knees among the fagots. Before he could rise the door clanged horridly on him, the key grated in the lock, he was in darkness, a prisoner!

The men, reckless and half-drunk, roared with delight at the jest. "Welcome, my lord duke!" the ringleader cried, holding aloft his light, and bowing to the ground before the thick oaken door. "Welcome to Villeneuve!"

"Welcome!" cried the others, waving their lights, and clutching one another in fits of laughter. "Welcome to Villeneuve! A good night to you! An appetite to your supper, my lord duke!"

So they gibed awhile. Then, beginning to weary of it, they turned and, still shaking with laughter, discovered an addition to their party: Roger stood before them, his eyes glittering with excitement. The lad had not been able to look on and see the trick played on a guest; the more as that guest represented his one solitary, feeble hope of help. The men might still be sober enough to listen; at any rate he would try. Much against their wills he had broken away from the girls. He was here.

"Open that door!" he said.

The man to whom he spoke, the ringleader, looked almost as much astonished as he was. The others ceased to laugh, and waited to see what would happen.

"That door?" the man concerned answered slowly as soon as he could bring his thoughts to bear on the emergency.

"Yes, that door!" Roger cried imperiously, all the

Villeneuve in him rising to the surface. "And instantly, fellow!"

"So be it, if you will have it so," the man replied, shrugging his shoulders. "But it was only a jest, and——"

"There is enough of the jest, and too much!" Roger retorted. He spoke so bravely that not a man remembered his crooked shoulders. "Open, I say!"

The man shook his head. "Best not," he said.

"It shall be done!"

"Well, you can open, if you please," the man replied. "But I am M. de Vlaye's man and take orders nowhere else!" And with an insolent gesture he flung the key on the ground.

To punish him for his insolence, when they were a score to one, was impossible. Roger took up the key, set it in the lock, turned, opened, and, tricked in his turn, plunged head first into the darkness, impelled by a treacherous thrust from behind. Crash! The door was shut on him.

But he knew naught of that. As he fell forward a savage blow from the front, from the darkness, hurled him breathless against a pile of fagots. At the same moment a voice cried in his ear, "There is one is spent, Deo Laus!" A hand groped for him, a foot was set hard against him, and something wrenched at his clothes.

"Why," quoth the same voice a second later—the darkness was almost perfect—"did I not run the rascal through?"

"No!" Roger said, and as the stranger's sword, which had only passed through his clothes, was dragged clear, he nimbly shifted his place. "And I beg you will not," he continued hurriedly. "I was coming to your aid, and those treacherous dogs played the same trick on me!"

"Then who are you?"

"I am Roger de Villeneuve, my father's son."

"Then it *is* Villeneuve, this place? They did not lie in that?"

"No, it is Villeneuve, but these scoundrels are Vlaye's people," Roger answered. He was in the depths of despair, for the girls were alone now and unprotected. "They are in possession here," he continued, almost weeping. "M. de Vlaye——"

"The Captain of Vlaye, do you mean?"

"Yes. He tried to seize the Countess of Rochechouart as she passed this way yesterday. She took refuge here and he did not dare to drag her away. So he left these men to guard her, as he said; but really to carry her off as soon as they should be drunk enough to venture on it." Poor Roger's voice shook. He was lamenting his folly, his dreadful folly, in leaving the women.

The stranger took the news, as was natural, after a different fashion, and one strange enough. First he swore with a deliberate fluency that shocked the country lad; and then he laughed with a light-hearted joyousness that was still more alien from the circumstances. "Well, it is an adventure!" he cried. "It is an adventure! And for what did I come? To the fool his folly! And one fool makes many! But do you think, my friend," he continued, speaking in a different strain, "that they will carry off the Countess while we lie here?"

Roger, raging in the dark, had no other thought. "Why not?" he cried. "Why not? And there are other women in the house." He groaned.

"Young?"

"Yes, yes."

"And one of them—lovely?" There was amusement in the stranger's tone.

"One of them is my sister," Roger retorted fiercely. And for an instant the other was silent.

Then, "With what attendance?" he asked. "Whom have they with them that you can trust?"

"The Countess's steward and one old man. And my father, but he is old also."

"Pheugh!" the stranger whistled. "An adventure indeed!" From the sound of the fagots it seemed that he was moving. "We must out of this," he said, "and to the rescue! But how? There is no other door than the one by which we entered?"

"There is one, but the key is lost, and it has not been opened for years."

"Then we must go out as we came in," the stranger answered gaily. "But how? But how? Let me think! Let me think, lad!"

The smell of damp earth mingled with rotting wood pervaded the darkness in which they stood. They could not see one another, but at a certain height from the ground a shaft of reddish light pierced the gloom and disclosed about a foot of the cobweb vault above them. This light entered through an arrow-slit which looked toward the bonfire, and apparently it suggested a plan, for presently the stranger could be heard stumbling and groping towards it.

"You cannot go out that way!" Roger said.

"No, but I can get them in!" the other answered drily, and from certain noises which came to his ear Roger judged that the man was piling wood under the

opening that he might climb to it. He succeeded by-
and-by; his head and shoulders became darkly visible
at the window—if window that could be called which
was but a span wide.

"There is some one in command?" he asked. "Who
is it? His name, my friend?" And when Roger, who
fortunately remembered Ampoule's name, had told him:
"Do you pile," he said, "some wood behind the door,
so that it cannot be opened to the full or too quickly.
It is only to give us time to transact the punctilios."

Roger complied. He hoped—but with doubt—that
the man was not mad. He supposed that out in the
world men were of these odd and surprising kinds.
The Lieutenant had impressed him. This strange man,
who after coming within an ace of killing him jested,
who laughed and blasphemed in a breath, and who
was no sooner down than he was up, impressed him
more vividly, though differently. And was to impress
him still more. For when he had set the wood behind
the door, the unknown, raised on his pile of fagots, thrust
his face into the opening of the arrow-slit, and in a shrill
voice of surprising timbre began to pour on the ill-
starred Ampoule a stream of the grossest and most
injurious abuse. Amid stinging gibes and scalding epithets, and words that blistered, the name rang out at
intervals only to sink again under the torrent of vile
charges and outrageous insinuations. The lad's ears
burned as he listened; burned still more hotly as he
reflected that the girls might be within hearing. As
for the men at the fire, twenty seconds saw them silent
with amazement. Their very laughter died out under
that steady stream of epithets, for any one of which
a man of honour must have cut his fellow's throat.

A moment or two passed in this stark surprise; still the voice, ever attaining lower depths of abuse, went on.

At length, whether some one told him or he heard it himself, the lieutenant came out, and, flushed with drink, listened for a while incredulous. But when he caught his name, undoubtedly his name, "Ampoule! Ampoule!" again and again, and the tale was told him, and he began to comprehend that in the tower was a man who dared to say of him, Vlaye's right hand in many a dark adventure, of him who had cut many a young cock's comb—to say of him the things he heard—he stood an instant in the blaze of the fire and bellowed like a bull.

"His own sister, fifteen years old," the pitiless voice repeated. "Sold her to a Spanish Jew and divided the money with his mother!"

Ampoule's mouth opened wide, but this time breath failed him. He gasped.

"And being charged with it at Fontarabie," continued the voice, "as he returned, showed the white feather before four men at the inn, who took him and dipped him in a dye vat."

"Son of a dog!" Ampoule shrieked, getting his voice at last. "This is too much! This is——"

"Why, he never bullies when he is unsupported!" his tormentor went on. "But a craven he has always been when put to it! If he be not, let him say it now, and face me in a ring!"

The exasperated man ground his teeth and flung out his arms. "Face you!" he roared. "You! You! Face me, and I will cut out your heart!"

"Fine talk! Fine talk!" came the answer. "So

you have said many a time and run!   Meet me in a ring, foot to foot and fairly, in your shirt!"

"I'll meet you!" the lieutenant answered passionately. "I'll meet you, fool of the world. Little you know whom you have bearded. You must be mad; but mad or not, say your prayer, for 'twill be the last time!"

There was a momentary pause. Then "Promise me a ring and fair-play!" cried the high, delicate voice, "and a clear way of escape if I kill you!"

"Ay, ay! That will I! All that! And much good may it do you!"

"Nay, but swear it," the stranger persisted, "by—by our Lady of Rocamadour!"

"I swear it! I swear it!"

"Then," the stranger replied with a sneer, "it is for you to open. I've no key!" And he leapt lightly from his pile of fagots to the floor.

CHAPTER VIII.

FATHER ANGEL.

As he groped his way towards the door, he came into contact with Roger, who was also making for it. Roger gripped him and tried to hold him. "Is there no other way?" the lad muttered. The situation appalled him. "No other way? You are no match for him!"

"That we shall see!" the stranger retorted curtly.

"Then I shall help you!" the lad declared.

"Would you take on another of them?" the stranger answered eagerly. "But no, you are over young for it! You are over young by your voice." Then, as the key grated in the lock, "Stand at my back if you will," he continued, "and if they—would play me foul, it may serve. But I shall give him brief occasion! You will see a pretty thing, my lad."

Crash! The door was forced open, letting a flood of smoky light into the dark place. He who had opened the door, Ampoule himself, strode back, when he had done it, across the wooden bridge, and flinging a hoarse taunt, a "Come if you dare!" over his shoulder, swaggered to the farther end of the hollow space which the men had formed by ranging themselves in three lines; the bridge and moat forming the fourth. One

141

in every three or four held up a blazing firebrand, plucked
from the flames; the light of which, falling on the intervening space, rendered it as clear as in the day.

The stranger, a little to Roger's surprise, but less to
the surprise of Ampoule's comrades, did not obey the
summons with much alacrity. He waited in the doorway, accustoming his eyes to the light, and the lad,
whose heart overflowed with pity and apprehension—
for he could not think his ally a match for Ampoule's
skill and strength—had time to mark the weird mingling
of glare and shadow, and to wonder if this lurid space
encircled by unreal buildings were indeed the peaceful
courtyard which he had known from childhood. Meanwhile Ampoule waited disdainfully at the other end of
the lists, and as one who scarcely expected his adversary to appear made his blade whistle in the air. Or,
in turn, to show how lightly he held the situation, he
aimed playful thrusts at the legs of the man who stood
nearest, and who skipped to escape them.

"Must we fetch you out, dirty rogue?" he cried, after a minute of this. "Or——"

"Oh, *tace! tace!*" the stranger answered in a peevish
tone. He showed himself on the drawbridge, and with
an air of great caution began to cross it. He still wore
his mask. "You are more anxious than most to reach
the end of your life," he continued in the same querulous
tone. "You are ready?"

"Ready, when you please!" Ampoule retorted fum-
ing. "It is not I——"

"Who hang back?" the stranger answered. As he
spoke he stepped from the end of the bridge like a man
stepping into cold water. He even seemed to hold
himself ready to flee if attacked too suddenly. "But

you are sure you are ready now?" he queried. "Quite ready? Do not let me"—with a backward glance— "take you by surprise!"

Ampoule began to think that it would not be without trouble he would draw his adversary within reach. The duels of those days, be it remembered, were not formal. Often men fought without seconds; sometimes in full armour, sometimes in their shirts. Advantages that would now be deemed dishonourable were taken by the most punctilious. So, to lure on his man and show his own contempt for the affair, Ampoule tossed up his sword, and caught it again by the hilt. "I'm ready!" he said. He came forward three paces, and again tossing up his sword, recovered it.

But the masked man seemed to be unwilling to quit the shelter of the drawbridge; so unwilling that Roger, who had taken up his position on the bridge behind him, felt his cheek grow hot. His ally had proved himself such a master of tongue fence as he had never imagined. Was he, ready as he had been to provoke the quarrel, of those who blench when the time comes to make good the taunt?

It seemed so. For the stranger still hung undecided, a foot as it were either way. "You are sure that I should not now take you by surprise?" he babbled, venturing at length a couple of paces in the direction of the foe—but glancing behind between his steps.

"I am quite sure," Ampoule answered scornfully, "that I see before me a poltroon and a coward!"

The word was still on his lips, when like a tiger-cat, like that which in all the world is most swift to move, like, if you will, the wild boar that will charge an army, the mask darted rather than ran upon his opponent.

But at the same time with an incredible lightness. Before Ampoule could place himself in the best posture, before he could bring his sword-point to the level, or deal one of those famous *"estramaçons"* which he had been wasting on the empty air, the other was within his guard, they were at close quarters, the advantage of the bigger man's length of arm was gone. How it went after that, who struck, who parried, not the most experienced eye could see. So quick on one another, so-furious, so passionate were the half-dozen blows the masked man dealt, that the clearest vision failed to follow them. It was as if a wild cat, having itself nine lives, had launched itself at Ampoule's throat, and gripped, and stabbed, and struck, and in ten seconds borne him to the ground, falling itself with him. But whereas in one second the masked man was up again and on his guard, Ampoule rose not. A few twitches of the limbs, a stifled groan, an arm flung wide, a gasp, and as he had seen many another pass, through the gate by which he had sent not a few, Ampoule passed himself. Of so thin a texture is the web of life, and so slight the thing that suffices to tear it. Had the masked stranger ridden another road that night, had he been a little later, had he been a little sooner; had the trooper refrained from his jest or the men from the wine-pot, had Roger kept his distance, or the arrow-slit looked another way—had any one of these chance occasions fallen other than it fell, Ampoule had lived, and others perchance had died by his hand!

All passed, it has been said, with incredible swiftness; the attack so furious, the end a lightning-stroke. Roger on the bridge awoke from a doubt of his ally's courage to see a whirl, a blow, a fall; and then on the ground ill-lighted and indistinct—for half the men had dropped their lights in their excitement—he saw a grim picture, a man dying, and another crouching a pace from him, watching with shortened point and bent knees for a possible uprising.

But none came; Ampoule had lived. And presently, still watching cautiously, the mask raised himself and dropped his point. A shiver, a groan passed round the square. A single man swore aloud. Finally three or four, shaking off the stupor of amazement, moved forwards, and with their eyes assured themselves that their officer was dead.

At that Roger, still looking on as one fascinated, shook himself awake, in fear for his principal. He expected that an attack would be made on the masked man. None was made, however, no one raised hand or voice. But as he moved towards him, to support him were it needful, the unexpected happened. The unknown tottered a pace or two, leant a moment on his sword-point, swayed, and slowly sank down on the ground.

With a cry of despair Roger sprang to him, and by the gloomy light of the three brands which still remained ablaze, he saw that blood was welling fast from a wound in the masked man's shoulder. Ampoule had passed, but not without his toll.

Roger forgot the danger. Kneeling, following his instinct, he took the fainting man's head on his shoulder. But he was helpless in his ignorance; he knew not how to aid him. And it was one of the troopers, late his enemies, who, kneeling beside him, quickly and deftly cut away the breast of the injured man's shirt, and

with a piece of linen, doubled and redoubled, staunched
the flow of blood. The others stood round the while,
one or two lending a light, their fellows looking on in
silence. Roger, even in his distress, wondered at their
attitude. It would not have surprised him if the men
had fallen on the stranger and killed him out of hand.
Instead they bent over the wounded man with looks
of curiosity; with looks gloomy indeed, but in which
awe and admiration had their part. Presently at his
back a man muttered.

"The devil, or a Joyeuse!" he said. "No other, I'll
be sworn!"

No one answered, but the man who was dressing the
wound lifted the unknown's hand and silently showed
a ring set with stones that even by that flickering and
doubtful light dazzled the eye. They were stones such
as Roger had never seen, and he fancied that they
must be of inestimable value.

"Ay, ay!" the man who had spoken muttered. "I
thought it was so when I saw him join! I mind his
brother, the day he died, taking two of his own men so,
and—pouf! I saw him drown an hour after, and he
took the water just so, cursing and swearing; but the
Tarn was too strong for him."

"That was Duke Antony?" a second whispered.

"Antony Scipio."

"I never saw him," the second speaker answered
softly. "Duke Anne at Coutras—I saw him die; and
des Ageaux, that is now Governor of Périgord, got just
such a wound as that in trying to save him."

"Pouf! All the world knew *him!*" he who had first
spoken rejoined with the scorn of superior knowledge.
"But"—to the man who was binding up the hurt, and

who had all but finished his task—"you had better look and make sure that we shall not have our trouble for nothing."

The trooper nodded and began to feel for the fastening of the mask, which was of strong silk on a stiff frame. Roger raised his hand to prevent him, but as quickly repressed the impulse. The men were saving the man's life, and had a right to learn who he was. Besides, sooner or later, the thing must come off.

Its removal was not easy. But at length the man found the catch, it gave way, and the morsel of black fell and disclosed the pale, handsome face of an effeminate, fair-haired man of about thirty. "Ay, it is he! It is he, sure enough!" went around the circle, with here and there an oath of astonishment.

"Has any one a mouthful of Armagnac?" the impromptu surgeon asked. "No, not wine. There now, gently between his lips. When he has swallowed a little we must lift him into the house. He will do well, I think."

"But," Roger asked, after in vain interrogating their faces with his eyes, "who is it? Who it is, if you please? You know him?"

"Ay, we know him," the trooper answered sententiously. And, rising to his feet, he looked about him. "Best close that gate," he said, raising his voice. "If his people be on his track, as is likely, and come on us before we can make it clear, it may be awkward! See to it, some of you. And do you, Jasper, take horse and tell the Captain, and get his orders."

Two or three of the men, whom the event had most sobered, strode across the court to do his bidding. Roger looked from one to another of those who remained. "But who is he?" he asked. His curiosity was piqued, the more sharply as it was evident that the presence of this man who lay before him, wounded and unconscious, altered, in some fashion, the whole position.

"Who is he?" the former spokesman answered roughly. "Father Angel, to be sure! You have heard of him, I suppose, young sir?"

"Father Angel?" Roger repeated incredulously. "A priest? Impossible!"

"Well, a monk."

"A monk?"

"Ay, and a marshal for the matter of that!" the trooper rejoined impatiently. "Here, lift him, you! Gently, gently! Man, it is the Duke of Joyeuse," he continued, addressing Roger. "You have heard of him, I take it? Now, step together, men, and you won't shake him! We must lay him in the dining-hall. He will do well there." And again to Roger, who walked with him behind the bearers, "If you don't believe me, see here," he said. "'Tis plain enough still!" And taking a burning splinter of wood from one of the others he held it so that the light fell on the crown of the wounded man's head. There discernible amid the long fair hair was the pale shadow of a tonsure.

"Father Angel?" Roger repeated in wonder, as the men bearing their burden stepped slowly and warily on to the bridge.

"Ay, no other! And riding on what mad errand God knows! It was an unlucky one for Ampoule. But they are all mad in that house! Coutras saw the end of one brother, Villemar of another; there are but this one and the Cardinal left! Look your fill," he continued, as the men under his direction carried their burden up the three or four steps that led from the outer hall—where the fire Ampoule had knocked together still burned on the dogs—to the dining-hall. "Monk and Marshal, Duke and Capuchin, angel and devil, you'll never see the like again!"

Probably his words were not far from the mark. Anne, the eldest of the four brothers, by whom and by whose interest with King Henry the Third the house had risen from mediocrity to greatness, from respectability to fame, had fallen at Coutras encircled by the old nobility whom he had led to defeat. His brother, Antony Scipio, young as he was, had taken charge for the League in Languedoc, had pitted himself against the experience of Montmorency, and for a time had carried it. But his minor successes had ended in a crushing defeat at Villemar on the Tarn, and he had drowned his chagrin in its icy waters, cursing and swearing, says the old chronicler, to the last. The event had drawn from his monastery the singular man on whom Roger now looked, Henry, third of the brothers, third Duke of the name, the fame of whose piety within the cloister was only surpassed by that of his excesses in the world; who added to an emotional temperament and its sister gift of eloquence the feverish energy and headlong courage of his race. Snatching the sword fallen from his brother's hands, in five and twenty months he had used it with such effect as to win from the King the baton of a marshal as the price of his obedience.

"M. de Joyeuse!" Roger muttered, as he watched them lay the unconscious man on an improvised couch in the corner. "M. de Joyeuse? It seems incredible!"

"There is nothing credible about them," the man answered darkly. "The old fool who keeps the gate here would try the belief of most with his fables. But he'll never put the handle to their hatchet," with a nod of meaning. "Yet to listen to him, Charlemagne and the twelve were not on a level with his master—once! But where are you going, young sir?" in an altered tone.

"To tell the Vicomte what has occurred," Roger answered, his hand on the latch of the inner door—the door that led to the stairs and the upper rooms.

"By your leave!"

"I don't understand."

"By your leave, I say!" the trooper answered more sharply, and in a twinkling he had intervened, turned the key in the lock and withdrawn it. "I am sorry, young sir," he continued, coolly facing about again, "but until we know what is to do, and what the Captain's orders are—he has a trump card in his hand now, or I am mistaken—I must keep you here, by your leave."

"Against my leave!"

"As you please for that."

"I should have though that you had had enough of keeping people!" Roger retorted angrily.

"May-be Ampoule has," the man answered with a faint sneer. "I'll see if I have not better luck. Come, young sir," he continued with good-humour, "you cannot say that I have been aught but gentle so far. You've fared better with me, ay, a *mort* better, than you'd have fared if the Captain had been here. But I don't want to have to hurt you if it comes to blows upstairs. You are safer here looking after the Duke. And trust me, you'll thank me, some day."

Roger glared at him in resentment. He felt that he who lay helpless in the corner would have known how to deal with the man and the situation; but, for himself, he did not. To attempt force was out of the question, and the trooper had withdrawn and closed the door, leaving Roger alone with the patient, before the idea of bribery occurred to the lad. It was as well perhaps; for what was there at Villeneuve, what had they in that poverty-stricken home of such a value as to outweigh the wrath of Vlaye? Or to corrupt men who had seen, without daring to touch, a ring worth a King's ransom?

Nothing, for certain, which it was in Roger's power to give. Moreover, the situation, though full of peril, seemed less desperate. The Duke's act, if it had wrought no more, had sobered the men, and his presence, wounded as he was, was a factor Roger could not estimate. The respect with which the men treated him when he lay at their mercy, and their care to do the best for him, to say nothing of the feelings of awe and admiration in which they held him—these things promised well. The question was, how would his presence affect M. de Vlaye? And his pursuit of the Countess?

Roger had no notion. The possession of the person of a prince who ruled a great part of Languedoc might touch the Captain of Vlaye—a minnow by comparison, but in his own water—in a number of ways. It might strengthen him in his present design, or it might turn him from it by opening some new prospect to his ambition. Again, M. de Vlaye might treat the Duke in one of several modes; as an enemy, as a friend, as a hostage. He might use the occasion well or ill. He might work on fears or gratitude. All to Roger was dark and uncertain; as dark as the courtyard, where the flames of the huge fire had sunk low, and men by the dull glow of the red embers were removing in a cloak the body of the unfortunate Ampoule. Ay, and as uncertain as the breathing of the wounded man in the corner, which now seemed to stop, and now hurried weakly on.

Roger paced the room. He did not know for certain what had become of the Countess, or of his sister, or of his father. He took it for granted that they had sought the greater safety of the upper rooms. He had himself, earlier in the evening, suggested that if the worst threatened they might retreat to the tower chamber, and there defend themselves; but the Vicomte had pooh-poohed the suggestion, and though Bonne, who persisted in expecting help from outside, had supported it, the plan had been given up. Still they were gone, and they could have retired no other way. He listened at the locked door, hoping to hear feet on the stairs; for they must be anxious about him. But all was still. His sister, the Countess, the Vicomte, might have melted into the air—as far as he was concerned.

And this, anxious as he was for them, vexed him. He had failed! The long silence that had brooded over the decaying house, the dull life against which he and his brother had fretted, were come to an end with a vengeance. But what use had he made of the opportunity? When he should have been playing the hero upstairs, when he should have been the head and front of the defence, directing all, inspiring all, he lay here in a locked room like a naughty child who must be shielded from harm.

A movement on the part of the sick man cut short his thoughts. The Duke was making futile attempts to raise himself on his elbow. "Ageaux! Des Ageaux!" he muttered. "You are satisfied now! I struck him fairly."

Roger hurried to him and leant over him. "Lie still and do not speak," he said, hoping to soothe him.

"We are quits now," the Duke whispered. "We are quits now. Say so, man!" he continued querulously. "I tell you Vlaye will trouble you no more. I struck him fairly in the throat."

"Yes, yes," Roger replied. It was evident that the Duke was rambling in his mind, and took him for some one else. "We are quits now."

"Quits," the wounded man muttered, as if he found some magic in the words. And he drowsed off again into the half-sleep, half-swoon of exhaustion.

Roger could make nothing of it, except that the Duke had Vlaye in his mind, and fancied that it was he whom he had killed. But des Ageaux, whom he fancied he was addressing? Roger knew him by name and that he was Governor of Périgord, a man of name and position beyond his rank. But how came he in this galley? Oh, yes. He remembered now. His name had been mentioned in connection with the death of the eldest Joyeuse at Coutras.

Roger snuffed the candles, and mixing a little wine with water, put it by the Duke's side. Then he wandered to the locked door, and again listened fruitlessly. Thence, for he could not rest, he went to the window, where he pressed his forehead against the cool glass. The fire had sunk lower; it was now no more than an angry eye glowing in the darkness. He could discern little by its light. No one moved, the courtyard seemed as vacant and deserted as the house. Or no. In the direction of the gate he caught the glint of a lanthorn and the movement of several figures, revealed for an instant and as suddenly obscured. He continued to watch the place where the light had vanished, and presently out of the obscurity grew a black mass that slowly took the form of a number of men crossing the court in a silent body, five or six abreast. The tramp of their feet, inaudible on the soil, rumbled hollowly as they mounted the bridge, which creaked beneath them. He caught the gleam of weapons, heard a low order given, fell back from the window. He had little doubt what they were about to do.

He was right. The heavy, noisy entry into the outer hall had scarcely prepared him before the door was thrown open and they filed into the room in which he stood.

What could he do? Resistance was out of the question. "What is it?" he asked, making a show of confronting them.

"No matter, young sir," the man who had before taken charge answered gruffly. "Stand you on one side and no harm will happen to you."

"But——"

"Stand back! Stand back!" the man answered sternly. "We are on no boy's errand!" Then to his party, "Bring the lights," he continued, and advancing to the inner door he unlocked it. "Who has the hammer? Good, do you come first with me. And let the last two stand here and keep the door."

He went through without more words, and disappeared up the staircase, followed by his men in single file. The two last remained on guard at the door, and they and Roger waited in the semi-darkness listening to the lumbering tread of the troopers as they stumbled on the wooden stairs, or their weapons clanged against the wall. Roger clenched his hands hard, vowing vengeance; but what could he do? And he had one consolation. Ampoule's death had sobered the men. They would execute their orders, but the fear of outrage and excess which had dwelt on his mind earlier in the evening no longer seemed serious.

The sound of the men's feet on the stairs had ceased; he guessed that they were searching the rooms overhead. A moment later their movements made this clear. He heard their returning footsteps and their raised voices in the upper passage. They seemed to confer, and to halt for a minute undecided. Then a door, doubtless the one which led to the roof, was tried, and tried again. But in vain, for the next moment a voice cried harshly, "Open! Open!" and after an interval a crash, twice repeated, proclaimed that the hammer was being brought into use. A scrambling of hasty feet followed, and then silence—doubtless they were crossing the roof—and then a pistol shot! One pistol shot!

Roger glared at the men who had been left with him. They opened the door more widely, and stepping through seemed to listen. For a moment the wild notion of locking the door on them, of locking the door on all, occurred to Roger. But he discarded it.

CHAPTER IX.

SPEEDY JUSTICE.

THE elder of the Villeneuve brothers was less happy than Roger, in that the Vicomte had passed to him a portion of his crabbed nature. Something of the bitterness, something of the hardness of the father lurked in the son; who in the like unfortunate circumstances might have grown to be such another as his sire, but with more happy surroundings and a better fate still had it in him to become a generous and kindly gentleman.

It was this latent crabbedness that had kept the injustice of his lot ever before his gaze. Roger bore lightly with his heavier burden, and only the patient sweetness of his eyes told tales. Bonne was almost content; if she fretted it was for others, and if she dreamed of the ancient glories of the house, it was not for the stiff brocades and jewelled stomacher of her grandame that she pined.

But with Charles it was otherwise. The honour of the family was more to him, for he was the heir. Its dignity and welfare were his in a particular sense; and had he been of the most easy disposition, he must still have found it hard to see all passing; to see the end, and to stand by with folded arms. But when to the

155

misery of inaction and the hopelessness of the outlook were added the Vicomte's daily and hourly taunts, and all fell on a nature that had in it the seeds of unhappiness, what wonder if the young man broke away and sought in action, however desperate, a remedy for his pains?

A step which he would now have given the world to undo. As he rode a prisoner along the familiar track, which he had trodden a thousand times in freedom and safety, the iron entered into his soul. The sun shone, the glades were green, in a hundred brakes the birds sang, in shady dells and under oaks the dew sparkled; but he rode, his feet fastened under his horse's belly, his face set towards Vlaye. In an hour the dungeon door would close on him. He would have given the world, had it been his, to undo the step.

Not that he feared the dungeon so much, or even death; though the thought of death, amid the woodland beauty of this June day, carried a chill all its own, and death comes cold to him who awaits it with tied hands. But he could have faced death cheerfully—or he thought so—had he fallen into a stranger's power; had the victory not been so immediately, so easily, so completely with Vlaye—whom he hated. To be dragged thus before his foe, to read in that sneering face the contempt which events had justified, to lie at his mercy who had treated him as a silly clownish lad, to be subjected, may-be, to some contemptuous degrading punishment—this was a prospect worse than death, a prospect maddening, insupportable! Therefore he looked on the woodland with eyes of despair, and now and again, in fits of revolt, had much ado not to fight with his bonds, or hurl unmanly insults at his captors.

They, for their part, took little heed of him. They had not bound his hands, but had tied the reins of his horse to one of their saddles, and, satisfied with this precaution, they left him to his reflections. By-and-by those reflections turned, as the thoughts of all captives turn, to the chance of escape; and he marked that the men—they numbered five—seemed to be occupied with something which interested them more than their prisoner. What it was, of what nature or kind, he had no notion; but he observed that as surely as they recalled their duty and drew round him, so surely did the lapse of two or three minutes find them dispersed again in pairs—it might be behind, it might be before him.

When this happened they talked low, but with an absorption so entire that once he saw a man jam his knee against a sapling which he failed to see, though it stood in his path; and once a man's hat was struck from his head by a bough which he might have avoided by stooping.

Naturally the trooper to whose saddle he was attached had no part in these conferences. And by-and-by this man, a grizzled, thick-set fellow with small eyes, grew impatient, and even, it seemed, suspicious. For a time he vented his dissatisfaction in grunts and looks, but at last, when the four others had got together and were colloguing with heads so close that a saddle-cloth would have covered them, he could bear it no longer.

"Come, enough of that!" he cried surlily. "One of you take him, and let me hear what you have settled. I'd like my say as well as another."

"Ay, ay, Baptist," one of the four answered. "In a minute, my lad."

Baptist swore under his breath. Still he waited, and by-and-by one of the men came grudgingly back, took over the prisoner, and suffered Baptist to join the council. But Villeneuve, whose attention was now roused, noted that this man also, after an interval, became restless. He watched his comrades with jealous eyes, and from time to time he pressed nearer, as if he would fain surprise their talk. Things were in this position when the party arrived at a brook, bordered on either side by willow beds and rushes, and passable at a tiny ford. Beyond the brook the hill rose suddenly and steeply. Charles knew the place as he knew his hand, and that from the brook the track wound up through the brushwood to a nick in the summit of the hill, whence Vlaye could be seen a league below.

The four troopers paused at the ford, and letting their horses drink, permitted the prisoner and his guard to come up. The man they called Baptist approached the latter. "If you will wait here," he said, with a look of meaning, "we'll look to the—you know what."

"I? No, cursed if I do!" the man answered plumply, his swarthy face growing dark. "I'm not a fool!"

"Then how in the devil's name are we to do it?" Baptist retorted with irritation.

"Stay yourself and take care of him!"

"And let you find the stuff!" with an ugly look. "A nice reckoning I should get afterwards."

"Well, I won't stay, that's flat!"

The men looked at one another, and their lowering glances disclosed their embarrassment. The prisoner could make no guess at the subject of discussion, but he saw that they were verging on a quarrel, and his heart beat fast. Given the slightest chance he was resolved to take it. But, that his thoughts might not be read, he kept his eyes on the ground, and feigned a sullenness which he no longer felt.

Suddenly, "Tie him to a tree!" muttered one of the men with a sidelong look at him.

"And leave him?"

"Ay, why not?"

"Why not?" Baptist, the eldest of the men, rejoined with an oath. "Because if harm happen to him, it will be I will pay for it, and not you! That is why not!"

"Tie him well and what can happen?" the other retorted. And then, "Must risk something, Baptist," he added with a grin, which showed that he saw his advantage, "since you are in charge."

The secret was simple. The men had got wind that morning of a saddle and saddle-bags—and a dead horse, but that counted for nothing—that in the search after the attack on the Countess's party had been overlooked in the scrub. Detached to guard the prisoner to Vlaye they had grinned at the chance of forestalling their comrades and gaining what there was to gain; which fancy, ever sanguine, painted in the richest colours. But the five could neither trust one another nor their prisoner; for Charles might inform Vlaye, and in that case they would not only lose the spoil but taste the strapado—the Captain of Vlaye permitting but one robber in his band. Hence they stood in the position of the ass between two bundles of hay, and dared not leave their prisoner, nor would leave the spoil.

At length, after some debate, made up in the main of oaths, "Draw lots who stays!" one suggested.

"We have no cards."

"There are other ways."

"Well," said he who had charge of the prisoner, "whose horse stops drinking first—let him stay!"

"Oh, yes!" retorted Baptist. "And we have watered our horses and you have not!"

The man grinned feebly; the others laughed. "Well," he said, "do you hit on something then! You think yourself clever."

Villeneuve bethought him of the prince who set. his guards to race, and, when their horses were spent, galloped away laughing. But he dared not suggest that, though he tingled with anxiety. "Who sees a heron first," said one.

But "Pooh!" with a grin, "we are all liars!" put an end to that.

"Well," said Baptist sulkily, "if we stay here a while longer we shall all lie for nothing, for we shall have the Captain upon us."

Thus spurred a man had an idea that seemed fair. "We've no two horses alike," he said. "Let us pluck a hair from the tail of each. He"—pointing to Charles— "shall draw one with his eyes shut, and whoever is drawn shall stay on guard."

They agreed to this, and Charles, being applied to, consented with a sulky air to play his part. The hairs were plucked, a grey, a chestnut, a bay, a black, and a sorrel; and the prisoner, foreseeing that he would be left with a single trooper, and determined in that case to essay escape, shut his eyes and felt for the five hairs, and selected one. The man drawn was the man who had last had him in charge, and to whose saddle his reins were still attached.

The man cursed his ill-fortune; the others laughed,

"All the same," he cried, "if you play me false you'll laugh on the other side of your faces!"

"Tut, tut, Martin!" they jeered in answer. "Have no fear!" And they scarce made a secret of their intention to cheat him.

The four turned, laughing, and plunged into the undergrowth which clothed the hill. Still their course could be traced by the snapping of dry sticks, the scramble of a horse on a steep place, or the scared notes of blackbirds, fleeing low among the bushes. Slowly Martin's eyes followed their progress along the hill, and as his eyes moved, he moved also, foot by foot, through the brook, glaring, listening, and now and then muttering threats in his beard.

Had he glanced round once, however impatiently, and seen the pale face and feverish eyes at his elbow, he had taken the alarm. Charles knew that the thing must be done now or not at all; and that there must be one critical moment. If nerve failed him then, or the man turned, or aught happened to thwart his purpose midway, he had far better have left the thing untried.

Now or not at all! He glanced over his shoulder and saw the sun shining on the flat rushy plat beyond the ford, which the horses' feet had fouled while their riders debated. He saw no sign of Vlaye coming up, nor anything to alarm him. The road was clear were he once free. Martin's horse had stepped from the water, his own was in act to follow, his guard sat, therefore, a little higher than himself; in a flash he stooped, seized the other's boot, and with a desperate heave flung him over on the off side.

He clutched, as the man fell, at his reins; they were life or death to him. But though the fellow let them slip, the frightened horse sprang aside, and swung them out of reach. There remained but one thing he could do; he struck his own horse in the hope it would run away and drag the other with it.

But the other, rearing and plunging, backed from him, and the two, pulling in different directions, held their ground until the trooper had risen, run to his horse's head and caught the reins. "Body of Satan!" he panted with a pale scowl; the fall had shaken him. "I'll have your blood for this! Quiet, beast! Quiet!"

In his passion he struck the horse on the head; an act which carried its punishment. The beast backed from him and dragged him, still clinging to the reins, into the brook. In a moment the two horses were plunging about in the water, and he following them was knee deep. Unfortunately Villeneuve was helpless. All he could do was to strike his horse and excite it further. But the man would not let go, and the horses, fastened together, circled round one another until the trooper, notwithstanding their movements, managed to shorten the reins, and at last got his horse by the bit.

"Curse you!" he said again. "Now I've got you! And in a minute, my lad, I'll make you pay for this!"

But Villeneuve, seeing defeat stare him in the face, had made use of the last few seconds. He had loosened the stirrup-leather from the trooper's saddle, and as the fellow, thinking the struggle over, grinned at him, he swung the heavy iron in the air, and brought it down on the beast's withers. It leapt forward, maddened by pain, dashed the man to the ground, and dragging Villeneuve's horse with it, whether it would or no, in a moment both were clear of the brook and plunging along the bank.

Villeneuve struck the horses again to urge them forward; but only to learn that which he should have recognised before; that to escape on a horse, fastened to a second, over difficult ground and through a wood, was not possible. Half-maddened, half-bewildered, they bore him into a mass of thorns and bushes. It was all he could do to guard his eyes and head, more than they could do to keep their feet. A moment and a tough sapling intervened, the rein which joined them snapped, and his horse, giving to the tug at its mouth, fell on its near shoulder.

Bound to his saddle, he could not save himself, but fortunately the soil was soft, the leg that was under the horse was not broken, and for a moment the animal made no effort to rise. Villeneuve, despair in his heart, and the sweat running down his face, had no power to rise. Nor would the power have availed him, for before he could have gone a dozen paces through the tangle of thorns, the troopers, some on horseback, and some on foot, were on him.

The man from whom he had escaped was a couple of paces in front of the others. He had snatched up a stick, and black with rage, raised it to strike the prostrate horse. Had the blow fallen and the horse struggled to his feet, Villeneuve must have been trampled. Fortunately Baptist was in time to catch the man's arm and stay the blow. "Fool!" he said. "Do you want to kill the man?"

"Ay, by Heaven!" the fellow shrieked. "He nearly killed me!"

"Well, you'll not do it!" Baptist retorted, and he

pushed him back. "Do you hear? I have no mind to account for his loss to the Captain, if you have."

"Do you think that I am going to be pitched on my head by a Jack-a-dandy like that," the fellow snarled, "and do naught? And where is my share?"

The grizzled man stooped, and, while one of his comrades held down the horse's head, untied Villeneuve's feet, and drew him from under the beast. "Share?" he answered with a sneer as he rose. "What time had we to find the thing?"

"You have not found it?"

"No—thanks to you! What kind of a guard do you call yourself?" Baptist continued ferociously. "By this time, had you done your part, we had done ours! If there is to be any accounting, you'll account to us!"

"Ay," the others cried, "Baptist is right, my lad!"

The man, seeing himself outnumbered, cast a devilish look at them. He turned on his heel. When he was gone a couple of paces, "Very good," he said over his shoulder, "but when I get you alone——"

"You!" Baptist roared, and took three strides towards him. "You, when you get me alone! Stand to me now, then, and let them see what you will do!"

But the malcontent, with the same look of hate, continued to retreat. Baptist jeered. "That is better!" he said. "But we knew what you were before! Now, lads, to horse, we've lost time enough!"

Flinging a mocking laugh after the craven the troopers turned. But to meet with a surprise. By their horses' heads stood a strange man smiling at them. "I arrest all here!" he said quietly. He had nothing but a riding switch in his hand, and Villeneuve's eyes opened wide as he recognised in him the guest of the Tower Chamber. "In the King's name, lay down your arms!"

They stared at him as if he had fallen from the skies. Even Baptist lost the golden moment, and, in place of flinging himself upon the stranger, repeated, "Lay down our arms? Who, in the name of thunder, are you?"

"No matter!" the other answered. "You are surrounded, my man. See! And see!" He pointed in two directions with his switch.

Baptist glared through the bushes, and saw eight or ten horsemen posted along the hill-side above him. He looked across the brook, and there also were two or three stalwart figures, seated motionless in their saddles.

The others looked helplessly to Baptist. "Understand," he said, with uneasy defiance. "You will answer for this. We are the Captain of Vlaye's men!"

"I know naught of the Captain of Vlaye," was the stern reply. "Surrender, and your lives shall be spared. Resist, and your blood be on your own heads!"

Baptist counted heads rapidly, and saw that he was outnumbered. He gave the word, and after one fashion or another, some recklessly, some stolidly, the men threw down their arms. "Only—you will answer for this!" Baptist repeated.

"I shall answer for it," des Ageaux replied gravely. "In the meantime I desire a word with your prisoner. M. de Villeneuve, this way if you please."

He was proceeding to lead Charles a little apart. But his back had not been turned three seconds when a thing happened. The man who had slunk away before Baptist's challenge had got to horse unnoticed. At a little distance from the others, he had not surrendered his arms. Whether he could not from where he was see the horsemen who guarded the further side of the brook, and so thought escape in that direction open, or he could not resist the temptation to wreak his spite on Baptist at all risks, he chose this moment to ride up behind him, draw a pistol from the holster, and fire it into the unfortunate man's back. Then with a yell that echoed his victim's death-cry he crashed through the undergrowth in the direction of the brook.

But already, "Seize him! Seize him!" rose above the wood in a dozen voices. "On your life, seize him!"

The order was executed almost as soon as uttered. As the horse leaping the water alighted on the lower bank, it swerved to avoid a trooper who barred the way. The turn surprised the rider; he lost his balance. Before he could get back into his seat, a trooper knocked him from the saddle with the flat of his sword. In a trice he was seized, disarmed, and dragged across the brook.

But by that time Baptist, with three slugs under his shoulder-blade, lay still among the moss and briars, the hand that had beaten time to a thousand camp-ditties in a thousand quarters from Fontarabie to Flanders flung nerveless beside a wood-wren's nest. As they gathered round him Charles, who had never seen a violent death, gazed on the limp form with a pale face, questioning, with that wonder which the thoughtful of all times have felt, whither the mind that a minute before looked from those sightless eyes had taken its flight.

He was roused by the Lieutenant's voice, speaking in tones measured and stern as fate. "Let him have five minutes," he said, "and then—that tree will be best!"

They began to drag the wretch, now pale as ashes, in the direction indicated. Half way to the tree the man began to struggle, breaking into piercing shrieks that he was Vlaye's man, that they had no right——

"Stay, right he shall have!" des Ageaux cried solemnly. "He is judged and doomed by me, Governor of Périgord, for murder in Curia. In the King's name! Now take him!"

The wretch was dragged off, his judge to all appearance deaf to his cries. But Charles could close neither his ears nor his heart. The man had earned his doom richly. But to stand by while a fellow-creature, vainly shrieking for mercy, mercy, was strangled within his hearing, turned him sick and faint.

Des Ageaux read his thoughts. "To spare here were to kill there," he said coldly. "Learn, my friend, that to rule men is no work for a soft heart or a gentle hand. But you are shaken. Come this way," he continued in a different tone; "you will be the better for some wine." He took out a flask and gave it to Charles, who, excessively thirsty now he thought of it, drank greedily. "That is better," des Ageaux went on, seeing the colour return to his cheeks. "Now I wish for information. Where are the nearest Crocans?"

The young man's face fell. "The nearest Crocans?" he muttered mechanically.

"Yes."

"I——"

"Are there any within three hours' ride of us?"

But Charles had by this time pulled himself together. He held out his wrists. "I am your prisoner," he said. "Call up your men and bind me. You can do with me as you please. But I am a Villeneuve, and I do not betray."

"Not even——"

"You saw me turn pale?" the young man continued. "Believe me, I can bear to go to the tree better than to see another dragged there!"

Des Ageaux smiled. "Nay, but you mistake me, M. de Villenueve," he said. "I ask you to betray no one. It is I who wish to enlist with you."

"With us?" Charles exclaimed. And he stared in bewilderment.

"With you. In fact you see before you," des Ageaux continued, his eyes twinkling, his hand stroking his short beard, "a Crocan. Frankly, and to be quite plain, I want their help; a little later my help may save them. They fear an attack by the Captain of Vlaye? I am prepared to aid them against him. Afterwards——"

"Ay, afterwards."

"If they will hear reason, what can be done in their behalf I will do! But there must be no Jacquerie, no burning, and no plundering. In a word," with a flitting smile, "it is now for the Crocans to say whether the Captain of Vlaye shall earn the King's pardon by quelling them—or they by quelling him."

"But you are the Governor of Périgord?" Charles exclaimed.

"I am the King's Lieutenant in Périgord, which is the same thing."

"And in this business?"

"I am in the position of the finger which is set between the door and the jamb! But no matter for that, you will not understand. Only do you tell me where these Crocans lie, and we will visit them if it can be done before night. To-night I must be back"—with a peculiar look—"for I have other business."

Charles told him, and with joy. Ay, with joy. As a sail to the raft-borne seaman awash in the Biscayan Gulf, or a fountain to the parched wanderer in La Mancha, this and more to him was the prospect suddenly opened before his eyes. To be snatched at a word from the false position in which he had placed himself, and from which naught short of a miracle could save him! To find for ally, instead of the broken farmers and ruined clowns, the governor of a great province! To be free to carve his fortune with his right hand where he would! These, indeed, were blessings that a minute before had seemed as far from him as home from the seaman who feels his craft settling down in a shoreless water.

CHAPTER X.

MIDNIGHT ALARMS.

BONNE'S first thought when her brother darted to the stranger's rescue was to seek aid from Ampoule, who, it will be remembered, sat drinking beside the fire in the outer hall. But the man's coarse address, and the nature of his employment at the moment, checked the impulse; and the girl returned to the window, and, flattening her face against the panes, sought to learn what fortune her brother had. The fire, still burning high, cast its light as far as the gateway. But the tower to which Roger had hastened, being in a line with the window, was not visible, and though Bonne pressed her face as closely as possible against the panes, she could discover nothing. Yet her brother did not come back. The murmur of jeers and laughter persisted, but he did not appear.

She turned at last, impelled to seek aid from some one. But at sight of the room, womanish panic took her by the throat, and the hysterical fit almost overcame her. For what help, what hope of help, lay in any of those whom she saw round her? The Countess indeed had crept to her side, and cast her arm about her, but she was a child, and ashake already. For the others, the Vicomte sat sunk in lethargy, heeding no

171

one, ignorant apparently that his son had left the room; and Fulbert, whose wits had exhausted themselves in the effort that had saved his mistress, stood faithful indeed, but brainless, dull, dumb. Only Solomon, who leant against the wall beside the door, his old face gloomy, his eyebrows knit, only to him could she look for a spark of comfort or suggestion. He, it was clear, appreciated the crisis, for he was listening intently, his head inclined, his hand on a weapon. But he was old, and there was not a man of Vlaye's troopers who was not more than a match for him foot to foot.

Still, he was her only hope, if her brother did not return. And she turned again to the casement, and, scarcely breathing, listened with a keenness of anxiety almost indescribable. If only Roger would return! Roger, who had seemed so weak a prop a few minutes before, and who, now that she had lost him, seemed everything! But the voices of Ampoule and his companion disputing in the outer hall rose louder, drowning more distant sounds; and the minutes were passing. And still Roger did not return.

Then a thought came to her; or rather two thoughts. The first was that all now hung on her—and that steadied her. The second, that he whose grasp had brought the blood to her cheeks that morning had bidden her hold out to the last, fight to the last, play the man to the last; and this moved her to action. Better do anything than succumb like her father. She flew to Solomon, dragging the Countess with her.

"We are not safe here," she said. "These men are drinking. They have kept Roger, and that bodes us no good. Were it not better to go upstairs to the Tower Room?"

"It were the best course," the old man answered slowly, with his eyes on the Vicomte. "Out and away the best course, mademoiselle. Fulbert and I could guard the stairs awhile at any rate."

"Then let us go!"

But he looked at the Vicomte. "If my lord says so," he answered. All his life the Vicomte's word had been his law.

In a moment she was at her father's side. "The Countess will be safer upstairs, sir," she said, speaking with a boldness that surprised herself—but who could long remain in fear of the failing old man whose leaden eyes met hers with scarce a gleam of meaning? "The Countess is frightened here, sir," she continued. "If you would guard us upstairs——"

"Have done!" he struck at her with feeble passion, and waved her off. "Let me alone."

"But——"

"Peace, girl, I say!" he repeated irascibly. "Who are you to fix comings and goings? Get to your stool and your needle. God knows," in a burst of childish petulance, "what the world is coming to—when children order their elders! But since—there, begone! Begone!"

She wrung her hands in despair. Outside, fuel was beginning to fail, the fire was burning low, the court growing dark. Within, the two guttering candles showed only the Vicomte's figure sunk low in his chair, and here and there a pale face projected from the shadow. But the noise of riot and disorder did not slacken, rather it grew more menacing; and what was she to do? Desperate, she returned to the attack.

"Sir," she said, "there is no one to escort the Countess of Rochechouart to her room. She wishes to retire, and it is late."

He got abruptly to his feet, and looked about him with something of his ordinary air. "Where is the Countess?" he asked peevishly. And then addressing Solomon, "Take candles! Take candles!" he continued. "And you, sirrah, light the way! Don't you know your duty? The Countess to her room! Mordieu, girl, we are fallen low indeed if we don't know how to behave to our guests. Madame—or, to be sure, Mademoiselle la Comtesse," with a puzzled look at the shrinking child, "let me have the honour. Things are out of gear to-night, and we must do the best we can. But to-morrow—to-morrow all shall be in order."

He marshalled Solomon out and followed, bowing the young Countess before him. Bonne overjoyed went next; Fulbert, like a patient dog, brought up the rear. All was not done yet, however, as Bonne knew; and she nerved herself for the effort. On the landing her father would have stopped, but she passed him lightly and opened the door that led by way of the roof, to the Tower Chamber. "This way!" she muttered to Solomon, as he hesitated. "The Countess is timid to-night, sir," she continued aloud, "and craves leave to lie in the Tower as the room is empty."

He frowned. "Still this silliness!" he exclaimed, and then passing his hand over his brow, "There was something said about it, I remember. But I thought I——"

"Gave permission, sir? Yes!" Bonne murmured, pushing the girl steadily forward. "Solomon, do you hear? Light along the leads!"

Great as was his fear of the Vicomte, the old porter succumbed to her will, and all were on the point of following, when a door on the landing opened, and the Abbess appeared on the threshold of her room. She held a light above her head, and with a sneer on her handsome face, contemplated the group.

"What is this?" she asked. And then, gathering their intention from their looks—possibly she had had some inkling of it, "You do not mean to tell me," she continued, partly in temper, and partly in feigned surprise, "that a half-dozen of roystering troopers, sir, are driving the Vicomte de Villeneuve from his own chamber? To take refuge among the owls and bats? For shame, sir, for shame!"

Bonne tried to stay her by a gesture.

In vain. "A fine tale they will have to tell to-morrow!" the elder sister continued in tones of savage raillery. "M. de Villeneuve afraid of a handful of rascals, whom their master keeps within bounds with a stick! The Lord of Villeneuve bearded in his own house by a scum of riders!"

"Peace, daughter!" the Vicomte cried; he even raised his hand in anger. "You lie! It is not I"—his head trembling—"I indeed, but the Countess! You don't see her. The Countess of Rochechouart——"

"Oh!" said the Abbess. And, the light she held shining on her arrogant beauty, she swept a great curtsy, as if she had not seen her intended guest before; as if her scornful eyes had not from the first descried the girl; as if the small beginnings of hate, hate that scarcely knew itself, were not already in her breast. "Oh," she said again, "it is the Countess of Rochechouart, is it, who is afraid?"

"And with reason," Bonne answered, intervening hurriedly, but in a low voice. "The men are drinking and growing violent. Roger went to them some time ago, and has not come back."

"Roger!" the Abbess ejaculated, shrugging her shoulders. "Did you think that he could do anything?"

But she who of all those present seemed least likely to interfere spoke up at that. Whether the young Countess resented—Heaven knows why she should—the sneer at Roger's expense, or only the contempt of herself which the Abbess's manner expressed, she plucked up a spirit. After all she was not only a Rochechouart, but she was a woman; and there is in all women, even the meekest, a spark of temper that, being fanned by one of their own sex, blazes up. "It is true," she replied coldly, her face faintly pink. "It is I who am afraid, mademoiselle. But it is not of the men downstairs. It is their master whom I fear."

"You fear M. de Vlaye?" the Abbess repeated. And she laughed aloud, a little over merrily, at the absurdity of the notion. "You—fear M. de Vlaye? Why? If I may venture to ask?"

"Why?" the Countess replied. She had learned somewhat during the day, and was too young to hide her knowledge, being provoked. "Do you ask why, mademoiselle? Because, to be plain, I fear that which it may be you do'not fear."

The Abbess flushed crimson to her very throat. "And what, to be plain, do you mean by that?" she retorted in a tone that shook with passion. "If you think that this story is true that they tell——"

"That M. de Vlaye waylaid and would have seized me?" the little Countess retorted undismayed. "It is quite true."

"You say that!" The young Abbess was pale and

red by turns. "How do you know? What do you know?"

"I know the Captain of Vlaye," the girl answered firmly. "I have seen him more than once at Angoulême, His mask fell yesterday, and I could not be mistaken. It was he!"

The Abbess bit her lip until the blood came in the vain attempt to mask feelings which her temper rendered her impotent to control. She no longer doubted the story. She saw that it was true; and jealousy, rage, and amazement—amazement at Vlaye's treachery, amazement at the discovery of a rival in one so insignificant in all save rank—deprived her of the power of speech. Fortunately at this moment the clash of steel reached Solomon's ears, and, startled, the porter gave the alarm.

"My lord, they are fighting!" he cried. And then emboldened by the emergency, "Were it not well," he continued, "to put the ladies in a place of safety?"

The Vicomte, urged up the steps by the women, leant over the parapet, and learned the truth for himself. Bonne, the Countess, the Abbess and her women, all followed, and in a twinkling were standing on the roof in the dark night, the round tower rising beside them, and the croaking of the frogs coming up to them from below.

But the brief clash of weapons was over, and they could make out no more than a group of figures gathered about two prostrate men. The movement of the lights, now here now there, augmented the difficulty of seeing, and for a while Bonne's heart stood still. She made no lamentations, for she came of the old blood, but she thought Roger dead. And then a man raised a light, and she distinguished his figure leaning over one of the injured men.

"Thank God!" she murmured. "There is Roger. He is not hurt!"

"Who are they? Who are they?" the Vicomte babbled, clinging to the parapet. "Eh? Who are they? Cannot any one see?"

But no one could see, and the Abbess's women began to cry. She paid no heed to them. She leant with the others over the parapet, and she listened with them to the shuffling feet of the men below, as slowly in a double line they bore the cloaked form towards the house. But whether their thoughts were her thoughts, their anxiety her anxiety, whether she was wrapt, as they were, in the scene that passed below, or chewed instead the cud of other and more bitter reflections, was known only to herself. Her proud spirit, whose worst failings hitherto had not gone beyond selfishness and vanity, hung, it may be, during those moments between good and evil, the better and the worse; took, perhaps, the turn that must decide its life; flung from it, perhaps, in passionate abandonment the last heart-strings that bound it to the purer and more generous affections.

Perhaps; but none of those who stood beside her had an inkling of her mood. For the troopers had passed with their mysterious burden into the house, and no sooner were they gone than one of the Abbess's women cried in a panic that they would be murdered, and in a trice all, succumbing to the impulse, made for the Tower Chamber, and herded into it pell-mell, some shrugging their shoulders and showing that they gave way to the more timid, and the men not knowing from whom to take orders. In the chamber were already two or three of the house-women, who had sought that refuge earlier in the evening, and these, seeing the

Vicomte, looked for nothing but slaughter, and by their shrill lamentations added to the confusion.

The security of all depended entirely on their holding the way across the leads, and here the men should have remained; but the women would not part with them and all entered together. Some one locked the outer door, and there they were, in all eleven or twelve persons, in the great, dreary chamber, where a few feeble candles that served to make darkness visible disclosed their blanched faces. At the slightest sound the women shrieked or clung to one another, and with every second the boldest expected to hear the tramp of feet without, and the clatter of weapons on the oak.

There was something ridiculous in this noisy panic; yet something terrifying also to those who, like Bonne, kept their heads. She strove in vain to make herself heard; her voice was drowned; the disorder overwhelmed her as a flood overwhelms a strong swimmer. She seized a girl by the arm to silence her: the wench took it for a fresh alarm and squalled the louder. She flew to her father and begged him to interpose; flurried, he fell into a rage with her, and stormed at her as if it were she who caused the confusion. For the others, the young Countess, though quiet, was scared; and Odette, seated at a distance, noticed her companions only at intervals in the dark current of her thoughts—and then with a look of disdain.

At length Bonne betook herself to Solomon. "Some one should hold the roof!" she said.

He shrugged his shoulders. "Ay, ay, mademoiselle," he said, "but we have no orders and the door is locked, and he has the key."

"You could do something there?"

"Ay, if we had orders."

She flew to the Vicomte at that. "Some one should be holding the roof, sir," she said. "Solomon and Fulbert could maintain it awhile. Could you not give them orders?"

He swore at her. "We are mad to be here," he exclaimed, veering about on an instant. "This comes of letting women have a voice! Silence, you hell-babes!" he continued, turning with his staff raised upon two of the women, who had chosen that moment to raise a new outcry. "We are all mad! Mad, I say!"

"I will silence them, sir," she answered. And stepping on a bed, "Listen! Listen to me!" she cried stoutly. "We are in little danger here if we are quiet. Therefore let us make no noise. They will not then know where to find us. And let the men go to the door, and the maids to the other end of the room. And——"

Shrieks stopped her. The two whom the Vicomte had upbraided flung themselves screaming on Solomon. "The window! The window!" they cried, glaring over their shoulders. And before the astonished old man could free himself, or the Vicomte give vent to his passion, "The window! They are coming in!" they shrieked.

The words were the signal for a wild rush towards the door. Two or three of the candles were knocked down, the Vicomte was well-nigh carried off his legs, the Abbess, who tried to rise, was pinned where she was by her women; who flung themselves on their knees before her and hid their faces in her robe. Only Bonne, interrupted in the midst of her appeal, retained both her presence of mind and her freedom of action. After obeying the generous instinct which bade her thrust the young Countess behind her, she remained motionless, staring intently at the window—staring in a mixture of hope and fear.

The hope was justified. They were the faces of friends that showed in the dark opening of the window. They were friends who entered—Charles first, that the alarm might be the sooner quelled, des Ageaux second; if first and second they could be called, when the feet of the two touched the floor almost at the same instant. But Charles wore a new and radiant face, and des Ageaux a look of command, that to Bonne after what she had gone through was as wine to a fainting man. There were some whom that look did not reach, but even these—women with their faces hidden—stilled their cries, and raised their heads when he spoke. For a trumpet could not have rung more firm in that panic-laden air.

"We are friends!" he said. "And we are in time! M. le Vicomte, we must act and ask your leave afterwards." Turning again to the window he spoke to the night.

Not in vain. At the word troopers came tumbling in man after man; the foremost, a lean, lank-visaged veteran, who looked neither to right nor left, but in three strides, and with one salute in the Vicomte's direction, put himself at the door and on guard. He had a long, odd-looking sword with a steel basket hilt, with which he signed to the men to stand here or there.

For they continued to come in, until the Vicomte, stunned by the sight of his son, awoke to fresh wonder; and, speechless, counted a round dozen and three to boot, besides his guest and Charles. Moreover they were men of a certain stamp, quiet but grim, who, being bidden, did and asked no questions.

When they had all filed through the group of staring women now fallen silent, and had ranged themselves beside the Bat—for he it was—at the door, des Ageaux spoke.

"Do you hear them?"

"No, my lord."

"Unlock softly, then, but do not open! And wait the word! M. le Vicomte"—he turned courteously to the old man—"the occasion presses, or I would ask your pardon. Mademoiselle"—but as he turned to Bonne he lowered his voice, and what he said escaped other ears. Not her ears, for from brow to neck, though he had but praised her courage and firmness, she blushed vividly.

"I did only what I could," she replied, lifting her eyes once to his and as quickly dropping them. "Roger——"

"Ha! What of Roger?"

She told him as concisely as she could.

He knit his brows. "That was not of my contrivance," he said. And then with a gleam of humour in his eyes, "Masked was he? Another knight-errant, it seems, and less fortunate than the first! You do not lack supporters in your misfortunes, mademoiselle. But—what is it?"

"They come, my lord," the Bat answered, raising his hand to gain attention.

All, at the word, listened with quickened pulses, and in the silence the harsh rending of wood came to the ear, a little dulled by distance. Then a murmur of voices, then another crash! The men about the door poised themselves, each with a foot advanced, and his weapon ready; their strained muscles and gleaming eyes told of their excitement. A moment and they would be let loose! A moment—and then, too late, Bonne saw Charles beside the Bat.

Too late; but it mattered nothing. She might have spoken, but he, panting for the fight, exulting in the occasion, would not have heeded if an angel had spoken. And before she could find words, the thing was done. The Bat flung the door open, and with a roar of defiance the mob of men charged out and across the roof, Charles among the foremost.

A shot, a scream, a tumult of cries, the jarring of steel on steel, and the fight rolled down through the house in a whirl of strident voices. The candles, long-wicked and guttering, flamed wildly in the wind; the room was half in shadow, half in light. The Vicomte, who had seen all in a maze of stupefaction, stiffened himself— as the old war-horse that scents the battle. Bonne hid her face and prayed.

Not so the Abbess. She sat unmoved, a sneer on her face, a dark look in her eyes. And so Bonne, glancing up, saw her; and a strange pang shot through the younger girl's breast. If he had praised *her* courage— and that with a look and in a tone that had brought the blood to her cheeks—what would he think of her handsome sister? How could he fail to admire her, not for her beauty only, but for her stately pride, for the composure that not even this could alter, for the challenge that shone in her haughty eyes?

The next moment Bonne reproached herself for entertaining such a thought, while Charles's life and perhaps Roger's hung in the balance, and the cries of

men in direst straits still rung in her ears. What a
worm she was, what a crawling thing! God pardon her!
God protect them!

The Abbess's voice—she had risen at last and moved
—cut short her supplications. "Who is he?" Odette
de Villeneuve muttered in a fierce whisper. "Who is
he, girl?" She pointed to des Ageaux, who kept his
station on the threshold, his ear following the course of
the fight. "Who is that man? They call him my
lord! Who is he?"

"I do not know," Bonne said.

"You do not know?"

"No."

The candles flared higher. The Lieutenant turned
and saw the two sisters standing together looking at
him.

He crossed the room to them, halting midway to
listen, his attention divided between them and the conflict below. His eyes dwelt awhile on the Abbess, but
settled, as he drew nearer, on Bonne. He desired to
reassure her. "Have no fear, mademoiselle," he said
quietly. "Your brother runs little risk. They were
taken by surprise. By this time it is over."

The Vicomte heard and his lips trembled, but no
words came. It was the Abbess who spoke for him.
"And what next?" she asked harshly.

Des Ageaux, still lending an ear to the sounds below,
looked at her with attention, but did not answer.

"What next?" she repeated. "You have entered
forcibly. By what right?"

"The right, mademoiselle," he replied, "that every
man has to resist a wrong. The right that every man
has to protect women, and to save his friends. If you

desire more than this," he continued, with a change of tone that answered the challenge of her eyes, "in the King's name, mademoiselle, and my own!"

"And you are?"

"His Majesty's Lieutenant in Périgord," he answered, bowing. His attention was fixed on her, yet he was vividly conscious of the colour that mounted suddenly to Bonne's cheeks, dyed her brows, shone in her eyes.

"Of Périgord?" the Abbess repeated in astonishment.

"Of Périgord," he replied, bowing again. "It is true," he continued, shrugging his shoulders, "that I am a league or two beyond my border, but great wrongs beget little ones, mademoiselle."

She hated him. As he stood there successful, she hated him. But she had not found an answer, nor had Bonne stilled the fluttering, half painful, half pleasant, of her heart, when the tread of returning feet heralded news. The Bat and two others entered, bearing a lanthorn that lit up their damp swarthy faces. The first was Roger.

He was wildly excited. "Great news!" he cried, waving his hand. "Great news! I have downstairs——"

One look from des Ageaux's eyes silenced him. Des Ageaux looked from him to the Bat. "What have you done?" he asked curtly.

"Taken two unwounded, three wounded," the tall man answered as briefly. "The others escaped."

"Their horses?"

"We have their horses."

Des Ageaux paused an instant. Then, "You have closed the gates?"

"And set a guard, my lord!" the Bat answered. "We have no wounded, but——"

"The Duke of Joyeuse lies below, and is wounded!" Roger cried in a breath. He could restrain himself no longer.

If his object was to shatter des Ageaux's indifference, he succeeded to a marvel. "The Duke of Joyeuse?" the Lieutenant exclaimed in stupefaction. "Impossible!"

"But no!" Roger retorted. "He is lying below—wounded. It is not impossible!"

"But he was not—of those?" des Ageaux returned, indicating by a gesture the men whom they had just expelled. For an instant the notion that he had attacked and routed friends instead of foes darkened his face.

"No!" Roger explained fluently—excitement had rid him of his diffidence. "No! He was the man who rode into the courtyard—but you have not heard? They were going to maltreat him, and he killed their leader, Ampoule—that was before you came!" Roger's eyes shone; it was evident that he had transferred his allegiance.

Des Ageaux's look sought the Bat and asked a question. "There is a dead man below," the Bat answered. "He had it through the throat."

"And the Duke of Joyeuse?"

"He is there—alone apparently."

"Alone?"

The Bat's eyes sought the wall and gazed on it stonily. "There are more fools than one in the world," he said gruffly.

Des Ageaux pondered an instant. Then, "I will see him," he said. "But first," he turned courteously to the Vicomte, "I have to provide for your safety, M. le

Vicomte, and that of your family. I can only ensure it, I fear, by removing you from here. I have not sufficient force to hold the château, and short of that I see no way of protecting you from the Captain of Vlaye's resentment.''

The Vicomte, who had aged years in the last few days, as the old sometimes do, sat down weakly on a bed. "Go—from here?" he muttered, his hands moving nervously on his knees. "From my house?"

"It is necessary."

"Why?" A younger and stronger voice flung the question at des Ageaux. The Abbess stood forward beside her father. "Why?" she repeated imperiously. "Why should we go from here—from our own house? Or why should we fear M. de Vlaye?"

"To the latter question—because he does not lightly forgive, mademoiselle," des Ageaux replied drily. "To the former because I have neither men nor means to defend this house. To both, because you have with you"—he pointed to the Countess—"this lady, whom it is not consonant with the Vicomte's honour either to abandon or to surrender. To be plain, M. de Vlaye's plans have been thwarted and his men routed, and to-morrow's sun will not be an hour high before he takes the road. To remain here were to abide the utmost of his power; which," he added drily, "is at present of importance, however it may stand in a week's time.''

She looked at him darkly beautiful, temper and high disdain in her face. And as she looked there began to take shape in her mind the wish to destroy him; a wish that even as she looked, in a space of time too short to be measured by our clumsy methods, became a fixed

thought. Why had he intervened? Who had invited
him to intervene? With a woman's inconsistency she
left out of sight the wrong M. de Vlaye would have
done her, she forgot the child-Countess, she overlooked
all except that this man was the enemy of the man she
loved. She felt that but for him all would have been
well! But for him—for even that she laid at his door—
and his hostility the Captain of Vlaye had never been
driven to think of that other way of securing his fortunes.

These thoughts passed through her mind in a pause
so short that the listeners scarcely marked it for a
pause. Then, "And if we will not go?" she cried.

"All in the house will go," he replied.

"Whither?"

"I shall decide that," he answered coldly. And he
turned from her. Before she could retort he was giving orders, and men were coming and going and calling
to one another, and lights were flitting in all directions
through the house, and all about her was hubbub and
stir and confusion. She saw that resistance was
vain. Her father was passive, her brothers were des
Ageaux's most eager ministrants. The servants were
awed into silence, or, like old Solomon, who for once
was mute on the glories of the race, were anxious to
escape for their own sakes.

Then into her hatred of him entered a little of that
leaven of fear which makes hatred active. For amid
the confusion he was cool. His voice was firm, his eye
commanded on this side, his hand beckoned on that,
men ran for him. She knew the dread in which M. de
Vlaye was held. But this she saw was not the awe in
which men hold him whose caprice it may be to punish,

but the awe in which men stand of him who is just; whose nature it is out of chaos to create order, and who to that end will spend himself and all. A man cold of face and something passionless; even hard, we have seen, when a rope, a bough, and a villain forced themselves on his attention.

She would not have known him had she seen him leaning over Joyeuse a few minutes later, while his lean subaltern held a shaded taper on the other side of the makeshift pallet. The door was locked on them, they had the room to themselves, and between them the Duke lay in the dead sleep of exhaustion. "I do not think that we can move him," des Ageaux muttered, his brow clouded by care.

The Bat, with the light touch of one who had handled many a dying man, felt the Duke's pulse, without rousing him. "He will bear it," he said, "in a litter."

"Over that road? Think what a road it is!"

"Needs must!"

"He brought the money, found me gone, and followed," des Ageaux murmured in a voice softening by feeling. "You think we dare take him?"

"To leave him to the Captain of Vlaye were worse."

"Worse for us," des Ageaux muttered doubtfully. "That is true."

"Worse for all," the Bat grunted. He took liberties in private that for all the world he would not have had suspected.

Still his master, who had been so firm above-stairs, hung undecided over the sick man's couch. "M. de Vlaye would not be so foolish as to harm him," he said.

"He would only pluck him!" the Bat retorted. "And wing us with the first feather, the Lady Countess with the second, the Crocans with the third, and the King with the fourth." He stopped. It was a long speech for him.

Des Ageaux assented. "Yes, he is the master-card," he said slowly. "I suppose we must take him. But Heavens knows how we shall get him there."

"Leave that to me!" said the Bat, undertaking more than he knew. Nor did he guess with whose assistance he was to perform the task.

CHAPTER XI.

THE CHAPEL BY THE FORD.

It was after midnight, and the young moon had set when they came, a long procession of riders, to the ford in which des Ageaux had laved his horse's legs on the evening of his arrival. But the night was starlight, and behind them the bonfire, which the men had rekindled that its blaze might aid their preparations, was reflected in a faint glow above the trees. As they splashed through the shallows the frogs fell silent, scared by the invasion, but an owl that was mousing on the slope of the downs between them and the dim lifted horizon continued its melancholy hooting. The women shivered as the cool air embraced them, and one here and there, as her horse, deceived by the waving weeds, set a foot wrong, shrieked low.

But no one hesitated, for the Bat had put fear into them.

He had told them in the fewest possible words that in ninety minutes M. de Vlaye would be knocking at the gate they left! And how long the pursuit would tarry after that he left to their imaginations. The result justified his course; the ford, that in daylight was a terror to the timid, was passed without demur. One by one their horses stepped from its dark smooth-sliding

191

water, turned right-handed, and falling into line set their heads up-stream towards the broken hills and obscure winding valleys whence the river flowed.

Hampered by the wounded man's litter and the night, they could not hope to make more than a league in the hour, and with the first morning light might expect to be overtaken. But des Ageaux considered that the Captain of Vlaye, ignorant of his force, would not dare to follow at speed. And in the beginning all went well.

Over smooth turf, they made for half a league good progress, the long bulk of the chalk hill accompanying them on the left, while on the right the vague gloom of the wooded valley, teeming with mysterious rustlings and shrill night cries, drew many a woman's eyes over her shoulder. But, as the bearers of the litter could only proceed at a walking pace, the long line of shadowy riders had not progressed far before a gap appeared in its ranks and insensibly grew wider. Presently the two bodies were moving a hundred yards apart, and henceforward the rugged surface of the road, which was such as to hamper the litter without delaying the riders, quickly augmented the interval.

The Vicomte was mounted on his own grizzled pony, and with his two daughters and Roger rode at the head of the first party. They had not proceeded far before Bonne remarked that her sister was missing. She was sure that the Abbess had been at her side when she crossed the ford, and for a short time afterwards. Why had she left them? And where was she?

Not in front, for only the Bat and Charles, who had attached himself to the veteran, and was drinking in gruff tales of leaguer at his lips, were in front. Behind, then?

Bonne turned her head and strove to learn. But the light of the stars and the night—June nights are at no hour quite dark—allowed her to see only the persons who rode immediately behind her. They were Roger and the Countess. On their heels came two more—men for certain. The rest were shadows, bobbing vaguely along, dim one moment, lost the next.

Presently Charles, also, missed the Abbess, and asked where she was.

Roger could only answer: "To the rear somewhere."

"Learn where she is," Charles returned. "Pass the word back, lad. Ask who is with her."

Presently, "She is not with us," Roger passed back word. "She is with the litter, they say. And it has fallen behind. But the Lieutenant is with it, so that she is safe there."

"She were better here," Charles answered shortly. "She is not wanted there, I'll be sworn!"

Wanted or not, the Abbess had not put herself where she was without design. Her passage of arms with des Ageaux had not tended to soften her feelings. She was now bent on his punishment. The end she knew; the means were to seek. But with the confidence of a woman who knew herself beautiful, she doubted not that she would find or create them. Bitterly, bitterly should he rue the day when he had forced her to take part against the man she loved. And if she could involve in his fall this child, this puling girl on whom the Captain of Vlaye had stooped an eye, not in love or adoration, but solely to escape the toils in which they were seeking to destroy him—so much the better! The two were linked inseparably in her mind. The guilt was theirs, · the cunning was theirs, the bait was theirs; and M. de

Vlaye's the misfortune only. So women reason when they love.

If she could effect the ruin of these two, and at the same time save the man she adored, her triumph would be complete. If—but, alas, in that word lay the difficulty; nor as she rode with a dark face of offence had she a notion how to set about her task. But women's wits are better than their logic. Men spoke in her hearing of the litter and of the delay it caused, and in a flash the Abbess saw the means she lacked, and the man she must win. In the litter lay the one and the other.

For the motives that led des Ageaux to bear it with him at the cost of trouble, of delay, of danger, were no secret to a quick mind. The man who lay in it was the key to the situation. She came near to divining the very phrase—a master-card—which des Ageaux had used to the Bat in the security of the locked room. A master-card he was; a card that at all costs must be kept in the Lieutenant's hands, and out of Vlaye's power.

Therefore, even in this midnight flight they must burden themselves with his litter. A Duke, a Marshal of France, in favour at Court, and lord of a fourth of Languedoc, he had but to say the word, and Vlaye was saved—for this time at any rate. The Duke need but give some orders, speak to some in power, call on some of those to whom his will was law, and his *protégé* would not fall for lack of means. Up to this point indeed, after a fashion which the Abbess did not understand—for the man had fallen from the clouds—he was ranged against her friend. But if he could be put into Vlaye's hands, or fairly or foully led to take Vlaye's side, then the Captain of Vlaye would be saved. And if she could effect this, would be saved by her. By her!

The sweetness of such a revenge only a woman can understand. Her lover had fancied the Rochechouart's influence necessary to his safety, and to gain that influence he had been ready to repudiate his love. What a sweet savour of triumph if she—*she* whom he was ready to abandon—could save him by this greater influence, and in the act show him that a mightier than he was at her feet!

She had heard stories of the Duke's character, which promised well for her schemes. At the time of her short sojourn at Court, he had but lately left his cloister, drawn forth by the tragical death of his brother. He was then entering upon that career of extravagance, eccentricity, and vice which, along with his reputation for eloquence and for strange fits of repentance, astonished even the dissolute circles of the Court. His name and his fame were in all mouths; a man quick to love, quick to hate, report had it; a man in whom remorse followed sharp on sin, and sin on remorse. A man easy to win, she supposed, if a woman were beautiful and knew how to go about it.

Ay, if she knew; but there was the difficulty. For he was no common man, no man of narrow experience, and the ordinary bait of beauty might not by itself avail. The Abbess, high as her opinion of her charms stood, perceived this. She recognised that in the circles in which he had moved of late beauty was plentiful, and she bent her wits to the point. After that she might have been riding in daylight, for all she saw of her surroundings. She passed through the ford and in her deep thinking saw it not. The long, dark hill on her left, and the low woods on her right with their strange night noises, and their teeming evidences of that tragedy

of death which fills the world, did not exist for her.
The gleam of the star-lit river caught her eye, but
failed to reach her brain. And if she fell back slowly
and gradually until she found herself but a few paces
before the litter and its convoy, it was not by design
only, but in obedience to a subtle attraction at work
within her.

When her women presently roused her by their complaints that she was being left behind with the litter,
she took it for an omen, and smiled in the darkness.
They, on the contrary, were frightened, nor without
reason. The road they pursued followed the bank of
the river; but the wide vale had been left behind.
They had passed into a valley more strait and gloomy;
a winding trough, close pressed by long, hog-shaped
hills, between which the travellers became every
moment more deeply engaged. The stars were fading
from the sky, the darkness which comes before the
dawn was on them, and with the darkness a chill.

This change alarmed the women. But it did not
terrify them one half as much as the marked anxiety
of the litter-party. More than once des Ageaux'
voice could be heard adjuring the bearers to move
faster. More than once a rider passed between them
and the main body, and on each of these occasions men
fell back and took the places of the old carriers. But
still the cry was "Faster! Faster!"

In truth the day was on the point of breaking, and
the fugitives were still little more than two leagues
from Villeneuve. At any moment they might be
overtaken, when the danger of an attack would be
great, since the light must reveal the paucity of their
numbers. In this pinch even the Lieutenant's stoicism

failed him, and moment by moment he trembled lest the sound of galloping horses reach his ear. Less than an hour's riding at speed would place his charges in safety; yet for the sake of a wounded man he must risk all. No wonder that he cried again, "Faster, men, faster!" and pressed the porters to their utmost speed.

Soon out of the darkness ahead loomed the Bat. "This will never do, my lord," he said, reining in his horse beside his leader. He spoke in a low voice, but the Abbess, a dozen paces ahead, could hear his words, and even the heavy breathing of the carriers. "To go on at this pace is to hazard all."

"You must go forward with the main body!" des Ageaux replied shortly. "Let the women who are with us ride on and join the others, and do you—but, no, that will not do."

"For certain it will not do!" the Bat answered. "It is I must stay, for the fault is mine. But for me you would have left him, my lord."

"Do you think we could support him on a horse?"

"It would kill him!" the Bat rejoined. "But it is not two hundred paces to the chapel by the ford that you remarked this morning. If we leave him there, and M. de Vlaye finds him, he will be as anxious to keep life in him as we are. If, on the other hand, M. de Vlaye overlooks him, we can bring him in to-morrow."

"If it must be," des Ageaux answered reluctantly, "we must leave him. But we cannot leave him without some assistance. Who will stay with him?"

"*Diable!*" the Bat muttered.

"I will not leave him without some one," des Ageaux repeated firmly. "Some one must stay."

Out of the darkness came the answer. "I," the Abbess said, "will stay with him!"

"You, mademoiselle?" in a tone of astonishment.

"I," she repeated, "and my women. I," she continued haughtily, "have nothing to fear from the Captain of Vlaye or his men."

"And mademoiselle's robe," the Bat muttered with the faintest suspicion of irony in his tone, "protects her."

Charles, who had joined them with the Bat, thoughtlessly assented. "To be sure!" he cried. "Let my sister stay! She can stay without danger."

Alone of the three des Ageaux remained silent— pondering. He had seen enough of the Abbess to suspect that it was not humanity alone which dictated her offer. Probably she desired to rejoin her admirer. In that case, did she know enough of the fugitives' plans and strength to render her defection formidable?

He thought not. At any rate it seemed well to take the chance. He was taking, he was beginning to see that he was taking a good many chances. "It seems a good plan, if mademoiselle be indeed willing," he said. He wished that he could see her face.

"I have said," she replied coldly, "that I am willing."

But her women showed forthwith that they were not. What? Remain in this wilderness in the dark with a dying man? They would be eaten by wolves, they would be strangled by witches, they would be ravished by thieves! Never! And in a trice one was in hysterics, deaf to her mistress's threats and to the Bat's grim hints. The other, after a conflict, allowed herself to be browbeaten, and sullenly, and with tears, yielded. But not until the water of the ford rippled about their horses' hoofs, and the tiny spark of light that through the open door beaconed the shallows shone in their eyes.

Had it been day they would have had before them a scene at once wild and peaceful. On their right, below the ford—which was formed by the passage of the stream from one side of the narrow valley to the other —a lofty bluff overhung a black pool. Above the ford, on the level meadow, and a stone's-throw from the track—if track that could be called which was not used by a hundred persons in a year—stood a tiny chapel and cell, which some hermit in past ages had built with his own hands. The approach of the Crocans had driven his latest successor from his post; but des Ageaux, passing that way in the day, had noted the chapel, and with the forethought of the soldier who expected to return in the dark he had seen the earthen lamp relit. Its light, he knew, would, in case of need, direct him to the ford.

At present that lamp, a tiny spark in the blackness, was all they saw. They made for it through the shallows and over a bed of shingle across which the horses clattered noisily. In haste they reached the door of the chapel, and there in a trice—for if the thing was to be done it must be done quickly—they aided the Abbess and the lay sister to alight, bore in the litter with the wounded man, and closed the door on all; this last, that the light might no longer be visible from the ford. Then they, the men, got themselves to horse again, and away at a round trot.

Not without repugnance on the part of several; not without regret and misgiving. Des Ageaux's heart smote him as his horse's feet carried him farther and farther away; it seemed so cowardly a thing to leave women to bear in that wild and lonely place the brunt of whatever might befall. And Charles, ready as he had been to acclaim the notion, wondered if he had erred in leaving his sister thus lightly. But in truth they were embarked in an enterprise whose full perils it lay with time to disclose. And other and more pressing anxieties soon had possession of their minds.

They had been less troubled had they been able to witness the Abbess's demeanour in her solitude. While her companion, overcome by her fears, sank down in a fit of hysterical weeping, Odette de Villeneuve remained standing within the low doorway, and with head erect listened frowning until the last sound of the horses' hoofs died to the ear. Then she drew a deep breath, and, turning slowly, she allowed her eyes to take stock of the place in which she so strangely found herself.

It was a tiny building of rough-hewn stones, with an altar and crucifix, also of stone, erected at the end remote from the door. Along either wall ran a stone bench, on one or other of which the good fathers must have spent many a summer day watching the ford; for at a certain point the stone was polished and worn by friction. The litter and the wounded man filled half the open space, leaving visible only a floor of trodden earth foul with the droppings of birds and sheep, and betraying in other respects the results of neglect. Here and there on some stone larger than its fellows, and particularly on the lintel, a prentice hand had carved symbols; but, this notwithstanding, the whole wore by the light of the smoky lamp an aspect far from sacred.

Yet the prospect of spending several hours in so

poor a place did not appear to depress the Abbess. Her inspection finished, she nodded an answer to her thoughts, and sitting down on the bench beside the litter, rested her elbow on her knee and her chin on her hand, and fixing her large dark eyes on the wounded man, gave herself up, as completely as if she had been in her own chamber, to her thoughts.

Her woman, whose complaining, half fractious, half fearful, had sunk to an occasional sob, presently looked at her, and fascinated by that gloomy absorption— which might have dealt with the mysteries of the faith, but turned in fact on the faithlessness of man— she could not look away. And moments passed; the first pale glimmer of dawn appeared, and still the two women faced one another across the insensible man whose heavy breathing, broken from time to time by some obstruction, was the one sound that vied with the low murmur of the stream.

Suddenly the Abbess lifted her head. Mingled with the water's chatter was a harsher sound—a sound of rattling stones, of jingling steel and, a second later, of men's voices. She rose slowly to her feet, and as the other woman, alarmed by the expression of her features, would have screamed, she silenced her by a fierce gesture. Then she stood, her hand resting against the wall beside her, and listened.

She had no doubt that it was *he.* Her parted lips her eyes, half fierce, half tender, told as much. It was he, and she had but to open the door, she had but to show herself in the lighted doorway, and he would come to her! As the voices of the riders grew, and the rattle of hoofs among the pebbles ceased, she pictured him abreast of the hermitage; she fancied, but it must have been fancy, that she could distinguish his voice. Or no, he would not be speaking. He would be riding, silent, alone, his hand on his hip, the grey light of morning falling on his stern face. And at that, at that picture of him, his deeds and his career, his greatness who had made himself, his firmness whom no obstacle stayed, rose before her embodied in the solitary figure riding foremost through the dawn. Her breast rose and fell tumultuously. The hand that rested on the wall shook. She had only to open the door, she had only to cry his name aloud, only to show herself, and he would be at her side! And she would be no longer against him but with him, no longer would be ranked with his foes—who were so many—but for him against the world!

The temptation was so strong that her form seemed to droop and sway as if a physical charm drew her in the direction of the man she loved, the man to whom, in spite of his faults, or by reason of them, she clung in the face of defection. But powerful as was the spell laid upon her, pride—pride and her will proved stronger. She stiffened herself; for an instant she did not seem to breathe. Nor was it until the last faint clink of iron died away that she turned feverish eyes in search of some crevice, some loophole, some fissure, through which she might yet see him; yet see, if it were but the waving of his plume.

She found none. The only windows, two tiny arrow-slits that had never known glass, were in the wall remote from the track. On that she set her teeth to control the moan of disappointment that rose from her heart; and slowly she sank into her old seat.

But not into her old reverie. The eyes which she bent

on the sick man were no longer dreamy. On the contrary, they were fixed in a gaze of eager scrutiny that sought to drag from the Duke's pallid features the secret of his weakness and waywardness, of his strange nature and bizarre fame. And unconsciously as she gazed, she bent nearer and nearer to him; her look grew sharper and more imperious. All hung on him now— all! Her mind was made up. Fortune had not cast him so timely in her path, fate had not afforded her the opportunity of which she had dreamed, without intending her to profit by it, without proposing to crown the scheme with success. The spell of her lover's presence, the spell that had obsessed her so short a time before that the interval could be reckoned by seconds, was broken! Never should it be hers to play that creeping part, to regain him that way, to return to him tamely, empty-handed, a suppliant for his love! No, not while it might be hers to return a conqueror, an equal, with a greater than the Captain of Vlaye in her toils!

She rose to her feet, and tasting triumph in advance, she smiled. With a firm hand, disregarding her woman's remonstrance, she extinguished the lamp. The pale light of early morning stole in through the narrow slits, and then for a brief instant the Abbess held her breath; for the light falling on the Duke's face so sharpened his thin temples and nervous features, showed him so livid and wan and death-like, that she thought him gone. He was not gone, but she acted upon the hint. If he died, where were her schemes and the clever combinations she had been forming? Quickly she drew from the litter a flagon of broth that had been mixed with a cunning cordial; and first moistening his lips with the liquor, by-and-by she contrived to make him swallow some. In the act he opened his eyes, and they were clear and sensible; but it was only to close them again with a sigh, half of satisfaction, half of weakness. Nevertheless, from this time his state was rather one of sleep, the sleep craved by exhausted nature, than of insensibility or fever, and with every hour the forces of his youth and constitution wrought at the task of restoration.

Odette, brooding over him, watched with satisfaction the return of a more healthy colour to his cheeks. Time passed, and presently, while the light was still cold and young, there came an interruption. A murmur of voices, and the jingle of spur and bit, warned her that M. de Vlaye, baffled in his attempt to cut off the fugitives before they found refuge, was returning through the valley. This time, how different were her sensations. She started to her feet and listened, and her face grew hard, but under pressure of suspense, not of desire. Suspense—for if they turned aside, if they entered the deserted chapel and discovered her, her plan—and her very soul was now set on its success—perished still-born.

It was a trying moment, but it passed. Probably Vlaye knew the chapel of old, and knew that the good father had fled from it. At any rate he passed by it, and rode on his way. She heard the trampling of the horses break the singing of the ford; and then she heard only the murmur of the water and the morning hymn of a lark that, startled by the passage of the riders, soared above the glen, and with the sunshine on its throbbing breast, hailed the warm rising of another day.

Whether the lark's song appealed to the softer strain in her, or she began to hate the sordid interior with its grey half-light, the moment she was sure that the riders had gone on their way she opened the door and went out. The sun was peeping into the valley and all nature was astir. The laughing waters of the ford, the steep bluff, darksome by night, now clad in waving tree-tops, the floor of meadow emerald-green, all reflected the brightness of a sky in which not one but half a dozen songsters trilled forth the joy of life. After the gloom, the vigil, the danger of the night, the scene appealed to her strongly; and for a brief time, while she stood gazing on the vale unmarred by human works or human presence, she felt a compunction; such a feeling as in a similar scene invades the breast of the veteran hunter, and whispers to him that to carry death into the haunts of nature is but a sorry task.

A feeling as quickly suppressed in the one case as in the other. A few minutes later the Abbess appeared in the doorway, and beckoned to the woman to join her outside.

"Give me your hood and veil," she said in a tone that forestalled demur. "And I need your outer robe! Don't stare, woman!" she continued fiercely. "Is there any one to see you? Can the hills hurt you? Obey. It is my pleasure to wear the dress of the order, and I have it not with me!"

"But, madam——"

"Obey, woman, and take my cloak!" the Abbess retorted. "Wrap yourself in that!" And when the change was made, and she had assumed over her dress the loose black and white robe of the order, "Now wait for me here," she said. "And if he call, as is possible, do not go to him, but fetch me!"

She departed towards the pool below the ford, and, disappearing behind a clump of low willows, made, using the still water for a mirror, some further changes in her toilet.

Not fruitlessly, for when she returned to the door of the chapel, the woman who awaited her stared, thinking that she had never seen her mistress show fairer in her silks than in this black and white, which she so seldom favoured. And soon there was another who thought—if not that thought, a similar one. The Duke, opening on the glory of sunshine and summer warmth, the eyes that had so nearly closed for good, saw at the foot of his litter a wondrous figure kneeling before the altar.

The face of the figure was turned from him, and for a time, between sleeping and waking, he considered her idly, supposing her now an angel interceding for him in the other life on which he had entered, now a nun praying beside his bier; for he took it for certain he was dead. By-and-by he passed over to the theory of the angel, for the figure moved, and the sunlight passing in through a tiny window-slit formed a nimbus about her head. And then again, moving afresh, as in an ecstacy of devotion, she lifted her eyes to the crucifix, and the hood falling back with the movement revealed a profile of a beauty and purity almost unearthly.

The Duke sighed. He had sighed before, but apparently, for the sigh had not changed her rapt expression, she had not heard. Now she did hear. She rose, and with a deep genuflection turned from the altar, and glided with downcast eyes to his side. Eyes softened to the meekness of a dove's looked into his, and found that he was awake. Then, angel or saint, or whatever she was, she made a sign to him not to speak; and producing, by magic as it seemed, ambrosial food, she fed him, and with a finger on his lip bade him in gentle accents, "Sleep!"

Sleep? To think he could sleep when an angel—and while he laughed in ridicule of the notion he slept, that heavenly face framed in its nun's hood, that drooping form with the hands crossed upon the breast moving before him into the land of visions. He was back again in those earliest days of his cloistered existence, when to live in an atmosphere, pure and apart, innocent of the passions and desires of the world, had been his dream. He had learned—only too soon—that that atmosphere and that innocence were not to be maintained, though the walls of a monastery be ten feet through. For the nature which the thought of such a life had charmed was of all natures the one most open to worldly fascinations. He had fallen; and he had presently replaced the vision of being good by the enthusiasm of doing good. He had lifted his voice, and the preaching of Père Ange had moved half Paris to a twenty-four hours' repentance. His own had lasted a little longer.

Now, weak and unnerved, he reverted at sight of this beautiful nun's face to his old visions of a saintly life; and in innocent adoration he dreamt of naught but her countenance. When he awoke again and found her still at her devotions, though the sun was high, still at his service when she found him waking, still moving dove-like and silent about her ministrations—he watched her everywhere. Several times he wished to speak, but she laid a finger on her lips, and covering her hands with her sleeves, sat on the bench beside him, reading her book of hours. And so during the hazy period of his return to consciousness he saw her. Awake or drowsing, stung to life by the smart of his hurt or lulled to sleep by the music of the stream, he had her face always before him.

At length there came a time, a little before high noon, when he awoke with a clearer eye and a mind capable of feeling surprise at his position. He saw her sitting beside him, but he saw also the rough grey walls, the altar, the crucifix; and to wonder succeeded curiosity. What had happened, and how came he there? His eyes sought her face and remained riveted to it.

"Where am I?" he whispered.

She marked that his eyes were clear and his strength greater, and, "You are in the chapel in the upper valley of the Dronne," she answered.

"But I——" He stopped and closed his eyes, brought up by some confusion in his thoughts. At last, "I fancied I fought with some one," he whispered. "It was in a courtyard—at night? And there were lights? It was one of Vlaye's men, and the place was——" He broke off in the painful effort to remember. His lips moved without sound.

"Villeneuve," she said.

"Villeneuve," he whispered gratefully. "But this is not Villeneuve?"

"We are two leagues from Villeneuve."

"How come I here?"

She told him, preserving the gentle placidity which, not without thought, she had adopted for her *rôle*. The repulse of Vlaye's men and the Lieutenant's decision to quit the château, that and the night retreat up to the arrival of the party at the ford—all were told. Then she broke off.

"But des Ageaux?" he murmured. "Where is he?"

And again, that he might look round him, he tried to rise. "Where are they all?" he continued in wonder. "They have not left me?" with a querulous note in his voice.

"They are not here," she answered. And gently she induced him to lie back again. "Be still, I pray," she said. "Be still. You do yourself no good by moving."

He sighed. "Where are they?" he persisted.

"We were hard pressed at the ford," she answered with feigned reluctance. "And your litter delayed them. It was necessary to leave you or all had been lost."

He lay in silence awhile with closed eyes, considering what she had told him. At last, "And you stayed?" he murmured in so low a voice that the words were barely audible. "You stayed!"

"It was necessary," she answered.

"And you have been beside me all night?"

She bowed her head.

His eyes filled with tears, and his lips trembled, for he was very weak. He groped for her hand, and would have carried it to his lips, but as men kiss relics or the hands of saints—if she had not withheld it from him. Settling the thin coverings more comfortably round him, she gave him to drink again, softly chiding him and bidding him be silent—be silent and sleep.

But, "You have been beside me all night!" he repeated. "All night, alone here, and a woman! A woman!"

She did not tell him that she was not alone; that her woman was even then sitting outside, under strict orders not to show herself. For now she was assured that she was in the right path. She had had opportunities of studying his countenance while he slept, and she had traced in it those qualities of enthusiasm and weakness, of the libertine and the ascetic, which his career so remarkably displayed. The beauty which in ordinary circumstances his jaded eye, versed in woman's wiles, might neglect, would appeal with irresistible force in a garb of saintliness. Nay, more; as he recovered his strength and returned to his common feelings, it would prove, she felt sure, more provocative than the most worldly lures. Her resolve to carry the matter through was now fixed and immutable: and with her eye on the goal, she neglected no precaution that occurred to her mind.

CHAPTER XII.

THE PEASANTS' CAMP.

SOMETHING after high noon des Ageaux appeared and, whatever the Abbess's feelings, he was overjoyed to find the three undisturbed. He despatched a flying party down the valley that he might have notice if the enemy approached, and then he bent himself to remove the Duke in safety to his camp. In this the Abbess had her own line to take, and took it with decision. She represented the patient as worse than he was, described the fever as still lingering upon him, and using the authority which her devotion of the night gave her, she insisted that the Duke should see no one. A kind of shelter from the sun was woven of boughs, and placed over the litter. He was then lifted and borne out with care, the Abbess walking on one side, and her woman on the other. In the open air des Ageaux would have approached and spoken to him, for between gratitude and remorse the Lieutenant was much touched. But the authority of the sick-nurse was great then as it is now. The Abbess repelled him firmly, and, refusing the horse which had been brought for her, she persisted in walking the whole distance to the camp—a full league—by the side of the litter. In this way she fenced others off, and the Duke had her

211

always before him. Always the opening at the side of the litter framed her face.

She gave her mind so completely to him that she took no note of their route, save that they kept the valley, which preserving its flat bottom now ran between hills of a wilder aspect. It was only when the troopers, at a word from the Lieutenant, closed in about the litter, that she observed—though it had been some time in sight—the object which caused the movement. This was a small hill-town, girt by a ruinous wall, and buckled with crazy towers, which topped an acclivity on the right of the valley, and commanded the road. The suspicion with which her escort regarded the place did not surprise her when she remarked the filthy forms and wild and savage faces which swarmed upon the wall. There were women and children as well as men in the place, and all, ragged and half naked, mopped and mowed at the passers, or, leaping to their feet, defied them with unspeakable words and gestures.

The Abbess looked at them with daunted eyes. There was something inhuman in their squalor and wildness. "Who are they?" she asked.

"Crocans," the nearest rider answered.

"But we are not going to them?" she returned in astonishment. She had heard that they were bound for the peasants' camp, and her lip had curled at the information. But if these were Crocans—horror!

The man spat on the ground. "That is one band, and ours is another," he replied. "All canaille, but—not all like that, or we had some strange bed-fellows indeed!"

He would have said more, but he caught the Lieutenant's eye, and was silent and five minutes later the

Abbess saw a strange sight. The riders before her wheeled to the left, and, bending low in their saddles, vanished bodily in the rock that walled the road on that side.

A moment later she probed the mystery. In the rock wall which fenced the track on the left, as the river fenced it on the right, was an arched opening, resembling the mouth of a cave—of one of those caves so common in the Limousin. Within was no cave, however, but a spacious circus of smooth green turf open to the heaven, though walled on every side by grassy slopes which ran steeply to a height of a hundred feet. There was no entrance to the basin, but neither its defensible strength, nor the wisdom of the Crocans in choosing it, was apparent until the green rampart cast about it by nature was examined and found to be so scarped on the outer side as to form here a sheer precipice, there a descent trying to the most active foot.

A spring near the inner margin of this natural amphitheatre fed a rivulet which, after passing across it, and dividing it into two unequal parts, escaped to the river through the rocky gateway.

The smaller portion of the sward thus divided, a portion raised very slightly above the rest, had something of the aspect of a stage on a great scale. About its middle a flat-topped rock rising to a man's height from the ground had the air of an altar, and this was shaded by the only tree in the enclosure, a single plane-tree of vast size, which darkened with its ancient smooth-barked limbs a half-acre of ground. Probably this rock and this tree had witnessed the meetings of some primitive people, had borne part in their human sacrifices, and echoed the cries with which they acclaimed the moment of the summer solstice.

To-day this basin, long abandoned to the solitude of the hills, presented once more a scene of turmoil, such as for strangeness might rival the gatherings of that remote age. Nor, save for a circumstance presently to be named, could even the Abbess's sullen curiosity have withheld a meed of admiration as the panorama unfolded itself before her.

Round the edge of the larger half of the amphitheatre ran a long line—in parts double and treble, of booths open at the front, and formed, some of branches of trees, some of plaited rushes or osier. Under these, swarms of men, women, and children lounged in every posture, while others strolled about the ground before the sheds, which, crowded with sheep, oxen and horses, wore the aspect of a rustic fair. The turf that had been so fair a fortnight before was trodden bare in places, and in others poached and stained by the crowds that moved on it. Only the immediate bank of the rivulet had been kept clear.

The smaller portion of the sward had been given up to des Ageaux and his band of troopers and refugees. A dozen horses tethered in an orderly row at the rear of the plane-tree, with a pile of gear at the head of each, spoke of military order, as did the three or four booths which had been erected for the accommodation of the Vicomte's party. But as in such a place and under such circumstances it was impossible to enforce strict discipline, the curious among the peasants, and not men only, but women and children, roved in small parties on this side also, staring and questioning; some with furtive eyes as expecting a trap and treachery,

others watching in clownish amazement the evolutions
of a picked band of three score peasants whom the Bat
was beginning to instruct in the use of their weapons
and in the simplest movements of the field. Here and
there on the steep slopes about the saucer were groups
of peasants; and on the top of the ridge, which was forbidden to the crowd, were five sentinels, stationed beside as many cairns of stones piled for the purpose at
fixed distances from one another. These were of the
Lieutenant's institution, for though the safety of the
camp hung wholly on the command of its natural bat-
tlement, which captured would convert the basin into a
death-trap, the Crocans had kept no regular guard on
it. He on his arrival had entrusted its oversight to
the two young Villeneuves, and one or the other was
ever patrolling the length of the vallum, or from the
highest point searching the chaos of uninhabited hills
and glens that stretched on every side.

This hasty sketch of the scene leaves to be fancied
those worst traits of the camp, of its wildness and
savagery, that could not fail to disquiet the mind even
of a bold woman. Many of the peasants were half
naked, others were clad in cow-skins, in motley armour,
in sordid, blood-stained finery. All went unshaven,
and many had long, filthy elf-locks hanging about their
faces, and ragged beards reaching to their girdles.
Some had squalid bandages on head or limb, and all
were armed grotesquely with bill-hooks or scythes, or
with stakes pointed and hardened in the fire, or with
knotty clubs. M. de Vlaye and his kind would have
seen in them only a horde to be exterminated without
pity or remorse. Nor could their looks have failed to
startle the Abbess, high as was her natural courage—

if a thing had not at the very entrance engaged her attention.

For there, under the archway, a group of six men sat on their hams, their backs against the rock. And these were so foul in garb, and repulsive in aspect, that the common peasants of the camp seemed by comparison civilised. The Abbess shuddered at the mere look of them, and would have averted her eyes if they had not, as des Ageaux entered, risen and barred the way. The foremost, a tall, meagre figure with a long white beard, and the gleam of madness in his eyes, seized the Lieutenant's bridle and raising his other hand seemed to forbid his entrance. "Give us," he cried in a strange patois, "our man! Our man!"

The Abbess expected des Ageaux to strike him from his path, or bid his men ride him down. But the Lieutenant considered with patience the strange figure clad much as John the Baptist is protrayed in pictures, and when he answered he spoke calmly. "You are from the town on the hill?" he said.

"Ay, and we claim our man!"

"The man, you mean, whom we took from your hands last night?"

"Ay, that man!"

"For what?"

"That we may burn him," the savage answered, his face lit up by a gleam of frightful cruelty. "That we may do to him as he has done to us and our little ones. That we may burn him as he and his have burned us, from father to son, father to son, by the light of our own thatch. They have smoked us in our holes," he continued with ferocity, "as they smoke foxes; and we will smoke him. He has done to us that! And that!" He turned, and at a sign two of his five fellows stepped forward and held aloft the maimed and ghastly stumps of their arms. "And that! And that!" Again two stepped forward and pointed to their eyeless sockets. "And what he has done to us we will do to him!"

The Abbess turned sick at the sight. But des Ageaux answered with quietness. "Yet what has he done to you, old man," he asked, "that you stand foremost?"

"He has blinded me there!" the madman answered, and with a strangely dramatic gesture pointed to his brow. "I am dark at times, and boys mock me! But to-day I am whole and well!"

"I will not give him up to you!" the Lieutenant replied with calm decision. "But if he has done the things of which you tell me, I will judge him myself and punish him. Nay"—staying them sternly as they began to cry out upon him, "listen to me now! I have listened to you. For all who come in to me, and cease from pillage, and burning, and murder, I give my warrant that the past shall be overlooked. They shall be free to go back to their villages, or if they dare not go back they shall be settled elsewhere, with pardon for life and limb. But for those who do not come in, the burden of all will fall upon them! The law will pass upon them without mercy, and their gibbets will be on every road!"

"Not so!" the other cried, raising himself to his full height and flinging his lean arms to heaven. "Not so, lord, for the time is full! Hear me, too, man of blood. We know you. You speak softly because the time is full, and you would fain cast in your lot with us and escape. But you are of those who ride in blood, and

who trust in the strength of your armour, and who eat
of the fat and drink of the strong, while the poor man
perishes under the feet of your horses, while the earth
groans under the load of your wickedness, and God
is mocked. But the time is full, and there comes an
end of your gyves and your gibbets, your wheels and
your molten lead! The fire is kindled that shall burn
you. Is there one of you for ten of us? Can your
horses bear you through the sea when the fire fills all
the land? Nay, three months have we burned all
ways, and no man has been able to withstand our fire!
For it grows! It grows!"

The fierce murmurings of the madman's fellows
almost drowned des Ageaux' voice when he went to
answer. "Your blood be on your own heads!" he
said solemnly. "I have spoken you fairly, I have
given you the choice of good and of evil."

"Nought but evil," the other cried, "can proceed
out of your mouth! Now give us our man!"

"Never!"

"Then will we burn you for him," the madman
shrieked, in sudden frenzy, "when you fall into our
hands. You and these—women with breasts of flint
and hearts of the rock-core, who bathe in the blood of
our infants, and make a holiday of our torments! Beware, for when next we meet, you die!"

"Be it so!" des Ageaux replied, sternly restraining
his men, who would have fallen on the hideous group.
"But begone!"

They turned away, mopping and mowing—one was a
leper—and lifting hands of imprecation. And the Abbess, while the litter was being lifted, was left for a
moment with des Ageaux. She hated him, but she did

not understand him; and it was the desire to understand him that led her to speak.

"Why did you not seize the wretches," she asked, "and punish them?"

"Their turn will come," he replied coldly. "I would have saved them if I could."

"Saved them?" she exclaimed. "Why?"

"Who knows what they have suffered to bring them to this?"

She laughed in scorn of his weakness—who fancied himself a match for the Captain of Vlaye! His cold words, his even manner, had somewhat deceived her. But now she saw that he was a fool, a fool. She saw that if she detached Joyeuse there was nothing in this man M. de Vlaye need fear.

She left him then. She had had no sleep the previous night, and loth as she was to lose sight of the Duke or to give another the chance of supplanting her, she knew that she must rest. So weary was she after she had eaten that the rough couch in the hut set apart for her —her women after the mode of the day slept across the door or where they could—might have been a chamber in the heart of some guarded palace instead of a nook sheltered from curious eyes only by a wall of boughs. She had that healthiness which makes nerves and even conscience superfluous, and could not anywhere have slept better or been less aware of the wild life about her. The slow tramp of armed men, the voices of the watch upon the earth-wall, that to waking ears told of danger and suspicion—these were no more to her in her fatigue than the silent march of the summer stars across the sky.

When she awoke on the following morning, refreshed and full of energy, the sun was an hour high, and the peasants' camp was astir. In one place the Bat was drilling his three score men as if he had never ceased; in another food was being apportioned, and forage assigned. Neither des Ageaux nor her brothers were visible, but hard by her door the Vicomte, attended by Bonne and Solomon, sat with a hand on either knee, and gazed piteously on the abnormal scene.

The uppermost feeling in the old man's mind was a querulous wonder; first that he had allowed himself to be dragged from his house, secondly that, even since Coutras, things were suffered to come to this pass. How things had come to this, why his life and home had been broken up, why he had had no voice in the matter, and why his sons, even crooked-back Roger, went, and came, and ordered, without so much as a *by your leave* or an *if you please*—these were points that by turns puzzled and enraged him, and in the consideration of which he found no comfort so great as that which Solomon assiduously administered.

"Ah!" the old servant remarked more than once, as he surveyed with a jaundiced eye the crowded camp beyond the rivulet, "they are full of themselves! But I mind the day—it was when you entertained the Governors, my lord—when they'd have looked a few beside the servants we had to supper in the courtyard! A few they'd look. I'd sixty-two men, all men of their hands, and not naked gipsies like these, to my own table!"

Which was true; but Solomon forgot to add that it was the only table.

"Ay!" the Vicomte said, pleased, though he knew that Solomon was lying. "Times are changed."

"Since Coutras—devil take them!" Solomon rejoined, wagging his beard. "There were men then. 'Twas a word and a blow, and if we didn't run fast enough it was to the bilboes with us, and we smarted. Your lordship remembers. But now, Heaven help us," he continued with growing despondency as his eye alighted on des Ageaux, who had just appeared in the distance, "the men might be women! Might be women, and mealy-mouthed at that!"

The Vicomte laughed an elderly cackling laugh. "You didn't think, man, that the Villeneuves would come to this?" he said.

"Never! And would no wise ha' believed it!"

"Who were once masters of all from Barbesieux to Vlaye!"

"And many a mile further!" Solomon cried, leaping on the proffered hobby. "There were the twenty manors of Passirac"—he began to count on his hands. "And the farms of Perneuil, more than I have fingers and toes. And the twenty manors of Corde, and the great mill there—the five wind-mills of Passirac I don't think worth mentioning, though they would make many a younger son a portion. Then the Abbey lands of Vlaye, and the great mill there that took in toll as much as would keep a vicomte of these times, saving your lordship's presence. And then at Brenan——"

Bonne, listening idly, heard so much. Then the Abbess, who, unnoticed, had joined the group, touched her elbow, and muttered in her ear: "Do you see?"

"What?" Bonne asked innocently.

The Abbess raised her hand. "Why he has dragged us all here," she said.

Bonne followed the direction of her sister's hand, and slowly the colour mounted to her cheeks. But, "Why?" she asked, "I don't understand."

"You don't understand," Odette answered, "don't you? It is plain enough—for the blind." And she pointed again to the Lientenant, who was standing at some distance from the group in close talk with the Countess. "The Lieutenant of Périgord is a great man while the King pleases, and when the King no longer pleases is an adventurer like another! A broken officer living at ordinaries," with a sneer, "at other men's charges. Such another as the creature they call the Bat! No better and no worse! But the Lieutenant of Périgord with the lands and lordships of Roche-chouart were another and a different person. And none sees that more clearly than the Lieutenant of Périgord. He has made his opportunity, and he is not going to waste it. He has brought her here, and not for nothing."

Bonne had an easy retort. "At least he is not the first to see his interest there!" lay ready to her tongue. But she did not utter it. She was silent. Her colour fluttered, as the tender, weakling hope that she had been harbouring, for a few hours, died within her. Of course she should have known it! The prize that had attracted the Captain of Vlaye, the charm that had ousted her handsome sister from his heart—was it likely that M. des Ageaux would be proof against these —proof against them when she herself had no prior claim nor such counter-claims as beauty and brilliance? When she was but plain, homely, and country-bred, as her father often told her? She had been foolish; foolish in harbouring the unmaidenly hope, the forward thought; foolish now in feeling so sharp and numbing a pain.

But perhaps most foolish in her inability to await his

coming. For he and the little Countess were approaching the group, at a slow pace; the girl talking with an animation that showed she had quite forgotten her shyness. Bonne marked the manner, the smile, the confiding upward look, the lifted hand; and she muttered something, and escaped before the two came within earshot.

She wanted to be alone, quite alone, to have this out with herself; and she made for a tiny cup in the hillside, hidden from the camp by the thick branches of the plane-tree. She had discovered it the day before, but when she gained it now, there in the hollow sat Roger, looking down on the scene below.

He nodded as if he were not in the best of tempers; which was strange, for he had been in high spirits an hour before. She sat down beside him, having no choice, but some minutes elapsed before he opened his mouth. Then, "Lord," he exclaimed, with something between a groan and a laugh, "what a fool a man can be!"

She did not answer; perhaps for the word "man" she was substituting the word "woman." He moved irritably in his seat. "Hang it!" he exclaimed. "Say something, Bonne! Of course it seems funny to you that because she thanked me prettily the day I tried to cover her retreat to the house and—and because she talked to me the night before last as we rode—as if she liked it, I mean—I should forget who she is!"

"Who she is," Bonne repeated quietly, thinking of some one else who had forgotten.

"And who I am!" he answered. "As if the Vicomte had not ground it into me enough! If I were Charles, she would still be—who she is, and meat for my master.

But as I am what I am," he laughed ruefully, "would you have thought I could be such a fool, Bonne?"

"Poor Roger," she said gently.

"She clung to me that day, when I ran with her. But, dash it"—rubbing his head—"I must not think of it. I suppose she would have clung to old Solomon just the same!"

"I am afraid so!" Bonne said, smiling faintly. It was certain that she had not clung to any one. Yet there were analogies.

"I suppose you—you saw them just now?"

"Yes, I saw them."

"She never talked to me like that! Why should she—a thing like me." Poor Roger! "I knew the moment I cast eyes on them. You did, too, I suppose?"

"Yes," she answered.

Perhaps Roger had hoped in his heart for a different reply, for he stared gloomily at the swarming huts visible above the tree. And finally, "There is Charles," he said, "walking the ridge—against the sky-line there! Why cannot I be like him, as happy as a king, with my head full of battles and sieges, and the Bat more to me than any woman in the world! Why cannot I? With such a pair of shoulders as I have—"

"Dear lad!"

"I should be in his shoes and he in mine! Lord, what a fool!" with gloomy unction. "What a fool! I must needs think of *her* when a peasant girl would not look at me. I must needs think of the Countess of Rochechouart! Oh, Lord, as if I had anything to give her! Or aught I could do for her!"

Bonne did not reply on the instant. But presently,

"There is something you can do for her," she ventured. "It is not much, but——"

"What?" he said. "I know nothing."

"You can help him."

"I?"

"The mouse helped the lion. You can help him and be at his side, and guard him in danger—for her sake. Just as," Bonne continued, her voice sinking a little, "if you were a girl, and—and felt for him as you feel for her, you could watch over her and protect her and keep her safe—for his sake. Though it would be harder for a woman, because women are jealous," Bonne added thoughtfully.

"And men too!" Roger rejoined from the depths of his small experience. "All the same I will do it. And I am glad it is he. He won't beat her, or shut her up and leave her in some lonely house as Court people do. I believe," he continued gloomily, "I'd as soon it was he as any one."

Bonne nodded. "That is agreed then," she said softly, though a moment before she had sighed.

"Agreed?" rather grumpily. "Well, if one person can agree, it is!" And then, thinking he had spoken thanklessly to the sister who had been his friend and consoler in many a dark hour when the shadow of his deformity had hidden the sun, he laid his hand on hers and pressed it. "Well, agreed it is!" he said more brightly. "They came from their outside world to our poor little life, and we must help them back again, I suppose. I would not wish them ill, if—if it would make me straight again."

"That is a big bribe," she said, smiling. "But neither would I—if it would make me as handsome as Odette!"

"No!"

They sat silent then. Far away on their left, where lay the entrance to the camp from the river gorge, men were piling stones under the archway, so as to leave but a narrow passage. Below them on the right the Bat was drilling his pikemen, and alternately launching his lank form this way and that in a fever of impatience. On the sky-line men were pacing to and fro, searching with keen eyes the misty distance of glen and hill; and ever and anon the squeal of a war-horse rang above the multitudinous sounds of the camp. On every side, wherever the eye rested, it discovered signs of strife and turmoil, harbingers of pain and death.

But though the two who looked down on the scene neither knew it nor thought of it, with them in their little hollow was a power mightier than any, the power that in its highest form does indeed make the world go round; the one power in the world that is above fortune, above death, above the creeds—or, shall we say, behind them. For with them was love in its highest form, the love that gives and does not ask, and being denied—loves. In their clear moments men know that this love is the only real thing in the world; and a thousand times more substantial, more existent, than the objects we grasp and see.

CHAPTER XIII.

HOSTAGES.

THERE is born of the enthusiasm of self-denial a happiness that while the fervour lasts seems all-sufficing. The skirmish that has routed the van of jealousy stands for the battle; nor does the victor foresee that with the fall of night the enemy will flock again to the attack, and by many an insidious onset strive to change the fortune of the day.

Still once to have felt the generous impulse, once to have trodden self underfoot and risen god-like above the baser thoughts, is something. And if Bonne and her brother were destined to find the victory less complete than they thought, if they were to know moments when the worst in them raised its head, they were but as the best of us. And again—a reflection somewhat more humorous—had these two been able to read the mind of the man of whom each was thinking, they had met with so curious an enlightenment that they had hardly been able to look at one another. To say that des Ageaux entertained no tender feeling for any one were to say more than the truth; for during the last few days a weakness had crept unwelcome and unbidden into his heart. But he kept it sternly in the background—he who had naught to do with such

things—and it did not tend in the direction of the
Countess. In point of fact the Lieutenant had other
and more serious food for thought; other and more
pressing anxieties than love. Forty-eight hours had
disclosed the weakness of the position in which he
had chosen to place himself. He foresaw, if not the
certainty, the probability of defeat. And defeat in
the situation he had taken up might be attended by
hideous · consequences.

These were not slow to cast their shadows. The two
on the hill had not sat long in silent companionship
before the sounds which rose from the camp began to
take a sterner note. Roger was the first to mark the
change. Rousing himself and shaking off his lugu-
brious mood, "What is that?" the lad asked. "Do
you hear, Bonne? It sounds like trouble somewhere."

"Trouble?" she repeated, still half in dreams.

"Yes, by Jove, but—listen! And what has become"
—he was on his feet by this time—"of the Bat's ragged
regiment? They have vanished."

"They must be behind the tree," Bonne answered.
And moved by the same impulse they walked a little
aside along the slope until they could see the section
of the camp immediately below them, which had been
hidden hitherto by the branches of the great plane-tree.

The little group which Bonne had left when her
feelings compelled her to flight remained in the same
place. But all who formed it, the Vicomte and his
eldest daughter as well as des Ageaux and the Countess,
were now on their feet. The Vicomte and the ladies
stood together in the background, while des Ageaux,
who had placed himself before them, confronted an
excited body of men, some hundred in number, and

composed in part at least of those whom the Bat had been lately drilling. Whether these had broken from his control and gathered their fellows as they moved, or the impulse had come from outside and they were but recruits, their presence rendered the movement more formidable. They were not indeed of so low and savage a type as the creatures who had met des Ageaux in the gate the previous day, but viewed in this serried mass, their lowering brutish faces and clenched hands called up a vivid sense of danger. They must have made some outcry as they approached, or Roger had not noticed their assemblage. But now they were fallen silent. A grim mass of scowling, hard-breathing men, their small suspicious eyes glaring through tangled locks irresistibly reminded the observer of that quarry the most dangerous of all the beasts of chase, the wild boar.

Bonne's colour faded as her eyes took in the meaning of the scene. She grew still paler as her brain pictured for the first time the things that might happen in this camp of clowns of whose real sentiments the intruders had so little knowledge, at whose possible treachery it was so easy to guess. Time has not wiped, time never will wipe from the French memory the fear of a Jacquerie. The horrors of that hideous revolt, of its rise and its suppression are stamped on the minds of the unborn. "What is it?" she repeated more than once, her heart fluttering. How very, very near he stood—on whom all depended—to the line of scowling men!

"A mutiny, I fear!" Roger answered hastily. "Come!" And, with face slightly flushed, he hurried, running and sliding down the slope.

She was not three paces behind him when he reached the foot. Here they lost sight of the scene, but quickly passed between two huts and reached the Vicomte's side. Des Ageaux was speaking.

"I cannot give you the man," he was saying, "but I can give you justice."

"Justice?" the spokesman of the peasants retorted bitterly—he wore the dress of a smith, and belonged to that craft. "Who ever heard but of one sort of justice for the poor man? Justice, Sir Governor, is the poor man's right to be hung! The poor man's right to be scourged! The poor man's right to be broken on the wheel! To see his hut burned and his wife borne off! That is the justice"—rudely—"the poor man gets—be it high or low, king's or lord's!"

"Ay, ay!" the stern chorus rose from a hundred throats behind him, "that is the poor man's justice!"

"It is to put an end to such things I am here!" des Ageaux replied, marking with a watchful eye the faces before him. He was far from easy, but he had handled men of their kind before, and thought that he knew them.

"There was never a beginning of such things, and there will never be an end!" the smith returned, the hopelessness of a thousand years of wrong in his words. "Never! But give us this man—he has done all these things, he and his master, and we will believe you."

"I cannot give him to you," des Ageaux answered. The same prisoner, one of Vlaye's followers, was in question whom the Old Crocans had yesterday required to be given up to them. "But I have told you and I tell you again," the Lieutenant continued, reading mischief in the men's faces, "that you shall have justice. If this man has wronged you and you can prove it——"

"If!" the peasant cried, and baring his right arm he raised his clenched fist to heaven.

But the Lieutenant went on as if the man had not spoken. "If you can prove these things upon him by witnesses here present——"

"You will give him to us?"

"No, I will not do that!"

"You will give him to us!" the smith repeated, refusing to hear the denial. And all along the line of scowling faces—the line that wavered ominously at moments of emotion as if it would break about the little group—ran a swift gleam of white teeth.

But des Ageaux did not blench. He raised his hand for silence, and his voice was steady as a rock as he made answer. "No," he said, "I will not give him to you. He belongs neither to me nor to you, but to God and the King, whose is justice."

"To God!" the other snarled, "whose is justice! Rather, whose servants hold the lamb that the devils may flay it! And for the King, Sir Governor, a fig for him! Our own hands are worth a dozen kings!"

"Stay!" The line was swaying; in the nick of time des Ageaux' voice, and perhaps something in his eye, stayed it. "Listen to me one moment," he continued. "To-morrow morning—for I have not time to-day—the man you accuse shall be tried. If he be guilty, before noon he shall die. If he be not guilty, he shall go!"

A murmur of protest.

But des Ageaux raised his head higher and spoke more sternly. "He shall go!" he repeated—and for the moment he mastered them. "If he be innocent he shall go! What more do you claim? To what beyond have you a right? And now," he continued, as he saw them pause angry but undecided, "for yourselves! I have told you, I tell you again that this is your last chance. That I and the offer I make you are your last hope! There is a man there"—with his forefinger he singled out a tall youth with a long, narrow face and light blue eyes—"who promises that when you are attacked he will wave his arm, and Vlaye and his riders will fall on their faces as fell the walls of Jericho! Do you believe him? Will you trust your wives and children to him? And another"—again he singled out a man, a beetle-browed dwarf, hideous of aspect, survivor of some ancient race—"who promises victory if you will sacrifice your captives on yonder stone! Do you believe him? And if you do not trust these, in what do you trust? Can naked men stand before mailed horses? Can you take castles with your bare hands? You have left your villages, you have slain your oxen, you have burned your tools, you have slain your lords' men, you have taken the field. Have peasants ever done these things—and not perished sooner or later on gibbets and in dungeons? And such will be your fate, and the fate of your women and your children, if you will go your way and will not listen!"

"What do you promise us?" The question in various forms broke from a dozen throats.

"First, justice on the chief of your oppressors."

"The Captain of Vlaye?"

"The same."

"Ay, ay!" Their harsh cries marked approval. Some with dark looks spat on their hands and worked their right arms to and fro.

"Next," des Ageaux continued, "that which never peasant who took the field had yet—pardon for the past. To those who fear not to go back, leave to return to their homes. To those who have broken their lords' laws a settlement elsewhere with their wives and children. To every man of his hands, when he leaves, ten deniers out of the spoils of Vlaye to carry him to his home."

Nine out of ten marked their approval by a shout; and des Ageaux heaved a sigh of relief, thinking all well. But the smith turned and exchanged some words with the men nearest him, chiding them and reminding them of something. Then he turned again.

"Fine words! But for all this what pledge, Sir Governor?" he asked with a sneer. "What warranty that when we have done our part we shall not to gibbet or gallows like our fellows?"

"The King's word!"

"Ay? And hostages? What hostages?"

"Hostages?" The Lieutenant's voice rang sharp with anger.

"Ay, hostages!" the man answered sturdily, informed by the murmurs of his fellows that he had got them back into the road from which des Ageaux' arguments had led them. "We must have hostages."

Clearly they had made up their minds to this, they had determined on it beforehand. For with one voice, "We must have hostages!" they thundered.

Des Ageaux paused before he answered—paused in dismay. It looked as if—already he feared it—he had put out his hand too far. As if he had trusted too implicitly to his management of men, and risked not himself only, but women; women of the class to which these human beasts set down their wrongs, women on whom the least accident or provocation might lead them to wreak their vengeance! If it were so! But he dared not follow up the thought, lest the coolness on which all depended should leave him. Instead, "We are all your hostages," he said.

"And what of those? And those?" the smith answered. With a cunning look he pointed to the two knots of troopers whom des Ageaux had brought with him. "And by-and-by there will be more. Madame" —he pointed to the little Countess who had shrunk to Bonne's side, and stood witn the elder girl's arm about her—"Madame has sent for fifty riders from her lands in the north—oh, we know! And the Duke who is ill, for another hundred and fifty from Bergerac! When they come"—with a leer—"where will be our hostages? No, it is now we must talk, Sir Governor, or not at all."

Des Ageaux, his cheek flushed, reflected amid an uneasy silence. He knew that two of his riders were away bearing letters, and that four more were patrolling the valley; that two with Charles de Villeneuve were isolated on the ridge, unable to help; in a word, that no more than twelve or thirteen were within call, who, separated from their horses, were no match for a mob of men outnumbering them by five or six to one, and whom the first blow would recruit from every quarter of the seething camp. He had miscalculated, and saw it. He had miscalculated, and the consequences he dare not weigh. The men in whose power he had placed himself—and so much more than himself—were not the dull clods he had deemed them, but alike ferocious and suspicious, ready on the first hint of treachery to exact a fearful vengeance. No man had ever kept faith with them; why should they believe that he would keep faith? He shut his teeth hard. "I will consider the matter," he said, "and let you know my answer to-morrow at noon." He spoke as ending the conference, and he made as if he would turn on his heel.

"Ay, when madame's fifty spears are come?" the smith cried. "That will not do! If you mean us well give us hostages. If you mean us ill," taking one step forward with an insolent gesture——

"Fool, I mean you no ill!" the Lieutenant answered sternly. "If I meant you ill, why should I be here?"

But "Hostages! Hostages!" the crowd answered, raising weapons and fists.

Their cries drowned his words. A score of hands threatened him. Without looking, he felt that the Bat and his troopers, a little clump apart, were preparing to intervene, and he knew that on his next movement all depended. The pale faces behind him he could not see, for he was aware that if his eye left his opponents, they would fall upon him. At any second a hurried gesture, or the least sign of fear might unloose the torrent, and well was it for all that in many a like scene his nerve had been tempered to hardness. He shrugged his shoulders.

"Well," he said, "you shall have your hostages."

"Ay, ay!" A sudden relaxation, a falling back into quietude of the seething mass approved the consent.

"You shall have my lieutenant," he continued, "and——"

"And I will be the other," cried Roger manfully. He stepped forward. "I am the son of M. le Vicomte there! I will be your hostage," he repeated.

But the smith, turning to his followers, grinned. "We'd be little the better for them," he said. "Eh? No, Sir Governor! We must have our choice!"

"Your choice, rogues?"

"Ay, we'll have the pick!" the crowd shouted. "The best of the basket!" Amid ferocious laughter.

Des Ageaux had suspected for some hours past that he had done a foolish, a fatally foolish thing in trusting these men, whom no man had ever trusted. He saw now that only two courses stood open to him. He might strike the smith down at his feet, and risk all on the effect which the act might have on his followers; or he might yield what they asked, allow them to choose their hostages, and trust to time and skill for the rest. His instincts were all for the bolder course, but he had women behind him, and their chance in a conflict so unequal must be desperate. With a quietness and firmness characteristic of the man he accepted his defeat.

"Very well," he said. "It matters nothing. Whom will you have?"

"We'll have you," the smith replied grinning, "and her!" With a grimy hand he pointed to the little Countess who with Bonne's arm about her and Fulbert at her elbow was staring fascinated at the line of savage faces.

"You cannot have a lady!" the Lieutenant answered with a chill at his heart.

"Ay, but it is she who has the riders who are coming!" the smith retorted shrewdly. "It is her we want and it is her we'll have! We'll do her no harm, and she may have her own hut on our side, and her woman with her, and a man if she pleases. And you may have a hut beside hers, if one," with a wink, "won't do for the two."

"But, man," des Ageaux cried, his brow dark, "how can I take Vlaye and his castle while I lie a hostage?"

"Oh, you shall go to and fro, to and fro, Sir Governor!" the smith answered lightly. "We'll not be too strict if you are there of nights. And we will know ourselves safe. And as we live by bread," he continued stoutly, "we'll do her no harm if faith be kept with us!"

Des Ageaux endeavoured to hide his emotion, but the sweat stood on his brow. Defeat is bitter to all. To the man who has long been successful most bitter.

Suddenly, "I will go!" said the Countess bravely. And she stepped forward by the Lieutenant's side, a little figure, shrinking, yet resolute. "I will go," she repeated, trembling with excitement, yet facing the men.

"No!" Roger cried—and then was silent. It was not for him to speak. What could he do?

"We will all go!" Bonne said.

"Nay, but that will not do," the smith replied, with a sly grimace. "For then they"—he pointed to the little knot of troopers who waited with sullen faces a short arrow-shot away—"would be coming as well. The lady may bring a woman if she pleases, and her man there, as I said." He nodded towards Fulbert. "But no more, or we are no gainers!"

To the Lieutenant that moment was one of the bitterest of his life. He, the King's Governor, who had acted as master, who had forced the Vicomte and his party to come into his plans, whether they would or no, stood out-generalled by a mob of peasants, whom he had thought to use as tools! And not only that, but the young Countess, whose safety he had made the pretext for the abandonment of the chateau, must surrender herself to a risk more serious—ay, far

more serious, than that from which he had made this
ado to save her!

Humiliation could scarcely go farther. It was to
his credit, it was perhaps some proof of his capacity for
government that, seeing the thing inevitable, he refrained from useless words or protest, and sternly
agreed. He and the Countess would remove to the
farther side of the camp in the course of the day.

"With a man and a maid only?" the smith persisted,
knitting his brows. Having got what he had asked
he doubted.

"The Countess of Rochechouart will be so attended,"
the Lieutenant answered sternly.

"And you, Sir Governor?"

"I am a soldier," he retorted, so curtly that they
were abashed. With some muttering they began to
melt away. Awhile they stood in groups, discussing
the matter. Then gradually they retired across the
rivulet to their quarters.

The Lieutenant had been almost happy had that
ended it. But he had to face those whom he had led
into this trap, those whom he had forced to trust him,
those whom he had carried from their home. He was
not long in learning their views.

"A soldier!" the Vicomte repeated, taking up his
last word in a voice shaking with passion. "You call
yourself a soldier and you bring us to this! To this!"
With loathing he described the outline of the camp
with his staff. "You a soldier, and cast women to
these devils! Pah! Since Coutras there may be such
soldiers! But in my time, no!"

He did not reply: and the Abbess took up the tale.
"Excellent!" she said, with bitterest irony. "We are

all now assured of your prudence and sagacity, sir!
The safety and freedom which we enjoy here, the ease
of mind which the Countess will doubtless enjoy to-
night——"

"Do not frighten her, mademoiselle!" he said, repressing himself. Then, as if an impulse moved him,
he turned slowly to Bonne. "Have you nothing to
add, mademoiselle?" he asked, in a peculiar tone.

"Nothing!" she answered bravely. And then—it
needed some courage to speak before her father and
sister, "Were I in the Countess's place I should not
fear. I am sure she will be safe with you."

"Safe!" Odette cried, her eyes flashing. In the
excitement of the moment the plans she had so recently
made were forgotten. "Ay, as safe as a lamb among
wolves! As safe as a nun among robbers! So safe
that I for one am for leaving this moment. Ay, for
leaving, and now!" she continued, stamping her foot
on the sward "What is it t us if this gentleman,
who calls himself the Governor of Périgord—and may
be such, I care not whether he is or not—has a quarrel
with M. de Vlaye and would fain use us in it as he
uses these brute beasts? What, I say, is it to us? Or
why do we take part? M. le Vicomte"—she turned to
her father—"if you are still master of Villeneuve, you
will order our horses and take us thither. We have
naught to fear, I say it again, we have naught to fear
at M. de Vlaye's hands; and if we fall into them
between this and Villeneuve, so much the better! But
if we stay here we have all to fear." In truth she was
honestly frightened. She thought the case desperate.

"Mademoiselle——"

"No, sir!" she retorted, turning from him. "I did

not speak to you; but to you, M. le Vicomte! Sir,
you hear me? Is it not your will that we order the
horses and go from here?"

"If we can go safely——"

"You cannot go safely!" des Ageaux said, with returning decision. "If you have nothing to fear from the
Captain of Vlaye, the Countess has. Nor is that all.
These men"—he pointed in the direction of the peasants,
who were buzzing about their huts like a swarm of bees
—"have forced my hand, but through fear and distrust,
not in malice. They mean us no harm if we mean them
none. But the Old Crocans, as they call themselves, in
the town on the hill—if you fall into their hands, M. le
Vicomte—and beyond the lines of this camp no one is
safe from their prowling bands—then indeed God help
you!"

"God help us whether or no!" the Vicomte answered
in senile anger. "I wash my hands of it all, of it all!
I am nothing here, and have been nothing! Let who
will do! The world is mad!"

"Certainly we were mad when we trusted you!" the
Abbess cried, addressing des Ageaux. "Never so mad!
But if I mistake not, here is another with good news!
Oh!" to the Bat, who, with a shamefaced air, was
hovering on the skirts of the group, as if he were not
sure of his reception, "speak, sir, without reserve! We
all know"—in a tone of mockery—"how fair and safely
we stand!"

Des Ageaux turned to his follower. "What is it?"
he asked.

"The prisoner is missing, my lord."

The Abbess laughed bitterly. The others looked at
the Bat with faces of dismay. "Missing? The man we

have promised to hold for them. How?" des Ageaux exclaimed sternly. This was a fresh blow and a serious one.

"When I saw, my lord, that we were like to be in trouble here, I drew off the two men who were guarding him. He was bound, and—we had too few as it was."

"But he cannot have passed the ramparts."

"Anyway we cannot find him," the Bat answered, looking ashamed and uncomfortable. "I've searched the huts, and——"

"Is it known?"

"No, my lord."

"Then set the guards as before over the hut in which you had him, and see that the matter does not leak out to-night."

"But if," the Bat objected, "they discover that he is gone while you are with them to-night, my lord, they are in an ugly mood, and——"

"They must not discover it!" des Ageaux answered firmly. "Go, see to it yourself. And let two men whom you can trust continue the search, but as if they had lost something of their own."

The Bat went on his errand; and the Abbess, with this fresh weapon in her quiver, prepared to resume the debate. But the Lieutenant would not have it. "Mademoiselle," he said, with a look which silenced her, "if you say more to alarm the Countess, whose courage" —he bowed in the direction of the pale frightened girl —"is an example to us all, she will not dare to go this evening. And if she does not go, the lives of all will be in danger. An end of this, if you please!"

And he turned on his heel, and left them.

CHAPTER XIV.

SAINT AND SINNER.

AN hour later the Lieutenant was with the Duke in his quarters, and had imparted to him what he knew of the position. The Duke listened, not much affected; nay, with something approaching indifference.

"It is a question of four days then?" he rejoined, as he painfully moved himself on his litter. They had made him as comfortable as they could, screening the head of his couch, which was towards the hut door, with a screen of wattle. Against one wall, if wall that could be called which was of like make with the screen, ran a low bench of green turves, and on this des Ageaux was seated.

"Of four days—and nights," the Lieutenant made answer, masking a slight shiver. He was not thinking of his own position, but of the young Countess; neither her fears nor the courage with which she controlled them were a secret from him. "To-day is Saturday. The Countess's men should be here by Monday, your men, M. de Joyeuse, by Wednesday. All will be well then; and I doubt not with such support we can handle the Captain of Vlaye. But until then we run a double risk."

"Of Vlaye, of course."

"And of our own people if anything occur to exasperate them."

Joyeuse laughed recklessly. "*Vogue la galère!*" he cried. "The plot grows thicker. I came for adventure, and I have it. Ah, man, if you had lived within the four walls of a convent!"

Des Ageaux shook his head. He knew the wanton courage of the man, who, sick and helpless, found joy in the peril that surrounded them. But he was very far from sharing the feeling. The dangers that threatened the party lay heavy on the man who was responsible for all. The tremors of the young girl who must share his risk that evening, the bitter reproaches of the Abbess and her father, even the confidence that Bonne's eyes rather than her lips avowed, all tormented him; so that to see this man revelling in that which troubled him so sorely, insulted his reason.

"I fancy, my lord," he said, a faint note of resentment in his tone, "if you had had to face these rogues this morning you had been less confident this evening."

"Were they so spiteful?" The Duke raised himself on his elbow. "Well, I say again, you made a mistake. You should have run the spokesman through the throat! Ca! Sa!" He made a pass through the air. "And trust me, the rest of the knaves——"

"Might have left none of us alive to tell the tale!" the Lieutenant retorted.

"I don't know that!"

"But I suspect it!" des Ageaux replied warmly. "And I do beg you, my lord, to be guided in this. I am more than grateful for the impulse which led you to come to my assistance. But honestly I had been more glad if you had brought a couple of hundred spears with you. As it is, the least imprudence may cost us more than our own lives! And it behoves us all to remember that!"

"The least imprudence!"

"Certainly."

The Duke laughed softly—at nothing that appeared. "So!" he said. "The least imprudence may destroy us, may it? The least imprudence!" And then, suddenly sobered, he fixed his eyes on the Lieutenant. "But what of letting your prisoner go, eh? What of that? Was not that an imprudence, most wise Solomon?"

"A very great one!" des Ageaux replied with a sigh.

"What shall you do when, to-morrow morning, they claim his trial?"

"What I can," the Lieutenant answered, frowning and sitting more erect. "See that the Countess returns early to this side; where the Bat must make the best dispositions he can for your safety. Meanwhile, I shall tell them and make them see reason if I can!"

"Lord!" the Duke said with genuine gusto, "I wish I were in your place!"

"I wish you were," des Ageaux replied. "And still more that I had the rogue by the leg again."

"Do you?"

"Do I?" the Lieutenant repeated in astonishment. "I do indeed. The odds are they will maintain that we released him on purpose, and dearly we may pay for it!"

For a moment the Duke, flat on his back, looked thoughtful. Then, "Umph!" he said, "you think so? But you were always a croaker, des Ageaux, and you are making the worst of it! Still—you would like to lay your hand on him, would you?"

"I would indeed!"

The Duke rose on his elbow. "Would you mind giving me—I am a little cold—that cloak?" he said. "No," as des Ageaux moved to do it, "not that one under your hand—the small one! Thank you. I——"

He could not finish. He was shaking with laughter—which he vainly tried to repress. Des Ageaux stared. And then, "What have I done to amuse you so much, my lord?" he asked coldly, as he rose.

"Much and little," the Duke answered, still shaking.

"Much or little," des Ageaux retorted, "you will do yourself no good by laughing so violently. If your wound, my lord, sets to bleeding again——"

"Pray for the soul of Henry, Duke of Joyeuse, Count of Bouchage!" the Duke replied lightly. Yet on the instant, and by a transition so abrupt as to sound incredible to men of these days, he composed his face, groped for his rosary, and began to say his offices. The suddenness of the change, the fervour of his manner, the earnestness of his voice astonished the Lieutenant, intimately as he knew this strange man. Awhile he waited, then he rose and made for the door.

But Joyeuse—not the Duke of three minutes before, but Frère Ange of the Capuchin convent—stopped him with a movement of his eyes. "And why not," said he, "to-day as well as to-morrow? No man need be afraid to die who prepares himself. The soldier above all, Lieutenant, for the true secret of courage is to repent. Ay, to repent," he continued in a voice, sweet and thrilling, and with a look in his eyes strangely gentle and compelling. "Friend, are you prepared? Have you

confessed lately? If not, kneel down! Kneel, man,
and let us say a dozen aves, and a couple of Paternos-
ters! It will be no time wasted," he continued anxiously. "No man has sinned more than I have. No
man, no man! Yet I face death like one in a thousand!
And why? Why, man? Because it is not I, but——"

But there are things too high for the level of such nar-
rations as this, and too grave for such treatment as is
here essayed. The character of this man was so abnormal, he played with so much enthusiasm his alter-
nate *rôles*, that without this passing glimpse of his rarer
side—that side which in the intervals of wild revelry
led him to dying beds and sick men's couches—but one-
half of him could be understood. Not that he was
quite alone in the possession of this trait. It was a
characteristic of the age to combine the most flagrant
sins with the strictest observances; and a few like M.
de Joyeuse added to both a real, if intermittent and
hysterical, repentance.

On this occasion it was not long before he showed
his other face. The Abbess, after waiting without
and fretting much—for she had returned to the purpose momentarily abandoned, and the length of the
interview alarmed her—won entrance at last. She
exchanged a cold greeting with the departing Lieutenant,
then took his place, book in hand, on the green bench.
For a while there was silence. She had so far played
her part with success. The Duke knew not whether
to call her saint or woman; and that he might remain
in that doubt she now left it to him to speak. At
the same time she left him at liberty to look: for
she knew that bending thus at her devotions she must
appear more striking to his jaded senses. And he, for a

time, was mute also, and thoughtful; so much he gave to the scene just ended.

It is possible that the silence was prolonged by the chance of considering her at leisure which she was careful to afford him. He was still weak, the better side of him was still uppermost; and handsome as she was, he saw her through a medium of his own, in a halo of meekness and goodness and purity. Thus viewed she fell in with his higher mood, she was a part of it, she prolonged it. A time would come, would most certainly come, when one of the wildest libertines of his day would see her otherwise, and in the woman forget the saint. But it had not yet come. And the Abbess, with her pure, cold profile, bent over her book, and, with her thoughts apparently in heaven, knew also that her time had not yet come.

Though her face betrayed nothing, she was in an angry mood. She had gained little by the altercation with des Ageaux; and though the simplicity which he had betrayed in his. dealings with the peasants excited her boundless contempt—he, to pit himself against M. de Vlaye!—the peril which it brought upon all heightened that contempt to anger. If the peril had been his only, or included the Countess only, if it had threatened those only whom she could so well spare, and towards whose undoing her brain was busily working, she could have borne it bravely and gaily.

But the case was far other; and something she regretted that she had not bowed to her first impulse in the chapel and called to M. de Vlaye, and gone to him—ay, gone to him empty-handed as she was, without the triumph of which she had dreamed. For the jeopardy in which she and all her family now stood put her in a dilemma. If the Lieutenant kept faith with the peasants and all went well, it would go ill with her lover. If, on the contrary, M. des Ageaux failed to restrain the peasants, it might go ill with herself.

It came always to this: she must win over the Duke. Of the allies against Vlaye, he, with his hundred and fifty horse, due to arrive on the Wednesday, with the larger support which he could summon if it were necessary, and with his favour at Court, was by far the most formidable. Detach him, and the Lieutenant with his handful of riders, backed though he might be by the Countess's men, and the peasant rout would be very likely to fail. It came back then always to this: she must win the Duke. As she pondered, with her eyes on her book, as she considered again and anew this resolution, the noises of the camp, the Bat's sharp word of command—for he had fallen imperturbably to drilling as if that were the one thing necessary—the Vicomte's querulous voice, and the more distant babel of the peasants' quarter, all added weight to her thoughts. And then on a sudden an alien sound broke the current. The man lying beside her laughed.

She glanced at him, startled for the moment out of her *rôle*. The Duke was shaking with merriment. Confused, not understanding, she rose. "My lord," she said, half offended, "what is it? What moves you?"

"A rare joke," he answered. "I was loth to interrupt your thoughts, fair sister, but 'twas too much for me." He fell to laughing again.

"You will injure yourself, my lord," she said, chiding him gently, "if you laugh so violently."

"Oh, but——" The litter shook under him.

"At least," she said, with a look more tender and less

saintly than she had yet permitted herself, "you will tell me what it is! What——"

"Raise that—the cloak!" he said. He pointed with his hand. "Remove it, I mean, and you will see what— what you will see!"

She obeyed and immediately recoiled with a low cry, the cloak in her hand. "*Mon Dieu!*" she whispered, with the colour gone from her cheeks. "Who—who is he? Who is he?" She shuddered.

The man her act had revealed rose from his hiding-place, his face whiter than hers, his haggard, shifty eyes betraying his terror.

"My lord!" he cried, "you will not betray me? My lord, you passed your word!"

"Pah, coward, be silent!" the Duke answered. He turned to the Abbess, his eyes dancing. "Do you know him?" he asked.

"He is M. de Vlaye's man," she said. "The prisoner!" She was pale and she frowned, her hands pressed to her breast.

"Whom they are so anxious to hang!" the Duke replied, chuckling. "And whom des Ageaux is so anxious to have under his hand! Ha! ha! Those were his words! Under his hand! When he touched the cloak I thought I should have died. And you, rascal, what did you think? You thought you were going to die, I'll be sworn!"

"My lord—my lord!" the man faltered the words, holding out imploring hands.

"Ay, I'll wager you did!" Joyeuse replied. "Wished you had let me confess you then, I'll be sworn! He'd not have it, good sister, when I offered it, because it was too like the end—the rope and the tree!"

"My lord! My lord!" Fear had driven all but those two words from the man's mouth.

And certainly if man had ever ground for fear, he had. In that hut of wattle, open to the sky, open in a dozen places to the curious eye, he had heard the voices, the cries, the threats of his pursuers. The first that entered must see him, even if this mad lord who played with his life as lightly as he had in the beginning shielded it did not summon them to take him.

Verily, as he stood, the cloak plucked from him, with every opening in the hut's walls an eye, he tasted the bitterness of death. And in the amused face of his protector, in the girl's cold frowning gaze, what of sympathy, of feeling, of pity? Not a jot. Not a sign. To the one a jest, to the other a peril, he was to neither akin.

As it seemed. But a few seconds saw a change. The Abbess, in the first flush of amazement, had come near to forgetting her part. Under other circumstances the trembling wretch before her might have claimed and gained her sympathy, for he was one of Vlaye's men. At any rate, his punishment by des Ageaux would have added one more to the list of the Lieutenant's offences. But as it was she saw in him only a root, so long as he lay hidden, of utmost peril to all her party; a thing to be cast to the wolves, if she and those who rode in the chariot with her were to escape. Her first feeling, therefore—and her face must have betrayed it had the Duke looked at her at the first— had been one of fierce repulsion. Her natural impulse had been the impulse to call for help and give the man up!

But in time, with a kind of shock of the mind that

turned her hot, she remembered. The Duke was not one to see his will or his whim thwarted lightly. And she, the saint, whose book of offices still lay where it had fallen at her feet, she to lend herself to harshness! She to show herself void of pity! Hurriedly she forced words to her lips, and did what she could to match her face to their meaning.

"My lord, blessed are the merciful," she murmured with a slight but irrepressible shudder. "You who"—her words stuck a little—"have been spared so lately should be mercy itself."

"My sister," the Duke said slowly, "you are more than mercy!" And he looked at her, his lips still smiling, but his eyes grave. He knew—was ever Frenchman who did not know—the value of his own courage. He knew that to act as a mere whim led him to act was not in many, where life was in question; and to see a woman rise thus to his level, ay, and rise in a moment and unasked, touched him with a new and ardent admiration. His eyes, as he looked, grew tender.

"You, too, will protect him?" he said.

"Who am I that I should do otherwise?" she answered. She spoke the words so well she seemed to him an angel. And to the man——

The man fell at her feet, seized the hem of her robe, kissed it, clung to it, sobbed broken words of thanks over it, gave way to transports of gratitude. To him, too, she was an angel. And while she reflected, "I can still give him up if I think better of it," the Duke watched her with moist eyes, finding that holy in her case which in his own had been but a jest, the freak of a man in love with danger, and proud of seeking it by every road.

Presently "Now, man, to your cloak!" he said. "And you, sister," he continued, willing to hear the words again, "you are sure that you are not afraid?"

"I am no more afraid," she replied, with downcast eyes and hands crossed upon her breast, "than I was when I stayed alone with you by the river, my lord. There was no other who could stay."

"Say instead, who dared to stay."

"There is no other now who can shelter him!"

"*Mon Dieu!*" he whispered.

He followed her with his eyes after that, all his impressions confirmed; and as it was rare in those days to find the good also the beautiful, the imprint made on him was deep. She thrilled him as no woman had thrilled him since the days of his boyhood and his first gallantries. His feeling for her elevated him, purified him. As he watched her moving to and fro in his service, a great content stole over him. Once, when she bent to his couch to do him some office, he contrived to touch her hand with his. So might an anchorite have touched the wood of the true Cross—so reverent, so humble, so full of adoration and worship was the touch.

But it was the first step—that touch—and she knew it. She went back to her bench, and veiling her eyes with her long lashes that he might not read the triumph which shone in them, she fell again to her devotions—but with content in her breast. A little more, a little while, and she would have him at her beck, she would have him on his knees; and then it should not be long before his alliance with des Ageaux was broken, and his lances sent home. Not long! But meanwhile time pressed. There was the trouble; time pressed, yet she dared not be hasty. He was no simple boy, and one false move might open his eyes. He might see that she was no angel, but of the same clay as those of whom he had made toys all his life!

As she pondered, the near prospect of success set the possibility of failure, through some accident, through some mischance, in a more terrible aspect. She hated the trembling fugitive cowering in his hiding-place behind the Duke's bed; she wished to heaven he were in des Ageaux' hands again. The danger of a mutiny on his account, a danger that despite her courage chilled her, would then be at an end. True, such a mutiny menaced the Lieutenant in the first place and the Countess in the second; and she could spare them. But she could not be sure that it would go no farther. She could not be sure that its burning breath would not lap all in the camp. Had she been sure—that had been another matter. And behold, as she thought of it, from some cell of the brain leapt full-grown a plan; a plan wicked enough, cruel enough, terrible enough, to shock even her, but a clever plan if it could be executed!

She had little doubt that the Lieutenant would overcome the difficulty of the morning and succeed in persuading the peasants that he was guiltless of the escape of the prisoner. Suppose he succeeded, what would happen if it leaked out later that the prisoner had been hidden all the time in the Lieutenant's huts? Particularly if it leaked out at a time when the Lieutenant and the Countess lay in the peasants' power in the peasants' camp? And for choice after the arrival of the first batch of spears had secured the rest of the party from danger? What would happen to des Ageaux and the Countess in that event?

It was a black thought. The beautiful face bent over the book of offices grew perceptibly harder. But what better fate did they deserve who took on themselves to mar and meddle? They who incited her very brothers, clownish hobbledehoys, and her mawkish sister to rise up against her and against *him?* If fault there was, the fault lay with those who threw down the glove. The Lieutenant was come for naught else but her lover's destruction: and if he fell into the pit that he digged for another he could blame himself only. As for the girl, the white-faced puling child whose help M. de Vlaye's enemies were driving him to seek, if she, with her castles and her wealth, her lands and horse and foot, could not protect herself, the issue was her affair! Of a surety it was not her rival's!

Odette de Villeneuve's breath came a little quickly, a fine dew stood on her white forehead. Meantime the Duke watched her and wondered in an enthusiasm of piety what prayer it was that so stirred that angelic breast, what aspirations for the good of her sinning and suffering sisters swelled that saintly bosom! A vision of an ascetic life spent by her side, of Fathers read page by page in her company, of the good and the noble pursued with her under cloistered yews, of an Order such as the modern Church had never seen—such a vision wrapt him for a few blissful minutes from the cold, lower world of sense.

CHAPTER XV.

FEARS.

THE Abbess was not present that evening when the hostages transferred themselves to the peasants' side of the camp. Had she witnessed the scene she had found, it is possible, matter for reflection. Hard as he had struggled against the surrender, the Lieutenant struggled almost as hard, now it was inevitable, to put a good face on it. But his easy word and laugh fell flat in face of a crowd so watchful and so ominously silent that it was useless to pretend that the step was no more than a change from a hut in this part to a hut in that. He who knew that he must, in the morning, face the men and deny them their prisoner—knew this too well. But, in truth, the downcast faces of his troopers and the furtive glances of the Vicomte's party were evidence that the matter meant much, and that these, also, recognised it; nor did the peasants, who fell in beside the two when they started, and accompanied them in an ever growing mob, seem unaware of the fact. The movement was their triumph; a sign of victory to the dullest as he ran and stared, and ran again. A section indeed there were who stood aloof and eyed the thing askance: but two of the Vicomte's party, who recognised among these the men whom the Lieutenant had

255

denounced in the morning—the tall, light-eyed fanat-
ic and the dwarf—held it the worst sign of all; and
had it lain in their power they would even at that late
hour have called back their friends.

Those two were Roger and his younger sister. With
what feelings they saw des Ageaux and the Countess
ride away to share a solitude full alike of danger and
of alarm may be more easily imagined than described.
But this is certain; whatever pangs of jealousy gnawed
at Bonne's heart or reddened her brother's cheek, neither
forgot the bargain they had made on the hill-side, or
wished their rival aught but a safe deliverance.

As it was, could the one or the other, by the lifting of
a finger, have injured the person who stood in the way,
they had not lifted it or desired to lift it. But—to be in
her place! To be in his place! To share that solitude
and that peril! To know that round them lay half a
thousand savages, ready at the first sign of treachery to
take their lives, and yet to know that to the other it was
bliss to be there—this, to the two who remained in the
Vicomte's huts and gave their fancy rein, seemed happiness. Yet were they sorely anxious; anxious in view of
the abiding risk of such a situation, more anxious in view
of the crisis that must come when the peasants learned
that the prisoner had escaped. Nevertheless, they did
not talk of this, even to one another.

If Roger kept vigil that night his sister did not know
it. And if Bonne, whose secret was her own, started and
trembled at every sound—and such a camp as that bred
many a sound and some alarming ones—she told no one.
But when the first grey light fell thin on the basin in the
hills, disclosing here the shapeless mass of a hut, and
there only the dark background of the encircling ridge,

her pale face, as she peered from her lodging, confronted Roger's as he paced the turf outside. The same thought, the same fear was in the mind of brother and sister, and had been since earliest cock-crow; and for Roger's part he was not slow to confess it. Presently they found that there was another whom care kept waking. A moment and the Bat's lank form loomed through the mist. He found the two standing side by side; and the old soldier's heart warmed to them. He nodded his comprehension.

"The trouble will not be yet awhile," he said. "He will send the lady back before he tells them. I doubt"—he shrugged his shoulders with a glance at Bonne—"if she has had a bed of roses this night."

Bonne sighed involuntarily. "At what hour do you think she will be back?" Roger asked.

"My orders are to send six riders for her half an hour after sunrise."

"A little earlier were no worse," Roger returned, his face flushing slightly as he made the suggestion.

"Nor better," the Bat replied drily. "Orders are given to be obeyed, young sir."

"And the rest of your men?" Bonne asked timidly. "They will go to support M. des Ageaux as soon as she arrives, I suppose?"

The Bat read amiss the motive that underlay her words. "Have no fear, mademoiselle," he said, "we shall see to your safety. You know the Lieutenant little if you think he will look to his own before he has ensured that of others. My lady the Countess once back with us, not a man is to stir from here. And, with warning, and the bank behind us, it will be hard if with a score of pikes we cannot push back the attack of such a crew as this!"

"But you do not mean," Bonne cried, her eyes alight, "that you are going to leave M. des Ageaux alone—to face those savages?"

"Those are my orders," the Bat replied gently; for the girl's face, scarlet with protest, negatived the idea of fear. "And orders where the Lieutenant commands, mademoiselle, are made to be obeyed; and are obeyed. Moreover," he continued seriously, "in this case they are common sense, since with a score of pikes something may be done, but with half a score here, and half a score there"—shrugging his shoulders—"nothing! Which no one knows better than my lord!"

"But——"

"The Lieutenant allows no 'buts,'" the old soldier answered, smiling at her eagerness. "Were you with him, mademoiselle—were you under his orders, I mean—it would not be long before you learned that!"

Poor Bonne was silenced. With a quivering lip she averted her face: and for a few moments no one spoke. Then, "I wish M. de Joyeuse were on his feet," the Bat said thoughtfully. "He is worth a dozen men in such a pinch as this!"

"The sun is up!" This from Roger.

"Ah!"

"How will you know when half an hour is past?"

The Bat raised his eyebrows. "I can guess it within two or three minutes," he said. "There is no hurry for a minute or two!"

"No hurry?" Roger retorted. "But the Countess—won't she be in peril?"

The Bat looked curiously at him. "For the matter of that," he said, "we are all in peril. And may-be we shall be in greater before the day is out. We must take the rough with the smooth, young sir. However—perhaps you would like to make one to fetch her?"

Roger blushed. "I will go," he said.

"Very good," the old soldier answered. "I don't know that it is against orders. For you, mademoiselle, I fear that I cannot satisfy you so easily. Were I to send you," he continued with a sly smile, "to escort my lord back——"

"Could you not go yourself?" Bonne interrupted, her face reflecting the brightest colours of Roger's blush.

"I, indeed? No, mademoiselle. Orders! Orders!"

They did not reply. By this time the dense grey mist, forerunner of heat, had risen and discovered the camp, which here and there stirred and awoke. The open ground about the rivulet, which formed a neutral space between the peasants' hovels and the quarters assigned to the Vicomte, still showed untenanted, though marred and poached by the trampling of a thousand feet. But about the fringe of the huts that, low and mean as the shops of some Oriental bazaar, clustered along the foot of the bank, figures yawned and stretched, gazed up at the morning, or passed bending under infants, to fetch water. Everywhere a rising hum told of renewed life. And behind the Vicomte's quarters the brisk jingle of bits and stirrups announced that the troopers were saddling.

In those days of filthy streets, and founderous sloughy roads, the great went ever on horseback, if it were but to a house two doors distant. To ride was a sign of rank, no matter how short the journey. Across the street, across the camp it was the same; and Bonne, as she watched Roger and the five troopers proceeding

with three led horses across the open, saw nothing strange
in the arrangement.

But when some minutes had passed, and the little
troop did not emerge again from the ruck of hovels
which had swallowed them, Bonne began to quake.
Before her fears had time to take shape, however, the
riders appeared; and the anxiety she still felt—for she
knew that des Ageaux was not with them—gave way
for a moment to a natural if jealous curiosity. How
would she look, how would she carry herself, who had
but this moment parted from him, who had shared
through the night his solitude and his risk, his thoughts,
perhaps, and his ambitions? Would happiness or anxiety or triumph be uppermost in her face?

She looked; she saw. Her gaze left no shade of
colour, no tremor of eye or lip unnoticed. And certainly for happiness or triumph she failed to find a trace
of either in the Countess's face. The young girl, pale
and depressed, drooped in her saddle, drooped still
more when she stood on her feet. No blush, no smile
betrayed remembered words or looks, caresses or promises; and if it was anxiety that clouded her, she showed
it strangely. For when she had alighted from her
horse she did not wait. Although, as her feet touched
the ground, a murmur rose from the distant huts, she
did not heed it; but looking neither to right nor left,
she hastened to hide herself in her quarters.

She seemed to be in trouble, and Bonne, melted, would
have gone to her. But a sound stayed the elder girl at
the door. The murmur in the peasants' quarter had
risen to a louder note; and borne on this—as treble on
base—came to the ear the shrill screech that tells of
fanaticism. Such a sound has terrors for the boldest;

for, irrational itself, it deprives others of reason. It gathers up all that is weak, all that is flighty, all that is cruel, even all that is cowardly, and hurls the whole, imbued with its own qualities, against whatever excites its rage. Bonne, who had never heard that note before, but knew by intuition its danger, stood transfixed, staring with terrified eyes at the distant huts. She was picturing what one instant of time, one savage blow, one shot at hazard, might work under that bright morning sky! She saw des Ageaux alone, hemmed in, surrounded by the ignorant crowd which the enthusiast was stirring to madness! She saw their lowering brows, their cruel countenances, their small, fierce eyes under matted locks; and she looked trembling to the Bat, who, stationed a few paces from her, was also listening to the shrill voice.

Had he sworn she had borne it better. But his compressed lips told of a more tense emotion; of fidelity strained to the utmost. Even this iron man shook, then! Even he to whom his master's orders were heaven's first law felt anxiety! She could bear no more in silence.

"Go!" she murmured. "Oh, go! Surely twenty men might ride through them!"

He did not look at her. "Orders!" he muttered hoarsely. "Orders!" But the perspiration stood on his brow.

She saw that, and that his sinewy hands gripped nail to palm; and as the distant roar gathered volume, and the note of peril in it grew more acute, "Oh, go!" she cried, holding out her hands to him. "Go, Roger! Some one!" wildly. "Will you let them tear him limb from limb!"

Still "Orders! Orders!" the Bat muttered. And though his eyes flickered an instant in the direction of the waiting troopers, he set his teeth. And then in a flash, in a second, the roar died down and was followed by silence.

Silence; no one moved, no one spoke. As if fascinated every eye remained glued to the low, irregular line of huts that hid from sight the inner part of the peasants' camp. What had happened, what was passing there? On the earthen ramparts high overhead were men, Charles among them, who could see, and must know; but so taken up were the group below, from Bonne to the troopers, in looking for what was to come, that no one diverted eye or thought to these men who knew. And though either the abrupt cessation of sound, or the subtle excitement in the air, drew the Abbess at this moment from the Duke's hut, no one noted her appearance, or the Duke's pale eager face peering over her shoulder. What had happened? What had happened behind the line of hovels, under the morning sunshine that filled the camp and rendered only more grim the fear, the suspense, the tragedy that darkened all?

Something more than a minute they spent in that absorbed gazing. Then a deep blush dyed Bonne's cheeks. The Bat, who had not sworn, swore. The Duke laughed softly. The troopers, if their officer had not raised his hand to check them, would have cheered. Des Ageaux had shown himself in one of the openings that pierced the peasants' town. He was on horseback, giving directions, with gestures on this side and that. A score of naked urchins ran before him, gazing up at him; and a couple of men at his bridle were taking orders from him.

He was safe, he had conquered. And Bonne, uncertain what she had said in her anxiety, but certain that she had said too much, cast a shamed look at the Bat. Fortunately his eye was on the troopers; and it was not his look but her sister's smile which drove the girl from the scene. She remembered the Countess: she bethought her that, in the solitude of her hut, the child might be suffering. Bonne hastened to her, with the less scruple as the two shared a hut.

The impulse that moved her was wholly generous. Yet when her hasty entrance surprised the young girl in the act of rising from her knees, there entered into the embarrassment which checked her one gleam of triumph. While the other had prayed for her lover, she had acted. She had acted!

The next moment she quelled the mean thought. The girl before her looked so wan, so miserable, so forlorn, that it was impossible to think of her hardly, or judge her strictly. "I am afraid that I scared you," Bonne said, and stooped and kissed her. "But all is well, I bring you good news. He is safe! You can see him if you look from the door of the hut."

She thought that the child would spring to the door and feast her eyes on the happy assurance of his safety. But the young Countess did not move. She stared at Bonne as if she had a difficulty in taking in the meaning of her words. "Safe?" she stammered. "Who is safe?"

"Who?" Bonne ejaculated.

The young girl passed her hand over her brow. "I am very sorry," she replied humbly. "I did not understand. You said that some one was safe?"

"M. des Ageaux, of course!"

"Of course! I am very glad."

"Glad?" Bonne repeated, with indignation she could not control. "Glad? Only that?"

The girl, her lip trembling, her face working, cast a frightened look at her, and then with a piteous gesture, as if she could no longer control herself, she turned from her and burst into tears.

Bonne stared   What did this mean? Relief? Joy? The relaxation of nerves too tightly strained? No. She should have thought of it before. It was not likely, it was not possible that this child had already conceived for des Ageaux such an affection as casts out fear. It was not she, but he, who had to gain by the marriage; and prepared as the Countess might be to look favourably on his suit, ready as she might be to give her heart, she had not yet given it.

"You are overwrought!" Bonne said, to soothe her. "You have been frightened."

"Frightened!" the girl replied through her sobs. "I shall die—if I have to go through it again! And I have to go through it, I must go through it. And I shall die! Oh, the night I have spent listening and waiting and"—she cowered away, with a stifled scream. "What was that?" She stared at the door, her eyes wild with terror. "What was that?" she repeated, seizing Bonne, and clinging to her.

"Nothing! Nothing!" Bonne answered gently, seeing that the girl was thoroughly shaken and unnerved. "It was only a horse neighing."

The Countess controlled her sobs, but her scared eyes and white face revealed the impression which the suspense of the night had made on one not bold by nature, and only supported by the pride of rank. "A horse neighing?" she repeated. "Was it only that? I thought—oh! if you knew what it was to hear them creeping and crawling, and rustling and whispering every hour of the night! To fancy them coming, and to sit up gasping! And then to lie down again and wait and wait, expecting to feel their hands on your throat! Ah, I tell you"—she hid her face on Bonne's shoulder and clasped her to her passionately—"every minute was an hour, and every hour a day!"

Bonne held her to her full of pity. And presently, "But he was near you?" she ventured. "Did not his— his neighbourhood——"

"The Lieutenant's?"

."Yes. Did not that"—Bonne spoke with averted eyes: she would know for certain now if the child loved him!—"did not that make you feel safer?"

"One man!" the Countess's voice rang querulous. "What could one man do? What could he have done if they had come? Besides they would have killed him first. I did not think of him. I thought of myself. Of my throat!" She clasped it with a sudden movement of her two hands—it was white and very slender. "I thought of that, and the knife, and how it would feel—all night! All night, do you understand? And I could have screamed! I could have screamed every minute. I wonder I did not."

Bonne saw that the child had gone to the ordeal, and passed through it, in the face of a terror that would have turned brave men. And she felt no contempt for her. She saw indeed that the child did not love; for love, as Bonne's maiden fancy painted it, was an all-powerful impervious armour. She was sure that in the other's place she would have known fear, but it would have been fear on *his* account, not on her own. She might have shuddered as she thought of the steel, but it would have been of the steel at his breast. Whereas the Countess—no, the Countess did not love.

"And I must go again! I must go again!" the child wailed, in the same abandonment of terror. "Oh, how shall I do it? How shall I do it?"

The cry went to Bonne's heart. "You shall not do it," she said. "If you feel about it like this, you shall not do it. It is not right nor fit."

"But I cannot refuse!" the Countess shook violently as she said it. "I dare not refuse. Afraid and a Rochechouart! A Rochechouart and a coward! No, I must go. I must die of fear there; or of shame here."

"Perhaps it may not be necessary," Bonne murmured.

"No? Why, even if my men come I must go! If they come to-day I must still go to-night. And lie trembling, and starting, and dying a death at every sound!"

"But perhaps——"

"Don't—don't!" the Countess cried, moving feverishly in her arms. "And, ah, God, I was cold a moment ago, and now I am hot! Oh, I am so hot! So hot! Let me go." Her parched lips and bright eyes told of the fever of fear that ran through her veins.

But Bonne still held her.

"It may not be necessary," she murmured. "Tell me, did you see M. des Ageaux—after you went from here last night?"

"See him?" querulously. "No! He has his hut and I mine. I see no one! No one!"

"And he does not come and talk to you?"

"Talk? No. Talk? You do not know what it is like. I am alone, I tell you, alone!"

"Then if I were to take your place he would not find it out?"

The Countess started violently—and then was still. "Take my place?" she echoed in a different tone. "In their camp, do you mean?"

"Yes."

"But you would not," the other retorted. "You would not." Then before Bonne could answer, "What do you mean? Do you mean anything?" she cried. "Do you mean you would go?"

"Yes."

"In my place?"

"If you will let me," Bonne replied. She flushed a little, conscience telling her that it was not entirely, not quite entirely for the other's sake that she was willing to do this. "If you will let me I will go," she continued. "I am bigger than you, but I can stoop, and in a riding-cloak and hood I think I can pass for you. And it will be dusk too. I am sure I can pass for you."

The Countess shivered. The boon was so great, the gift so tremendous, if she could accept it! But she was Rochechouart. What would men say if they discovered that she had not gone, that she had let another take her place and run her risk? She pondered with parted lips. If it might be!

"You are not fit to go," Bonne continued. "You will faint or fall. You are ill now."

"But they will find out!" the Countess wailed, hiding her face on Bonne's shoulder. "They will find out!"

"They will not find out," Bonne replied firmly.

"And I—why should I not go? You have done one night. I will do one."

"Oh, if you would! But will you—not be afraid?" The Countess's eyes were full of longing. If only she could accept with honour!

"I shall not be afraid," Bonne answered confidently. "And no one need know, no one shall know. M. des Ageaux does not talk to you?"

"No. But if it be found out, everybody—ah, I shall die of shame! Your brother, Roger, too—and everybody!"

"No one shall know," Bonne answered stoutly. "No one. Besides, you have been once. It is not as if you had not been!"

And the child, with the memory of the night pressing upon her, jumped at that. "Then I shall go to-morrow night," she said. "I shall go to-morrow night."

Bonne was clear that she was not fit to go again. But she let that be for the moment. "That shall be as you wish," she answered comfortably. "We will talk about that to-morrow. For to-night it is settled. And now you must try if you cannot go to sleep. If you do not sleep you will be ill."

CHAPTER XVI.

TO DO OR NOT TO DO?

To do or not to do? How many a one has turned
the question in his mind; this one in the solitude of
his locked room, seated with frowning face and eyes
fixed on nothingness; that one amid the babble of
voices and laughter, masking anxious thought under
set smiles. How many a one has viewed the act she
meditated this way and that, askance and across, in
the hope of making the worse appear the better, and
so of doing her pleasure with a light heart. Others
again, trampling the scruple under foot, have none the
less hesitated, counting the cost and striving to view
dispassionately—with eyes that, the thing done, will
never see it in that light again—how it will be with
them afterwards, how much better outwardly, how
much worse inwardly, and so to strike a balance for or
against—to do or not to do. And some with burning
eyes, and minds unswervingly bent on the thing they
desire have yet felt hands pluck at them, and something—be it God or the last instinct of good—whispering them to pause—to pause, and not to do!

The Abbess pondered, while the Duke, reclining in
the opening of his hut, from which the screen had been
drawn back that he might enjoy the air, had no more

accurate notion of her thoughts than had the Lieutenant's dog sleeping a few paces away. The missal had
fallen from her hands and lay in her lap. Her eyes
fixed on the green slope before her betrayed naught
that was not dove-like; while the profound stillness of
her form which permitted the Duke to gaze at will
breathed only the peace of the cloister and the altar,
the peace that no change of outward things can long
disturb. Or so the Duke fancied; and eyeing her with
secret rapture, felt himself uplifted in her presence.
He felt that here was a being congenial with his better
self, and a beauty as far above the beauty to which he
had been a slave all his life as his higher moods rose
above his worst excesses.

He had gained strength in the three days which had
elapsed since his arrival in the camp. He could now
sit up for a short time and even stand, though giddily
and with precaution. Nor were these the only changes
which the short interval had produced. The Countess's
spears, to the number of thirty, were here, and their
presence augmented the safety of the Vicomte's party.
But indirectly, in so far as it fed the peasants' suspicions, it had a contrary effect. The Crocans sub-
mitted indeed to be drilled, sometimes by the Bat,
sometimes by his master; and reasonable orders were
not openly disobeyed. But the fear of treachery which
a life-time of ill-usage had instilled was deepened by
the presence of the Countess's men. The slightest
movements on des Ageaux' part were scanned with
jealousy. If he conferred too long with the Villeneuves or the Countess men exchanged black looks,
or muttered in their beards. If he strayed a hundred
paces down the valley a score were at his heels. Nor

were there wanting those who, moving secretly between the camp and the savage horde upon the hill—the Old Crocans, as they were called—kept these apprised of their doubts and fears.

To eyes that could see, the position was critical, even dangerous. Nor was it rendered more easy by a feat of M. de Vlaye's men, who, reconnoitring up to the gates one evening, cut off a dozen peasants. The morning light discovered the bodies of six of these hanged on a tree below the Old Crocans' station, and well within view from the ridge about the camp. That the disaster might not have occurred had des Ageaux been in his quarters, instead of being a virtual prisoner, went for nothing. He bore the blame, some even thought him privy to the matter. From that hour the gloom grew deeper. Everywhere, and at all times, the more fanatical or the more suspicious drew together in corners, and while simpler clowns cursed low or muttered of treachery, darker spirits whispered devilish plans. Those who had their eyes open noted the more frequent presence of the Old Crocans, who wandered by twos and threes through the camp; and though these, when des Ageaux' eye fell on them, fawned and cringed, or hastened to withdraw themselves, they spat when his back was turned, and with stealthy gestures they gave him to hideous deaths.

In a word, fear like a dark presence lay upon the camp; and to add to the prevailing irritation, the heat was great. The giant earth-wall which permitted the Lieutenant to mature his plans and await his reinforcements shut out the evening breezes. Noon grilled his men as in a frying-pan; all night the air was hot and heavy. The peasants sighed for the cool streams of Brantôme and the voices of the frogs. The troopers, accustomed to lord it and impatient of discomfort, were quick with word and hand, and prone to strike, when a blow was as dangerous as a light behind a powder screen. Without was Vlaye, within was fear; while, like ravens waiting for the carnage, the horde of Old Crocans on the hill looked down from their filthy eyrie.

No one knew better than the Abbess that the least thing might serve for a spark. And she pondered. Not for an hour since its birth had the plan she had imagined been out of her mind; and still—there was so much good in her, so much truth—she recoiled. The two whom she doomed, if she acted, were her enemies; and yet she hesitated. Her own safety, her father's, her sister's, the safety of all, those two excepted, was secured by the Rochechouart reinforcement. Only her enemies would perish, and perhaps the poor fool whose presence she must disclose. And yet she could not make up her mind. To do or not to do?

It might suffice to detach Joyeuse. But the time was short, and the Duke's opinion of her high; and she shrank from risking it by a premature move. He had placed her on a pinnacle and worshipped her: if she descended from the pinnacle he might worship no longer. Meantime, if she waited until his troopers rode in, and on their heels a second levy from Rochechouart, it might be too late to act, too late to detach him, too late to save Vlaye. To do or not to do?

A dozen paces from her, old Solomon was pouring garrulous inventions into the ear of the Countess's steward; who, dull, faithful man, took all for granted, and gaped more widely at every lie. Insensibly her mind began to follow and take in the sense of their words.

"Six on one tree!" Solomon was saying, in the contemptuous tone of one to whom Montfaucon was an every-day affair. "'Tis nothing. You never saw the like at Rochechouart, say you? Perhaps not. Your lady is merciful."

"Three I have!"

"And who were they?" Solomon asked, with a sniff of contempt.

"Cattle-stealers. At least so it was said. But the wife of one came down next day and put it on another, and it was complained that they had suffered wrongfully. But three they were."

"Three?" Solomon's nose rose in scorn. "If you had seen the elm at Villeneuve in my lord's father's time! They were as acorns on an oak. Ay, they were! Fifteen in one forenoon."

"God ha' mercy on us!"

"And ten more when he had dined!"

"God ha' mercy on us!" Fulbert replied, staring in stricken surprise. "And what had they done?"

"Done?" Solomon answered, shrugging his shoulders after a careless fashion. "Just displeased him. And why should he not?" he continued, bristling up. "What worse could they do? Was he not lord of Villeneuve?"

And she was making a scruple of two lives. Of two lives that stood in her path! Still—life was life. But what was that they were saying now? Hang Vlaye? Hang—the Captain of Vlaye?

It was Solomon had the word; and this time the

astonishment was on his side. "What is that you say?" he repeated. "Hang M. de Vlaye?"

"And why for not?" the steward replied doggedly, his face red with passion, his dull intelligence sharpened by his lady's wrongs. "And why for not?"

Solomon was scandalised by the mere mention of it. Hang like any clod or clown a man who had been a constant visitor at his master's house! "Oh, but he— you don't hang such as he!" he retorted. "The Captain of Vlaye? Tut, tut! You are a fool!"

"A fool? Not I! They will hang him!"

"Tut, tut!"

"Wait until *he* speaks!" Fulbert replied, nodding mysteriously in the direction of the Lieutenant, who, at no great distance from the group, was watching a band of peasants at their drill. "When he speaks 'tis the King speaks. And when the King speaks, it is hang a man must, whoever he be!"

"Tut, tut!"

"Whoever he be!" Fulbert repeated with stolid obstinacy. And then, "It is not for nothing," he added with a menacing gesture, "that a man stops the Countess of Rochechouart on the King's road! No, no!"

Not for nothing? No, and it is not for nothing, the Abbess cried in her heart, that you threaten the man I love with the death of a dog! Dogs yourselves! Dogs!

It was well that the Duke was not looking at her at that moment, for her heaving bosom, her glowing eyes, the rush of colour to her face all betrayed the force of her passion. Hang him? Hang her lover? So that was what they were saying, thinking, planning behind her back, was it! That was the camp talk! That!

She could have borne it better had the Lieutenant proclaimed his aim aloud. It was the sedateness of his preparations, the slow stealth of his sap, the unswerving calmness of his approaches at which her soul revolted. The ceaseless drilling, the arming, the watch by day and night, all the life about her, every act, every thought had her lover's ruin for their aim, his death for their end! A loathing, a horror seized her. She felt a net closing about her, a net that enmeshed her and fettered her, and threatened to hold her motionless and powerless, while they worked their will on him before her eyes!

But she could still break the net. She could still act. Two lives? What were two lives, lives of his enemies, in comparison of his life? At the thought a spring of savage passion welled up in her heart, and clouded her eyes. The die was cast. It remained only to do. To do!

But softly—softly. As she rose, having as yet no formed plan, a last doubt stayed her. It was not a doubt of his enemies' intentions, but of their power. He whose words had opened her eyes to their grim purpose was a dullard, almost an imbecile. He could be no judge of the means they possessed, or of their chances of success. The swarm of unkempt, ill-armed peasants, who disgusted her eyes, the troop of spears, who even now barely sufficed to secure the safety of her party, what chance had they against M. de Vlaye and the four or five hundred men-at-arms who for years had lorded it over the marches of the province, and made themselves the terror of a country-side? Surely a small chance if it deserved the name. Surely she was permitting a shadow to frighten her.

"Something," the Duke murmured near her ear, "has interrupted the even current of your thoughts, mademoiselle. What is it, I pray?"

"I feel the heat," she answered, holding her hand to her brow, that behind its shelter she might recover her composure. "Do not you?"

"It is like an oven," he answered, "within these earth-walls."

"How I hate them!" she cried, unable to repress the spirit of irritation.

"Do you? Well, so do I," he replied. "But within them—it is nowhere cooler than here."

"I will put that to the proof, my lord," she returned with a smile. And, gliding from him, in spite of the effort he made to detain her, she crossed the grass to her father. Sinking on the sward beside his stool, she began to fan herself.

The Vicomte was in an ill-humour of some days' standing; nor without reason. Dragged, will he nill he, from the house in which his whim had been law, he found himself not only without his comforts, but a cipher in the camp. Not once, but three or four times he had let his judgment be known, and he had looked to see it followed. He might have spoken to the winds. No one, not even his sons, though they listened respectfully, took heed of it. It followed that he saw himself exposed to dangers against which he was not allowed to guard himself, and to a catastrophe which he must await in inaction; while all he possessed stood risked on a venture that for him had neither interest nor motive.

In such a position a man of easier temper and less vanity might be pardoned if he complained. For the Vicomte, fits of senile rage shook him two or three times

a day. He learned what it was to be thwarted: and
if he hated any one or anything more than the filthy
peasants on whom his breeding taught him to look
with loathing, it was the man with whose success his
safety was bound up, the man who had forced him
into this ignominious position.

Of him he could believe no good. When the Abbess,
after fanning herself in silence, mentioned the arrival of
the Countess's troopers, and asked him if he thought
that the Lieutenant was now strong enough to attack, he
derided the notion.

"M. de Vlaye will blow this rabble to the winds," he
said, with a contemptuous gesture. "We may grill
here as long as we please, but the moment we show
ourselves outside, pouf! It will be over! What can a
handful of riders do against five hundred men as good
as themselves?"

"But the peasants?" she suggested, willing to know
the worst. "There are some hundreds of them."

"Food for steel!" he answered, with the same contemptuous pantomime.

"Then you think—we were wrong to come here?"

"I think, girl, that we were mad to come here. But
not so mad," he continued spitefully, "as those who
brought us!"

"Yet Charles thinks that the Governor of Périgord
will prevail."

"Charles had his own neck in the noose," the Vicomte
growled, "and was glad of company. Since Coutras
it is the young lead the old, and the issue you will see.
Lieutenant of Périgord? What has the Lieutenant of
Périgord or any other governor to do with canaille such
as this?"

Odette heaved a sigh of relief and her face lightened. "It will be better so," she said softly. "M. de Vlaye knows, sir, that we had no desire to hurt him, and he will not reckon it against us."

The Vicomte fidgeted in his stool. "I wish I could think so," he answered with a groan. "Curse him! Who is more to blame? If he had left the Countess alone, this would not have happened. They are no better one than the other! But what is this? Faugh!" And he spat on the ground.

There was excuse for his disgust. Across the open ground a group of men were making their way in the direction of the Lieutenant's quarters. They were the same men who had met him at the entrance on his return with the Abbess and Joyeuse: nor had the lapse of four or five days lessened the foulness of their aspect, or robbed them of the slinking yet savage bearing—as of beasts of prey half tamed—which bade beware of them. They shambled forward until they neared des Ageaux, who was writing at an improvised table not far from the Vicomte; then cringing they saluted him. Their eyes squinting this way and that from under matted locks—as if at a gesture they were ready to leap back—added to their beast-like appearance.

The Lieutenant's voice, as he asked the men with asperity what they needed, came clearly to the ears of the group about the Vicomte. But the Old Crocans' answer, expressed at length in a patois of the country, was not audible.

"Foul carrion!" the Vicomte muttered. "What do they here?" while the Abbess and Bonne, who had joined her, contemplated them with eyes of shuddering dislike.

"What, indeed?" Bonne muttered, her cheek pale. She seemed to be unable to take her eyes from them. "They frighten me! Oh, I hope they will not be suffered to remain in the camp!"

"Is it that they wish?" the Vicomte asked.

"Yes, my lord," Solomon answered: he had gone forward, listened awhile and returned. "They say that eleven more of their people were surprised by Vlaye's men three hours ago, and cut to pieces. This is the second time it has happened. They think that they are no longer safe on the hill, and wish to join us."

"God forbid!" Bonne cried, with a strange insistence.

The Abbess looked at her. "Why so frightened?" she said contemptuously. "One might suppose you were in greater danger than others, girl!"

Bonne did not answer, but her distended eyes betrayed the impression which the wretches' appearance made on her. Nor when Charles—who was seldom off the ridge which was his special charge—remarked that after all a man was a man, and they had not too many, could she refrain from a word. "But not those!" she murmured. "Not those!"

Charles, who in these days saw more of the Bat than of any one else, shrugged his shoulders. "I shall be surprised if he does not receive them," he answered. "They are vermin and may give us trouble. But we must run the risk. If we are to succeed we must run some risks."

Not that risk, however, it appeared. For he had scarcely uttered the words when des Ageaux was seen to raise his hand, and point with stern meaning to the entrance. "No," he said, his voice high and clear. "Begone to your own and look to yourselves! You chose to go your own way and a bloody one! Now your blood be on your own heads! Here is no place for you, nor will I cover you!"

"My lord!" one cried in protest. "My lord, hear us!"

"No!" the Lieutenant replied harshly. "You had your warning and did not heed it! M. de Villeneuve, when he came to you, warned you, and I warned you. It was your own will to withdraw yourselves. You would have naught but blood. You would burn and kill! Now, on your own heads," he concluded with severity, "be your blood!"

They would have protested anew, but he dismissed them with a gesture which permitted no denial. And sullenly, with stealthy gestures of menace, they retreated towards the entrance; and gabbling more loudly as they approached it, seemed to be imprecating vengeance on those who cast them out. In the gate they lingered awhile, turning about and scolding the man on guard. Then they passed out of sight, and were gone.

As the last of them disappeared des Ageaux, who had kept a vigilant eye on their retreat, approached the group about the Vicomte. The old man, though he approved the action, could not refrain from giving his temper vent.

"You are sure that you can do without them," he said, with a sneer. His shaking hand betrayed his dislike of the man to whom he spoke.

"I believe I can," the Lieutenant answered. He spoke with unusual gravity, but the next moment a smile—smiles had been rare with him of late—curved the corners of his mouth. His eyes travelled from one to another, and in a low voice, but one that betrayed his relief, "I will tell you why, if you wish to know, M. le Vicomte."

"Why?"

Des Ageaux' smile grew broader, but his tone remained low. "Because I have news," he returned. "And it is good news. I have had word within the last hour that I may expect M. de Joyeuse's levies about nightfall to-morrow, and a day or two later a reinforcement beyond my hope—fifty men-at-arms whom the Governor of Agen has lent me, and fifty from my garrison of Périgueux. With those we should have enough—though not too many."

They received the news with words of congratulation or with grunts of disdain, according as each felt about it. And all began to discuss the tidings, though still in the tone of caution which the Lieutenant's look enjoined. One only was silent, and with averted face saw the cup of respite dashed from her lips. A hundred men beyond those looked for! Such an accession must change hope to certainty, hazard to surety. A few days would enable the Lieutenant to match rider for rider with Vlaye, and still boast a reserve of four or five hundred undisciplined allies. While jubilant voices hummed in her ears, and those whom she was ready to kill because they hated him rejoiced, the Abbess rose slowly and, detaching herself from the group, walked away.

No one followed her even with the eye; for the Duke, fatigued, and a little hurt that she did not return, had retired into his quarters. Nor would the most watchful have learned much from her movements, or, unless jealous beyond the ordinary, have found aught to suspect in what she did.

She strolled very slowly along the foot of the slope, as if in pure idleness or to stretch limbs cramped by over-long sitting. Presently she came to some tethered horses, and stood and patted them, and looked them over; nor could any but the horses tell—and they could not speak—that while her hand was on them her eyes were roving the camp. Perhaps she found what she sought; perhaps it was chance only that guided her steps in the direction of the tall young man with pale eyes, whose violence had raised him to a certain leadership among the peasants.

It must have been chance, for when she reached his neighbourhood she did not address him. She stooped and—what could be more womanly or more natural? —she spoke to a naked child that rolled on the trampled turf within arm's length of him. What she said—in French or patois, or that infant language of which no woman's tongue is ignorant—the baby could not say, for, like the horses, it could not speak. Yet it must have found something unusual in her face, for it cowered from her, as in terror. And what she said could have no interest for the man who lounged near, though he seemed disturbed by it.

She toyed with the shrinking child a moment, then turned and walked slowly back to the Vicomte's quarters. Her manner was careless, but her face was pale. No wonder. For she had taken a step—and she knew it—which she could never retrace. She had done that which she could not undo. Between her and Bonne and Roger and Charles was a gulf henceforth, though they might not know it. And the Duke? She winced a little, recognising more plainly than before how far she stood below the notion he had of her.

Yet she felt no remorse. On the contrary, the uppermost feeling in her mind—and it ran riot there—was a stormy exultation. They who had dragged her at their chariot wheels would learn that in forcing her to take part against her lover they had made the most fatal of mistakes. They triumphed now. They counted on sure success now. They thought to hang him, as they would hang any low-bred thief! Very good! Let them wait until morning, and talk then of hanging!

Once or twice, indeed, in the afternoon she was visited by misgivings. The man she had seen was a mere savage; he might not have understood. Or he might betray her, though that could hurt her little since no one would believe him. Or the peasants, though wrought to fury, might recoil at the last like the cowards they were!

But these and the like doubts arose not from compunction, but from mistrust. Compunction was to come later, when evening fell and from the door of the Duke's quarters she viewed the scene, now familiar, of the hostages' departure in the dusk—saw the horses drawn up and the two whom she was dooming in act to mount. It was then that a sudden horror of what she was about seized her—she was young, a mere girl—and she rose with a stifled cry from her stool. It was not yet too late. A cry, a word would save them. Would save them still! Impulsively she moved a pace towards them, intending—ay, for a moment, intending to say that word.

But she stopped. A word would save them, but—she was forgetting—it would doom her lover! And on that thought, and to reinforce it, there rose before her mind's eye the pale puling features of the Countess—

her rival! Was she to be put aside for a thing like that? Was it to such a half-formed child as that she must surrender her lover? She pressed her hands together, and, returning to her seat, she turned it about that her eyes might not see them as they went through the dusk.

CHAPTER XVII.

THE HEART OF CAIN.

SEVEN hours had passed.

The moon had just dropped below the narrow horizon of the camp, but to eyes which looked up from the blackness of the hollow the form of the nearest sentinel, erect on the edge of the cup, showed plain against the paler background of sky. The hour was the deadest of the night; but, as the stillest night has its noises, the camp was not without noises. The dull sound of horses browsing, the breath of a thousand sleepers, the low whinny of a mare, or the muttered word of one who dreamed heavily and spoke in his dream, these and the like sounds fed a murmurous silence that was one with the brooding heaviness of a June night.

Odette de Villeneuve—the ears that drank in the voices of the slumbering host were hers—stood half-hidden in the doorway of her quarters and listened. The inner darkness had become intolerable to her. The wattled walls, though they were ventilated by a hundred crevices, stifled her. Pent behind them she fancied a hundred things; she saw on the curtain of blackness drawn faces and staring eyes; she made of the faintest murmur that entered now a roar of voices, and now the hoarse beginnings of a scream. Outside, with the cooler air fanning her burning face, she could at least lay hold on reality. She was no longer the sport and plaything of her own strained senses. She could at least be sure that nothing was happening, that nothing had happened —yet. And though she still breathed quickly and crouched like a fearful thing in the doorway, here she could call hate to her support, she could reckon her wrongs and think of her lover, and persuade herself that this was but a nightmare from which she would awake to find all well with herself and with him.

If only the thing were over and done! Ah, if only it were done! That was her feeling. If only the thing were done! She bent her ear to listen; but nothing stirred, no alarm clove the night; and it could want little of morning. She fancied that the air struck colder, laden with that chill which comes before the dawn: and eastwards she thought that she discerned the first faint lightening of the sky. The day was at hand and nothing had happened.

She could not say on the instant whether she was sorry or glad. But she was sure that she would be sorry when the sun rose high and shone on her enemy's triumph, and Charles and Roger and Bonne, whom she had taught herself to despise, saw their choice justified, and the side they had supported victorious. The triumph of those beneath us is hard to bear; and at that picture the Abbess's face grew hard, though there was no one to see it. The blood throbbed in her head as she thought of it; throbbed so loudly that she questioned the reality of a sound that a moment later forced itself upon her senses. It was a sound not unlike the pulsing of the blood; not terrible nor loud, but rhythmical, such as the tide makes when it rises slowly but irresistibly to fill some channel left bare at the ebb.

What was it? She stood arrested. Was it only the blood surging in her ears? Or was it the silent uprising of a multitude of men, each from the place where he lay? Or was it, could it be the stealthy march of countless feet across the camp?

It might be that. She listened more intently, staying with one hand the beating of her heart. She decided that it was that.

Thereon it was all she could do to resist the impulse to give the alarm. She had no means of knowing in which direction the unseen band was moving. She could guess, but she might be wrong; and in that case, at any moment the night might hurl upon her a hundred brutes whose first victim as they charged through the encampment she must be. She fancied that the darkness wavered; and here and there bred shifting forms. She fancied that the dull sound was drawing nearer and growing louder. And—a scream rose in her throat.

She choked it down. An instant later she had her reward, if that was a reward which left her white and shuddering—a coward clinging for support to the frail wall beside her.

It was a shrill scream rending the night; such an one as had distended her own throat an instant before —but stifled in mid-utterance in a fashion horrible and suggestive. Upon it followed a fierce outcry in several voices, cut short two seconds later with the same abruptness, and followed by—silence. Then, while she clung cold, shivering, half fainting to the wattle, the darkness gave forth again that dull shuffling, moving sound, a little quickened perhaps, and a little more apparent.

This time it caused an alarm. Sharp and clear came a voice from the ridge, "What goes there? Answer!"

No answer was given, and "Who goes there?" cried a voice from a different point, and then "To arms!" cried a third. "To arms! To arms!" And on a rising wave of hoarse cries the camp awoke.

The tall form of the Bat seemed to start up within a yard of the Abbess. He seized a stick that hung beside a drum on a post, and in a twinkling the hurried notes of the Alert pulsed through the camp. On the instant men rose from the earth about him; while frightened faces, seen by the rays of a passing light, looked from hut-doors, and the cries of a waiting-maid struggling in hysterics mingled with the words of command that brought the troopers into line and manned the ground in front of the Vicomte's quarters. A trooper flew up the sloping rampart to learn from the sentry what he had seen, and was back as quickly with the news that the guards knew no more than was known below. They had only heard a suspicious outcry, and following on it sounds which suggested the movement of a body of men.

The Bat, bringing order out of confusion—and in that well aided by Roger, though the lad's heart was bursting with fears for his mistress—could do naught at the first blush but secure his position. But when he had got his men placed, and lanthorns so disposed as to advantage them and hamper an attack, he turned sharply on the man. "Did they hear my lord's voice?" he asked.

"It was their fancy. Certainly the outcry came from that part of the camp."

"Then out on them!" Roger exclaimed, unable to control himself. "Out on them. To saddle and let us charge, and woe betide them if they stand!"

"Softly, softly," the Bat said. "Orders, young sir! Mine are to stand firm, whatever betides, and guard the women! And that I shall do until daylight."

"Daylight?" Roger cried.

"Which is not half an hour off!"

"Half an hour!" The lad's tone rang with indignation. "Are you a man and will you leave a woman at their mercy?" He was white with rage and shaking. "Then I will go alone. I will go to their quarters —I, alone!" As he thought of the girl he loved and her terrors his heart was too big for his breast.

"And throw away another life?" the Bat replied sternly. "For shame!"

"For shame, I?"

"Ay, you! To call yourself a soldier and cry fie on orders!"

He would have added more, but he was forestalled by the Vicomte. In his high petulant tone he bade his son stand for a fool. "There are women here," he continued, sensibly enough, "and we are none too many to guard them, as we are."

"Ay, but she" Roger retorted, trembling, "is alone there."

"A truce to this!" the Bat struck in, with heat. "To your post, sir, and do your duty, or we are all lost together. Steady, men, steady!" as a slight movement of the troopers at the breastwork made itself felt rather than seen. "Pikes low! Pikes low! What is it?"

He saw then. The commotion was caused by the approach of a group of men, three or four in number, whose neighbourhood one of the lights had just betrayed. "Who comes there?" cried the leader of the Countess's troopers, who was in charge of that end of the line. "Are you friends?"

"Ay, ay! Friends!"

If so, they were timorous friends. For when they were bidden to advance to the spot where the Bat with the Vicomte and Roger awaited them, their alarm was plain. The foremost was the man who had spoken for the peasants at the debate some days before. But the smith's boldness and independence were gone; he was ashake with fear. "I have bad news," he stammered. "Bad news, my lords!"

"The worse for some one!" the Bat answered with a grim undernote that should have satisfied even Roger. As he spoke he raised one of the lights from the ground, and held it so that its rays fell on the peasants' faces. "Has harm happened to the hostages?"

"God avert it! But they have been carried off," the man faltered through his ragged beard. It was evident that he was thoroughly frightened.

"Carried off?"

"Ay, carried off!"

"By whom? By whom, rascal?" The Bat's eyes glared dangerously. "By Heaven, if you have had hand or finger in it——" he added.

"Should I be here if I had?" the man answered, piteously extending his open hands.

"I know not. But now you are here, you will stay here! Surround them!" And when the order had been carried out, "Now speak, or your skin will pay for it," the Bat continued. "What has happened, spawn of the dung-heap?"

"Some of our folk—God knows without our knowledge"—the smith whined—"brought in a party of the men on the hill——"

"The Old Crocans from the town?"

"Ay! And they seized the—my lord and the lady—and got off with them! As God sees me, they were gone before we were awake!" he protested, seeing the threatening blade with which Roger was advancing upon him.

The Lieutenant held the lad back. "Very good," he said. "We shall follow with the first light. If a hair of their heads be injured, I shall hang you first, and the rest of you by batches as the trees will bear!" And with a black and terrible look the Bat swore an oath to chill the blood. The leader of the Countess's men repeated it after him, word for word; and Roger, silent but with rage in his eyes, stood shaking between them, his blade in his hand.

The Vicomte, his fears for the safety of his own party allayed, turned to see who were present. He discovered his eldest daughter, leaning as if not far from fainting, against the doorway of the Duke's quarters. "Courage, girl," he said, in a tone of rebuke. "We are in no peril ourselves, and should set an example. Where is your sister?"

"I do not know," the Abbess replied shakily. It was being borne in on her that not two lives, but the lives of many, of scores and of hundreds, might pay for what she had done. And she was new to the work. "I have not seen her," she repeated with greater firmness, as she summoned hate to her support, and called up before her fancy the Countess's childish attractions. "She must be sleeping."

"Sleeping?" the Vicomte echoed in astonishment. He was going to add more when another took the words out of his mouth.

"What is that?" It was Roger's voice fiercely raised. "By Heaven! It is Fulbert."

It was Fulbert. As the men, of whom some were saddling—for the light was beginning to appear—pressed forward to look, the steward crawled out of the gloom about the brook, and, raising himself on one hand, made painful efforts to speak. He looked like a dead man risen; nor did the uncertain light of the lanthorns take from the horror of his appearance. Probably he had been left for dead, for the smashing blow of some blunt weapon had beaten in one temple and flooded his face and beard with blood. The Abbess, faint and sick, appalled by this first sign of her handiwork, hid her eyes.

"Follow! Follow!" the poor creature muttered, swaying as he strove to rise to his feet. "A rescue!"

"With the first light," the Bat answered him. "With the first light! How many are they?"

But he only muttered, "Follow! A rescue! A rescue!" and repeated those words in such a tone that it was plain that he no longer understood them, but said them mechanically. Perhaps they had been the last he had uttered before he was struck down.

The Bat saw how it was with him; he had seen men in that state before. "With the first light!" he said, to soothe him. "With the first light we follow!" Then turning to his men he bade them carry the poor fellow in and see to his hurts.

Roger sprang forward, eager to help. And they were bearing the man to the rear, and the Abbess had taken heart to uncover her eyes, while still averting them, when a strange sound broke from her lips—lips blanched in an instant to the colour of paper. It caught the ear of the Bat, who stood nearest to her. He turned. The Abbess, with arm outstretched, was pointing to the door of the Countess's hut. There, visible, though she seemed to shrink from sight, and even raised her hand in deprecation, stood the Countess herself.

"By Heaven!" the Bat cried. And he stood. While Roger, in place of advancing, gazed on her as on a ghost.

She tried to speak, but no sound came. And for the Abbess she had as easily spoken as the dead. Her senses tottered, the slim figure danced before her eyes, the voices of those who spoke came from a great way off.

It was the Vicomte who, being the least concerned, was first to find his voice. "Is it you, Countess?" he quavered.

The Countess nodded. She could not speak.

"But how—how have you escaped?"

"Ay, how?" the Bat chimed in more soberly. He saw that it was no phantom, though the mystery seemed none the less for that. "How come you here, Countess? How—am I mad, or did you not go to their quarters at sundown?"

"No," she whispered. "I did not go." She framed the words with difficulty. Between shame and excitement she seemed ready to sink into the earth.

"No? You did not? Then who—who did go? Some one went."

She made a vain attempt to speak. Then command-
ing herself—

"Bonne went—in my place," she cried. And clapping her hands to her face in a paroxysm of grief, she
leant, weeping, against the post of the door.

They looked at one another and began to understand, and to see. And one had opened his mouth to
speak, when a strangled cry drew all eyes to the Abbess.
She seemed to be striving to put something from her.
Her staring eyes, her round mouth of horror, her
waving fingers made up a picture of terror comparable
only to one of those masks which the Greeks used in
their tragedies of fate. A moment she showed thus,
and none of those who turned eye on her doubted
that they were looking on a stress of passion beside
which the Countess's grief was but a puny thing.
The next moment she fell her length in a swoon.

.   .   .   .

When she came to herself an hour later she lay for
a time with eyes open but vacant, eyes which saw but
conveyed no image to the ailing brain. The sun was
still low. Its shafts darting through the interstices in
the wall of the hut were laden with a million dancing
motes, which formed a shifting veil of light between
her eyes and the roof. She seemed to have been gazing
at this a whole æon when the first conscious thought
pierced her mind, and she asked herself where she was.

Where? Not in her own lodging, nor alone. This
was borne in on her. For on one side of her couch
crouched one of her women; on the other knelt the
Countess, her face hidden. In the doorway behind the
head of the bed, and so beyond the range of her vision,
were others; the low drone of voices, her father's, the

Duke's, penetrated one by one to her senses still dulled by the shock she had suffered. Something had happened then; something serious to her, or she would not lie thus surrounded with watchers on all sides of her bed. Had she been ill?

She considered this silently, and little by little began to remember: the flight to the camp, the camp life, the Duke's hut in which she had passed most of her time in the camp. Yes, she was in the Duke's hut, and that was his voice. She was lying on his couch. They had been besieged, she remembered. Had she been wounded? From under half-closed lids she scrutinised the two women beside her. The one she knew. The other must be her sister. Yes, her sister would be the first to come, the first to aid her. But it was not her sister. It was——

She knew.

She called on God and lay white and mute, shaking violently, but with closed eyes. The women rose and looked at her, and suggested remedies, and implored her to speak. But she lay cold and dumb, and only from time to time by violent fits of trembling showed that she was alive. What had she done? What had she done?

The women could make nothing of her. Nor when they had tried their utmost could her father, though he came and chid her querulously; his tone the sharper for the remorse he was feeling. He had had an hour to think; and during that hour the obedience which his less cherished daughter had ever paid him, her cheerful care of him, her patience with him, had risen before him; and, alas, with these thoughts, the memory of many an unkind word and act, many a taunt flung at her as lightly as at the dog that cumbered the hearth. To balance the account, and a little perhaps because the way in which Odette took it was an added reproach to him, he spoke harshly to the Abbess—such is human nature! But, for all the effect his words had on her, he might have addressed a stone. That which she had done thundered too loudly in her ears for another's voice to enter.

She had not loved her sister over dearly, and into such love as she had given contempt had entered largely. But she was her sister. She was her sister! Memories of childish days in the garden at Villeneuve, when Bonne had clung to her hand and run beside her, and prattled, and played, and quarrelled, and yielded to her—being always the gentler—rose in her mind; and memories of little words and acts, and of Bonne's face on this occasion and on that! And dry-eyed she shook with horror of the thing she had done. Her sister! She had done her sister to death more cruelly, more foully, more barbarously, than if she had struck her lifeless at her feet.

An age, it seemed to her, she lay in this state, cold, paralysed, without hope. Then a word caught her ear and fixed her attention.

"They have been away two hours," Joyeuse muttered, speaking low to the Vicomte. "They should be back."

"What could they do?" the Vicomte answered in a tone of despair.

"Forty swords can do much," Joyeuse answered hardily. "Were I sound I should know what to do. And that right well!"

"They started too late."

"The greater reason they should be back! Were all over they would be back."

"I have no hope."

"I have. Had they desired to kill them only," the Duke continued with reason, "the brutes had done it here, in a moment! If they did not hope to use them why carry them off?"

But the Vicomte with a quivering lip shook his head. He was still thinking—with marvellous unselfishness for him—of the daughter who had borne with him so long and so patiently. For des Ageaux there might be hope and a chance. But a woman in the hands of savages such as those he had seen in the town on the hill! He shuddered as he thought of it. Better death, better death a hundred times than that. He did not wish to see her again.

But in one heart the mention of hope had awakened hope. The Abbess raised herself on her elbow. "Who have gone?" she asked in a voice so hollow and changed they started as at the voice of a stranger. "Who are gone?" she repeated.

"All but eight spears!" the Duke answered.

"Why not all?" she cried feverishly. "Why not all?"

"Some it was necessary to keep," Joyeuse replied gently. "Not one has been kept that could go. If your sister can be saved, she will be saved."

"Too late!" the Vicomte muttered. And he shook his head.

The Abbess sank back with a groan. But a moment later she broke into a passion of weeping. The cord that had bound her heart had snapped. The first horror of the thing which she had done was passing. The first

excuse, the first suggestion that for that which she had
not intended she was not answerable, was whispering at
the threshold of her ear. As she wept in passionate, in
unrestrained abandonment, regarding none of those
about her, wonder, an almost resentful wonder, grew in
the Vicomte's heart. He had not given her credit for a
tithe, for a hundredth part of the affection she felt for her
sister! For the Duke, he, who had seen her consistently
placid, garbed in gentle dignity, and as unemotional as
she was beautiful, marvelled for a different reason. He
hailed the human in her with delight; he could have
blessed the weeping girl for every tear that proclaimed
her woman. By the depth of her love for her sister he
plumbed her capacity for a more earthly passion. He
rejoiced, therefore, as much as he marvelled.

There was one other upon whom Odette's sudden
breakdown wrought even more powerfully; and that was
the Countess. While the sister remained stunned by the
dreadful news and deaf to consolation, the poor child, who
took all to herself and mingled shame with her grief, had
not dared to speak; she had not found the heart or the
courage to speak. Awed by the immensity of the catastrophe, and the Abbess's stricken face, she had cowered
on her knees beside the bed with her face hidden; and
weeping silently and piteously, had not presumed to
trouble the other with her remorse or her useless regret.
But the tears of a woman appeal to another woman after
a fashion all their own. They soften, they invite. No
sooner, then, had Odette proclaimed herself human by
the abandonment of her grief than the Countess felt the
impulse to throw herself into her arms and implore her
forgiveness. She knew, none better, that Bonne had
suffered in her place; that in her place and because of

her fears—proved only too real—she had gone to death or worse than death; that the fault lay with herself. And that she took it to herself, that her heart was full of remorse and love and contrition—all this she longed to say to the sister. Before Odette knew what to expect or to fear, the younger woman was in her arms.

One moment. The next Odette struck her—struck her with furious, frantic rage, and flung her from her. "It is you! You have done this! You!" she cried, panting, and with blazing eyes. "You have killed her! You!"

The young girl staggered back with the mark of the Abbess's fingers crimson on her cheek. She stood an instant breathing hard, the combative instinct awakened by the blow showing in her eyes and her small bared teeth. Then she flung her hands to her face. "It is true! It is true!" she sobbed. "But I did not know!"

"Know?" the Abbess cried back relentlessly; and she was going to add other and madder and more insulting words, when her father's face of amazement checked her. She fell back sullenly, and with a gesture of despair turned her face to the wall.

The Vicomte was on his feet, shocked by what had passed. He began to babble words of apology, of excuse; while Joyeuse, ravished, strange to say, by the spirit of the woman he had deemed above anger and above passion, smiled exultant, wondering what new, what marvellous, what incomparable side of herself this wonderful woman would next exhibit. He who had exhausted all common types, all common moods, saw that he had here the quintessence both of heaven and earth. Her beauty, her meekness, her indignation, her sorrow—what an amalgam was here! And how all qualities became her!

Had Roger been there he had taken, it is possible, another view. But he was not; and presently into the halting flow of the Vicomte's words crept a murmur, a tramp of feet, a sound indescribable, but proclaiming news. He broke off. "What is it?" he said. "What is it?"

"News! Ay, news, for a hundred crowns!" the Duke answered. He moved to the door.

The Countess, her face bedabbled with tears, tears of outraged pride as well as grief, stayed her sobs and looked in the same direction. Even the Abbess caught the infection, and raising her head from the pillow listened with parted lips and staring eyes. News! There was news. But what was it? Good or bad? The Abbess, her heart standing still, bit her lip till the blood came.

The murmur of voices drew nearer.

CHAPTER XVIII.

TWO IN THE MILL.

IT is possible that Bonne did not herself know in
what proportions pity and a warmer sentiment entered
into her motives when she undertook to pass for the
Countess and assume the girl's risks. Certainly her
first thought was for the Countess; and, for the rest, she
felt herself cleared from the reproach of unmaidenliness
by the danger of the step which she was taking. Even
so, as she rode across the camp in the dusk of the first
evening, into the half pain, half pleasure that burned
her cheeks under the disguising hood entered some
heat of shame.

Not that it formed a part of her plan that des Ageaux
should discover her. To be near him unknown, to share
his peril whom she loved, while he remained unwitting,
to give and take nothing—this was the essence of the
mystery that charmed her fancy, this was the heart of
the adventure on which her affection had settled. He,
by whose side she rode, and near whom she must pass
the dark hours in a solitude which only love could rob
of its terrors, must never know what she had done for
love of him; or know it only from her lips in a delicious
future on which reason forbade her to count.

In supporting her disguise she was perfectly successful. No suspicion that the girl riding beside him in depressed silence was other than the Countess, the unwilling sharer of his exile, crossed his mind. Bonne, hooded to the eyes and muffled in her cloak, sat low-hunched on her horse. Fulbert, who was in the secret, and to whom nothing which any one could do for his adored mistress seemed odd or extraordinary, helped her to mount and dismount, and nightly lay grim and stark across the door of her hut repelling inquiry. Add the fact that the Lieutenant on his side had his delicacy. Fortune compelled the Countess into his company, forced her on his protection. It behoved him to take no advantage, and, short of an indifference that might appear brutal, to leave her as much as possible to herself.

Bonne therefore had her wish. He had no slightest suspicion who was with him. She had, too, if she needed it, proof of his honour; proof certain that if he loved the great lady, he respected her to the same extent. Love her he might, see in her a grand alliance he might; but had he been the adventurer the Abbess styled him, he had surely made more of this opportunity, more of her helplessness and her dependence. The Countess's fortune, the wide lands that had tempted Vlaye, what a chance of making them sure was his! No great lady was here, but a young girl helpless, terrified, hedged in by perils. Such an one would be ready at the first word, at a sign, to fling herself into the arms of her only friend, her only protector, and promise him all and everything if he would but save her scatheless.

Bonne had imagination enough, and perhaps jealousy enough, to picture the temptation. And finding him superior to it—so that in the sweetness of her secret nearness to him was mingled no gall—she whispered to herself that if he loved he did not love overmuch. Was it possible that he did not love—in that direction? Was it possible that he had no more feeling for the Countess than she had for him?

Perhaps for an hour Bonne was happy—happy in these thoughts. Happy while the tones of his even and courteous voice, telling her that she need fear nothing, dwelt in her ears. For that period the pleasures of fancy overcame the tremors of the real. Then —for sleep was in no haste to visit her—a chance rustle, caused by something moving in her neighbourhood, the passage it might be of a prowling dog, made her prick her ears, forced her against her will to listen, sent a creepy chill down her back. After that she was lost. She did not wish to think of such things, it was foolish to think of such things; but how flimsy were the walls of her hut! How defenceless she lay, in the midst of the savage, grisly horde, whose looks even in the daylight had paled her cheeks. How useless must two swords prove against a multitude!

She must divert her thoughts. Alas, when she tried to do so, she found it impossible. It was in vain that she chid herself, in vain that she asked herself what she was doing there, if des Ageaux' presence were no charm against fear, if with him at hand she was a coward! Always some sound, something that seemed the shuffle of feet or the whisper of murder, brought her to earth with quivering nerves; and as by the Lieutenant's desire she burned no light, she could not interpret the most innocent alarm or learn its origin. She was no coward. But to lie in the dark, expecting and trembling, and thrice in the hour to sit up bathed in perspiration—a short experience of this left her no right to despise the younger girl whose place she had taken. When at last the longed-for light pierced the thin walls, and she knew that the night was past, she knew also that she looked forward to a second with dread. And she hated herself for it.

Not that to escape a hundred such nights would she withdraw. If she suffered, what must the child have suffered? She was clear that the Countess must not go again. But during the day she was more grave than usual; more tender with her father, more affectionate to her sister. And when she rode across the camp in the evening, exciting as little suspicion as before, she carried with her, hidden in her dress, a thing that she touched now and again to assure herself of its safety. She took it with her to the rough pallet on which she lay in her clothes; and her hand clasped it under the pillow. Something of a link it seemed between her and des Ageaux, so near yet so unwitting; for as she held it her mind ran on him. It kept at bay, albeit it was a strange amulet for a woman's hand, the thought that had troubled her the previous night; and though more than once she raised herself on her elbow, fancying that she heard some one moving outside, the panic-terror that had bedewed her brow was absent. She lay down again on these occasions with her fingers on her treasure. And towards morning she slept—slept so soundly that when the light touched her eyelids and woke her, she sprang up in pleased confusion. They were calling her, the horses were waiting at the door. And in haste she wrapped herself in her travesty.

"I give you joy of your courage, Countess!" the Lieutenant said, as he came forward to assist her to mount. Fortunately Fulbert, with apparent clumsiness, interposed and did her the office. "You have slept?" des Ageaux continued, as he swung himself into his saddle and took his place by her side. "That's good," accepting her inarticulate murmur for assent. "Well, one more night will end it, I fancy. I greatly, very greatly regret," he continued, speaking with more warmth than usual, "that it has been necessary to expose you to this strain, Countess."

Again she muttered something through her closely drawn hood. Fortunately a chill, grey mist, through which the huts loomed gigantic, swathed the camp, and he thought that it was to guard herself from this that she kept her mouth covered. He suspected nothing, though, at dismounting, Fulbert interposed again. In two minutes from starting she was safe within the shelter of the Countess's hut, with the Countess's arms about her, and the child's grateful kisses warm on her cheek.

He had praised her courage! That was something; nay, it was much if he learned the truth. But he should never learn it from her, she was resolved. She had the loyalty which, if it gives, gives nobly; nor by telling robs the gift of half its virtue. She had saved the younger woman some hours of fear and misery, but at a price too high were she ever to speak and betray her confidence. No one saw that more clearly than Bonne, or was more firmly resolved to hide her share in the matter.

The third night she set out, not with indifference, since she rode by his side whose presence could never be indifferent to her, but with a heart comparatively light. If she took with her the charm which had served her so well, if it attended her to her couch and lay beneath her pillow, it was no longer the same thing to her; she smiled as she placed it there. And if her fingers closed on it in silence and darkness and she derived some comfort from it, she fell asleep with scarce a thought of the things its presence imported. For two nights she had slept little; now, worn-out, she was proof against all ordinary sounds, the rustle of a dog prowling in search of food, or the restless movements of a horse tethered near. Ay, and against other sounds as stealthy as these and more dangerous, that by-and-by crept rustling and whispering through the camp; sounds caused by a cloud of low stooping figures that moved and halted, lurked behind huts, and anon swept forward across an open space, and again lurking showed like some dark shadow of the night.

A shadow fraught, when it bared its face, with horror! For what was that cry, sharp, wild, stopped in mid-utterance?

Even as Bonne sprang up palpitating, and glared at the open doorway, the cry rose again—close by her; and the doorway melted into a press of dark forms that hurled themselves on her as soon as they were seen. She was borne back, choked, stifled; and desperately writhing, vainly striving to shriek, or to free mouth or hands from the folds of the coverlets that blinded her, she felt herself lifted up in a grasp against which it was vain to struggle. A moment, and with a shock that took away what breath was left in her, she was flung head and heels across something—across a horse; for the moment the thing felt her weight it moved under her.

Whoever rode it held her pitilessly, cruelly heedless of the pain her position caused her. She could hardly breathe, she could not see, the movement was torture; for her arms, pinned above her head, were caught in the folds of the thing that swathed her, and she could not use them to support herself. Her one thought, her only thought was to keep her senses; her one instinct to maintain her grip on the long sharp knife which had lain under her pillow; and which had become more valuable to her than the wealth of the world. The hand that had rested on it in her sleep had tightened on it in the moment of surprise. She had it, she felt it, her fingers, even while she groaned in pain, stiffened about its haft.

It was useless to struggle, but by a movement she managed at last to relieve the pressure on her side. The blood ceased to run so tumultuously to her head. And by-and-by, under the mufflings, she freed her hands, and by holding apart the edges of the stuff was able to breathe more easily, and even to learn something of what was happening about her. Abreast of her horse moved another horse, and on either side of the two ran and trotted a score of pattering naked feet, feet of the unkempt filthy Crocans from the hill-town, or of the more desperate spirits in the camp—feet of men from whom no ruth or mercy was to be expected.

Were they clear of the camp? Yes, for to one side the water of the stream glimmered between the pattering feet. As she made the discovery the other horse sidled against the one that bore her, and all but crushed her head and shoulders between their bodies. She only saved herself by lifting herself convulsively; on which the man who held her thrust her down brutally with an oath as savage as the action. She uttered a moan of pain, but it was wrung from her against her will. She would have suffered twice as much and gladly to learn what she knew now.

The horse beside her also carried double; and the after rider was a prisoner, a man with his hands bound behind him, and his feet roped under the horse's body. A prisoner? If so it could be no other than des Ageaux. As she swung, painfully, to the movement of the horse across whose withers she lay, her pendant hands lacked little of touching, under cover of the stuff, his bound wrists.

Little? Nay, nothing. For suddenly the footmen, for a reason which she did not immediately divine, fell away leftwards, and the horse that bore the other prisoner strove to turn with them. Being spurred it sidled once more against hers, and though she raised herself, her head rubbed the rider's leg. The man noticed it, patted her head, and made a jest upon it. "She wants to come to me," he said. "My burden for yours, Matthias!"

"Wait until we are through the ford and I'll talk," her captor answered. "What will you offer for her? But it is so cursed dark here"—with an oath—"I can see nothing! We had better have crossed with them at the stepping-stones and led over." As he spoke he turned his horse to the ford.

She knew then that the footmen had crossed by the stepping-stones, a hundred yards short of the ford. And she felt that Heaven itself had given her, weak as she was, this one opportunity. As the men urged their horses warily into the stream she stretched herself out stiffly, and gripping the bound hands that hung within her reach, she cut recklessly, heeding little whether she cut to the bone if she could only cut the cords. The man who held her felt her body writhing under his hand; for she knew that any instant the other horse might move out of reach. But he was thinking most of his steed's footing, he had no fear that she could wrest herself from him, and he contented himself for the moment with a curse and a threat.

"Burn the wench," he cried, "she won't be still!"

"Don't let her go!" the other answered.

"No fear! And when we have her on the hill she shall pay for this! When——"

It was his last word. The keen long knife had passed from her hands to des Ageaux', from her weak fingers to his practised grip. As the man who held her paused to peer before him—for the ford, shadowed by spreading trees, was dark as pitch—des Ageaux drove the point straight and sure into the throat above the collar-bone. The action was so sudden, so unexpected, that the man he struck had no time to cry out, but with a low gurgling moan fell forward on his burden.

His comrade who rode before the Lieutenant knew little more. Before he could turn, almost before he could give the alarm, the weapon was driven in between his shoulders, and the Lieutenant, availing himself of the purchase which his bound feet gave him, hurled him over the horse's head. Unfortunately the man had time to utter one shriek, and the cry with the splash, and the plunging of the terrified horse, bore the alarm to his comrades on the bank.

"What is it? What is the matter?" a voice asked. And a score of feet could be heard pounding hurriedly along the bank.

The Lieutenant had one moment only in which to make his choice. If he remained on the horse, which he could not restrain, for the reins had fallen, he might escape, but the girl must perish. He did not hesitate. As the frightened horse reared he cut his feet loose, and slid from it. He made one clutch at the floating reins but missed them. Before he could make a second the terrified animal was on the bank.

There remained the girl's horse. But Bonne, drenched by the dying man's blood, had flung herself off—somehow, anyhow, in irrepressible horror. As des Ageaux turned she rose, dripping and panting beside him, her nerve quite gone. "Oh, oh!" she cried. "Save me! Save me!" and she clung to him.

Alas, while she clung to him her horse floundered out of the stream, and trotted after its fellow.

The pursuers were no more than thirty yards away, and but for the deep shadow which lay on the ford must have seen them. The Lieutenant had no time to think. He caught the girl up, and as quickly as he could he waded with her to the bank from which they had entered the water. Once on dry land he set her on her feet, seized her wrist and gripped it firmly.

"Courage!" he said. "We must run! Run for your life, and if we can reach the wind-mill we may escape!"

He spoke harshly, but his words had the effect he intended. She straightened herself, caught up her wet skirt and set off with him across the road and up the bare hill-side. He knew that not far above them stood a wind-mill with a narrow doorway in which one man might make some defence against numbers. The chance was slight, the hope desperate; but he could see no other. Already the pursuers were splashing through the ford and scattering on the trail, some running up the stream, some down, some stooping cunningly to listen. To remain beside the water was to be hunted as otters are hunted.

His plan answered well at first. For a few precious instants their line of retreat escaped detection. They even increased their start, and had put fifty or sixty yards of slippery hill-side between themselves and danger before a man of sharper ears than his fellows caught the sound of a stone rolling down the slope, and drew the hue and cry in the right direction. By that time the dark form of the wind-mill was faintly visible sixty or eighty yards above the fugitives. And the race was not ill set.

But Bonne's skirt hung heavy, her knees shook; and nearer and nearer she heard the pursuers' feet. She could do no more! She must fall, her lungs were bursting! But des Ageaux dragged her on ruthlessly, and on; and now the wind-mill was not ten paces before them.

"In!" he cried. "In!" And loosing her hand, he turned, quick as a hare, the knife gleaming in his hand.

But the nearest man—the Lieutenant's ear had told him that only one was quite near—saw the action and the knife, and as quickly sheered off, to wait for his companions. The Lieutenant turned again, and in half a dozen bounds was through the low narrow doorway and in the mill tower.

He had no sword, he had only the knife, still reeking. But he made no complaint. Instead, "There were sheep penned here yesterday," he panted. "There are some bars somewhere. Grope for them and find them."

"Yes!" she said. And she groped bravely in the

darkness, though her breath came in sobs. She found the bars. Before the half-dozen men who led the chase had squeezed their courage to the attacking point, the bars that meant so much to the fugitives were in their places. Then des Ageaux bade her keep on one side, while he crouched with his knife beside the opening.

The men outside were chattering and scolding furiously. At length they scattered, and instead of charging the doorway, fired a couple of shots into it and held off, waiting for reinforcements. "Courage, we have a fair chance now," the Lieutenant muttered. And then in a different tone, "Thanks to you! Thanks to you!" with deep emotion. "Never woman did braver thing!"

"Then do you one thing for me!" she answered, her voice shaking. "Promise that I shall not fall into their hands! Promise, sir, promise," she continued hysterically, "that you will kill me yourself! I have given you my knife. I have given you all I had. If you will not promise you must give it back to me."

"God forbid!" he said. And then, "Dear Lord, am I mad? Who was it I picked up at the ford? Am I mad or dreaming? You are not the Countess?"

"I took her place," she panted. "I am Bonne de Villeneuve." The place was so dark that neither could see the other's face, nor so much as the outline of the figure.

"I might have known it," he cried impulsively. And even in that moment of danger, of discomfort, of uncertainty, the girl's heart swelled at the inference she drew from his words. "I might have known it!" he repeated with emotion. "No other woman would have done it, sweet, would have done it! But how—

I am as far from understanding as ever—how come you to be here? And not the Countess?"

"I took her place," Bonne repeated—the truth must out now. "She is very young and it was hurting her. She was ill."

"You took her place? To-night?"

"This is—the third night."

"And I"—in a tone of wonder that a second time brought the blood to her cheeks—"I never discovered you! You rode beside me all those nights—all those nights and I never knew you! Is it possible?"

She did not answer.

He was silent a moment. Then, "By Heaven, it was well for me that you did!" he murmured. "Very well! Very well! Without you where should I be now?" His eyes strove to pierce the darkness in which she crouched on the farther side of the opening, scarce out of reach of his hand. "Where should I be now? A handsome situation," he continued bitterly, "for the Governor of Périgord to be seized and hurried to a dog's death by a band of brigands! And to be rescued by a woman!"

"Is it so dreadful to you," she murmured, "to owe your life to a woman?"

"Is it so dreadful to me," he repeated in an altered tone, "to owe my life to you, do you mean? I am willing to owe all to you. You are the only woman——"
But there, even as her heart began to flutter, he stopped. He stopped and she fell to earth. "They are coming!" he muttered. "Keep yourself close! For God's sake, keep yourself close!"

"And you too!" she cried impulsively. "Your life is mine."

He did not answer: perhaps he did not hear. The

Crocans who had spent some minutes in consultation
had brought a beam up the hill. They were about to
drive it against the stout wooden bars, of which they
must have guessed the presence, since they could not
see them. The plan was not unwise; and as they
fell into a ragged line on either side of the ram, while
three skirmished forward, with a view to leaping into
the opening before the defenders could recover from
the shock, the Lieutenant's heart sank. The form of
attack was less simple than he had hoped. He had
exulted too soon.

Whether Bonne knew this or not, she acted as if she
knew it. As the leader of the assault shouted to his men
to be ready, and the men lifted the beam hip high, she
flitted across the opening, and des Ageaux felt her
fingers close upon his arm.

He did not misunderstand her: he knew that she
meant only to remind him of his promise. But at the
touch a wave of feeling, as unexpected as it was irresistible, filled the breast of the case-hardened soldier;
who, something cold by nature, had hitherto found in
his career all that he craved. At that touch the admiration and interest which had been working within him
since his talk with Bonne in the old garden at Villeneuve
blossomed into a feeling infinitely more tender, infinitely
stronger—into a love that craved return. The girl
who had saved him, who had proved herself so brave,
so true, so gentle, what a wife would she be! What a
mother of brave and loyal and gentle children, meet
sons and daughters of a loyal sire! And even as he
thought that thought and was conscious of the love
that pervaded his being, he felt her shiver against him,
and before he knew it his arm was round her, he was

clasping her to him, giving her assurance that until the end—until the end he would not let her go! He would never let her go.

And the end was not yet. For his lips in that moment which he thought might be their last found hers in the darkness, and she knew seconds of a great joy that seemed to her long as hours as she crouched against him unresisting; while the last orders of the men who sought their lives found strange echo in his words of love.

Crash! The splinters flew to right and left, the two upper bars were gone, dully the beam struck the back of the mill. But he had drawn her behind him, and was waiting with the tight-grasped knife for the man bold enough to leap through the opening. Woe betide the first, though he must keep his second blow for her. After that—if he had to strike her—there would be one moment of joy, while he fought them.

But the stormers, poor-hearted, deemed the breach insufficient. They drew back the beam, intending to break the lowest bar, which still held place. Once more they cried, "One! Two!" But not "Three!" In place of the word a yell of pain rang loud, down crashed the battering-ram, and high rose—as all fled headlong—a clamour of shrieks and curses. A moment and the thunder of hoofs followed, and mail-clad men, riding recklessly along the steep hill-side, fell on the poor naked creatures, and driving them pell-mell before them amid stern cries of vengeance, cut and hacked them without mercy.

Trembling violently, Bonne clung to her lover. "Oh, what is it? What is it?" she cried. "What is it?" Her spirits could endure no more.

"Safety!" he replied, the harder nature of the man asserting itself. "Safety, sweetheart! Hold up your head, brave! What, swooning now when all is well!"

Ay, swooning now. The word safety sufficed. She fell against him, her head dropped back.

As soon as he was assured of it, he lifted her in his arms with a new feeling of ownership. And climbing, not without difficulty, over the bar that remained, he emerged into something that, in comparison of the darkness within the mill, was light—for the day was coming. Before the door two horsemen, still in their saddles, awaited him. One was tall, the other stout and much shorter.

"Is that you, Roger?" he asked. It was not light enough to discern faces.

The shorter figure to which he addressed himself did not answer. The other, advancing a pace and reining up, spoke.

"No," he said, in a tone that at once veiled and exposed his triumph, "I am the Captain of Vlaye. And you are my prisoner."

CHAPTER XIX.

THE CAPTAIN OF VLAYE'S CONDITION.

THE four who looked to the door of the Duke's hut, and waited for the news, were not relieved as quickly as they expected. When men return with no news they are apt to forget that others are less wise than themselves; and where, with something to impart, they had flown to relieve the anxious, they are prone to forget that the negative has its value for those who are in suspense.

Hence some minutes elapsed before Roger presented himself. And when he came and they cried breathlessly, "Well, what news?" his answer was a look of reproach.

"Should I not have come at once if there had been any?" he said. "Alas, there is none."

"But you must have some!" they cried.

"Nothing," he answered, almost sullenly. "All we know is that they quarrelled over their prisoners. The hill above the ford is a shambles."

The Vicomte repressed the first movement of horror. "Above the ford?" he said. "How came they there?"

Roger shrugged his shoulders. "We don't know," he said. And then reading a dreadful question in his sister's eyes, "No, there is no sign of them," he continued. "We crossed to the old town on the hill, but found it locked and barred. The brutes mopped and mowed at us from

317

the wall, but we could get no word of Christian speech from them. They seemed to be in terror of us—which looks ill. But we had no ladders and no force sufficient to storm it, and the Bat sent me back with ten spears to make you safe here while he rode on with Charles towards Villeneuve."

"Villeneuve?" the Vicomte asked, raising his eyebrows. "Why?"

"There were tracks of a large body of horsemen moving in that direction. The Bat hopes that some of the wretches quarrelled with the others, and carried off the prisoners, and are holding them safe—with an eye to their own necks."

"God grant it!" Odette muttered in a low tone, and with so much feeling that all looked at her in wonder. Nor had the prayer passed her lips many seconds before it was answered. The sound of voices drew their looks to the door, a shadow fell across the threshold, the substance followed. As the little Countess sprang forward with a shriek of joy and the Abbess dropped back in speechless emotion, Bonne stood before them.

"He has granted her prayer," the Duke muttered in astonishment. "*Laus Deo!*" While Roger, scarcely less surprised than if a ghost had appeared before them, stared at his sister with all his eyes.

She barely looked at them. "I am tired," she said. 'Bear with me a moment. Let me sit down." Then, as if she were not content with the surprise which her words caused, "Don't touch me!" she continued, recoiling before the Countess's approach. "Wait until you have heard all. You have little cause for joy. Wait!"

The Vicomte thought his worst fears justified. "But, my child," he faltered, "is that all you have to say to us?" And to the others, in a lower voice, "She is distraught! She is beside herself. Can those wretches——"

"I escaped them," she replied, in the same dull tones. "They have done me no harm. Let me rest a minute before I tell you."

Roger stayed the inquiry after the Lieutenant which was on his lips. It was evident to him and to all that something serious had happened: that the girl before them was not the girl who had ridden away yesterday with so brave a heart. But, freed from that fear of the worst which the Vicomte had entertained, they knew not what to think. Some signs of shock, some evidences of such an experience as she had passed through, were natural; but the reaction should have cast her into their arms, not withheld her—should have flung her weeping on her sister's shoulder, not frozen her in this strange apathy.

The Abbess, indeed, who had recovered from the paroxysm of gratitude into which Bonne's return had cast her, eyed her sister with the shadow of a terror. Conscience, which makes cowards of us all, suggested to her an explanation of her sister's condition, adequate and more than adequate. A secret alarm kept her silent therefore: while the young Countess, painfully aware that she had escaped all that Bonne had suffered, sank under new remorse. For the others, they did not know what to think: and stealthily reading one another's eyes, felt doubts that they dared not acknowledge. Was it possible, notwithstanding her denial, that she had suffered ill-treatment?

"Perhaps it were better," the Duke muttered, "if we left mademoiselle in the care of her sister?"

But low as he spoke, Bonne heard. She raised her

head wearily. "This does not lie with her," she said.

The Abbess breathed more freely. The colour came back to her cheeks. She sat upright, relieved from the secret fear that had oppressed her. "With whom, then, child?" she asked in her natural voice. "And why this mystery? But we—have forgotten"—her voice faltered, "we have forgotten," she repeated hardily, "M. des Ageaux. Is he safe?"

"It is of him I am going to speak," Bonne replied heavily.

"He has not—he has not fallen."

"He is alive."

"Thank Heaven for that!" Roger cried with heartiness, his eyes sparkling. "Has he gone on with Charles and the Bat?"

"No."

"Then where is he?" She did not answer, and, startled, Roger looked at her, the others looked at her. All waited for the reply.

"He is in the Captain of Vlaye's hands," she said slowly. And a gentle spasm, the beginning of weeping which did not follow, convulsed her features. "He saved me," she continued in trembling tones, "from the peasants, only to fall into M. de Vlaye's hands."

"Well, that was better!" Roger answered.

Her lips quivered, but she did not reply. Perhaps she was afraid of losing that control over herself which it had cost her much to compass.

But the Vicomte's patience, never great, was at an end. He saw that this was going to prove a troublesome matter. Hence his sudden querulousness. "Come, come, girl," he said petulantly. "Tell us what has happened, and no nonsense! Come, an end, I say! Tell us what has happened from the beginning, and let us have no mysteries!"

She began. In a low voice, and with the same tokens of repressed feeling, she detailed what had happened from the moment of the invasion of her hut by the peasants to the release of des Ageaux and the struggle in the river-bed.

"He owes us a life there," the Vicomte exclaimed, while Roger's eyes beamed with pride.

She paid no heed to her father's interjection, but continued the story of the succeeding events—the assault on the mill, and the arrival of Vlaye and his men.

"Who in truth and fact saved your lives then," Roger said. "I forgive him much for that! It is the best thing I have heard of him."

"He saved my life," Bonne replied, with a faint but perceptible shudder. She kept her eyes down as if she dared not meet their looks.

"But the Lieutenant's too," the Vicomte objected. "You told us that he was alive."

"He is alive," she murmured. And the trembling began to overpower her. "Still alive."

"Then——"

"But to-morrow at sunrise—" her voice shook with the pent-up misery, the long-repressed pain of her three hours' ride from Vlaye—"to-morrow at sunrise, he—he must die!"

"What?"

The word came from one who so far had been silent. And the Duke rising from his place by the door stood upright, supporting his weakened form against the wall of the hut. "What?" he repeated in a voice that in spite of his weakness rang clear and loud with anger. "He will not dare!"

"M. de Vlaye?" the Vicomte muttered in a discomfited tone, "I am sure—I am sure he will not—dream of such a thing. Certainly not!"

"M. de Vlaye says that if—if——" Bonne paused as if she could not force her pallid lips to utter the words —"he says that at sunrise to-morrow he will hang him as the Lieutenant last week hung one of his men."

"For murder! Clear proved murder!" Roger cried in an agitated voice. "Before witnesses!"

"Then by my salvation I will hang him!" Joyeuse retorted in a voice which shook with rage; and one of those frantic, blasphemous passions to which all of his race were subject overcame him. "I will hang him high as Haman, and like a dog as he is!" He snatched a glove from a peg on the wall beside him, and flung it down with violence. "Give him that, the miserable upstart!" he shrieked, "and tell him that as surely as he keeps his word, I, Henry of Joyeuse, who for every spear he boasts can set down ten to that, will hang him though God and all His saints stand between! Give it him! Give it him! On foot or on horse, in mail or in shirt, alone or by fours, I am his and will drag his filthy life from him! Go!" he continued, turning, his eyes suffused with rage, on Roger. "Or bid them bring me my horse and arms! I will to him now, now, and pluck his beard! I——"

"My lord, my lord," Roger remonstrated. "You are not fit."

Joyeuse sank back exhausted on his stool. "For him and such as he more than fit," he muttered. "More than fit—coward as he is!" But his tone and evident weakness gave him the lie. He looked feebly at his hand, opening and closing it under his eyes. "Well, let him wait," he said. "Let him wait awhile. But if he does this, I will kill him as surely as I sit here!"

"Ay, to be sure!" the Vicomte chimed in. "But unless I mistake, my lord, we are on a false scent. There was something of a condition unless I am in error. This silly girl, who is more moved than is needful, said —if, if—that M. de Vlaye would hang him, *unless*—— What was it, child, you meant?"

She did not answer.

It was Roger whose wits saved her the necessity. His eyes were sharpened by affection; he knew what had gone before. He guessed that which held her tongue.

"We must give up the Countess!" he cried in generous scorn. "That is his condition. I guess it!"

Bonne bowed her head. She had felt that to state the condition to the helpless, terrified girl at whose expense it must be performed was a shame to her; that to state it as if she craved its performance, expected its performance, looked for its performance, was a thing still baser, a thing dishonouring to her family, not worthy a Villeneuve—a thing that must smirch them all and rob them of the only thing left to them, their good name.

Yet if she did not speak, if she did not make it known? If she did not do this for him who loved her and whom she loved? If he perished because she was too proud to crave his life, because she feared lest her cloak be stained ever so little? That, too, was—she could not face that.

She was between the hammer and the anvil. The

question, what she should do, had bowed her to the
ground. She had seen as she rode that she must choose
between honour and life; her lover's life, her own
honour!

Meanwhile, "Give up the Countess?" the Vicomte
muttered, staring at his son in dull perplexity. "Give
up the Countess? Why?"

"Unless she is surrendered," Roger explained in a
low voice, "he will carry out his threat. He goes back,
sir, to his old plan of strengthening himself. It is very
clear. He thinks that with the Countess in his power
he can make use of her resources, and by their means
defy us."

"He is a villain!" the Vicomte cried, touched in his
tenderest point.

"Villain or no villain, I will cut his throat!" Joyeuse
exclaimed, his rage flaming up anew. "If he touch but
a hair of des Ageaux' head—who was wounded striving
to save my brother's life at Coutras, as all the world
knows—I will never leave him nor forsake him till I
have his life!"

"I fear that will not avail the Lieutenant," Roger
muttered despondently.

"No. No, it may not," the Vicomte agreed, "but
we cannot help that." He, in truth, was able to con-
template the Lieutenant's fate without too much vexation, or any overweening temptation to abandon the
Countess. "We cannot help it, and that is all that
remains to be said. If he will do this he must do it.
And when his own time comes his blood be upon his
own head!"

But the girl who shared with Bonne the tragedy of
the moment had something to say. Slowly the Countess

stood up.   Timid she was, but she had the full pride of her race, and shame had been her portion since the discovery of the thing Bonne had done to save her. The smart of the Abbess's fingers still burned her cheek and seared her pride.   Here, Heaven-sent, as it seemed, was the opportunity of redressing the wrong which she had done to Bonne and of setting herself right with the woman who had outraged her.

The price which she must pay, the costliness of the sacrifice did not weigh with her at this moment, as it would weigh with her when her blood was cool.   To save Bonne's lover stood for something; to assert herself in the eyes of those who had seen her insulted and scorned stood for much.

"No," she said with simple dignity.   "There is something more to be said, M. le Vicomte.   If it be a question of M. des Ageaux' life, I will go to the Captain of Vlaye."

"You will go?" the Vicomte cried, astounded. "You, mademoiselle?"

"Yes," she replied slowly, and with a little hardening of her childish features.   "I will go.   Not willingly, God knows!   But rather than M. des Ageaux should die, I will go."

They cried out upon her, those most loudly who were least interested in her decision.   But the one for whose protest she listened—Roger—was silent.   She marked that; for she was a woman, and Roger's timid attentions had not passed unnoticed, nor, it may be, unappreciated.   And the Abbess was silent.   She, whose heart this latest proof of her lover's infidelity served but to harden, she whose soul revolted from the possibility that the deed which she had done to sepa-

rate Vlaye from the Countess might cast the girl into
his arms, was silent in sheer rage. Into far different
arms had she thought to cast the Countess! Now, if
this were to be the end of her scheme, the devil had
indeed mocked her!

Nor did Bonne speak, though her heart was full. For
her feelings dragged her two ways, and she would not,
nay, she could not speak. That much she owed to her
lover. Yet the idea of sacrificing a woman to save a
man shocked her deeply, shocked alike her womanli-
ness and her courage; and not by a word, not by so
much as the raising of a finger would she press the
girl, whose very rank and power left her friendless
among them, and made her for the time their sport.
But neither—though her heart was racked with pity
and shame—would she dissuade her. In any other
circumstances which she could conceive, she had cast
her arms about the child and withheld her by force.
But her lover—her lover was at stake. How could she
sacrifice him? How prefer another to him? And after
all—she, too, acknowledged, she, too, felt the force of
the argument—after all, the Countess would be only
where she would have been but for her. But for her the
young girl would be already in Vlaye's power; or worse,
in the peasants' hands. If she went now she did but
assume her own perils, take her own part, stand on her
own feet.

"I shall go the rather," the Countess continued coldly,
using that very argument, "since I should be already
in his power had I gone myself to the peasants' camp!"

"You shall not go! You cannot go!" the Vicomte
repeated with stupid iteration.

"M. le Vicomte," she answered, "I am the Countess

of Rochechouart." And the little figure, the infantine face, assumed a sudden dignity.

"It is unbecoming!"

"It becomes me less to let a gallant gentleman die."

"But you will be in Vlaye's power."

"God willing," she replied, her spirit still sustaining her. Was not the Abbess, whom she was beginning to hate, looking at her?

Ay, looking at her with such eyes, with such thought, as would have overwhelmed her could she have read them. Bitter indeed, were Odette's reflections at this moment—bitter! She had stained her hands and the end was this. She had stooped to a vile plot, to an act that might have cost her sister her life, and with this for reward. The triumph was her rival's. Before her eyes and by her act this silly chit, with heroics on her lips, was being forced into his arms! And she, Odette, stood powerless to check the issue of her deed, impotent to interfere, unable even to vent the words of hatred that trembled on her lips.

For the Duke was listening, and she had still enough prudence, enough self-control, to remember that she must not expose her feelings in his presence. On him depended what remained: the possibility of vengeance, the chances of ambition. She knew that she could not speak without destroying the image of herself which she had wrought so patiently to form. And even when he added his remonstrances to her father's, and hot words imputing immodesty rose to the Abbess's lips—words that must have brought the blood to the Countess's cheeks and might have stung her to the renunciation of her project, she dared not utter them. She swallowed her passion, and showed only a cold mask of surprise.

Not that the Duke said much. For after a while, "Well, perhaps it is best," he said. "What if she pass into his power! It is better a woman marry than a man die. We can make the one a widow; whereas to bring the other to life would puzzle the best swordsman in France!"

The Vicomte persisted. "But there is no burden laid on the Countess to do this," he said. "And I for one will be no party to it! What? Have it said that I surrendered the Countess of Rochechouart who sought my protection?"

"Sir," the girl replied, trembling slightly, "no one surrenders the Countess save the Countess. But that the less may be said to your injury, my own people shall attend me thither, and——"

"They will avail you nothing!" the Vicomte replied with a frankness that verged on brutality. "You do not understand, mademoiselle. You are scarcely more than a child, and do not know to what you are going. You have been wont to be safe in your own resources, and now, were a fortnight given you to gather your power, you could perhaps make M. de Vlaye tremble. But you go from here, in three hours you will be there, and then you will be as much in his power, despite your thirty or forty spears, as my daughter was this morning!"

"I count on nothing else," she said. But her face burned. And Bonne, who suffered with her, Bonne who was dragged this way and that, and would and would not, in whom love struggled with pity and shame with joy, into her face, too, crept a faint colour. How cowardly, oh, how cowardly seemed her conduct! How base in her to buy her happiness at the price of this child's misery! To ransom her lover at a woman's cost! It was a bargain tnat in another's case she had repudiated with scorn, with pride, almost with loathing. But she loved, she loved. And who that loved could hesitate? One here and there perhaps, some woman of a rare and noble nature, cast in a higher mould than herself. But not Bonne de Villeneuve.

Yet the word she would not utter trembled on her tongue. And once, twice the thought of Roger shook her. He, too, loved, yet he bore in silence to see his mistress delivered, tied and bound, to his rival!

How, she asked herself, how could he do it, how could he suffer it? How could he stand by and see this innocent depart to such a fate, to such a lot!

That puzzled her. She could understand the acquiescence of the others; of her sister, whom M. de Vlaye's inconstancy must have alienated, of Joyeuse, who was under an obligation to des Ageaux, of the Vicomte, who, affecting to take the Countess's part, thought in truth only of himself. But Roger? In his place she felt that she must have spoken whatever came of it, that she must have acted whatever the issue.

Yet Roger, noble, generous Roger—for even while she blamed him with one half of her mind, she blessed him with the other—stood silent.

Silent, even when the Countess with a quivering lip and a fleeting glance in his direction—perhaps she, too, had looked for something else at his hands—went out, her surrender a settled thing; and it became necessary to give orders to her servants, to communicate with the Bat, and to make such preparations as the withdrawal of her men made necessary. The Duke's spears were expected that day or the next, but it needed no sharp eye to discern that Vlaye's capture of the Lieutenant had taken much of the spirit out of the attack. The Countess's men must now be counted on the Captain of Vlaye's side; while the peasants, weakened by the slaughter which Vlaye had inflicted on them at the mill, and by the distrust which their treachery must cause, no longer stood ·for much in the reckoning. It was possible that the Lieutenant's release might reanimate the forces of the law, that a second attempt to use the peasants might fare better than the first, that Joyeuse's aid might in time place des Ageaux in a position to cope with his opponent. But these were possibilities only, and the Vicomte for one put no faith in them.

He was utterly disgusted, indeed, with the turn which things were taking. Nor was his disgust at any time greater than when he stood an hour later and viewed the Countess and her escort marching out of the camp. If his life since Coutras had been obscure and ignoble, at least it had been safe. While his neighbours had suffered at the Captain of Vlaye's hands, he had been favoured. He had sunk something of his pride, and counted in return on an alliance for his daughter, solid if not splendid. Now, by the act of this meddling Lieutenant—for he ignored Vlaye's treatment both of his daughter and the Countess—all was changed. He had naught to expect now but Vlaye's enmity; Villeneuve would no longer be safe for him. He must go or he must humble himself to the ground. He had taken, he had been forced by his children to take, the wrong side in the struggle. And the time was fast approaching when he must pay for it, and smartly.

CHAPTER XX.

THE ABBESS MOVES.

THAT Bonne failed to read the dark scroll of her sister's thoughts need not surprise us; since apart from the tie of blood the two women had nothing in common. But that she failed also to interpret Roger's inaction; that, blaming herself for an acquiescence which love made inevitable, she did not spare him, whom love should have moved in the opposite direction —this was more remarkable. For a closer bond never united brother and sister. But misery is a grand engrosser. She had her lover in her thoughts, the poor girl whom she sacrificed on her mind; and she left the Duke's quarters without that last look at her brother which might have enlightened her.

Had she questioned him he had discovered his mind. She did not, and she had barely passed from sight before he was outside and had got a fresh horse saddled. One thing only it was prevented his leaving the camp in advance of the Countess, whose people were not ready. His foot was raised to the stirrup when he bethought him of this thing. He left the horse in charge of a trooper and hurried back to the Duke's quarters, found him alone and put his question.

"You made a man fight the other night against his

will," he said, his head high. "Tell me, my lord, how
I can do the same thing."

The Duke stared, then laughed. "Is it that you
want?" he answered. "Tell me first whom it is you
would fight, my lad?"

"The Captain of Vlaye."

"Ah?"

"You said a while ago," Roger continued, his eyes
sparkling, "that you would presently make her a
widow. Better a widow before she is wed, I say!"

The Duke smiled whimsically. "Sits the wind in
that quarter?" he answered. "You have no mind to
see her wed at all, my lad? That is it, is it? I had
some notion of it."

"Tell me how I can make him fight," Roger replied,
sticking to his question and refusing even to blush.

"Tell me how I can get the moon!" Joyeuse answered,
but not unkindly. "Why should he risk his life to rid
himself of you, who are no drawback to him? Tell me
that! Or why should he surrender the advantage of
his strong place and his four hundred spears to enter
the lists with a man who is naught to him?"

"Because if he does not I will kill him where I find
him!" Roger replied with passion. And the mode of
the day, which was not nice in the punctilios of the
duel, and forgave the most irregular assault if it were
successful, which cast small blame on Guise for the
murder of St. Pol, or on Montsoreau for the murder
of Bussy, justified the threat. "I will kill him!" he
repeated. "Fair or foul, light or dark——"

"He shall not wed her!" the Duke cried in a mocking tone and with an extravagant gesture. But in
truth the raillery was on the surface only. The lad's

spirit touched the corresponding note in his own nature. None the less he shook his head. "Brave words, brave words, young man," he continued; "but you are not Vitaux, who counted his life for nothing, and whose sword was a terror to all."

"But if I count my life for nothing?"

"Ay, if! If!"

"And why should I not?" Roger retorted, his soul rising to his lips. "Tell me, my lord, why should I count it for more? What am I, the son of a poor gentleman, misshapen, rough, untutored, that I should hold my life dear? That I should spare it, and save it, as a thing so valuable? What have I in prospect of all the things other men look to? Glory? See me! Fine I should be," with a bitter laugh covering tears, "in a triumph, or marching up the aisle to a Te Deum! Court favour? Ay, I might be the dwarf in a masque or the fool in motley! Naught besides! Naught besides, my lord! And for love?" He laughed still more bitterly. "I tell you my own father winces when he sees me! My own sister and my own brother— well, they are blind perhaps. They, they only, and old Solomon, and the woman who nursed me and dropped me—see in me a man like other men. Leave them out, and, as I live, until this man came——"

"Des Ageaux?"

"Des Ageaux—until he came and spoke gently to me and said, 'do this, and do that, and you shall be as Gourdon or as Guesclin!'—even he could not promise me love—as I live, till then no man pitied me or gave me hope! And shall I let him die to save my stunted life?"

"But it is not the saving him that is in question,"

the Duke replied gently, and with respect in his tone. He was honestly moved by this unveiling of poor Roger's thoughts. "She saved him."

"And I'll save her," Roger replied with fervour. "I will save her though I die a hundred deaths. For she, too——"

He paused. The Duke looked at him, a spice of humour mingling with his sympathy. "She, too, sees in you a man like other men," he said, "I suppose?"

"She pitied me," Roger answered. "No more; she pitied me, my lord! What more could she do, being what she is? And I being what I am?" His chin sank on his breast.

The Duke nodded kindly. "May-be," he said. "Less likely things have happened." And then, "But what will you do?" he asked.

"Go with her and see him, take him aside, and if he will fight me, well! And if he will not, I will strike him down where he stands!"

"But that will not save des Ageaux."

"No?"

"No! On the contrary, it will be he," Joyeuse retorted somewhat grimly, "who will pay for it. Do you not see that?"

"Then I will wait," Roger replied, "until he is released."

"And then," the Duke asked, still opposing, though the man and the plan were alike after his own heart, "what of the Countess? M. de Vlaye dead, who will protect her? His men——"

"They would not dare!" Roger cried, trembling. "They would not dare!"

"Well, perhaps not," the Duke answered, after a moment's thought. "Perhaps not. Probably his lieutenant would protect her, for his own sake. And des Ageaux free would be worth two hundred men to us. Not that, if I were well, he would be in question. But I am but half a man, and we need him!"

"You shall have him," Roger answered, his eyes glittering. "Have no doubt of it! But advise me, my lord. Were it better I escorted her to the gate and sought entrance later, after he had released des Ageaux? Or that I kept myself close until the time came?"

"The time? For what?"

The speaker was the Abbess. Unseen by the two men, she had that moment glided across the threshold. The pallor of her features and the brightness of her eyes were such as to strike both; but differently. To the Duke these results of a night passed in vivid emotions, and of a morning that had crowned her schemes with mockery, only brought her into nearer keeping with the dress she wore—only enhanced her charms. To her brother, on the other hand, who now hated Vlaye with a tenfold hatred, they were grounds for suspicion— he knew not why. But not even he came nearer to guessing the truth. Not even he dreamt that behind that mask were passions at work which, had they discovered them, would have cast the Duke into a stupor deeper than any into which his own mad freaks had ever flung a wondering world. As it was, the Duke's eyes saw only the perfection of womankind; the lily of the garden, drooping, pale, under the woes of her frailer sisters. Of the jealousy with which she contemplated the surrender of her rival to her lover's power, much less of the step which that surrender was pressing upon her, he caught no glimpse.

"The time for what?" the Duke repeated, with looks courteous to the point of reverence. "Ah—pardon, my sister, but we cannot take you into our counsel. Men must sometimes do things it is not for saints to know or women to witness."

"Saints!" The involuntary irony of her tone must have penetrated ears less dulled by prejudgment. "Saints!" and then, "I am no saint, my lord," she said modestly.

"Still," he answered, "it were better you did not know, mademoiselle. It is but a plan by which we think it possible that we may yet get the better of M. de Vlaye and save the child before—before, in fact——"

"Ay?" the Abbess said, a flicker of pain in her eyes. "Before—I understand.".

"Before it be too late."

"Yes. And how?"

The Duke shook his head with a smile meant to propitiate. "How?" he repeated. "That—pardon me—that is the point upon which—we would fain be silent."

"Yet you must not be silent," she replied. "You must tell me." And pale, almost stern, she looked from one to the other, dominating them. "You must tell me," she repeated. "Or perhaps," fixing Roger with a glance keen as steel, "I know already. You would save her by killing him. It is of that you are thinking. It is for that your horse is waiting saddled by the gate. You would ride after her, and gain access to him—and——"

"She has not started?" Roger exclaimed.

"She started ten minutes ago," the Abbess answered coldly. "Nay, stay!" For Roger was making for the door. "Stay, boy! Do you hear?"

"I cannot stay!"

"If you do not stay you will repent it all your life!" the Abbess made answer in a voice that shook even his resolution. "And she all hers! Ha! that stays you?" with a gleam of passion she could not restrain. "I thought it would. Now, if you will listen, I have something to say that will put another complexion on this."

They gazed expectant, but she did not at once continue. She stood reflecting deeply; while each of her listeners regarded her after his knowledge of her; Roger sullenly and with suspicion, doubting what she would be at, the Duke in admiration, expecting that with which gentle wisdom might inspire her.

Secretly she was heart-sick, and the sigh which she could not restrain declared it. But at last, "There is no need of violence," she said wearily. "No," addressing Roger, who had raised his hand in remonstrance, "hear me out before you interrupt me. How will the loss of a minute harm you? Or of five or ten? I repeat, there is no need of violence. Heaven knows there has been enough! We must go another way to work to release her. It is my turn now."

"I would rather trust myself," Roger muttered; but so low that the words, frank to rudeness, did not reach Joyeuse's ears.

"Yet you must trust me," she answered. "Do so, trust me, and follow my directions, and I will take on myself to say that before nightfall she shall be free."

"What are we to do?" the Duke asked.

"You? Nothing. I, all. I must take her place, as she has taken M. des Ageaux'."

For an instant they were silent in sheer astonishment. Then, "But M. de Vlaye may have something to say to that!" Roger ejaculated before the Duke could find words. The lad spoke on impulse. He knew a little and suspected more of the lengths to which Vlaye's courtship of his sister had gone.

If she had not put force on herself, she had flung him a retort that must have opened the Duke's eyes. Instead, "I shall not consult M. de Vlaye," she replied coldly. "I have visited him on various occasions, and we are on terms. My appearance in Vlaye, seeing that the Abbey of Vlaye is but a half-league from the town, will cause no surprise. Once in the town, if I can enter the castle and gain speech of the Countess, she may escape in my habit."

"I hate this shifting and changing!" Roger grumbled.

"But if it will save her?"

"Ay, but will it?" Roger returned, shrugging his shoulders. He suspected that her aim was to save M. de Vlaye rather than the Countess. "Will it? Can you, in the first place, get speech of her?"

"I think I can," the Abbess answered quietly. "Many of the men know me. And I will take with me Father Benet, who is at the Captain of Vlaye's beck and call. He will serve me within limits, if a friend be needed. I shall wear my robes, and though she is shorter and smaller I see no reason why she should not pass out in them in the twilight or after dark."

"But what of you?" the Duke asked, staring much.

"I shall remain in her place."

"Remain in her place?" Joyeuse said slowly, in the

voice he would have used had Our Lady appeared before him. "You will dare that for her?"

A faint colour stole into the Abbess's cheeks. "It is my expiation," she murmured modestly. "I struck her —God forgive me!"

"But——"

"And I run no risk. M. de Vlaye knows me, and this"—with a gesture which drew attention to her conventual garb—"will protect me."

The Duke gazed at the object of his adoration in a kind of rapture, seeing already the wings on her shoulders, the aureole about her head. "Mademoiselle, you will do that?" he cried. "Then you are no woman! You are an angel!" In his enthusiasm he knelt—not without difficulty, for he was still weak—and kissed her hand. To him the thing seemed an act of pure heroism, pure self-denial, pure good-doing.

But Roger, who knew more of his sister's nature and past history, and whose knowledge left less room for fancy's gilding, stood lost in gloomy thought. What did she mean? Was she going as friend or enemy? Influence with Vlaye she had, or lately had; but, the Countess released, in what a position would she, his sister, stand? Could he, could her father, could her friends let her do this thing?

Yet the chance—to a lover—was too good to reject; the position, moreover, was too desperate for niceties. The thought that she was going, not for the sake of the Countess, but of the Captain of Vlaye, the suspicion that she was not unwilling to take the Countess's place and the Countess's risks, occurred to him. But he thrust, he strove to thrust the suspicion and the thought from him. Her motive and her meaning, even though that motive and meaning were to save the Captain of Vlaye, were small things beside the Countess's safety.

"At any rate I shall go with you," he said at length, and with more of suspicion than of gratitude in his tone. " When will you be ready?"

"I think it likely that he will have bidden Father Benet to be with him at sunset," she answered. " If we are at the priest's, therefore, an hour earlier, it should do."

"And for safe-conduct?"

"I will answer for that," she replied with boldness, "so far as M. de Vlaye's men are concerned."

The answer chafed Roger anew. Her reliance on her influence with Vlaye and Vlaye's people—he hated it; and for an instant he hesitated. But in the end he swallowed his vexation: had he not made up his mind to shut his eyes? And the three separated after a few more words relating to the arrangements to be made. The Duke, standing with a full heart in the doorway, watched her to her quarters, marked the grace of her movements, and in his mind doomed the Captain of Vlaye to unspeakable deaths if he harmed her; while she, as she passed away, thought—but we need not enter into her thoughts. She was doing this, lest a worse thing happen; doing it in a passion of jealousy, in a frenzy of disgust. But she had one consolation. She would see the Captain of Vlaye! She would see the man she loved. Through the dark stuff of her thoughts that prospect ran like a golden thread.

Roger, on the other hand, should have been content. He should have been more than satisfied, as an hour later he rode beside her down the river valley to the chapel beside the ford, and thence to the open country about Villeneuve. For if things were still dark, there was a prospect of light. A few hours earlier he had despaired; he had seen no means of saving the woman he adored, save at the expense of his own life. Now he had hope and a chance, now he had prospects, now he might look, if fortune favoured him, to be her escort into safety before the sun rose again.

Surely, then, he should have been content; yet he was not. Not even when after a journey of four hours the two, having passed Villeneuve, gained without misadventure the summit of that hill on the scarped side of which the Countess had met with her first misfortune. From that point, they and the two armed servants who followed them could look down upon the wide green valley that framed the town of Vlaye, and that, somewhat lower, opened into the wide plain of the Dronne. They could discern the bridge over the river; they could almost count the red roofs of the small town that crept up from the water to the coronet of grey walls and towers that crowned all. Those walls and towers basking in the sunshine were the eyrie that lorded it over leagues of country seen and unseen—the hawk's nest, the *plebis flagellum*, as the old chronicler has it. They might, in sight of those towers, count the preliminaries over and all but the supreme risk run.

For quite easily they might have fallen in with Vlaye's people on the road and been taken; or with M. de Vlaye himself, and with that there had been an end of the plan. But they had escaped these dangers. And yet Roger was not content; still he rode with a gloomy brow and pinched lips. The longer he thought of his sister's plan, the more he suspected and the less he liked it. There was in it a little which he did not understand, and more which he understood too well. His sister and M. de

Vlaye! He hated the collocation; he hated to think
that she must be left, willingly and by her own act, in
the adventurer's power; and this at a moment when disappointment would aggravate a temper tried by the
attack on him and by the part which the Vicomte had
played in it. On what did she depend for her safety,
for her honour, for all that she put wantonly at stake?
On his respect? His friendship? Or his love?

"I will take her place," she had said. Could it be that
she was willing, that she desired, to take it altogether?
Was she, after the rebuffs, after the scornful and con-
tumelious slight which M. de Vlaye had put upon her,
willing still to seek him, willing still to be in his power?

It seemed so. Certainly it could not be denied that
she was seeking him, and that he, her brother, was es-
corting her. In that light people would look upon his
action.

The thought stung him, and he halted midway on the
woodland track that descended the farther side of the
hill. His face wore a mixture of shame and appeal—
with ill-humour underlying both. "See here, Odette,"
he said abruptly, "I do not see the end of this."

Though she raised her eyebrows contemptuously, a
faint tinge of colour crept into her face.

"I thought," she replied, "that the end was to save
this little fool who is too weak to save herself!"

"But you?"

"Oh, for me?" contemptuously. "Take no heed of
me. I am of other stuff, and can manage my own affairs."

"You think so," he retorted. "But the Captain of
Vlaye, he, too, is of other stuff."

"Do you fancy I am afraid of M. de Vlaye?" she

answered. And her eyes flashed scorn on him. "You may be! You should be!" with a glance which marked his deformity and stabbed the sense of it deep into his heart. "How should you be otherwise, seeing that in no circumstances could you be a match for him! But I? I say again that I am of other stuff."

"All the same," he muttered darkly, "I would not go on——"

"Would not go on?" she retorted in mockery. "Not with your sweet Countess in danger? Not with the dear light of your eyes in Vlaye's arms? Not go on? Oh, brave lover! Oh, brave man! Not go on, and your Countess, your pretty Countess——"

"Be silent!" he cried. She stung him to rage.

"Ah! We go back then?"

But he could not face that, he could not say yes to that; and, defeated, he turned in dumb sullen anger and resumed the road.

Necessarily the danger of arrest increased as they approached the town. The last mile, which brought them to the bridge over the river, was traversed under the eyes of the castle; it would not have surprised Roger had they been met and stopped long before they came to the town gate. But the Captain of Vlaye, it seemed, held the danger still remote, and troubled his followers with few precautions. The place lay drowsing in the late heat of the summer afternoon. It was still as the dead, and though their approach was doubtless seen and noted, no one issued forth or challenged them. Even the men who lounged in the shade of the low-browed archway—that still bore the scutcheon of its ancient lords—contented themselves with a long stare and a sulky salute. The bridge passed, a narrow street paved and steep, and overhung by ancient houses of brick and timber, opened before them. It led upwards in the direction of the castle, but after pursuing it in single file some fifty paces, the Abbess turned from it into a narrow lane that brought them in a bow-shot—for the town was very small—to the wall again. This was their present destination. For crowded into an angle of the wall under the shadow of one of the old brick watch-towers stood the chapel and cell that owned the lax rule of M. de Vlaye's chaplain, Father Benet.

CHAPTER XXI.

THE CASTLE OF VLAYE.

ROGER had little faith in the priest's power, and less in his willingness to aid them. But at worst he was not to be kept in suspense. By good luck, Father Benet was walking at the moment of their arrival in his potherb garden. As they dismounted, they espied the Father peeping at them between the tall sunflowers and budding hollyhocks; his ruddy face something dismayed and fallen, and his mien that of a portly man caught in the act of wrong-doing. Finding himself detected, he came forward with an awkward show of joviality.

"Welcome, sister," he said. "There is naught the matter at the Abbey, I trust, that I see you thus late in the day?"

"No, the matter is here," the Abbess replied, with a look in her eyes that told him she knew all. "And we are here to see about it. Let us in, Father. The time is short, for at any moment your master"—she indicated the castle by a gesture—"may hear of our arrival and send for us."

"I am sure," the priest answered glibly, "that anything that I can do for you, sister——"

345

She cut him short. "No words, no words, but let us in!" she said sharply. And when with pursed lips and a shrug of resignation he had complied, and they stood in the cool stone-floored room—communicating by an open door with the chapel—in which he received his visitors, she came with the same abruptness to the point.

"At what hour are you going up to the castle?" she asked.

He tried to avoid her eyes. "To the castle?" he repeated.

"Ay," she said, watching him keenly. "To the castle. Are there more castles than one? Or first, when were you there last, Father?"

His look wandered, full of calculation. "Last?" he said. "When was I at the castle last?"

"The truth! The truth!" she cried impatiently.

He chid her, but with a propitiatory smile akin to those which the augurs exchanged. "Sister! Sister!" he said. "*Nil nisi verum clericus!* I was there no more than an hour back."

"And got your orders? And got your orders, I suppose?" she repeated with rude insistence. "Out with it, Father. I see that you are no more easy than I am!"

He flung out his hands in sudden abandonment. "God knows I am not!" he said. "God knows I am not! And that is the truth, and I am not hiding it. God knows I am not! But what am I to do? He is a violent man—you know him!—and I am a man of peace. I must do his will or go. And I am better than nothing! I may "—there was a whine in his voice—"I may do some good still. You know that, sister. I may do some good. I baptise. I bury. But if I go, there is no one."

"And if you go, you are no one," she answered keenly. "For your suffragan has you in no good favour, I am told. So that if you go you happen on but a sackcloth welcome. So it is said, Father. I know not if it be said truly."

"Untruly! Untruly!" he protested earnestly. "He has never found fault with me, sister, on good occasion. But I have enemies, all men have enemies——"

"You are like to make more," Roger struck in, with a dark look.

The priest wrung his hands. "I know! I know!" he said. "He carries it too highly. Too highly! They say that he has caught the King's governor now, and has him in keeping there."

"It is true."

"Well, I have warned him; he cannot say I have not!"

"And what said he to your warning?" the Abbess asked with a sneer.

"He threatened me with the stirrup leathers."

"And you are now to marry him?"

He turned a shade paler. "You know it?" he gasped.

"I know it, but not the time," she answered. And as he hesitated, silent and appalled, "Come," she continued, "the truth, Father. And then I will tell you what I am going to do."

"At sunset," he muttered, "I am to be there."

"Good," she said. "Now we know. Then you will go up an hour earlier. And I shall go with you."

He protested feebly. He knew something of that which had gone before, something of her history, something of her passion for the Captain of Vlaye; and he was sure that she was not bent on good. "I dare not!" he said, "I dare not, sister! You ask too much."

"Dare not what?" the Abbess retorted, bending her handsome brows in wrath. "Dare not go one hour earlier?"

"But you—you want to go?"

"If I go with you, what is that to you?"

"But——"

"But what, Father, but what?"

"You want something of me?" he faltered. He was not to be deceived. "Something dangerous, I know it!"

"I want your company to the door of the room where she lies," the Abbess replied. "That is all. You have leave to visit her? Do not"—overwhelming him with swift fierce words—"deny it. Do not tell me that you have not! Think you I do not know you, Father? Think you I do not know how well you are with him, how late you sit with him, how deep you drink with him, when he lacks better company? And that this—though you are frightened now, and would fain be clear of it, knowing who she is—is the thing which you have vowed to do for him a hundred times and a hundred times to that, if it would help him!"

"Never! Never!" he protested, paler than before.

"Father," she retorted, stooping forward and speaking low, "be warned. Be warned! Get you a foot in the other camp while you may! You are over-well fed for the dry crust and the sack bed of the bishop's prison! You drink too much red wine to take kindly to the moat puddle! And that not for months, but for years and years! Have you not heard of men who

lay forgotten, ay, forgotten even by their gaoler at
last, until they starved in the bishop's prison? The
bishop's prison, Father!" she continued cruelly. "Who
comes out thence, but the rats, and they fat? Who
comes out thence——"

"Don't! Don't!" the priest cried, his complexion
mottled, his flabby cheeks trembling with fear of the
thing which her words called up, with fear of the thing
that had often kept him quaking in the night hours.
"You will not do it?"

"I?" she answered drily. "No, not I perhaps. But
is a Countess of Rochechouart to be abducted so lightly,
or so easily? Has she so few friends? So poor a kin-
dred? A cousin there is, I think—my lord Bishop of
Comminges—who has one of those very prisons. And,
if I mistake not, she has another cousin, who is in
Flanders now, but will know well how to avenge her
when he returns."

"What is it you want me to do?" he faltered.

"Go with me to her door—that I may gain admis-
sion. Then, whether you go to him or not, your silence, for one half-hour."

"You will not do her any harm?" he muttered.

"Fool, it is to do her good I am here."

"And that is all? You swear it?"

"That is all."

He heaved a deep sigh. "I will do it," he said. He
wiped his brow with the sleeve of his cassock. "I will
do it."

"You are wise," she replied, "and wise in time,
Father, for it is time we went. The sun is within an
hour of setting." Then, turning to Roger, who had
never ceased to watch the priest as a cat watches a

mouse, "The horses may wait in the lane or where you please," she said. "They are hidden from the castle where they stand, and perhaps they are best there. In any case"—with a meaning glance—"I return to this spot. Expect me in half an hour. After that, the rest is for you to contrive. I wash my hands of it."

The words in which he would have assented stuck in the lad's throat. He could not speak. She turned again to the priest. "One moment and I am ready," she said. "Have you a mirror?"

"A mirror?" he exclaimed in astonishment.

"But of course you have not," she replied. She looked about her an instant, then with a quick step she passed through the doorway into the chapel. There her eye had caught a polished sheet of brass, recording in monkish Latin the virtues of that member of the old family who had founded this " Capella extra muros," as ancient deeds style it. She placed herself before the tablet, and paying as little heed to her brother or the priest— though they were within sight—as to the sacred emblems about her, or the scene in which she stood, she cast back her hood, and drew from her robes a small ivory case. From this she took a morsel of sponge, and a tiny comb, also of ivory; and with water taken from the stoup beside the door, she refreshed her face, and carefully recurled the short ringlets upon her forehead. With a pencil drawn from the same case, she retouched her eyelashes and the corners of her eyes, and with deft fingers she straightened and smoothed the small ruff about her neck. Finally, with no less care, she drew the hood of her habit close round her face, and after turning herself about a time or two before the mirror went back to the others. They had not taken their eyes off her.

"Come," she said. And she led the way out without a second word, passed by the waiting horses and the servants, and, attended by the reluctant Father, walked at a gentle pace along the lane towards the main street.

The priest went in fear, his stout legs trembling under him. But until the two reached a triangular open space, graced by an Italian fountain, and used, though it sloped steeply, for a market site, the street they pursued was not exposed to view from the castle. Above the market-place, however, the road turned abruptly to the left, and, emerging from the houses, ascended between twin mounds, of which the nearer bore the castle, and the other, used on occasion as a tilt-yard, was bare. The road ascended the gorge between the two, then wound about, this time to the right, and gained the summit of the unoccupied breast; whence, leaping its own course by a drawbridge, it entered the grey stronghold that on every other side looked down from the brow of a precipice—here on the clustering roofs of the town, and there, and there again, on the wide green vale and silvery meanders of the Dronne.

Looking to the south, where the valley opened into a plain, the eye might almost discern Coutras—that famous battlefield that lies on the Dronne bank. Northward it encountered the wooded hills beyond which lay Villeneuve, and the town of Barbesieux on the great north road, and the plain towards Angoulême. Fairer eyrie, or stronger, is scarce to be found in the width of three provinces.

Until they came to the market-place the Abbess and her unwilling companion had little to fear unless they met M. de Vlaye himself. As far as others were con-

cerned, Father Benet's coarse, plump face, albeit less
ruddy than ordinary, was warrant enough to avert both
suspicion and inquiry. But thence onwards they walked
in full view not only of the lounge upon the ramparts
which the Captain of Vlaye most affected at the cool
hour, but of a dozen lofty casements from any one of
which an officious sentry or a servant might mark their
approach and pass word of it. Father Benet pursued
this path as one under fire. The sun was low, but at its
midday height it had not burned the stout priest more
than the fancied fury of those eyes. The sweat poured
down his face as he climbed and panted and crossed himself in a breath.

"Believe me, you are better here than in the bishop's
prison," his companion said, to cheer him.

"But he will see us from the ramparts," he groaned,
not daring to look up and disprove the fact. "He will
see us! He will meet us at the gate."

"Then it will be my affair," the Abbess answered.

"We are mad—stark, staring mad!" he protested.

"You were madder to go back," she said.

He looked at her viciously, as if he wished her dead.
Fortunately they had reached the narrow defile under
the bridge, and a feverish longing to come to an end of
the venture took place of all other feelings in the priest's
breast. Doggedly he panted up the Tilt Mound, as it
was called, and passed three or four groups of troopers,
who were taking the air on their backs or playing at
games of chance. Thence they crossed the drawbridge.
The iron-studded doors, with their clumsy grilles, above
which the arms of the old family still showed their
quarterings, stood open; but in the depths of the low-
browed archway, where the shadows were beginning to

gather, lounged a dozen rogues whose insolent eyes the Abbess must confront.

But she judged, and rightly, that the priest's company would make that easy which she could not have compassed so well alone, though she might have won entrance. The men, indeed, were surprised to see her, and stared; some recognised her with respect, others with grins half-knowing, half-insolent. But no one stepped forward or volunteered to challenge her entrance. And although a wit, as soon as her back was turned, hummed

> " Je suis amoureuse,
> Malheureuse,
> J'ai perdu mon galant!"

and another muttered, "Oh, la, la, the bridesmaid!" with a wink at his fellows, they were soon clear of the gate and the starers, and crossing the wide paved court, that, bathed in quiet light, was pervaded none the less by an air of subdued expectation. Here a man cleaned a horse or his harness, there a group chatted on the curb of the well; here a white-capped cook showed himself, and there, beside the entrance, a couple teased the brown bear that inhabited the stone kennel, and on high days made sport for the Captain of Vlaye's dogs.

Vlaye's quarters and those of his household and officers lay in the wing on the left, wnich overlooked the town; his men were barracked and the horses stabled in the opposite wing. The fourth side, facing the entrance, was open, but was occupied by a garden raised two steps above the court and separated from it, first by a tall railing of curiously wrought iron, and secondly by a row of clipped limes, whose level wall of foliage hid the pleasaunce from the come-and-go of the vulgar.

The Abbess knew the place intimately, and she felt

no surprise when the Father, in place of making for the common doorway on the left, which led into M. de Vlaye's wing, bore across the open to the floriated iron gates of the garden. He passed through these and turned to the left along the cool green lime walk, which was still musical with the hum of belated bees.

"She is in the demoiselles' wing then?" the Abbess murmured. She had occupied those rooms herself on more than one occasion. They opened by a door on the garden and enjoyed a fair and airy outlook over the Dronne. As she recalled them and the memories they summoned up her features worked.

"Where else should she be—short of this evening?" Father Benet answered, with full knowledge of the sting he inflicted. Her secret was no secret from him. "But I need come no farther," he added, pausing awkwardly.

"To the door," she answered firmly. "To the door! That is the bargain."

"Well, we are there," he said, halting when he had taken another dozen paces, which brought them to the door in the garden end of the left wing. "Now, I will retire by your leave, sister."

"Knock!"

He complied with a faltering hand, and the moment he had done so he turned to flee, as if the sound terrified him. But with an unexpected movement she seized his wrist in her strong grasp, and though he stammered a remonstrance, and even resisted her weakly, she held him until the opening door surprised them.

A grim-faced woman looked out at them. "To see the Countess," the Abbess muttered. Then to the priest, as she released him, "I shall not be more than ten minutes, Father," she continued. "You will wait for me, perhaps. Until then!"

She nodded to him after a careless, easy fashion, and the door closed on her. In the half-light of the passage within, which faded tapestry and a stand of arms relieved from utter bareness, the woman who had admitted her faced her sourly. "You have my lord's leave?" she asked suspiciously.

"Should I be here without it?" the Abbess retorted in her proudest manner. "Be speedy, and let me to her. My lord will not be best pleased if the priest be kept waiting."

"No great matter that," the woman muttered rebelliously. But having said it she led the visitor up the stairs and ushered her into the well-remembered room. It was a spacious, pleasant chamber, with a view of the garden, and beyond the garden of the widening valley spread far beneath. Nothing of the prison-house hung about it, nor was it bare or coldly furnished.

The woman did not enter with her, but the gain was not much. For the Abbess had no sooner crossed the threshold than she discovered a second gaoler. This was a young waiting-woman, who, perched on a stool within the door, sat eyeing her prisoner with something of pity and more of ill-humour. The little Countess, indeed, was a pitiful sight. She lay, half-crouching, half-huddled together, in the recess of the farther window, on the seat of which she hid her face in the abandonment of despair. Her loosened hair flowed dishevelled upon her neck and shoulders; and from minute to minute a dry, painful sob—for she was not weeping—shook the poor child from head to foot.

The Abbess, after one keen glance, which took in

every particular, from the waiting-woman's expression
to the attitude of the captive, nodded to the attendant.
Then for a moment she did not speak. At last, "She
takes it ill?" she muttered under her breath.

The other slightly shrugged her shoulders. "She
has been like that since he left her," she whispered.
Whether the words and the movement expressed more
pity, or more contempt, or more envy, it was hard
to determine; for all seemed to meet in them. "She
could not take it worse."

"I am here to mend that," the Abbess rejoined.
And she moved a short way into the room. But there
she came to a stand. Her eyes had fallen on a pile of
laces and dainty fabrics arranged upon one of the seats
of the nearer window. Her face underwent a sudden
change; she seemed about to speak, but the words stuck
in her throat. At last "Those are for her?" she said.

"Ay, but God knows how I am to get them on," the
girl answered in a low tone. "She is such a baby! But
there it is! Whatever she is now, she'll be mistress
to-morrow, and I—I am loath to use force."

"I will contrive it," the Abbess replied, a light in
her averted eyes. "Do you leave us. Come back in a
quarter of an hour, and if I have succeeded take no
notice. Take no heed, do you hear," she continued,
turning to the girl, "if you find her dressed. Say
nothing to her, but let her be until she is sent for."

"I am only too glad to let her be."

"That is enough," the Abbess rejoined sternly. "You
can go now. Already the time is short for what I have
to do."

"You will find it too short, my lady, unless I am mistaken," the waiting-woman answered under her breath.

But she went. She was glad to escape; glad to get rid of the difficulty. And she went without suspicion. How the other came to be there, or how her interest lay in arraying this child for a marriage with her lover —these were questions which the girl proposed to put to her gossips at a proper opportunity; for they were puzzling questions. But that the Abbess was there without leave—the Abbess who not a month before had been frequently in Vlaye's company, hawking and hunting, and even supping—to the scandal of the convent, albeit no strait-laced one nor unwont to make allowance for its noble mistresses—that the Abbess was there without the knowledge of her master she never suspected. It never for an instant entered the woman's mind.

Meanwhile Odette, the moment the door closed on the other, took action. Before the latch ceased to rattle her hand was on the Countess's shoulder, her voice was in her ear. "Up, girl, if you wish to be saved!" she hissed. "Up, and not a word!"

The Countess sprang up—startled simultaneously by hand and voice. But once on her feet she recoiled. She stood breathing hard, her hands raised to ward the other off. "You?" she cried. "You here?" And shaking her head as if she thought she dreamed, she retreated another step. Her distrust of the Abbess was apparent in every line of her figure.

"Yes, it is I," Odette answered roughly. "It is I."

"But why? Why are you here? Why you?"

"To save you, girl," the Abbess answered. "To save you—do you hear? But every moment is of value. Hold your tongue, ask no questions, do as I tell you, and all may be well. Hesitate, and it will be too late. See, the sun still shines on the head of that tall tree! Before it leaves that tree you must be away from here. Is it true that he weds you to-night?"

The other uttered a cry of despair. "And for naught!" she said. "Do you understand, for naught! He has not let him go! He lied to us! He has not released him! He holds me, but he will not release him."

"And he will not!" the Abbess replied, with something like a jeer. "So, if you would not give all for naught, listen to me! Put some wrapping about your shoulders, and a kerchief on your head to heighten you, and over these my robes and hood. And be speedy! On your feet these"—with a rapid movement she drew from some hiding-place in her garments a pair of thick-soled shoes. "Hold yourself up, be bold, and you may pass out in my place."

"In your place?" the girl stammered, staring in astonishment.

The Abbess had scant patience with her rival's obtuseness. "That is what I said," she replied, with a look that was not pleasant in her eyes.

The Countess saw the look, and, fearful and doubting, hung back. She could not yet grasp the position. "But you!" she murmured. "What of you?"

"What is that to you?"

"But——"

"Fear nothing for me!" the Abbess cried vehemently. "Think only of yourself! Think only of your own safety. I"—with scorn—"am no weak thing to suffer and make no cry. I can take care of myself. But, there"—impatiently—"we have lost five minutes! Are you going to do this or not? Are you going to stay here, or are you going to escape?"

"Oh, escape!   Escape, if it be possible!" the Countess answered, shuddering.   "Anywhere, from him!"

"You are certain?"

"Oh, yes, yes!   But it is not possible!   He is too clever."

"We will see if that be so," the Abbess answered, smiling grimly.   And taking the matter into her own hands, she began to strip off her robe and hood.

That decided the girl.   Gladly would she have learned how the other came to be there, and why and to what she trusted.   Gladly would she have asked other things. But the prospect of escape—of escape from a fate which she dreaded the more the nearer she saw it—took reality in view of the Abbess's actions.   And she, too, began.   Escape?   Was it possible?   Was it possible to escape?   With shaking fingers she snatched up a short cloak, and wrapped it about her shoulders and figure, tying it this way and that.   She made in the same way a turban of a kerchief, and stood ready to clothe herself.   By this time the Abbess's outer garments lay on the floor, and in three or four minutes the travesty, as far as the younger woman was concerned, was effected.

Meantime, while they both wrought, and especially while the Countess, stooping, stuffed the large shoes and fitted them and buckled them on, the Abbess never ceased explaining the remainder of the plan.

"Go down the stairs," she said, "and if you have to speak mutter but a word.   Outside the door, turn to the right until you come to the gate in the iron railing. Pass through it, cross the court, and go out through the great gate, speaking to no one.   Then follow the road, which makes a loop to the left and passes under itself.   Descend by it to the market-place, and then to the right until you see the town gate fifty paces before you. At that point take the lane on the left, and a score of yards will show you the horses waiting for you, and with them a friend. You understand? Then I will repeat it."

And she did so from point to point in such a way and so clearly that the other, distracted as she was, could not but learn the lesson.

"And now," the Abbess said, when all was told, "give me something to put on." Her beautiful arms and shoulders were bare. "Something—anything," she continued, looking about her impatiently. "Only be quick! Be quick, girl!"

"There is only this," the Countess answered, producing her heavy riding-cloak. "Unless"—doubtfully—"you will put on those." She indicated the little pile of wedding-clothes, of dainty silk and lace and lawn, that lay upon the window-seat.

"Those!" the Abbess exclaimed. And she looked at the pile as at a snake. "No, not those! Not those! Why do you want me to put on those? Why should I?" with a suspicious look at the other's face.

"If you will not——"

"Will not?" —violently. "No, I will not. And why do you ask me? But I prate as badly as you, and we lose time. Are you ready now? Let me look at you." And feverishly, while she kicked off her own shoes and donned the riding-cloak and drew its hood over her head, she turned the Countess about to assure herself that the disguise was tolerable—in a bad light.

Then, "You will do," she said roughly, and she pushed the girl from her. "Go now. You know what you have to do."

"But you?" the little Countess ventured. Words of gratitude were trembling on her lips; there were tears in her eyes. "You—what will you do?"

"You need not trouble about me," the Abbess retorted. "Play your part well; that is all I ask."

"At least," the Countess faltered, "let me thank you." She would have flung her arms round the other's neck.

But the Abbess backed from her. "Go, silly fool!" she cried savagely, "unless, after all, you repent and want to keep him."

The insult gave the needed fillip to the other's courage. She turned on her heel, opened the door with a firm hand, and, closing it behind her, descended the stairs. The waiting-maid and the grim-faced woman were talking in the passage, but they ceased their gossip on her appearance, and turned their eyes on her. Fortunately the place was ill-lit and full of shadows, and the Countess had the presence of mind to go steadily down to them without word or sign.

"I hope mademoiselle has succeeded," the waiting-woman murmured respectfully. "It is not a business I favour, I am sure."

The Countess shrugged her shoulders—despair giving her courage—and the grim-faced woman moved to the door, unlocked it, and held it wide. The escaping one acknowledged the act by a slight nod, and, passing out, she turned to the right. She walked, giddily and uncertainly, to the open gate in the railing, and then, with some difficulty—for the shoes were too large for her—she descended the. two steps to the court. She began to cross the open, and a man here and there, raising his head from his occupation, turned to watch her.

CHAPTER XXII.

A NIGHT BY THE RIVER.

THE Countess knew that her knees were shaking under her. The gaze, too, of the men who watched was dreadful to her. She felt her feet slipping from the shoes; she felt the kerchief, that, twined in her hair, gave her height, shift with the movement; she felt her limbs yielding. And she despaired. She was certain that she could not pass; she must faint, she must fall. Then the scornful words of the woman she had left recurred to her, stung her, whipped her courage once more; and, before she was aware of it, she had reached the gateway. She was conscious of a crowd of men about her, of all eyes fixed on her, of a jeering voice that hummed:

> " Amoureuse,
> Malheureuse,
> J'ai perdu mon galant!"

and—and then she was beyond the gate! The cool air blowing in the gorge between the two breasts fanned her burning cheeks—never breeze more blessed!—and with hope, courage, confidence all in a moment revived and active, she began to descend the winding road that led to the town.

There were men lounging on the road, singly or in groups, who stared at her as she passed; some with thinly-veiled insolence, others in pure curiosity. But they did not dare to address her; though they thought, looking after her, that she bore herself oddly. And she came unmolested to the spot where the road passed under the drawbridge. Here for an instant sick fear shook her anew. Some of the men in the gateway had come out to watch her pass below; she thought that they came to call her back. But save for a muttered jeer and the voice of the jester repeating slyly;

> " Malheureuse,
> Amoureuse,
> A perdu son galant!"

no one spoke; and as pace by pace her feet carried her from them, carried her farther and farther, her courage returned, she breathed again. She came at the foot of the descent, to the carved stone fountain and the sloping market-place. She took, as ordered, the road that fell away to the right, and in a twinkling she was hidden by the turn from the purview of the castle.

She ventured then—the town seemed to stifle her— to move more quickly; as quickly as her clumsy shoes would let her move on stones sloping and greasy. Here and there a person, struck by something in her walk, turned to take a second glance at her; or a woman in a low doorway bent curious eyes on her as she came and went. She could not tell whether she bred suspicion in them or not, or whether she seemed the same woman —but a trifle downcast—who had passed that way before. For she dared not look back nor return their gaze. Her heart beat quickly, and more quickly as the end drew near. Success that seemed within her grasp impelled her at last almost to a run. And then —she was round the corner in the side lane that had been indicated to her, and she saw before her the horses and the men gathered before the chapel gate. And Roger—yes, Roger himself, with a face that worked strangely and words that joy stifled in his throat, was leading her to a horse and lending his knee to mount her. And they were turning, and moving back again into the street.

"There is only the gate now," he muttered, "only the gate! Courage, mademoiselle! Be steady!"

And the gate proved no hindrance. Though not one moment of all she had passed was more poignant, more full of choking fear, than that which saw them move slowly through, under the gaze of the men on guard, who seemed for just one second to be rising to question them. Then—the open country! The open country with its air, its cool breezes, its spacious evening light and its promise of safety. And quick on this followed the delicious moment when they began to trot, slowly at first and carelessly, that suspicion might not be awakened; and then more swiftly, and more swiftly, urging the horses with sly kicks and disguised spurrings until the first wood that hid them saw them pounding forward at a gallop, with the Countess's robe flapping in the wind, her kerchief fallen, her hair loosened. Two miles, three miles flew by them; they topped the wooded hill that looked down on Villeneuve. Then, midway in the descent on the farther side, they left the path at a word from Roger, plunged into the scrub and rode at risk—for it was dark—along a deer-trail with which he was familiar. This brought them presently, by many windings and through thick brush, to a spot where the brook was fordable. Thence, in silence, they plodded and waded and jogged along damp woodland ways and through watery lanes that attended the brook to its junction with the river.

Here, at length, in the lowest bottom of the Villeneuve valley, they halted. For the time they deemed themselves safe; since night had fallen and hidden their tracks, and Vlaye, if he followed, would take the ordinary road. It had grown so dark indeed, that until the moon rose farther retreat was impossible; and though the river beside which they stood was fordable at the cost of a wetting, Roger thought it better to put off the attempt. One of the servants, the man at the Countess's bridle, would have had him try now, and rest in the increased security of the farther bank. But Roger demurred, for a reason which he did not explain; and the party dismounted where they were, in a darkness which scarcely permitted the hand to be seen before the face.

"The moon will be up in three hours," Roger said. "If we cannot flee they cannot pursue. Mademoiselle," he continued, in a voice into which he strove to throw a certain aloofness, "if you will give me your hand," he felt for it, "there is a dry spot here. I will break down these saplings and put a cloak over them, and you may get some sleep. You will need it, for the moment the moon is up we must ride on."

The snapping of alder boughs announced that he was preparing her resting-place. She felt for the spot, but timidly, and he had to take her hand again and place her in it.

"I fear it is rough," he said, "but it is the best we can do. For food, alas, we have none."

"I want none," she answered. And then hurriedly, "You are not going?"

"Only a few yards."

"Stay, if you please. I am frightened."

"Be sure I will," he answered. "But we are in little danger here."

He made a seat for himself not far from her, and he sat down. And if she was frightened he was happy, though he could not see her. He was in that stage of love when no familiarity has brought the idol too near, no mark of favour has declared her human, no sign of preference has fostered hope. He had done her, he was doing her a service; and all his life it would be his to recall her as he had seen her during their flight—battered, blown about, with streaming hair and draggled clothes, the branches whipping colour into her cheeks, her small brown hand struggling with her tangled locks. In such a stage of love to be near is enough, and Roger asked no more. He forgot his sister's position, he forgot des Ageaux' danger. Listening in the warm summer night to the croaking of the frogs, he gazed unrebuked into the darkness that held her, and he was content.

Not that he had hope of her, or even in fancy thought of her as his. But this moment was his, and while he lived he would possess the recollection of it. All his life he would think of her, as the monk in the cloister bears with him the image of her he loved in the world; or as the maid remembers blamelessly the lover who died between betrothal and wedding, and before one wry word or one divided thought had risen to dim the fair mirror of her future.

Alas, of all the dainty things in the world, too delicate in their nature to be twice tasted, none is more evanescent than this first worship; this reverence of the lover for her who seems rather angel than woman, framed of a clay too heavenly for the coarse touch of passion.

Once before, in the hay-field, he had tried to save her, and he had failed. This time—oh, he was happy when he thought of it—he would save her. And he fell into a dream of a life—impossible in those days, however it might have been in the times of Amadis of Gaul, or Palmerin of England—devoted secretly to her service and her happiness; a beautiful, melancholy dream of unrequited devotion, attuned to the solemnity of the woodland night with its vast spaces, its mysterious rustlings and gurgling waters. Those who knew Roger best, and best appreciated his loyal nature, would have deemed him sleepless for the Lieutenant's sake—whose life hung in the balance; or tormented by thoughts of the Abbess's position. But love is of all things the most selfish; and though Roger ground his teeth once and again as Vlaye's breach of faith occurred to him, his thoughts were quickly plunged anew in a sweet reverie, in which she had part. The wind blew from her to him, and he fancied that some faint scent from her loosened hair, some perfume of her clothing came to him.

It was her voice that at last and abruptly dragged him from his dream. "Are you not ashamed of me?" she whispered.

"Ashamed?" he cried, leaping in his seat.

"Once—twice, I have failed," she went on, her voice trembling a little. "Always some one must take my place. Bonne first, and now your other sister! I am a coward, Monsieur Roger. A coward!"

"No!" he said firmly. "No!"

"Yes, a coward. But you do not know," she con-

tinued in the tone of one who pleaded, "how lonely I
have been, and what I have suffered. I have been
tossed from hand to hand all my life, and mocked
with great names and great titles, and been with them
all a puppet, a thing my family valued because they
could barter it away when the price was good—just
as they could a farm or a manor! I give orders, and
sometimes they are carried out, and sometimes not—
as it suits," bitterly. "I am shown on high days as
Madonnas are shown, carried shoulder high through
the streets. And I am as far from everybody, as
lonely, as friendless," her voice broke a little, "as
they! What wonder if I am a coward?"

"You are tired," Roger answered, striving to control
his voice, striving also to control a mad desire to throw
himself at her feet and comfort her. "You will feel
differently to-morrow. You have had no food, mademoiselle."

"You too?" in a voice of reproach.

He did not understand her, and though he trembled
he was silent.

"You too treat me as a child," she continued. "You
talk as if food made up for friends and no one was lonely
save when alone! Think what it must be to be always
alone, in a crowd! Bargained for by one, snatched at
by another, fawned on by a third, a prize for the boldest!
And not one—not one thinking of me!" pathetically.
And then, as he rose, "What is it?"

"I think I hear some one moving," Roger faltered.
"I will tell the men!" And without waiting for her
answer, he stumbled away. For, in truth, he could listen
no longer. If he listened longer, if he stayed, he must
speak! And she was a child, she did not know. She

did not know that she was tempting him, trying him, putting him to a test beyond his strength. He stumbled away into the darkness, and steering for the place where the horses were tethered he called the men by name.

One answered sleepily that all was well. The other, who was resting, snored. Roger, his face on fire, hesitated, not knowing what to do. To bid the man who watched come nearer and keep the lady company would be absurd, would be out of reason; and so it would be to bid him stand guard over them while they talked. The man would think him mad. The only alternative, if he would remove himself from temptation, was to remain at a distance from her. And this he must do.

He found, therefore, a seat a score of paces away, and he sat down, his head between his hands. But his heart cried—cried pitifully that he was losing moments that would never recur—moments on which he would look back all his life with regret. And besides his heart, other things spoke to him; the warm stillness of the summer night, the low murmur of the water at his feet, the whispering breeze, the wood-nymphs—ay, and the old song that recurred to his memory and mocked him—

> " Je ris de moi, je ris de toi,
> Je ris de ta sottise!"

Here, indeed, was his opportunity, here was such a chance as few men had, and no man would let slip. But he was not as other men—there it was. He was crook-backed, poor, unknown! And so thinking, so telling himself, he fixed himself in his resolve, he strove to harden his heart, he covered his ears with his hands. For she was a child, a child! She did not understand!

He would have played the hero perfectly but for one fatal thought that presently came to him—a thought fatal to his rectitude. She would take fright! Left alone, ignorant of the feeling that drove him from her— what if she moved from the place where he had left her, and lost herself in the wood, or fell into the river, or— and just then she called him.

"Monsieur Roger! Where are you?"

He went back to her slowly, almost sullenly; partly in surrender to his own impulse, partly in response to her call. But he did not again sit down beside her. "Yes," he said. "You are quite safe, mademoiselle. I shall not be out of earshot. You are quite safe."

"Why did you go away?"

"Away?" he faltered.

"Are you afraid of me?" gently.

"Afraid of you?" He tried to speak gaily.

"Pray," she said in a queer, stiff tone, "do not repeat all my words. I asked if you were afraid of me, Monsieur Roger?"

"No," he faltered, "but—but I thought that you would rather be alone."

"I?" in a tone that went to poor Roger's heart. "I, who have told you that I am always alone? Who have told you that I have not"—her voice shook—"a friend—one real friend in the world!"

"You are tired now," Roger faltered, finding no other words than those he had used before.

"Not one real friend!" she repeated piteously. "Not one!"

He was not proof against that. He bent towards her in the darkness—almost in spite of himself. "Yes, one," he said, in a voice as unsteady as hers. "One you have, mademoiselle, who would die for you and ask not a look in return! Who would set, and will ever set, your honour and your happiness above the prizes of the world! Who asks only to serve you at a distance, by day and dark, now and always! If it be a comfort for you to know that you have a friend, know it! Know——"

"I do not know," she struck in, in a voice both incredulous and ironical, "where I am to find such an one save in books! In the Seven Champions or in Amadis of Gaul—perhaps. But in the world—where?"

He was silent. He had said too much already. Too much, too much!

"Where?" she repeated.

Still he did not answer.

Then, "Do you mean yourself, Monsieur Roger?" She spoke with a certain keenness of tone that was near to, ay, that threatened offence.

He stood, his hands hanging by his side. "Yes," he faltered. "But no one knows better than myself that I cannot help you, mademoiselle. That I can be no honour to you. For the Countess of Rochechouart to have a crook-backed knight at the tail of her train— it may make some laugh. It may make women laugh. Yet——" he paused on the word.

"Yet what, sir?"

"While he rides there," poor Roger whispered, "no man shall laugh."

She was silent quite a long time, as if she had not heard him. Then,

"Do you not know," she said, "that the Countess of Rochechouart can have but one friend—her husband?"

He winced. She was right; but if that was her feeling, why had she complained of the lack of friends?

"Only one friend, her husband," the Countess continued softly. "If you would be that friend—but perhaps you would not, Roger? Still, if you would, I say, you must be kind to her ever and gentle to her. You must not leave her alone in woods on dark nights. You must not slight her. You must not,"—she was half laughing, half crying, and hanging towards him in the darkness, her childish hands held out in a gesture of appeal, irresistible had he seen it—but it was dark, or she had not dared—"you must not make anything too hard for her!"

He stepped one pace from her, shaking.

"I dare not! I dare not!" he said.

"Not if I dare?" she retorted gently. "Not if I dare, who am a coward? Are you a coward, too, that when you have said so much and I have said so much you will still leave me alone and unprotected, and—and friendless? Or is it that you do not love me?"

"Not love you?" Roger cried, in a tone that betrayed more than a volume of words had told. And beaten out of his last defence by that shrewd dilemma, he threw his pride to the winds; he sank down beside her, and seized her hands and carried them to his lips—lips that were hot with the fever of sudden passion. "Not love you, mademoiselle? Not love you?"

"So eloquent!" she murmured, with a last flicker of irony. "He does not even now say that he loves me. It is still his friendship, I suppose, that he offers me."

"Mademoiselle!"

"Or is it that you think me a nun because I wear this dress?"

He convinced her by means more eloquent than all the words lovers' lips have framed that he did not so think her; that she was the heart of his heart, the desire of his desire. Not that she needed to be convinced. For when the delirium of his joy began to subside he ventured to put a certain question to her—that question which happy lovers never fail to put.

"Do you think women are blind?" she answered. "Did you think I did not see your big eyes following me in and out and up and down? That I did not see your blush when I spoke to you and your black brow when I walked with M. des Ageaux? Dear Roger, women are not so blind! I was not so blind that I did not know as much before you spoke as I know now."

And in the dark of the wood they talked, while the water glinted slowly by them and the frogs croaked among the waving weeds, and in the stillness under the trees the warmth of the summer night and of love wrapped them round. It was an hour between danger and danger, made more precious by uncertainty. For the moment the world held for each of them but one other person. The Lieutenant's peril, Bonne's suspense, the Abbess—all were forgotten until the moon rose above the trees and flung a chequered light on the dark moss and hart's-tongue and harebells about the lovers' feet. And with a shock of self-reproach the two rose to their feet.

They gave to inaction not a moment after that. With difficulty and some danger the river was forded by the pale light, and they resumed their journey by devious ways until, mounting from the lower ground that fringed the water, they gained the flank of the hills. Thence, crossing one shoulder after another by paths known to Roger, they reached the hill at the rear of the Old Crocans' town. In passing by this and traversing the immediate neighbourhood of the peasants' camp lay their greatest danger. But the dawn was now at hand, the moon was fading; and in the cold, grey interval between dawn and daylight they slipped by within sight of the squalid walls, and with the fear of surprise on them approached the gate of the camp. Nor, though all went well with them, did they breathe freely until the challenge of the guard at the gate rang in their ears.

After that there came with safety the sense of their selfishness. They thought of poor Bonne, who, somewhere in the mist-wrapped basin before them, lay waiting and listening and praying. How were they to face her? with what heart tell her that her lover, that des Ageaux, still lay in his enemy's power. True, Vlaye had gone back on his word, and, in face of the Countess's surrender, had refused to release him; so that they were not to blame. But would Bonne believe this? Would she not rather set down the failure to the Countess's faint heart, to the Countess's withdrawal?

"I should not have come!" the girl cried, turning to Roger in great distress. "I should not have come!" Her new happiness fell from her like a garment, and, shivering, she hung back in the entrance and wrung her hands. "I dare not face her!" she said. "I dare not, indeed!" And, "Wait!" to the men who wished to hurry off and proclaim their return. "Wait!" she said imperatively.

The grey fog of the early morning, which had sheltered their approach and still veiled the lower parts of the camp, seemed to add to the hopelessness of the news they bore. Roger himself was silent, looking at the waiting men, and wondering what must be done. Poor Bonne! He had scarcely thought of her—yet what must she be feeling? What had he himself felt a few hours before?

"Some one must tell her," he said presently. "If you will not——"

"I will! I will!" she answered, her lip beginning to tremble.

Roger hesitated. "Perhaps she is sleeping," he said; "and then it were a pity to rouse her."

But the Countess shook her head in scorn of his ignorance. Bonne would not be sleeping. Sleeping, when her lover had not returned! Sleeping, at this hour of all hours, the hour M. de Vlaye had fixed for —for the end! Sleeping, when at any moment news, the best or the worst, might come!

And Bonne was not sleeping. The words had scarcely passed Roger's lips when she appeared, gliding out of the mist towards them, the Bat's lank form at her elbow. Their appearance in company was, in truth, no work of chance. Six or seven times already, braving the dark camp and its possible dangers, she had gone to the entrance to inquire; and on each occasion—so strong is a common affection—the Bat had appeared as it were from the ground, and gone silently with her, learned in silence that there was no news, and seen her in silence to her quarters again. The previous afternoon she had got some rest. She had lain some hours in the deep sleep of exhaustion; and longer in a heavy doze, conscious of the dead weight of anxiety, yet resting in body.

Save for this she had not had strength both to bear

and watch. As it was, deep shadows under her eyes told of the strain she was enduring; and her face, though it had not lost its girlish contours, was white and woeful. When she saw them standing together in the entrance a glance told her that they bore ill news. Yet, to Roger's great astonishment, she was quite calm.

"He has not released him?" she said, a flicker of pain distorting her face.

The Countess clasped her hand in both her own, and with tears running down her face shook her head.

"He is not dead?"

"No, no!"

"Tell me."

And they told her. "When I said 'You will release him?'" the Countess explained, speaking with difficulty, "he—he—laughed. 'I did not promise to release him,' he answered. 'I said if you did not accept my hospitality, I should hang him!' That was all."

"And now?" Bonne murmured. A pang once more flickered in her eyes. "What of him now?"

"I think," Roger said, "there is a hope. I do indeed."

Bonne stood a moment silent. Then, in a voice so steady that it surprised even the Bat, who had experience of her courage, "There is a hope," she said, "if it be not too late. M. de Joyeuse, whose father's life he would have saved—I will go to him! I will kneel to him! He must save him. There must still be ways of saving him, and the Duke's power is great." She turned to the Bat. "Take me to him," she said.

He stooped his rugged beard to her hand, and kissed it with reverence. Then, while the others stood astonished at her firmness, he passed with her into the mist in the direction of the Duke's hut.

CHAPTER XXIII

THE BRIDE'S DOT.

THE Abbess left alone in the garden-chamber listened intently; looking now on the door which had closed on her rival, now on the windows, whence it was just possible that she might catch the flutter of the girl's flying skirts. But she did not move to the windows, nor make any attempt to look down. She knew that her ears were her best sentinels; and motionless, scarcely breathing, in the middle of the floor, she strained them to the utmost to catch the first sounds of discovery and alarm.

None reached her, and after the lapse of a minute she breathed more freely. On the other hand, the waiting-maid—glad to prolong her freedom—did not return. The Abbess, still listening, still intent, fell to considering, without moving from the spot, other things. The light was beginning to wane in the room —the room she remembered so well—the corners were growing shadowy. All things promised to favour and prolong her disguise. Between the inset windows lay a block of deep gloom; she had only to fling herself down in that place and hide her face on her arms, as the Countess, in her abandonment, had hidden hers, and the woman would discover nothing when she entered

377

—nothing until she took courage to disturb the bride —and would dress her.

The bride? Even in the last minute the room had grown darker—dark and vague as her sombre thoughts. But it happened that amid its shadows one object still gleamed white—a tiny oasis of brightness in a desert of gloom. The pile of dainty bride-clothes, lawn and lace, that lay on the window-seat caught and gave back what light there was. It seemed to concentrate on itself all that remained of the day. Presently she could not take her eyes from the things. They had at first repelled her. Now, and more powerfully, they fascinated her. She dreamed, with her gaze fixed on them; and slowly the colour mounted to her brow, her face softened, her breast heaved. She took a step towards the bride-clothes and the window, paused, hesitated; and, flushed and frowning, looked at the door.

But no one moved outside, no footstep threatened entrance; and her eyes returned to the lace and lawn, emblems of a thing that from Eve's day to ours has stirred women's hearts. She was not over-superstitious. But it could not be for nothing, a voice whispered her it could not be for nothing that the things lay there and, while night swallowed all besides, still shone resplendent in the gloaming. Were they not only an emblem, but a token? A sign to her, a finger pointing through the vagueness of her future to the clear path of safety?

The Abbess had thought of that path, that way out of her difficulties, not once only, nor twice. It had lain too open, too plain to be missed. But she had marked it only to shrink from it as too dangerous, too bold even for her. Were she to take it she must come into fatal collision, into irremediable relations with the man whom she loved; but whom others feared, and of whom his little world stood in an awe so dire and so significant.

Yet still the things beckoned her; and omens in those days went for more than in these. Things still done in sport or out of a sentimental affection for the past—on All-hallows' E'en or at the new moon—were then done seriously, their lessons taken to heart, their dictates followed. The Abbess felt her heart beat high. She trembled and shook on the verge of a great resolve.

Had she time? The cloak slipped a little lower, discovering her bare shoulders. She looked at the door and listened, looked again at the pale bride-clothes. The stillness encouraged her, urged her. And, for the rest, had she not boasted a few minutes before that, whoever feared him, she did not; that, whoever drifted helpless on the tide of fate, she could direct her life, she could be strong?

She had the chance now if she dared to take it! If she dared? Already she had thwarted him in a thing dear to him. She had released his prisoner, conveyed away his bride, wrecked his plans. Dared she thwart him in this last, this greatest thing? Dared she engage herself and him in a bond from which no power could free them, a bond that, the deed done, must subject her to his will and pleasure—and his wrath—till death?

She did fear him, she owned it. And she had not dared the venture had she not loved him more. But love kicked the beam. Love won—as love ever wins in such contests. Swiftly her mind reviewed the position: so much loss, so much gain. If he would stand worse here he would stand better there. And then she did not come empty-handed. Fain would she have come to him openly and proudly, with her dower in her hands, as she had dreamed that she would come. But that was not possible. Or, if it were possible, the prospect was distant, the time remote; while, this way, love, warm, palpitating, present love, held out arms to her.

The end was certain. For all things, the time, the gathering darkness, her gaoler's absence, seconded the temptation. Had she resisted longer she had been more than woman. As it was, she had time for all she must do. When the waiting-maid returned, and glanced around the darkened room, she was not surprised to find her crouching on the floor in the posture in which she had left her, with head bowed on the window-seat. But she was surprised to see that she had donned the bride-clothes set for her. True, the shimmer of white that veiled the head and shoulders agreed ill with the despondency of the figure; but that was to be expected. And at least—the woman recognised with relief—there would be no need of force, no scene of violence, no cries to Heaven. She uttered a word of thanksgiving for that; and then, thinking that light would complete the improvement and put a more cheerful face on the matter, she asked if she should fetch candles.

"For I think the priest is below, my lady," she continued doubtfully; she had no mind to quarrel with her future mistress if it could be avoided. "And my lord may be looked for at any moment."

The crouching figure stirred a foot fretfully, but did not answer.

"If I might fetch them——"

"No!" sharply.

"But, if it please you, it is nearly dark.   And——"

"Am I not shamed enough already?"   The bride as she spoke—in a tone half ruffled, half hysterical—raised her arms with a passionate gesture.   "If I must be married against my will, I will be married thus!   Thus!   And without more light to shame me!"

"Still it grows—so dark, my lady!" the maid ventured again, though timidly.

"I tell you I will have it dark!   And"—with another movement as of a trapped animal—"if they must come, bid them come!"   Then, in a choking voice, "God help me!" she murmured, as she let her head fall again on her arms.

The woman wondered, but felt no suspicion; there was something of reason in the demand.   She went and told the elder woman who waited below.   She left the room door ajar, and the Abbess, raising her pale, frowning face from the window-seat, could hear the priest's voice mingling in the whispered talk.   Light steps passed hurriedly away through the garden, and after an interval came again; and by-and-by she heard more steps, and voices under the window—and a smothered laugh, and then a heavier, firmer tread, and —his voice—his!   She pictured them making way for the master to pass through and enter.

She had need of courage now, need of the half-breathed prayer; for there is no cause so bad men will not pray in it.   Need of self-control, too, lest she give way and fall in terror at his feet.   Yet less need of this last; for fear was in her part, and natural to the right playing of it.   So that it was not weakness or modest tremors or prostration would betray her.

She clutched this thought to her, and had it for

comfort. And when the door opened to its full width, and they appeared on the threshold and entered, the priest first, the lord of Vlaye's tall presence next, and after these three or four witnesses, with the two women behind all, those less concerned found nothing to marvel at in the sight; nor in the dim crouching figure, lonely in the dark room, that rose unsteadily and stood cowering against the wall, shrinking as if in fear of a blow. It was what they had looked to see, what they had expected; and they eyed it, one coveting, another in pity, seeing by the half-light which was reflected from the pale evening sky little more than is here set down. For the priest, appearances might have been trebly suspicious, and he had suspected nothing; for he was terribly afraid himself. And M. de Vlaye, ignorant of the Abbess's visit and exulting in the success of his plan, a success won in the teeth of his enemy, had no grounds for suspicion. Even the marriage in the gloaming seemed only natural; for modesty in a woman seems natural to a man. He was more than content if the little fool would raise no disturbance, voice no cries, but let herself be married without the need of open force.

With something of kindness in his tone, "The Countess prefers it thus, does she?" he said, raising his head, as he took in the scene. "Then thus let it be! Her will is mine, and shall be mine. Still it is dark! You do, in fact, Countess," he continued smoothly, "prefer it so? I gathered your meaning rightly—from those you sent?"

With averted face she made a shamed gesture with her hand.

"You do not——"

"If it must be—let it be so!" she whispered. "And now!" And suddenly she covered her face—they could picture it working pitifully—with her hands.

M. de Vlaye turned to his witnesses. "You hear all present," he said, "that it is with the Countess of Rochechouart's consent that I wed her. For me it is my part now and will be my part always to do her pleasure." Then turning his face again to the shrinking figure, that uttered no protest or word of complaint, "Father, you hear?" he continued, a note of triumph in his voice. "Do your office on us I pray, and quickly." And he advanced a step towards his bride.

The Romish sacrament of marriage is short, and reduced to its essentials is of the simplest. Father Benet had his orders, and thankful to be so cheaply quit of his task—for she might have appealed to him, might have shrieked and struggled, might have made of his work a public crime—he hastened to bind the two together. For one second, at the most critical part of the rite—if that could be said to have parts which was done within the minute—the bride hung, wavered, hesitated—seemed about to protest or faint. The next, as by a supreme effort, she tottered a step nearer to the bridegroom, and placed her hand, burning with fever, in his. In a few seconds the words that made them man and wife, the irrevocable "*Conjungo vos*," were spoken.

Then followed a single moment of awkwardness. The Captain of Vlaye's heart was high and uplifted. All had gone well, all had gone better than his hopes. Yet he was prudent as he was bold. He would fain have raised her veil before them all and kissed her, and proved beyond cavil her willingness. But he doubted the wisdom of the act. He reflected that women were strange beings and capricious. She might be foolish enough to shriek—more, to faint, to resist, to speak; she might realise, now that it was too late, the thing which she had done. And a dozen curious eyes were on them, were watching them, were judging them. He contented himself with bowing over her hand.

"Would you be alone, madame?" he said gently. "If so, say so, sweet. And you shall be alone, while you please."

The answer, low and half-stifled as it was, astonished him. "With you," she murmured, with face half-averted. And as the others, smiling and with raised eyebrows, looked at one another, and then at a glance from him turned to withdraw, "And a light," she added, in the same subdued tone, "if you please."

"Bring a light," he said to the waiting-woman. "And, mark you, see that when your lady wants supper it be ready for her."

She had still, before they withdrew, a surprise for him. "I would have a draught of wine—now," she murmured.

He passed the order to them with a gay air, thinking the while of the queer nature of women. And he stood waiting by the door until the order was carried out. The footsteps of the witnesses and their laughter rose from the garden below as the maid brought in lights and wine and set them on the table beside him. "You can go," he said; and after a fleeting glance, half of envy, half of wonder at her new mistress—who had sunk into a sitting posture on the window-seat—the woman went out.

"May I serve you?" he murmured gallantly. And he poured for her.

With her face turned from him she lifted the gauzy veil with one hand and with the other—it trembled violently—she raised the wine to her lips. Still with her shoulder to him—but he set this down to modesty—she gave him back the empty cup, and he went and set it down on the table beside the door. When he turned again to her she had raised her veil and risen to her feet, and stood facing him with shining eyes.

"By Heaven!" he cried. And he recoiled a pace, his swarthy face gone sallow. Was he mad? Was he dreaming? The priest had been silent on the Abbess's visit. He believed her leagues distant. He had no reason to think otherwise. And he had not been more astonished if the one woman had turned into the other before his eyes. "By Heaven!" he repeated. For the moment sheer astonishment, the stupor of bewilderment, held him dumb.

She did not speak, but neither did she quail. She stood confronting him, erect and stately, her beauty never more remarkable than now, her breast heaving slightly under the lace.

"Am I mad?" he muttered again. And he closed his eyes and opened them. "Or dreaming?"

"Neither!" she replied.

"Then who in God's name are you?" he retorted, in something approaching his natural voice; though the awe of the unnatural still held his mind.

"Your wife," she answered.

"My wife!" With the words the full shock of that which had happened struck him.

"Your wife," she rejoined unblenching, though her

heart beat wildly, furiously, in her bosom, and she feared, ah, how she feared! "Your wife! And which of us two"—she continued proudly—"has a better right to be your wife? I,"—and with the word she flung the lace superbly from her head and shoulders, and stood before him in the full splendour of her beauty —"or that child? That puny weakling? That doll? I," with increasing firmness—he had not struck her yet!—"who have your vows, sir, your promises, your sacred oath—and all my due, as God knows and you know—or that puppet? I, who dare, and for your sake have dared—you know it only too well!—or that craven, puling and weeping and waiting for the first chance to flee you or betray you? What I have done for you"— and proudly she held out her hands to him—"you know, sir. What she would have done you know not."

"I know that you have ruined me," he said, looking darkly at her.

"And in return for—what?" she answered, with a look as dark.

His nostrils quivered, a pulse beat hard in his cheek. Only the sheer boldness of that which she had done, only the appeal of the lioness in her to the lion in him— and her beauty—held his hand; held his hand from striking her down, woman though she was, at his feet. Had she faltered, had she turned pale or trembled, had she uttered but one word of supplication, or done aught but defy him, he had flung her brutally to the floor and trampled upon her.

For the Captain of Vlaye was no knight of romance. And no scruple on his part, no helplessness on hers would have restrained his hand. But he loved her after his fashion. He loved her beauty, which had never been more brilliant or alluring; he loved the spirit that proved her fit helpmeet for such as he. And thwarted, tricked, baffled, hanging still on the verge of violence over which the least recoil on her part would push him, he still owned reason in her claim. She was the more worthy—of the two; such beauty, such spirit, such courage would go far. And not many weeks back he had looked no higher, aimed no farther, but had deemed her birth fit dower. But love sits lightly on the ambitious, and driven by a new danger to a new shift, forced to look abroad for aid, he had put her aside at the first temptation—not without a secret thought that she might be still what she had been to him.,

Her eyes, her words told a different story, and in his secret heart he gave her credit for her act; and he held his hand. But his looks were dark and bitter and passionate, as he told her again that she had ruined him, and flung it coarsely in her face that she brought herself, and naught besides to the bargain.

"It is but a little since you thought that enough!" she replied, with flashing eyes.

"You are bold to speak to me thus!" he said between his teeth. "What? You that call yourself my wife, to beard me!"

"That am your wife!" she answered, though sick fear rapped at her heart.

"Then for that the greater need to heed what you say!" he replied. "Wives that come empty-handed to husbands that ask them not had best be silent and be patient! Or in a very little time they creep as low as before they went high! You beautiful fool!"

he continued, in a tone of mingled rage and admiration, "to do this in haste and forget I could punish at leisure! To do me ill, ay, to ruin me, and forget that henceforth my pleasure must be yours, my will your rule! My wife, say you?" with increasing bitterness. "Ay! And therefore my creature, helpless as the scullion I send to the scourge, or the trooper I hang up by the heels for sleeping! You—you——" and with a movement as fierce as it was sudden he grasped her wrist and twisted her round forcibly so that her eyes at close quarters looked into his. "Do you not yet repent? Do you not begin to see that in tricking the Captain of Vlaye you have made your master?"

She could have screamed with pain, for the bones of her slender wrist seemed to be cracking in his cruel grip—but she knew that in her courage, and in that only, lay her one hope. "I know this," she replied hardily, forcing herself to meet his eyes without flinching, "that you mistake! I do not come empty—or I had not come," with pride. "I bring you that will save you—if you treat me well. But if you hold me so——"

"What will you do?" savagely.

"Release me and I will tell you," she answered. "I shall not fly. And if I say nothing to the purpose, I shall still be in your power."

He yielded, moved in secret by her spirit. "Well," he said, "speak! But let it be to the purpose, madam, that is all."

"Said I not it should be to the purpose?" she answered, her eyes bright. "And I keep my word, if you do not. Tell me, sir, frankly, what had that child, that doll"—bitterly—"to put in the scales against me? Beauty?"

"Nay!"

"A skin as white as mine or arms as round?" She held them out to him. "Or brighter eyes? You have looked in mine often enough and sworn you loved me, sworn that you would do me no wrong! You should know them—and hers!"

"It was none of these."

"Her birth? Nay, but she is no better born than I am! A Rochechouart is what a Villeneuve was. Her rank? No. Then what was it?"

"No one thing," he answered drily. "But five hundred things."

"Spears?"

"You are quick-witted. Spears."

"And her manors also, I suppose?" with contempt. "Her lordships here and there! Her farms and castles in Poitou and the Limousin and Beauce and the Dordogne! Her mills in the Bourbonnais and her fishings in Sologne!"

"Not one of these!"

"No?"

"The spears only, as God sees me!" he answered firmly. "For without these I could enjoy not the smallest of those. Without these, of which you, beautiful fool, have robbed me—robbing me therewith of my last chance—I take no farm nor smallest mill, nor hold one groat of that I have won! Do you think, my girl," he continued grimly, "that I was not pressed when I gave up your lips and your kisses for that child's company? Do you think it was for a whim, a fancy, a light thing that I turned my back on you and your smiles, and at risk sought a puling girl, when I could have had you without risk? Bah! I tell you it was not to gain, but to hold—because he had no other choice and no other way—it was not for love but for life, that the King went to his Mass! And I to mine!"

"All this I thought," she said quietly. She was no longer afraid of him.

"You thought it?"

"I knew it."

"You knew it? You knew, madam," he repeated, his face darkening, "on what a narrow edge I stood, and you dashed away my one holdfast?"

"To replace it by another," she replied, her figure welling with confidence. "I tell you, sir, I come not to you empty-handed, if I come unasked. I bring my dowry."

He eyed her gloomily. "It should be a large one," he muttered, "if it is to take the place of that I have lost."

"It is a large one," she answered. "But," with a change to gentleness, "do me credit. I have not puled nor wept. I have uttered no cry, I have made no complaint. But I have righted myself, doing what not one woman in a hundred would have dared to do! I have wit that has tricked you, and courage that has not quailed before you. And henceforward I claim to be no puppet for your play, no doll for your dull hours! But your equal, my lord, and your mate; deepest in your counsels, the heart of your plans, your other brain, your other soul! Make me this, hold me thus—close to you, and——

"Is that the thing you bring me?" he said, with sarcasm. Yet she had moved him.

"No!" She fell a little from her height, she looked

appeal. "My dowry is different. But say first, sir, I shall be this!"

"Bring me the spears," he answered, his eyes gleaming, "and you shall be that and more. Bring me the spears, and——" He made as if he would take her forcibly in his arms.

She recoiled, but her eyes shone. "I am yours," she said, "when you will! Do you not know it? But, for the present, listen. I have a husband, but I have also a lover. A lover of whom"—she continued more slowly, marking with joy how he started at the word—"my lord and master has no need to be jealous. He has not touched of me more than the tips of my fingers; yet if I raise but those fingers he has spears and to spare— five hundred and five hundred to that!—and I have but to play the laggard a little, and dangle a hope, and they dance to my piping."

He understood. A deep flush tinged the brown of his lean face. "You have brought,". he said, "the Duke to parley."

"To parley!" She pointed superbly to the floor. "Nay, but to my feet! What will you of him? Spears, his good word, his intercession with the King, a post? Name what you will, and it shall be yours."

He looked at her shrewdly, with a new admiration, a new and stronger esteem. Already she filled the place which she had claimed, already she was to him what she had prayed to be. "You are sure?" he said.

"In a week, had I not loved you, I had had him and his Duchy, and all those spears! And mills and manors and lordships and governments, all had been mine, sir! Mine, had I wished this man; mine, had I been willing to take him! But I"—letting her arms fall by her sides

and standing submissive before him—"am more faithful than my master!"

He stood staring at her. "But if this be so," he
said at last, his brows coming together, "what of it?
How does it help us? You are now my wife?"

"He need not know that yet."

"No?"

"He need not know it," she continued firmly, "until
he has played his part, and wrung your pardon from
the King! Or at the least—for that may take time—
until he has drawn off his power and left you to face
those whom you can easily match!"

"He would have wedded you?" he asked, eyeing her
in wonder.

"For certain."

"But, sweet——"

"I am sweet now!" she said, with tender raillery.

"To do this you must go to him?"

"He shall touch of me no more than the tips of my
fingers," she answered smiling. "Nor"—and at the
word a blush stole upward from her neck to her brow,
"need I go on the instant, if your men can be trusted
not to talk, my lord."

"He is soon without a tongue," he replied grimly,
"who talks too fast here! You should know that of
old."

She lowered her eyes, the colour mounting anew to
her brow. "Yes," she murmured. "I know that your
people can be silent. But the Lieutenant of Périgord
is here. You have not"—with a quick, frightened
look—"injured him?"

"Have no fear."

"For that were fatal," she continued anxiously.

"Fatal! If things go wrong, he may prove our safety."

"Pooh, I know it well," Vlaye replied, with a nod of intelligence. "None better, my girl. But have no fear, he will hear naught of our doings. Not, I suppose"—with a searching look, half humorous, half suspicious—"that he is also a captive of your bow and spear."

"I hate him," she answered.

Her tone, vehement, yet low, struck the corresponding chord in his nature. He took her into his arms with a reckless laugh. "You were right and I was wrong!" he cried, as he fondled her. "You will bring me more than a clump of spears, my beauty! More than that foolish child! God! In a month I had strangled her! But you and I—you and I, sweet, will go far together! And now, to supper! To supper! And the devil take to-morrow and our cares!"

CHAPTER XXIV.

FORS L'AMOUR.

THOUGH it was not des Ageaux' fate to lie in one of those underground dungeons, noisome and dark, which the lords of an earlier century had provided in the foundations of the castle, he was not greatly the better for the immunity. The humiliations of the mind are sometimes sharper than the pains of the body; and the Lieutenant of Périgord, defeated and a prisoner, was little the happier though a dry strong-room looking on a tiny inner court held him, and though he suffered nothing from cold or the slimy companionship of the newt and frog. On the ambitious man defeat sits more heavily than chains; into the nature that would fain be at work inaction gnaws deeper than a shackle-bolt. Never while he lived would des Ageaux forget the long hours which he spent, gazing drearily on the blank wall that faced his window, while his mind measured a hundred times over the depth and the completeness of his fall.

He feared little for his life if he deigned to fear at all. He knew that he was a prize too valuable to be wasted. In the last resort, indeed, when all hopes had failed the Captain of Vlaye, and ruin stared him in the face, he might wreak his vengeance on the King's governor.

But short of that moment—and it depended upon many things—the Lieutenant accounted himself safe. Safe as to life, but a beaten man, a prisoner, a failure; a blot, every moment he lay there, on the King's dignity, whose deputy he was; an unfortunate, whose ill hap would never be forgiven by the powers he nad represented so ill.

The misfortune was great, and, to a proud man, well-nigh intolerable. Moreover, this man was so formed that he loved the order which it was his mission to extend, and the good government which it was his to impose. To make straight the crooked—gently, if it might be, but by the strong hand if it must be—was his part in life, and one which he pursued witn the utmost zest. Every breach of order, therefore, every trespass in his province, every outrage wounded him. But tne breach and the trespass which abased in his person the King's name—he writhed, he groaned as he thought of this! Even the blow to his career, fatal as it promised to be, scarce hurt him worse or cut him so deeply.

The more as that career which had been all in all to him yesterday was not quite all in all to him to-day. Bonne's voice, the touch of her hands as she appealed to him, the contact of her figure with his as he carried her, these haunted him, and moved him, in his solitude and his humiliation. Her courage, her constancy, her appeal to him, when all seemed lost, he could not think of them—he who had thought of naught but himself for years—without a softening of his features, without a flood of colour invading the darkness of his face. Strong, he had estranged himself from the tender emotions, only to own their sway now. With half his mind he dwelt upon his mishap; the other half, the better half, found consolation in the prospect of her sympathy, of her fidelity, of her gentle eyes and quivering lips—who loved him. He found it strange to remember that he filled all a woman's thoughts; that, as he sat there brooding in his prison, she was thinking of him and dreaming of him, and perhaps praying for him!

It is not gladly, it is never without a pang that the man of affairs sees the world pass from him. And if there be nothing left, it is bad for him. Des Ageaux acknowledged that he had something left. A hand he could trust would lie in his, and one brave heart, when all others forsook him would accompany him whither he went. He might no longer aspire to government and the rule of men, the work of his life was over; but Bonne would hold to him none the less, would love him none the less, would believe in him truly. The cares of power would no longer trouble his head, or keep it sleepless; but her gentle breast would pillow it, her smiles would comfort him, her company replace the knot of followers to whom he had become accustomed. He told himself that he was content. He more than half believed it.

In the present, however, he had not her company; and the present was very miserable. He did not fear for his life, but he lay in ignorance of all that had happened since his capture, of all that went forward; and the tedium of imprisonment tried him. He knew that he might lie there weeks and months and come forth at last—for the world moved quickly in this period of transition—to find himself forgotten. Seventy years earlier, a king, misnamed the Great, standing where he stood, had said that all was lost but honour

—and had hastened to throw that also away. For him all was lost but love. All!

He had passed four days—they seemed to him a fortnight—in this weary inaction, and on the last evening of the four he was expecting his supper with impatience, when it occurred to him that the place was more noisy than ordinary. For some time sounds had reached him without making any definite impression on his mind; now they resolved themselves into echoes of distant merry-making. Little spirts of laughter, the catch of a drinking-song, the shrill squeal of a maid pinched or kissed, the lilt of a hautboy—he began with quickened ears to make these out. And straightway that notion which is never out of a prisoner's mind and which the least departure from routine fosters raised its head. Escape! Ah, if he could escape! Freedom would set him where he had been, freedom would undo the worst of his mishap. It might even give him the victory he had counted lost.

But the grated window or the barred door, the paved floor or the oaken roof—one of these must be pierced; or the gaoler, who never visited him without precautions and company, must be overcome and robbed of his keys. And even then, with that done which was well-nigh impossible, he would be little nearer to freedom than before. He would be still in the heart of his enemy's fortress, with no knowledge of the passages or the turnings, no clue to the stone labyrinth about him, no accomplice.

Yet, beyond doubt, there was merry-making afoot—such merry-making as accounted for the tarrying of his supper. Probably the man had forgotten him. By-and-by the notes of the hautboy rose louder and fuller, and on the wave of sound bursts of applause and laughter came to him. He made up his mind that some were dancing and others were looking on and encouraging them. Could it be that the Captain of Vlaye had surprised the peasants' camp? and that this was his way of celebrating his success? Or was it merely some common-place orgie, held, it might be, in the Captain's absence? Or—— But while he turned this and that in his thoughts the footsteps he had been expecting sounded at the end of the stone passage and approached. A light shone under the door, a key turned in the lock, and the man who brought him his meals appeared on the threshold. He entered, his hands full, while his comrade, who had opened for him, remained in the passage.

"You are gay this evening?" the Lieutenant said as the man set down his light.

The fellow grinned. "Ay, my lord," he replied good-humouredly, "you may say it. Wedding-bells and the rest of it!" He was not drunk, but he was flushed with wine. "That is the way the world goes—and comes."

"A wedding?" des Ageaux exclaimed. The news was strange.

"To be sure, my lord.

> ' En revenant des noces,
> Barabim!' "

he hummed.

"And whose, my man?"

The fellow, in the act of putting a bowl of soup on the table, held his hand. He looked at the Lieutenant with a grin. "Ay, whose?" he said. "But that would be talking. And we have orders not to talk, see you, my lord. Still, it is not many you'll have the chance of telling. And, if I tell you it is the Captain himself, what matter? Should we be footing it and drinking it and the rest for another?"

"M. de Vlaye married?" des Ageaux exclaimed in astonishment. "To-day?"

"Married for sure, and as tight as Father Benet could marry him! But to-day"—with his head on one side—"that is another matter."

"And the bride?"

"Ay, that is another matter, too!" with a wink. "Not that you can let it out to many either! So, if you must know——"

"Best not," intervened his comrade in the passage, speaking for the first time.

"Perhaps you do not know yourself?" the Lieutenant said shrewdly. He saw that the man was sufficiently in drink to be imprudent. With a little provocation he would tell.

"Not know?"—with indignation. "Didn't I——"

"Know or not, don't tell!" growled the other.

"Of course," said des Ageaux, "if you don't know you cannot tell."

"Oh!" the fool rejoined. "Cannot I? Well, I can tell you it is Mademoiselle de Villeneuve. So there's for knowing!"

Des Ageaux sprang to his feet, his face transformed. "What!" he cried. "Say that again!"

But his excitement overreached itself. His movement warned the other that he had spoken too freely. With an uneasy look—what had he done?—he refused to say more, and backed to the door. "I have said too much already," he muttered sullenly.

"But ——"

"Don't answer him!" commanded the man in the passage. "And hurry! You have stayed too long as it is! I would not be in your shoes for something if the Captain comes to know."

Des Ageaux stepped forward, pressing him again to speak. But the man, sobered and frightened, was obdurate. "I've said too much already," he answered with a resentful scowl. "What is it to you, my lord?" And he slipped out hurriedly, and secured the door behind him.

Des Ageaux remained glaring at the closed door. Bonne de Villeneuve had been taken with him. Bonne de Villeneuve also was a prisoner. Was it possible that she had become by force or willingly Vlaye's bride? Possible? Ah, God, it must be so! And, if so, by force surely! Surely, by force; his faith in her told him that! But if by force, what consolation could he draw from that? For that, if he loved her, were worst of all, most cruel of all! That were a thing intolerable by God or man!

So it seemed to this man, who only a few days before had not known what love was. But who now, stung with sudden passion, flung himself from wall to wall of his narrow prison. Now, when he saw it snatched from him, now, when he saw himself denuded of that solace at which he had grasped, but for which he had not been sufficiently thankful, now he learned what love was, its pains as well as its promise, its burning fevers, its heart-stabbing pity! He lost himself in rage. He who for years had practised himself in calmness, who had made it his aim to hide his heart, forgot his lesson, flung to the night his habit. He seized the iron bars of his window and shook them in a paroxysm of fury, as if only by violence he could retain his sanity. When the bars, which would have resisted the strength of ten, declined to leave the stone, he flung himself on the door, and beat on it and shouted, maddened by the thought that she was under the same roof, that she was within call, yet he could not help her! He called Vlaye by dreadful names, challenging him, and defying him, and promising him terrible deaths. And only when echo and silence answered all and the iron sense of his helplessness settled down slowly upon him and numbed his faculties did he, too, fall silent and, covering his face with his hands, stagger to a seat and sit in a stupor of despair.

He had put love aside, he had despised it through years—for this! He had held it cheap when it promised to be his—for this! He had accepted it grudgingly, and when all else was like to fail him—for this! He was punished, and sorely. She was near him. He pictured her in the man's power, in the man's hands, in the man's arms! And he could not help her.

Had his impotent cries and threats been heard they had only covered him with humiliation. Fortunately they were not heard: the merry-making was at its height, and no one came near him. The Captain of Vlaye, aware that his marriage could not be hidden from his own men—for he had made no secret of it beforehand—had not ventured to forbid some indulgence. He could make it known that the man who named his bride outside the gate would lose his tongue; but, that arranged, he must wink—for every despotism is tempered by something—at a few hours of riot, and affect not to see things that at another time had called for swift retribution.

The men had used his permission to the full. They had brought in some gipsies to make sport for them, a treble allowance of wine was on draught, and the hour that saw des Ageaux beating in impotent fury on his door saw the license and uproar of which he had marked the beginning grown to a head. In the great hall the higher officers, their banquet finished, were deep in their cups. In the cavernous kitchens drunken cooks probed cauldrons for the stray capon that still floated amid the spume; or half-naked scullions thrust a forgotten duck or widgeon on the spit at the request of a hungry friend. About the fires in the courtyard were dancing and singing and some romping; for there were women within the walls, and others had come in with the gipsies. Here a crowd surrounded the bear, and laid furious bets for or against; while yelps and growls and fierce barkings deafened all within hearing. There a girl, the centre of a leering ring, danced to the music of her tambour; and there again a lad tumbled, and climbed a pole at risk of his limbs. Everywhere, save in the dark garden under the "demoiselle's" windows, where a sentry walked, and at the great gates, where were some sober men picked for the purpose, wantonness and jollity held reign, and the noise of brawling and riot cast fear on the town that listened and quaked below.

A stranger entering the castle would have judged the reins quite fallen, all discipline fled, all control lost. But he had been wrong. Not only did a sentry walk the garden path—and soberly and shrewdly too—but no man in his wildest and tipsiest moment ventured a foot within the railing that fenced the lime avenue, or even approached the gates that led to it without lowering his voice and returning to something like his normal state. For in the rooms looking over the garden M. de Vlaye entertained his bride of two days— and he had relaxed, not loosed, the reins.

They sat supping in the room in which they had been wedded, and, unmoved by the sounds of uproar that came fitfully to their ears, discussed their plans; she, glowing and handsome, animated by present love and future hope; he, content, if not enraptured, conquered by her wit, and almost persuaded that all was for the best—that her charms and beauty would secure him more than the dowry of her rival. Their brief honeymoon over, they were to part on the morrow; she to pursue her plans for the Duke's detachment, he to take the field and strike such a blow as should scatter the peasants and dissipate what strength remained in them. They were to part; and some shadow of the coming separation had been natural. But her nerves as well as his were strong, and the gloom of parting had not yet fallen on them. The lights that filled the room were not brighter than her eyes; the snowy linen that covered the round table at which they sat was not whiter than her uncovered shoulders. He had given her jewels, the spoils of many an enterprise; and they glittered on her queenly neck and in her ears, gleamed through the thin lace of her dress, and on her round and beautiful arms. He called her his Abbess and his nun in fond derision; and she, in answering badinage, rallied him on his passion for the Countess and his skill in abduction. So cleverly had she wrought on him, so well managed him, that she dared even that.

The room had been hung for her with tapestries brought from another part of the house; the windows more richly curtained; and a door, long closed, had been opened, through which and an ante-room the chambers connected with M. de Vlaye's apartments. Where the wedding robes had lain on the window-seat a ribboned lute and a gay music-book lay on rich draperies, and elbowed a gilded head-piece of Milanese work surmounted by M. de Vlaye's crest, which had been brought in for his lady's approval. A mighty jar of Provence roses scented the apartment; and intoxicated by their perfume or their meaning, she presently seized the lute, and gaily, between jest and earnest, broke into the old Angoumois song:—

> "Si je suis renfermée.
> Ah, c'est bien sans raison;
> Ma plus belle journée,
> Se pass'ra-z-en prison.
> Mais mon amant sans peine
> Pourra m'y venir voir,
> Son cœur sait bien qu'il m'aime,
> Il viendra'-z-au parloir!"

And he answered her—

> "Oh, Madame l'Abbesse,
> Qu'on tire les verrous,
> Qu'on sorte ma maîtresse
> Le plus beau des bijoux;
> Car je suis capitaine,
> Je suis son cher amant,
> J'enfoncerai sans peine
> Les portes du couvent!"

As he finished, disturbed by some noise, he turned his head. "I told your wench to go," he said, rising.

"I suppose she took herself off?" With a frown, he strode to the screen that masked the door, and made sure by looking behind it that they had no listeners.

She smiled as she laid aside the lute. "I thought that your people obeyed at a word?" she said.

"They do, or they suffer," he answered.

"And is that to apply to me?" with a mocking grimace.

"When we come to have two wills, sweet, yes!" he retorted. "It will not be yet awhile. In the meantime I would this enterprise of yours were over. I doubt your success, though all looks well."

"If I had been half as sure of you two days ago as I am of him to-morrow!" she retorted.

"Yet you must not go too far with him."

She waved her finger-tips across the table. "So far, and no farther," she said lightly. "Have I not promised you? For the rest—what I have done I can do. Am I not armed?" And she rose from her seat, and stood before him in all the seduction of her charms. "Count it done, my master. Set Joyeuse aside. He is captive of *my* bow and spear. The question is, can you deal with the rest?"

"The peasants?"

"And what remains of des Ageaux' power? And the Countess's levies?"

"For certain, if the Duke be out of the reckoning," he answered. "He is a man. Remove him and des Ageaux—and the latter I have already—and there is no one. Your brothers——"

"Bah!" She dismissed them with a contemptuous gesture.

"Just so. And the Countess's people have no leader.

The Vicomte is old. There is no one. Detach the Duke, and there will be a speedy end of them. And before a new governor can set to work to make head against me, many things may happen, my girl!"

"Many things will happen," she answered with confidence. "If I can win one man, why not another? If a Duke, why not"—she made an extraordinary face at him, half-sportive, half-serious—"why not a greater? Eh, my lord?"

He stared. "No!" he answered, striking the table with sudden violence. "No!" He knew well what she meant and whom she meant. "Not that! Even to make all good, not that!" Yet his eyes glittered as he looked at her; and it was plain that his thoughts travelled far and fast on the wings of her words. While she, in the pride of her mastery, returned his look fondly.

"No, not that—never that!" she replied in a voice that more than reassured him. "It is for you and only for you that I do this. I am yours, all and always—always! But, short of that, something may be done. And, with friends at Court, from Captain of Vlaye to Governor of Périgord is but a step!"

He nodded. "And a step that might save his Majesty much trouble," he said with a smile. "Do that—— But I doubt your power, my girl."

"I have done that already should persuade you."

"You have tricked me," he said, smiling. "That is true. And it is no mean thing, I grant."

"More than that!" she retorted. The wine she had drunk had flushed her cheek and perhaps loosed her tongue. "More than that I have done! Who took the first step for you? Who put the Lieutenant in your hands—and my sister? And so, in place of my sister, the Countess?"

He looked at her in astonishment. "Who?" he rejoined. "Why, who but I myself? Did I not take them with my own hands—at the old windmill on the hill? What had you to do with that?"

"And who sent them to the windmill?"

"Why, the rabble to be sure, who seized them, took them as far as the ford."

"And who set the rabble on them?" As she asked the question she rose from her seat. In the excitement of her triumph, in the intoxication of her desire to please him she forgot the despair into which the act which she boasted had cast her but a week before. She forgot all except that she had done it for him whom she loved, for him who now was hers, and whose she was! "Who," she repeated, "set the rabble upon them?"

"You?" he murmured. "Not you?"

"I!" she said, "I!"—and held out her hands to him. "It was I who told the brute beasts that he—des Ageaux —had your man in hiding! It was I who wrought them to the attempt and listened while they did it! I thought, indeed, that it was your Countess who was with him. And I hated her! I was jealous of her! But, Countess or no Countess, 'twas done by me!—by me! And now do you think that there is anything I will not do for you? That there is anything I cannot do for you?"

He was not shocked; it took much to shock the Captain of Vlaye. But he was so much astonished, he marvelled so much that he was silent. And she, reading the astonishment in his face, and seeing it grow, felt a qualm—now she had spoken—and lost colour, and faltered. Had she been foolish to tell it? Perhaps. Had she passed some boundary, sacred to him, unknown to her? It must be so. For as she gazed, no word spoken, there came into his face a change, a strange hardening. He rose.

"My lord!" she cried, clapping her hands to her head, "what have I done?" She recoiled a pace, affrighted. "I did it for you!"

"Some one has heard you," he answered between his teeth. And then she saw that he was looking not at her, but beyond her—beyond her. "There is some one behind that screen."

She faced about, affrighted, and instinctively seized his arm and hung on it, her eyes on the screen. Her attitude as she listened, and her pallor, were in strange contrast with the gay glitter of the table, the lights, the luxury, the fairness of her dress.

"Yes, listening," he said grimly. "Some one has been listening. The worse for them! For they will never tell what they have heard!"

And bounding forward without warning, he dashed the screen down and aside—and recoiled. Face to face with him, cowering against the doorpost, and pale as ashes, was the very man she had mentioned a minute before—that very man of his whose hidden presence in the camp she had betrayed to the malcontents. Vlaye glared at him. "You!" he cried. "You!"

"My lord!"

"And listening!"

"But——"

"But! But die, fool!" the Captain retorted savagely. "Die!" And, swift as speech, the dagger he had stealthily drawn gleamed above his shoulder and sank in the poor wretch's throat.

The man's hands groped in the air, his eyes opened wide; but he attempted no return-stroke. Choked by the life-stream that gushed from his mouth, he sank back inert like a bundle of clothes, while the Abbess's low shriek of terror mingled with his stifled cry.

And, with a sterner sound, another sound. For as the man collapsed, and fell in on himself, a figure hitherto hidden in the doorway sprang over his falling body, a long blade flashed in the candle-light, and the Captain of Vlaye staggered back, one hand pressed to his breast. He made a futile attempt to ward with his poniard, but it fell from his grasp. And the pitiless steel found his heart again. Silent, grim, with unquenchable hate in his eyes, he reeled against the table. And then from the table, dragging with him all—silver and glass and fruit—in one common crash, he rolled to the floor—dying.

Ay, in five seconds, dead! And she saw it with her eyes! Saw it! And frozen, stiff, clinging to the bare edge of the table, she stood looking at him, her brain numbed by the horror, by the suddenness, the hopelessness of the catastrophe. In a twinkling, in a time measured by seconds, it was done. The olives that fell from the dish had not ceased to roll, the wine still crept upon the floor, the man who had struck the blow still panted, his point delivered—but he was dead whom she had loved. Dead!

CHAPTER XXV.

HIS LAST RIDE.

THE man who had struck the blow, and whose eyes still sparkled with fury, turned them upon her. He took note of her stupor, frowned, and with a swift, cruel glance searched the room. The lights were in sconces on the walls, and had not suffered. The rest was wreck—a splendid wreck, mingled terror and luxury, with the woman's Medusa-like face gazing on it. The Duke—for he it was—still breathing quickly, still with malevolence in his eyes, listened and looked; but the alarm had not been taken. The lilt of a song and faint distant laughter, borne on the night air, alone broke the night silence. He passed to a window, and putting aside a curtain, peered into the darkness of the garden. Then he went to the door, and listened. Still all was quiet without and within. But to the scene in the room his gliding figure, his bent, listening head gave the last touch of tragedy.

Presently—before, it would appear, he had made up his mind how to act—he saw a change come over the woman. Her breathing, which had been no more apparent for a time than the breath of the dead at her feet, became evident, her figure relaxed. Her attitude lost its stoniness; yet she did not stir to the eye. Only

410

her eyes moved; and then at last her foot. Stealthily her foot—the man listening at the door marked it—slid from her robe, and unshod in its thin silken stocking— so thin of web that the skin showed through it—covered the poniard, still wet with blood, that had fallen from her husband's hand. Slowly she drew it nearer and nearer to her.

He at the door made as if he did not heed. But when she had drawn the weapon within reach, and furtive and silent as a cat, stooped to grasp it, he was before her—so far before her, at least, that, though she gained it, he clutched her wrist as she rose. "No, madam!" he cried fiercely. "No! Enough!" And he tried to force it from her hand.

No words came from her lips, but an animal cry of unutterable fury. She seized on his wrist with her left hand—she tried to seize it with her teeth; she fought to free herself, clinging to the knife and wrestling with him in the midst of the trampled fruit, the shivered glass, the mingled wine and blood that made the floor slippery.

"Let it fall!" he repeated, hard put to it and panting. "Enough, I say, enough!" If he had loved her once he showed scant tenderness now.

And she—her lips writhed, her hair uncoiled and fell about her. He began to wish that he had not dropped his sword when he sprang upon her. For he was still weak; and if she persevered she was more than a match for him. In her normal condition she had been more than a match for him; but the shock had left its secret sap. Suddenly, without cry or warning, her grasp relaxed, her head fell back, and she sank—all her length, but sideways—amid the ruin.

He nursed his wrist a moment, looking askance at her, and thinking deeply and darkly. Assured at length that the swoon was no feint to take him un-awares, he went to the door by which he had entered, passed through the empty ante-room, and thence into the Captain of Vlaye's apartments. In the passage outside the farther door of these a sleepy valet was on guard. He was not surprised by the Duke's appear-ance, for half an hour before—only half an hour!—he had allowed him and his guide to enter.

"M. de Vlaye wishes to see the Captain of the gate," the Duke said curtly. "Bid him come, and quickly." And to show that he looked for no answer he turned his back on the man, and, without looking behind him, passed through the rooms again to the one he had left.

Here he did a strange thing. On a side table which had escaped the general disaster stood some dishes removed from the chief table, a plate or two, a bread trencher, and a silver decanter of wine. After a moment's thought he drew a chair to this table, laid his sword on it beside the dishes, and, helping himself to food, began to eat and drink, with his eyes on the door. After the lapse of two or three minutes, during which he more than once scanned the room with a strange and inexplicable satisfaction, a knock was heard at the door.

"Enter!" said the Duke, his mouth half-full.

The door opened, and a grizzled man with a square-cut beard stepped in. He wore a breastpiece over a leather coat, and held his steel cap in his hand.

"Shut the door!" the Duke said sharply.

The man did so mechanically, and turned again, and

—his mouth opened. After a few seconds of silence "Mon Dieu!" he whispered. "Mon Dieu!"

"He is quite dead," the Duke said, raising his glass to his lips. "But you had better satisfy yourself. When you have done so, listen to me."

Had the Duke been in any other attitude it is probable that the man had turned in a panic, flung the door wide, and yelled for help. But, seeing a stranger calmly eating and drinking and addressing him with a morsel on the point of his knife, the man stared helplessly, and then did mechanically as he was told—stooped, listened, felt for the life that had for ever departed. When he rose again "Now, listen to me," said the other. "I am the Duke of Joyeuse—you know my name? You know me? Yes, I did it. That is not your affair—but I did it. Your affair is with the thing we have next to do. No—she is not dead."

"Mon Dieu!" the man whispered. Old war-dog as he was, his cheeks were sallow, his hand trembled. A hundred dead, in the open, on the rampart, under God's sky, had not scared him as this lighted room with its medley of horror and wealth, its curtained windows and its suffocating tapestry, scared him.

"Your affair," the Duke repeated, "is with what is to follow." He raised his glass, and held it between his eye and the light. "Do you take my side or his? He is dead—you see him. I am alive—you know me. Now hear my terms. But first, my man, what do you number?"

The man made an effort, vain for the most part, to collect himself. But he managed to whisper, after a moment's hesitation, that they mustered four hundred and thirty, all told.

"Fighting-men?"

The man moved his lips without sound, but the other understood that he assented.

"Very well," the Duke said. "All that is here I give you. Understand, all. Divide, sack, spoil; make your bundles. He is dead," with a glance at Vlaye's body, "he'll not say you nay. And a free pardon for all; and for as many as please—my service. All that I give, on condition that you open your gates to me and render the place three hours after sunrise to-morrow."

The man gaped. The position was new, but he began to see his way. "I can do nothing by myself," he muttered.

"You can have first search," Joyeuse retorted brutally. "There he lies, and his buttons are jewelled. And ten gold crowns I will give you for yourself when the place is mine. You know me, and I keep my word. I told your friend there, who got me entrance"—he pointed to the man Vlaye had stabbed—"that if his master laid a finger on him I would kill his master with these hands. I did it. And there's an end."

The grizzled man's face was changed. It had grown cunning. His eyes shone with cupidity. His cheekbones were flushed. "And if they will not come into your terms, my lord?" he asked, his head on one side, his fingers in his beard, "what must I say you will do?"

"Hang while rope lasts," the Duke answered. "But, name of God, man!"—staring—"beyond the spoils of the place what do you want? He is dead, you have no leader. What matter is it of yours or of theirs who leads?"

The old soldier nodded. "That is true," he said: "we follow our wages."

"One thing more—nay, three things," Joyeuse continued, pushing his cup and plate aside and rising to his feet. "The lady there—I trust her to you. Lock her up where she will be safe, and at daybreak see that she is sent to the convent. M. des Ageaux, whom you have below—not a hair of his head must be injured. Lastly, you must do no harm in the town."

"I will remember, my lord, and tell them."

"And now see me through the gates."

The man grinned cunningly; but as one who wished to prove his astuteness, not as one who intended to refuse. "That is number four, my lord," he said, "and the chiefest of all."

"Not so," the Duke answered. "It was on that condition I spared your life, fool, when you came in."

"Then you knew——"

"I knew that his buttons were jewelled."

"My lord," the man said with admiration, "I vow you'd face the devil."

"You will do that whether you will or no," the Duke replied drily, "some day. But that reminds me." He turned from his companion. He looked on the bloodshed about him, and gradually his face showed the first signs of compunction that had escaped him. Something of disgust, almost of distress, appeared in his manner. He glanced from one prostrate form to another as if he scarce knew what to do and presently he crossed himself. "Lift her to the couch there," he said. And when it was done, "My friend," he continued, in a lower tone, "wait without the door one minute. But do not go beyond call."

The old soldier raised his eyebrows, but he, thoroughly won over, obeyed. Once outside, however, he pondered

cunningly. Why had he been sent out? And thoughts
of his jewelled buttons overcame him. After a moment's
hesitation—for Joyeuse had put fear into him—he
dropped softly to his knee and set his eye to a crack in
the door.

M. de Joyeuse was kneeling between the dead, his
palms joined before his breast, his rosary between them.
The lights of the feast, that shone ghastly on the grim
faces and on the blood-pool about them, shone also on
his uplifted face, from which the last trace of the tremendous rages to which he was prone had fled, leaving
it pale indeed and worn—for the marks of his illness
were still upon it—but calm and sublime. His eyes
were upward bent. Those eyes that a few minutes
earlier had burned with a hatred almost sub-human
now shone with a light soft and ecstatic, such as shines
in the eyes of those who see visions and hear voices.
His lips moved without sound. The beads dropped
one by one through his fingers.

.   .   .   .

The hewers of wood and feeders of oxen who herded
together in the town under the castle walls were timidly
aware of the festivities above their heads. The sounds
of brawling and dancing, of the tambour and glee, descended to them and kept them waiting far into the
night. On occasions, rare, it is true, the war-lords above
had broken loose from their bonds, and, mad with
drink and frenzied with excitement, had harried their
own town. Once, to teach a lesson, the thing had
been done—but more completely and cruelly—by
Vlaye's express order. The memory of these occasions
remained, burned shamefully into the towns-folk's
mind; and many a cotter looked up this night in

trembling from his humble window, many a woman
with her hood about her head stood in the alley whispering to her neighbour and quaked as she listened.
Something beyond the ordinary was passing above, in
the stronghold that at once protected and plundered
them; something that a sad experience told them
boded no good. Two or three young women of the
better class went so far as to seek a sanctuary in Father
Benet's chapel; while their fathers hid their little
hoards, and their mothers took heed to quench the
fires, and some threw water on the thatch—sad precautions which necessity had made second nature in
many a hamlet and many a market-town of France.

Had they known, these poor folk who paid for all,
that their lord lay dead in the lighted room above, had
they guessed that the hand which had held those tur-
bulent troopers in order was nerveless at last, never
again to instil fear or strike a blow, not even these precautions had contented them. They would have risen
and fled, and in the marshes by the river or in remote
meadows would have hidden themselves from the first
violence of the troopers' outbreak. But they did not
know, and they remained. And though those who were
most fearful or least sleepy, women or men, noted that
the lights above burned all night and that the tumult,
albeit its note changed, held till dawn, they slept or
kept vigil in security. The Duke's command availed.
And no man, until the day was broad, left the castle.

Then the gates were opened, and a procession number-
ing four score troopers—those who had the most to
fear from justice or the least bent towards honest
service—issued from them, and rode two abreast down
the hill and through the town. They were in strange

guise. Every man had a great bundle on his crupper, and some a woman; and every man rode gorgeous in silk or Genoa, or rich furs, with feathers and such like gewgaws. One had a headpiece damascened beyond price swinging at his shoulders, another flaunted trappings of silver, a third had a jewelled hilt, a fourth a bunch of clinking cups or a swollen belt. Behind them came a dozen spare horses, roped head and tail and high laden with casks and skins of wine; while hunting-dogs ran at the stirrups, and two or three monkeys and thrice as many chained hawks balanced themselves on the swaying casks. The men rode jauntily, with high looks and defiant voices, jesting and singing as they passed; and now and again a one aimed a blow at a clown, or, with rude laughter, flung a handful of coppers to the townsfolk, who shrank into their doorways to see them pass. But no man vouchsafed a word of explanation; only the last rider as he passed under the arch of the town gate turned, and, with his hands joined, flung behind him a derisive gesture of farewell.

The townsfolk wondered, for the men were rich laden. Many a one carried a year's pay on his shoulders; and what they hid in their bundles might amount to many times as much. Moreover, they swaggered as men who mind no master. What then had happened? Nay, what was still happening? For it was plain that something was amiss above. From the castle proceeded a strange and continuous hum; a dull noise, as of bees swarming; a murmur compound of many sounds, and full of menace.

But no man who was not in the secret guessed the truth or even came near it. And the sun had travelled

far and the lads had driven the cows to pasture before
the green valley of the Dronne, that had lain so long
under the spell of fear, awoke to find its burden gone
and to learn that a better time, bringing law, order, and
justice, was at hand. About seven a body of horsemen were seen crossing the narrow plain which divided
the place from the northern heights; and as these
approached the bridge a lad, one of those who had
first espied them, was sent to carry the alarm to the
castle. The townsfolk looked to see a rush of armed
men to the outer gate; or, if not that, something akin.
But nothing of the kind followed, and while they stood
gaping, uncertain whether to stand their ground or
flee to hiding, the advancing horsemen, who numbered
about two hundred, marched across the bridge with
every sign of confidence.

The Duke was not among them. Fatigue and the
weakness caused by his wound had stood in the way
of his return, and at this hour he lay in utter collapse
in his quarters in the peasants' camp. His place was
occupied by the Bat, who rode in the van with Charles
de Villeneuve on his right and Roger on his left. The
young men's minds were clouded by thoughts of their
sister and her plight; but, in spite of this, it was a
day of pride to them, a day of triumph and revenge—
and they rode in that spirit. The Bat, to whom Hecuba
was naught—it was long since a woman had troubled
his peace—wore none the less a grave face. For time
had pressed, the Duke's explanation had been brief
though fervid, and the men had saddled and started
within an hour of his return. Consequently all might
be well, or it might be ill. The Captain of Vlaye's
troops might surrender the place without a blow, or

they might not. For his part, the Bat would not have risked his purse on their promise.

But to risk his life and his men was in the way of war. And he moved steadily up the street, and gave no sign of doubt. Nevertheless it was his ear that, as they debouched into the market-place, caught the tread of a galloping horse on the flat beyond the river; and it was his hand that halted the men—apparently that the stragglers might move up and take their places.

A minute or two later the galloping horse pounded under the gateway and clattered recklessly up the paved street. The sound of those hurrying hoofs told of news; and the men turned in their saddles and looked to learn who followed. The rider appeared in the open. It was Bonne de Villeneuve.

Charles wheeled his horse, and rode down the column to meet his sister. "You have not come alone?" he said in astonishment, mingled with anger.

She nodded, breathing quickly; and, supporting herself by one hand on the sweating horse, she pulled up. She was unable to speak for a moment. Then "I must go first!" she gasped. "I must go first."

"But——"

"I must! I must!" she replied. Her distress was painful.

Her brother frowned. The Bat eyed her, in doubt and perplexity. But Roger spoke. "Let her go," he said in a low voice. "I understand. She is right."

And though no one else understood, the Bat let her pass the head of the file of horsemen and ride alone up the way that led to the castle. The men, with wondering faces, watched her figure and her horse until the turn in the road hid her, and watched again until she was seen crossing the bridge which spanned the road. Immediately she vanished without let or hindrance.

"The gates are open," some one muttered in a tone of relief. And the men's faces lost their gravity. They fell into postures of ease, and began to talk and exchange jests. Some gazed up at the castle windows or at that rampart walk, high above the town, which had been the Captain of Vlaye's favourite lounge of evenings. Only the foremost ranks, who could see the road before them and the bridge that crossed it, continued to look to the front with curiosity.

It was one of these whose exclamation presently stilled all tongues and recalled all thoughts to the work in hand. An instant later the Bat's face turned a dull red colour. Roger laughed nervously. Some of the men swayed, and seemed inclined to cheer; others raised their hands, but thought better of it. The rear ranks rose in their stirrups. A moment and all could see des Ageaux coming down the road on foot. The Bat and the two Villeneuves went forward to meet him.

He nodded to them without speaking. Then, "Why are you waiting?" he asked in a low voice. "Is it not all arranged?"

"But mademoiselle," the Bat answered, staring. "Have you not seen her?"

"No."

"But I thought—she asked us to wait."

The Lieutenant of Périgord looked along the line of horsemen, whose bronzed faces and smiling eyes—all striving at once to catch his—gave him welcome. "I don't understand," he said. "I know nothing of this."

"I do," Roger muttered. "I think Charles and I should go forward, and——"

He did not continue. The Bat, by a movement which silenced him, called his attention to the bridge. On it a number of persons had that moment appeared, issuing from the castle gates, and directing their course to the tilt-yard crest. Their progress was slow, yet the gazers below could not, from the place where they stood, discern why; or precisely who they were. But presently, after an interval of suspense and waiting, the little company reappeared in the road below and began to descend the slope towards them. Then here and there a man caught his breath, and, as by one consent, all edged their horses to the side. M. des Ageaux bared his head, and the troopers, from front to rear, followed his example.

It was a brief and mournful procession. In the van, riding where he had ridden so often, to foray and skirmish, the Captain of Vlaye rode his last ride, with a man at either rein and either stirrup, his war-cloak about him, and his steel headpiece nodding above his clay-cold face. His lance, with its drooping pennon, rose upright from his stirrup, and the faithful four who brought him forth had so fixed it that he seemed to grasp its shaft rather than to be supported by it. The sun twinkled on his steel, the light breeze caught and lifted the ends of his sash. As the old war-horse paced slowly and quietly along, conscious of its burden and of death, it was hard to say at a glance that the Lord of all the Valley was not passing forth as of old to battle; that, instead, he was moving to his last rest in the cloister which rose among the trees a half-league from the walls.

A few paces behind him, in a mule-litter, was borne a woman swathed in black cloth from head to foot, so that not so much as her eyes appeared. On one side of the litter walked Bonne, her chin on her breast, and her hand resting on the litter's edge. On the other side walked a frightened waiting-woman.

M. de Vlaye passed, the litter passed, all passed. But until the procession disappeared in the narrow street that led to the town gate no man covered himself or moved. Then, at a low word of command, the line of troopers rode on with a sudden merry jingle of bits and spurs, and, winding up the little gorge between the crests, marched over the bridge and through the open gates.

The Lieutenant's first act was to go to a low rampart on the west side of the courtyard, whence it was possible to trace with the eye the road to the Abbey. Bonne had not looked at him as she passed, nor so much as raised her eyes. But he knew by some subtle sense that she had been aware of his presence and that he had her promise that she would return.

Doubtless he looked forward to the moment of meeting; doubtless he looked forward to other things. But it was characteristic of the man that as soon as he had assured himself of her safe passage he turned without more ado to the work of restoring order, of raising the King's standard, and enforcing the King's peace.

THE END.

CPSIA information can be obtained at www.ICGtesting.com
Printed in the USA
BVOW07s2029160414

350848BV00016B/669/P